image® comics presents

Wayward

Volume Five: Tethered Souls

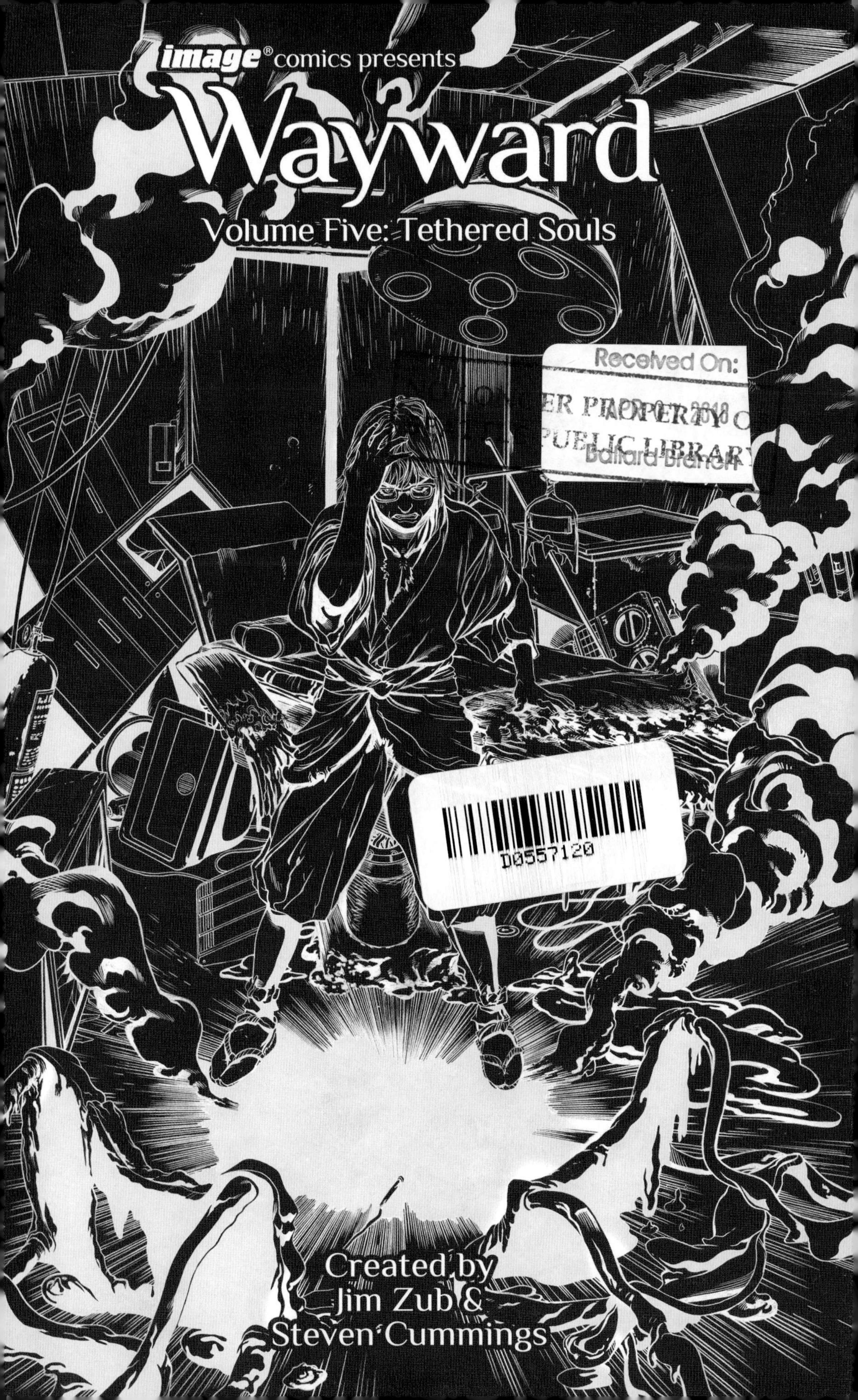

Created by
Jim Zub &
Steven Cummings

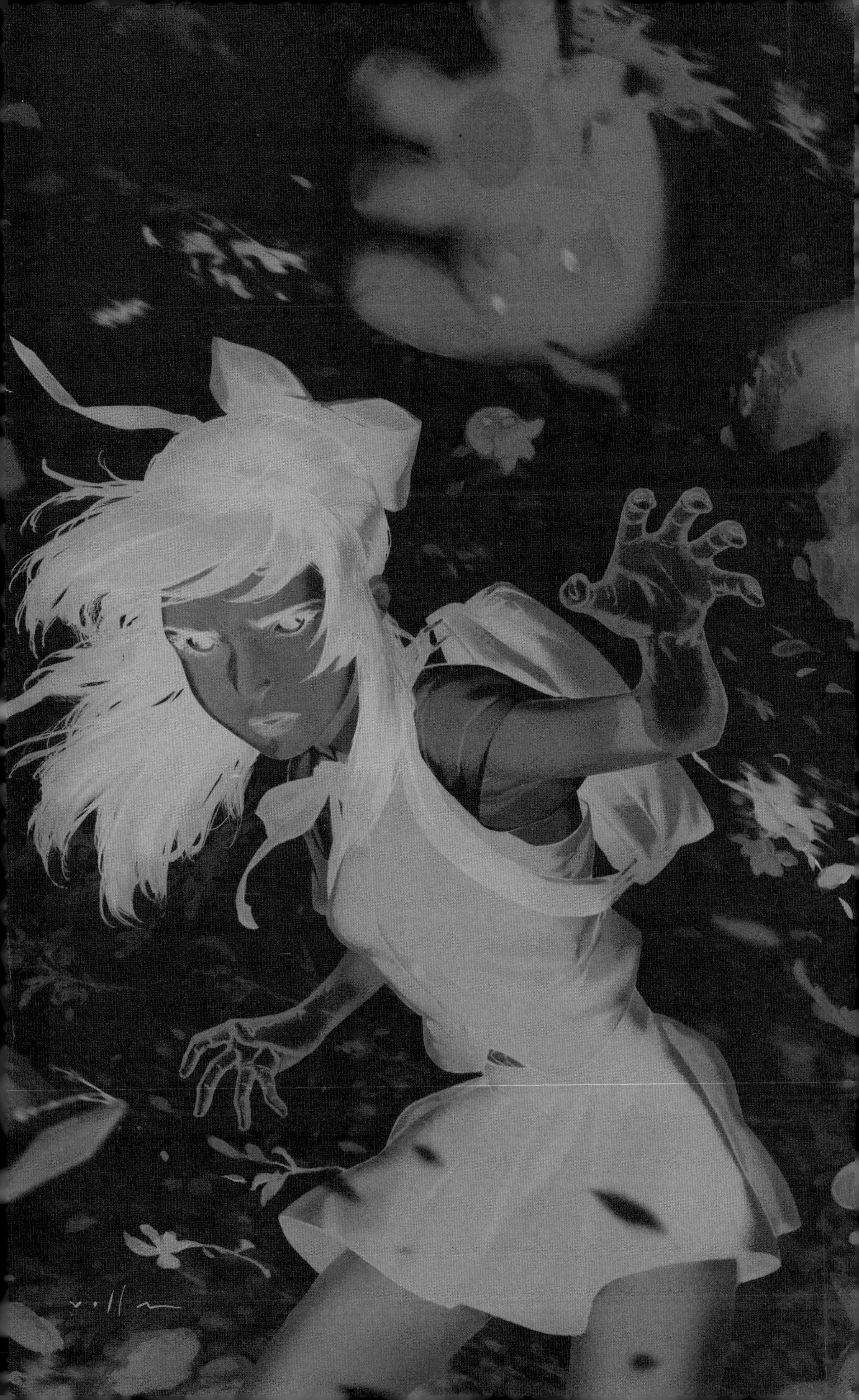

Previously

A group of teenagers in Japan discover they have strange supernatural powers. **Emi Ohara** can alter the form of manmade objects and change her body to match them. **Nikaido** senses and controls emotions. **Inaba** is a ronin kitsune, a shape-shifting fox warrior. **Segawa** can manipulate networks and technology. At the center is **Rori Lane**, a half-Japanese, half-Irish girl called a 'Weaver', a powerful conduit for the strings of fate that define power and destiny.

Soon after these powers emerge, the teens are hunted by **Yokai**, mythical Japanese creatures and spirits. The Yokai sense these striplings are the next generation of the supernatural in Japan, but they're not willing to relinquish the control they've built over the centuries.

Manipulated by the **Nurarihyon**, a powerful Yokai, the Japanese Self-Defense Force attacked Meguro, a temple the teens were using as their base of operations. The aftermath of the battle saw Inaba and Segawa separated from the others and Nikaido taken away in an ambulance...

story
Jim Zub

line art
Steven Cummings

color art
Tamra Bonvillain

color assist
Brittany Peer

color flats
Ludwig Olimba

letters
Marshall Dillon

back matter
Zack Davisson
Ann O'Regan

IMAGE COMICS, INC.
Robert Kirkman—Chief Operating Officer
Erik Larsen—Chief Financial Officer
Todd McFarlane—President
Marc Silvestri—Chief Executive Officer
Jim Valentino—Vice President

Eric Stephenson—Publisher
Corey Hart—Director of Sales
Jeff Boison—Director of Publishing Planning
    & Book Trade Sales
Chris Ross—Director of Digital Sales
Jeff Stang—Director of Specialty Sales
Kat Salazar—Director of PR & Marketing
Drew Gill—Art Director
Heather Doornink—Production Director
Branwyn Bigglestone—Controller
IMAGECOMICS.COM

WAYWARD VOL. 5: TETHERED SOULS. First Printing. JANUARY 2018. Published by Image Comics, Inc. Office of publication: 2701 NW Vaughn St., Suite 780, Portland, OR 97210. Copyright © 2018 Jim Zub and Steven Cummings. All rights reserved. Originally published in single magazine form as WAYWARD #21-25. WAYWARD™ (including all prominent characters featured herein), its logo and all character likenesses are trademarks of Jim Zub and Steven Cummings, unless otherwise noted. Image Comics® and its logos are registered trademarks of Image Comics, Inc. No part of this publication may be reproduced or transmitted, in any form or by any means (except for short excerpts for review purposes) without the express written permission of Image Comics, Inc. All names, characters, events and locales in this publication are entirely fictional. Any resemblance to actual persons (living or dead), events or places, without satiric intent, is coincidental. PRINTED IN THE USA. For information regarding the CPSIA on this printed material call: 203-595-3636 and provide reference # RICH-773933. ISBN: 978-1-5343-0350-8.

For international rights contact: foreignlicensing@imagecomics.com.

special thanks
Jon Gilmour
Jerome Mazandarani
Carlos Villa

Chapter Twenty-One

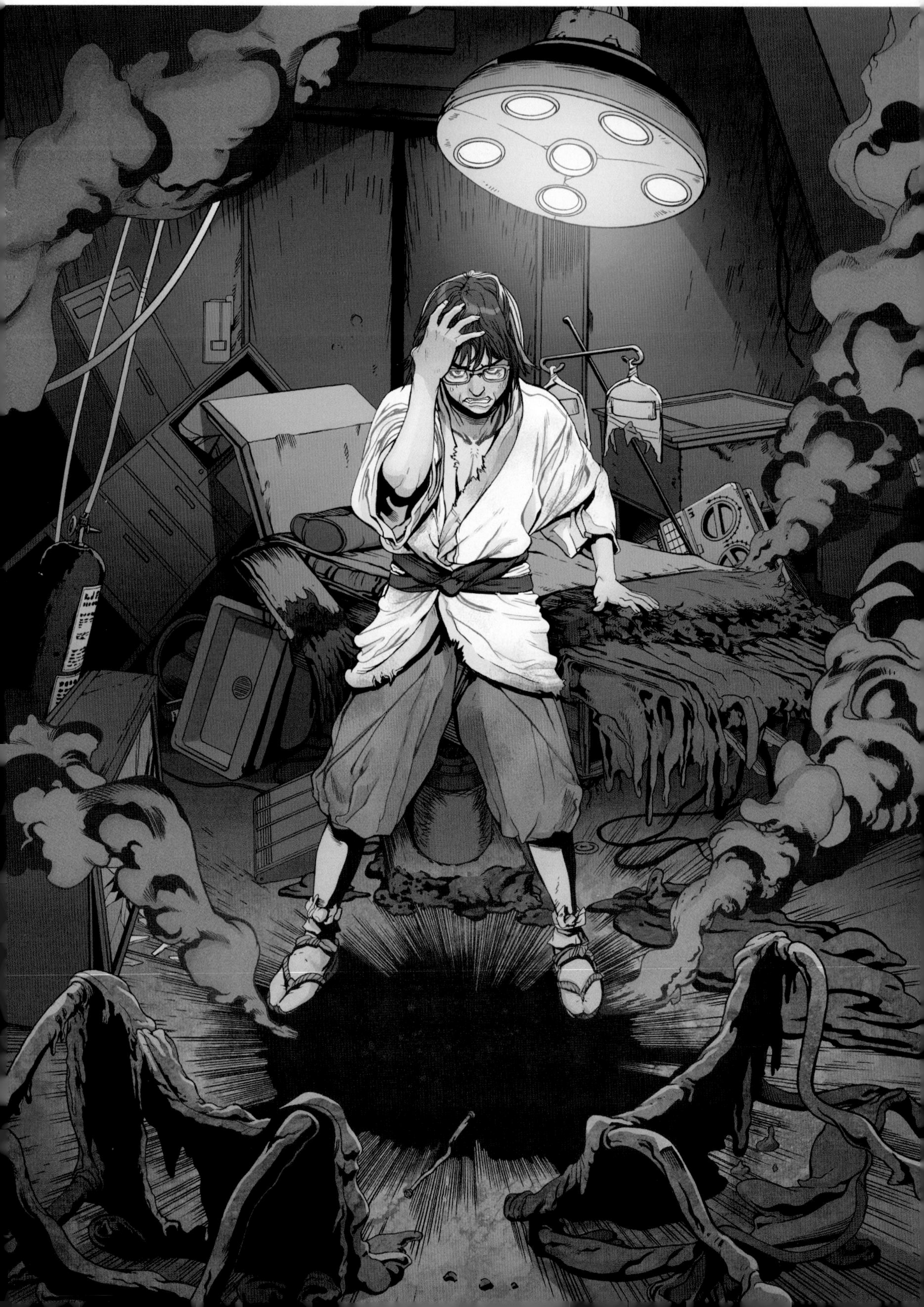

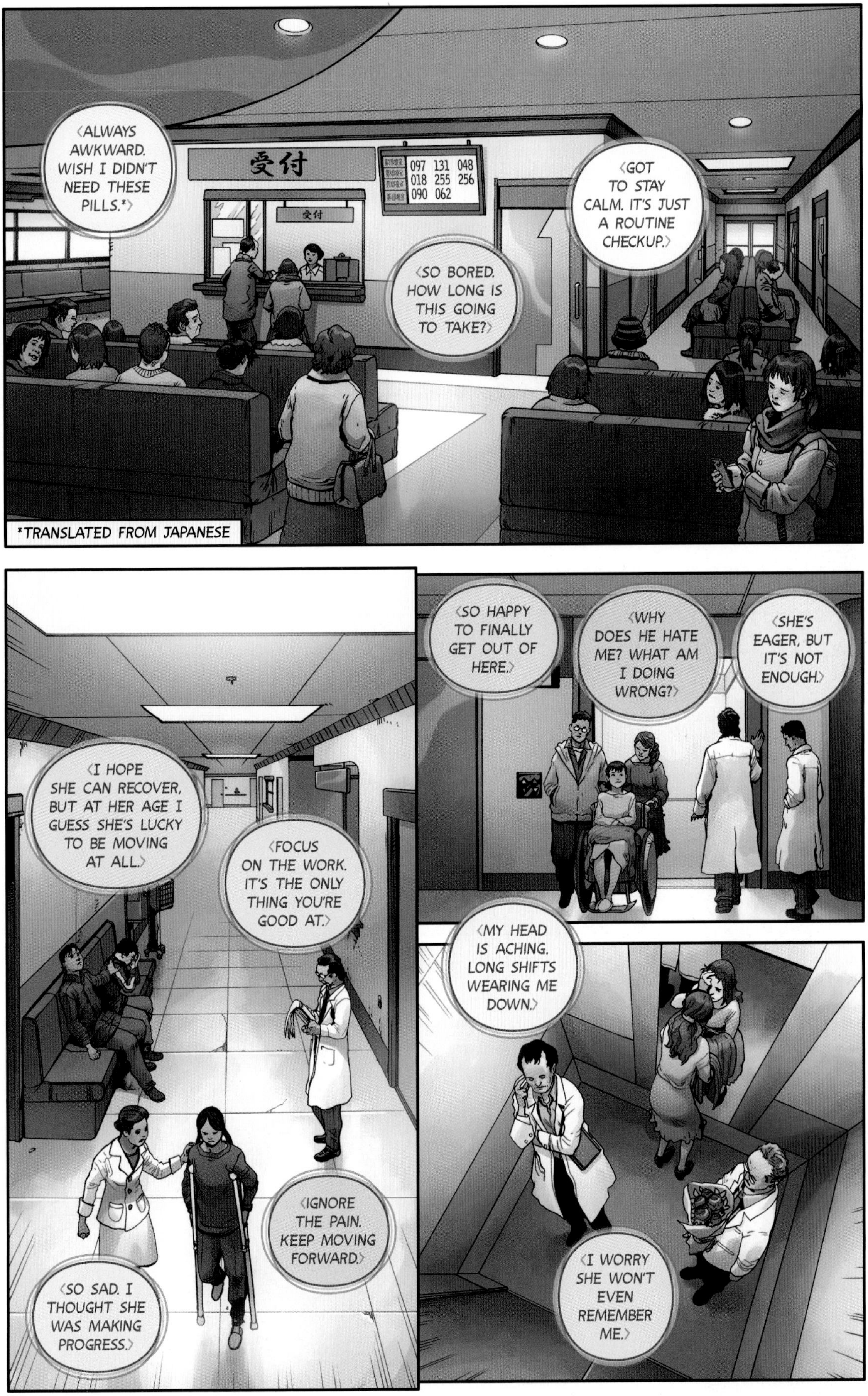
‹ALWAYS AWKWARD. WISH I DIDN'T NEED THESE PILLS.*›
受付
097 131 048
018 255 256
090 062
受付
‹SO BORED. HOW LONG IS THIS GOING TO TAKE?›
‹GOT TO STAY CALM. IT'S JUST A ROUTINE CHECKUP.›
*TRANSLATED FROM JAPANESE
‹I HOPE SHE CAN RECOVER, BUT AT HER AGE I GUESS SHE'S LUCKY TO BE MOVING AT ALL.›
‹FOCUS ON THE WORK. IT'S THE ONLY THING YOU'RE GOOD AT.›
‹IGNORE THE PAIN. KEEP MOVING FORWARD.›
‹SO SAD. I THOUGHT SHE WAS MAKING PROGRESS.›
‹SO HAPPY TO FINALLY GET OUT OF HERE.›
‹WHY DOES HE HATE ME? WHAT AM I DOING WRONG?›
‹SHE'S EAGER, BUT IT'S NOT ENOUGH.›
‹MY HEAD IS ACHING. LONG SHIFTS WEARING ME DOWN.›
‹I WORRY SHE WON'T EVEN REMEMBER ME.›

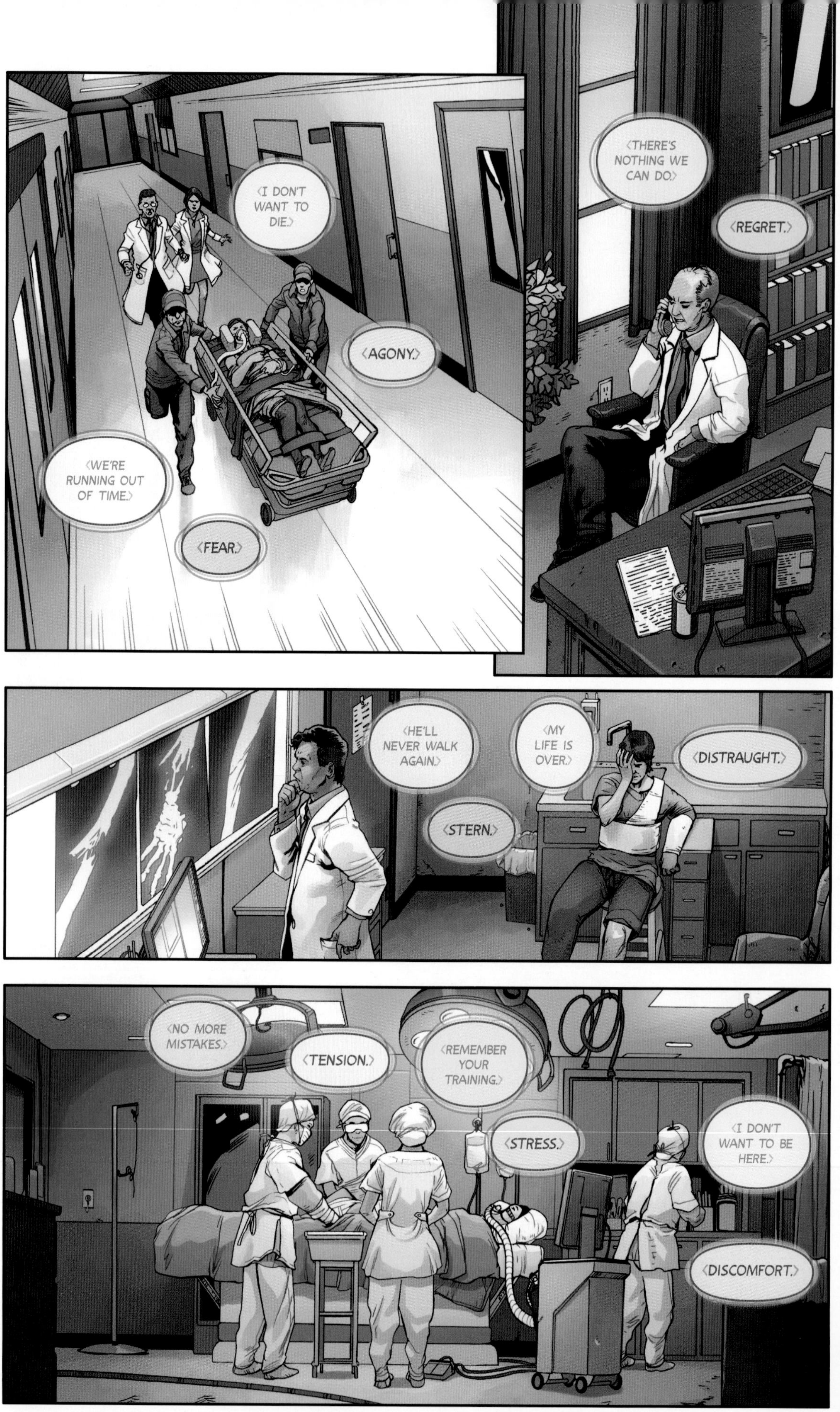
〈I DON'T WANT TO DIE.〉
〈AGONY.〉
〈WE'RE RUNNING OUT OF TIME.〉
〈FEAR.〉
〈THERE'S NOTHING WE CAN DO.〉
〈REGRET.〉
〈HE'LL NEVER WALK AGAIN.〉
〈STERN.〉
〈MY LIFE IS OVER.〉
〈DISTRAUGHT.〉
〈NO MORE MISTAKES.〉
〈TENSION.〉
〈REMEMBER YOUR TRAINING.〉
〈STRESS.〉
〈I DON'T WANT TO BE HERE.〉
〈DISCOMFORT.〉

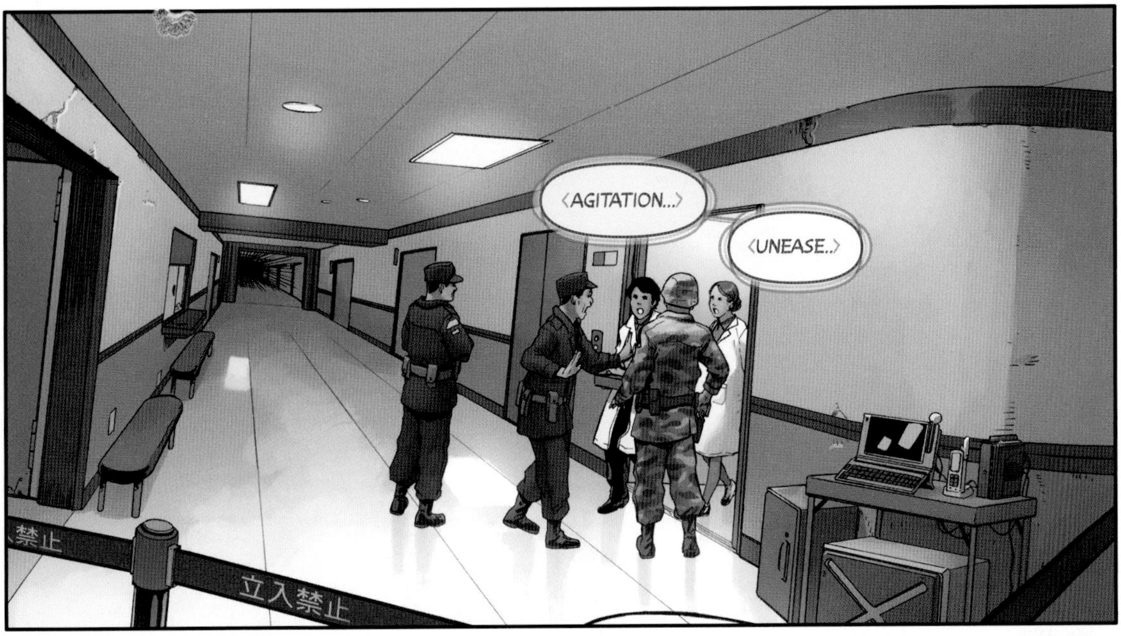
<AGITATION...>
<UNEASE..>
立入禁止

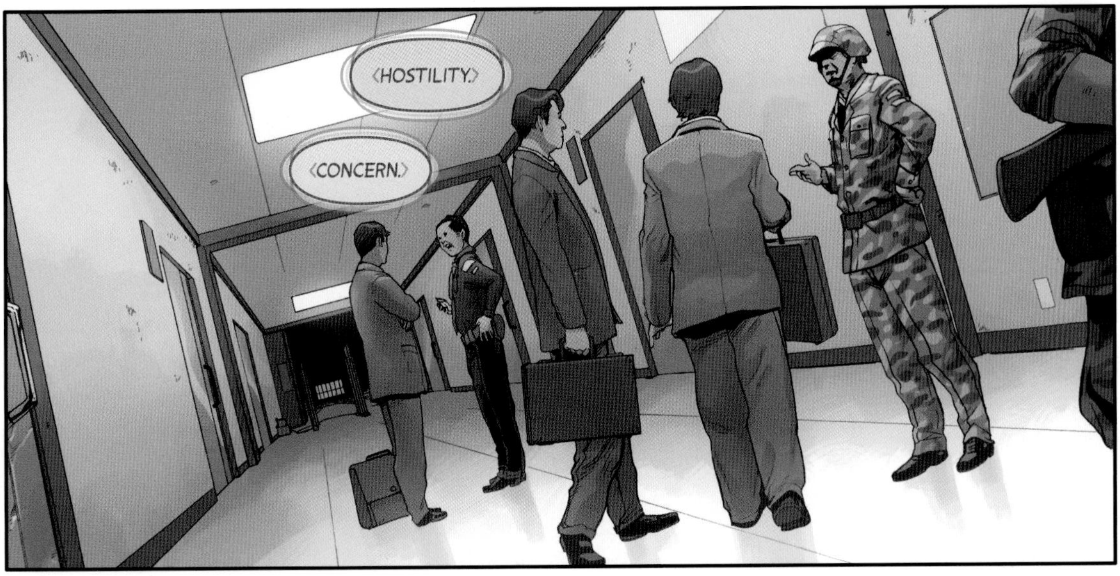
<HOSTILITY.>
<CONCERN.>

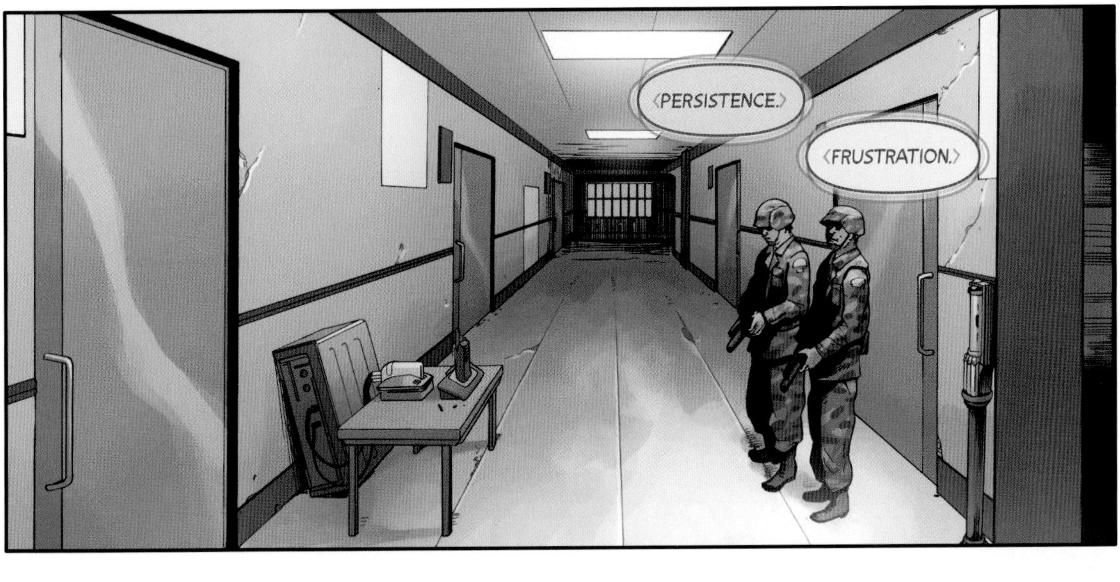
<PERSISTENCE.>
<FRUSTRATION.>

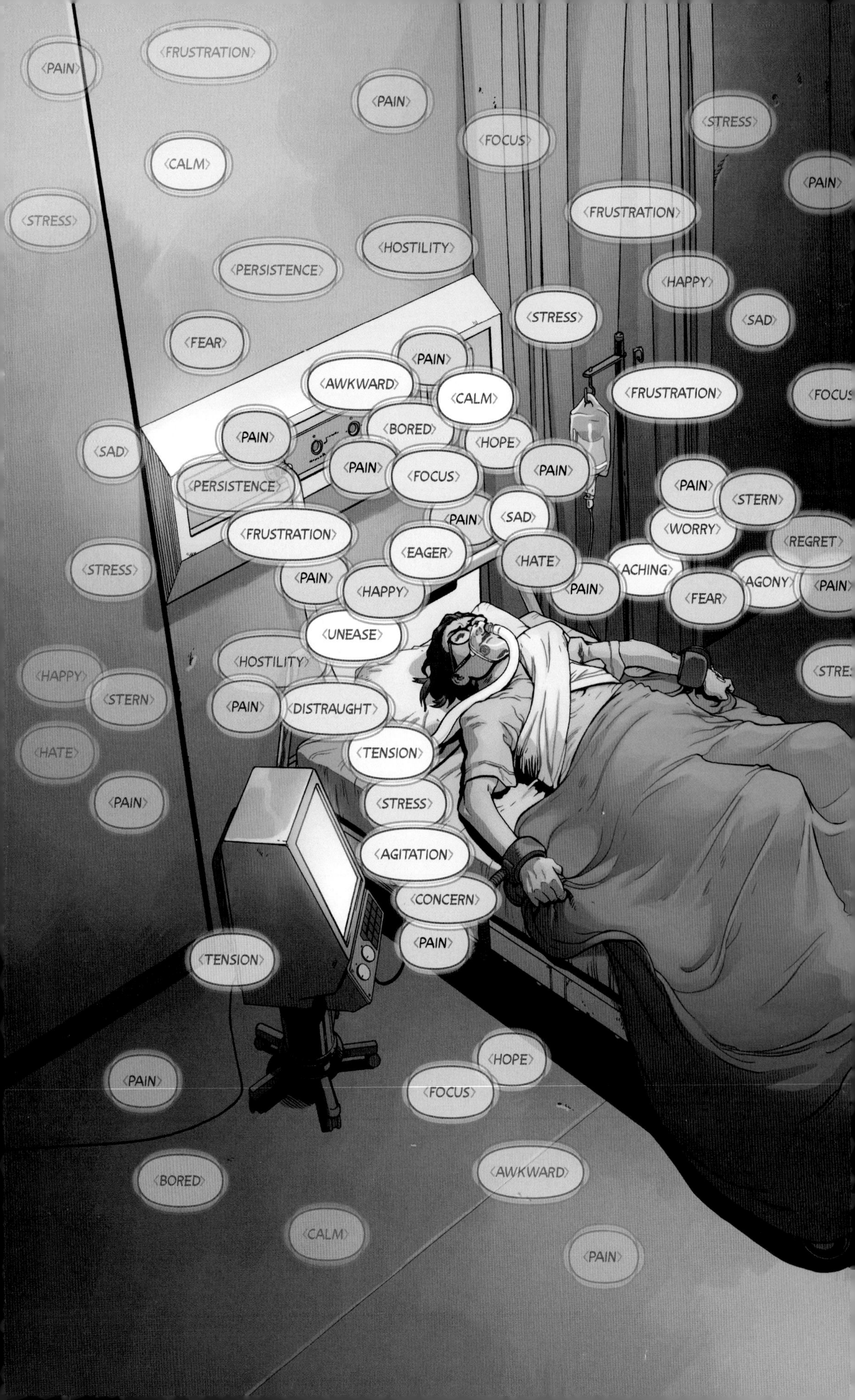
<PAIN>
<FRUSTRATION>
<PAIN>
<STRESS>
<FOCUS>
<CALM>
<PAIN>
<STRESS>
<FRUSTRATION>
<HOSTILITY>
<PERSISTENCE>
<HAPPY>
<STRESS>
<SAD>
<FEAR>
<PAIN>
<AWKWARD>
<CALM>
<FRUSTRATION>
<BORED>
<PAIN>
<HOPE>
<SAD>
<PAIN>
<FOCUS>
<PAIN>
<PERSISTENCE>
<PAIN>
<STERN>
<PAIN>
<SAD>
<WORRY>
<FRUSTRATION>
<REGRET>
<EAGER>
<HATE>
ACHING>
<STRESS>
<PAIN>
<AGONY>
<PAIN>
<PAIN>
<HAPPY>
<FEAR>
<UNEASE>
<HOSTILITY>
<HAPPY>
<STERN>
<PAIN>
<DISTRAUGHT>
<HATE>
<TENSION>
<PAIN>
<STRESS>
<AGITATION>
<CONCERN>
<PAIN>
<TENSION>
<HOPE>
<PAIN>
<FOCUS>
<BORED>
<AWKWARD>
<CALM>
<PAIN>

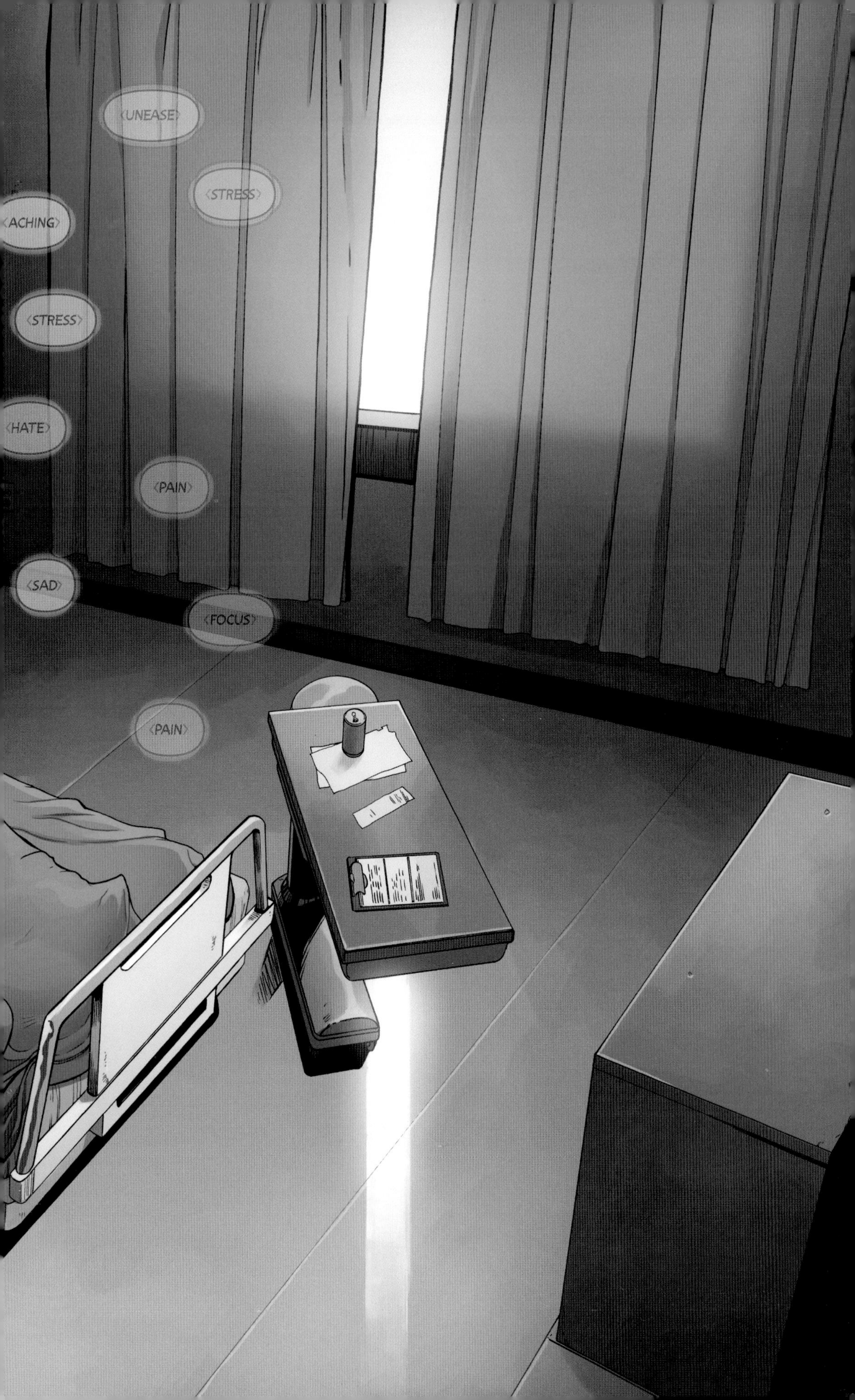
<UNEASE>
<STRESS>
<ACHING>
<STRESS>
<HATE>
<PAIN>
<SAD>
<FOCUS>
<PAIN>

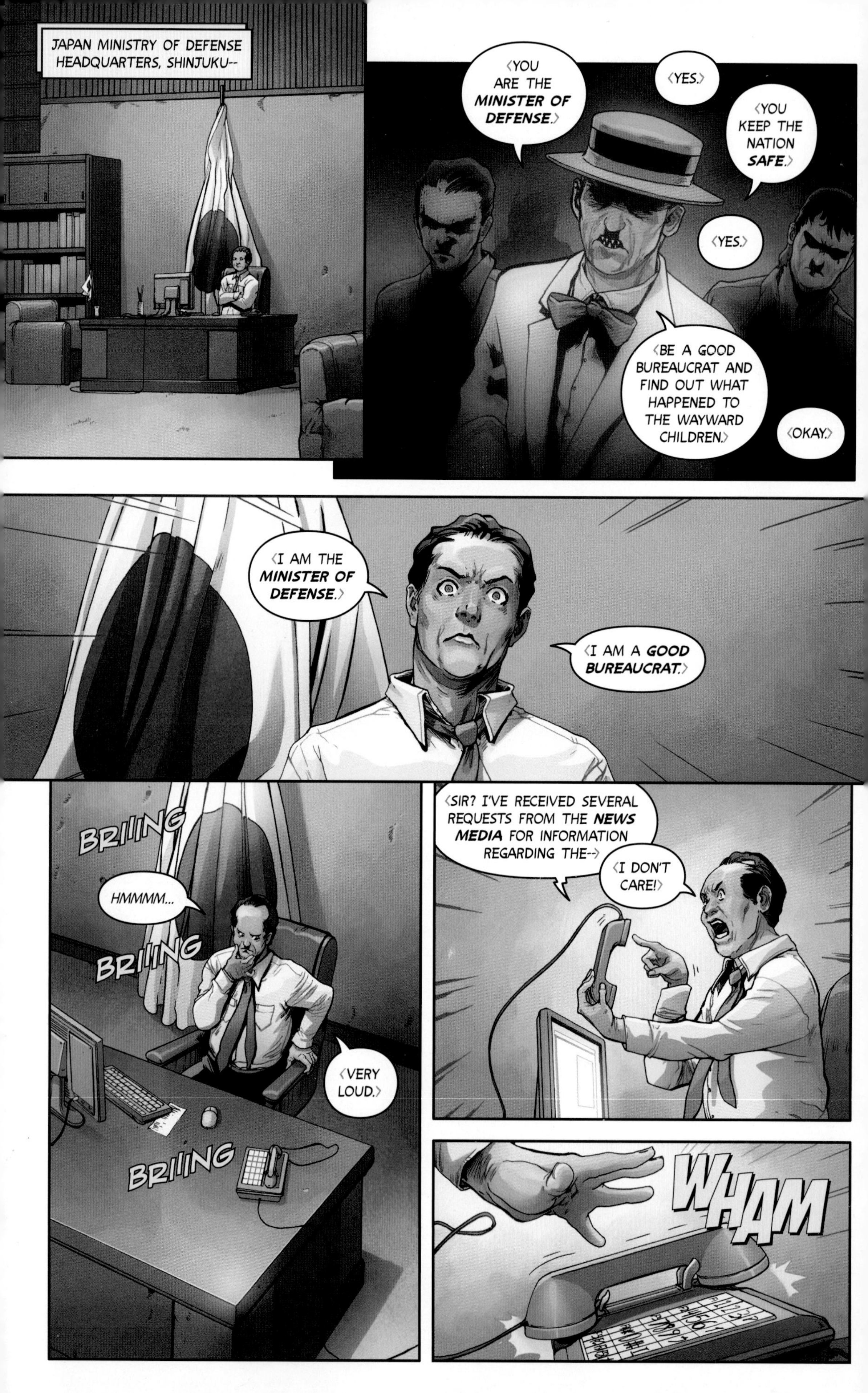

JAPAN MINISTRY OF DEFENSE HEADQUARTERS, SHINJUKU--
‹YOU ARE THE MINISTER OF DEFENSE.›
‹YES.›
‹YOU KEEP THE NATION SAFE.›
‹YES.›
‹BE A GOOD BUREAUCRAT AND FIND OUT WHAT HAPPENED TO THE WAYWARD CHILDREN.›
‹OKAY.›
‹I AM THE MINISTER OF DEFENSE.›
‹I AM A GOOD BUREAUCRAT.›
BRIIING
HMMMM...
BRIIING
‹VERY LOUD.›
BRIIING
‹SIR? I'VE RECEIVED SEVERAL REQUESTS FROM THE NEWS MEDIA FOR INFORMATION REGARDING THE--›
‹I DON'T CARE!›
WHAM

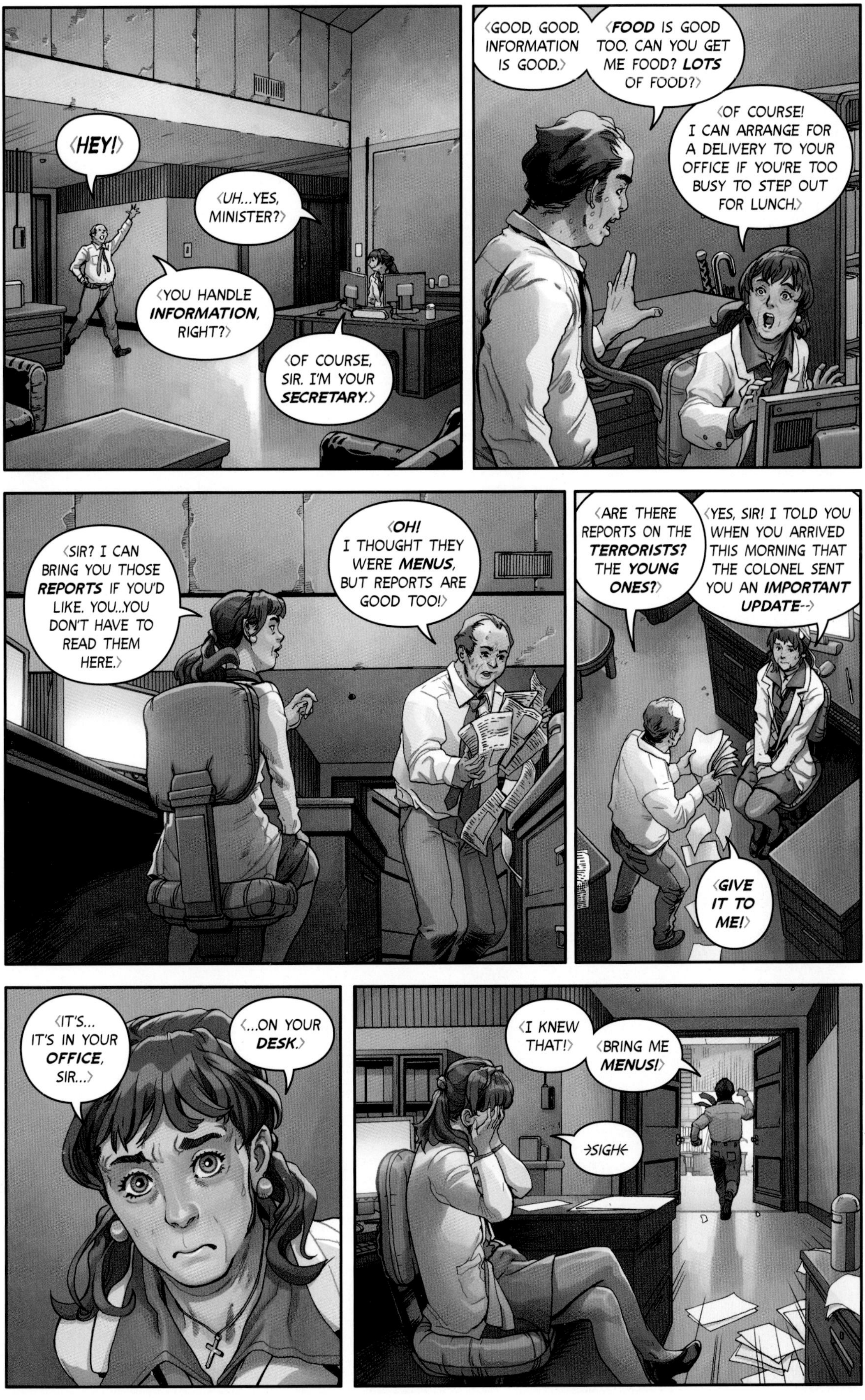

⟨HEY!⟩
⟨UH...YES, MINISTER?⟩
⟨YOU HANDLE INFORMATION, RIGHT?⟩
⟨OF COURSE, SIR. I'M YOUR SECRETARY.⟩
⟨GOOD, GOOD. INFORMATION IS GOOD.⟩
⟨FOOD IS GOOD TOO. CAN YOU GET ME FOOD? LOTS OF FOOD?⟩
⟨OF COURSE! I CAN ARRANGE FOR A DELIVERY TO YOUR OFFICE IF YOU'RE TOO BUSY TO STEP OUT FOR LUNCH.⟩
⟨SIR? I CAN BRING YOU THOSE REPORTS IF YOU'D LIKE. YOU...YOU DON'T HAVE TO READ THEM HERE.⟩
⟨OH! I THOUGHT THEY WERE MENUS, BUT REPORTS ARE GOOD TOO!⟩
⟨ARE THERE REPORTS ON THE TERRORISTS? THE YOUNG ONES?⟩
⟨YES, SIR! I TOLD YOU WHEN YOU ARRIVED THIS MORNING THAT THE COLONEL SENT YOU AN IMPORTANT UPDATE--⟩
⟨GIVE IT TO ME!⟩
⟨IT'S... IT'S IN YOUR OFFICE, SIR...⟩
⟨...ON YOUR DESK.⟩
⟨I KNEW THAT!⟩
⟨BRING ME MENUS!⟩
→SIGH←

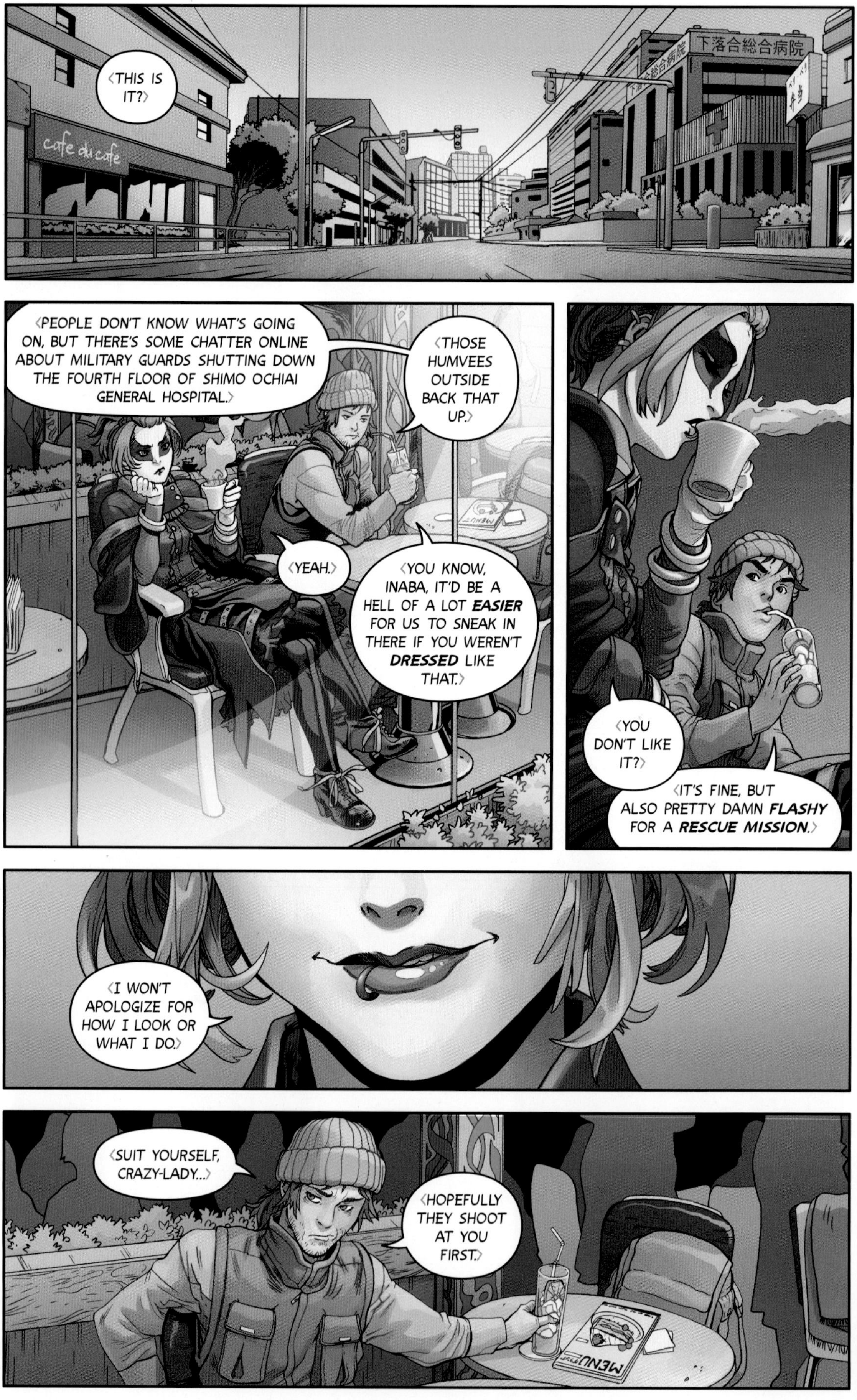
‹THIS IS IT?›
cafe du cafe
下落合総合病院
‹PEOPLE DON'T KNOW WHAT'S GOING ON, BUT THERE'S SOME CHATTER ONLINE ABOUT MILITARY GUARDS SHUTTING DOWN THE FOURTH FLOOR OF SHIMO OCHIAI GENERAL HOSPITAL.›
‹THOSE HUMVEES OUTSIDE BACK THAT UP.›
‹YEAH.›
‹YOU KNOW, INABA, IT'D BE A HELL OF A LOT **EASIER** FOR US TO SNEAK IN THERE IF YOU WEREN'T **DRESSED** LIKE THAT.›
MENU
‹YOU DON'T LIKE IT?›
‹IT'S FINE, BUT ALSO PRETTY DAMN **FLASHY** FOR A **RESCUE MISSION**.›
‹I WON'T APOLOGIZE FOR HOW I LOOK OR WHAT I DO.›
‹SUIT YOURSELF, CRAZY-LADY...›
‹HOPEFULLY THEY SHOOT AT YOU FIRST.›
MENU

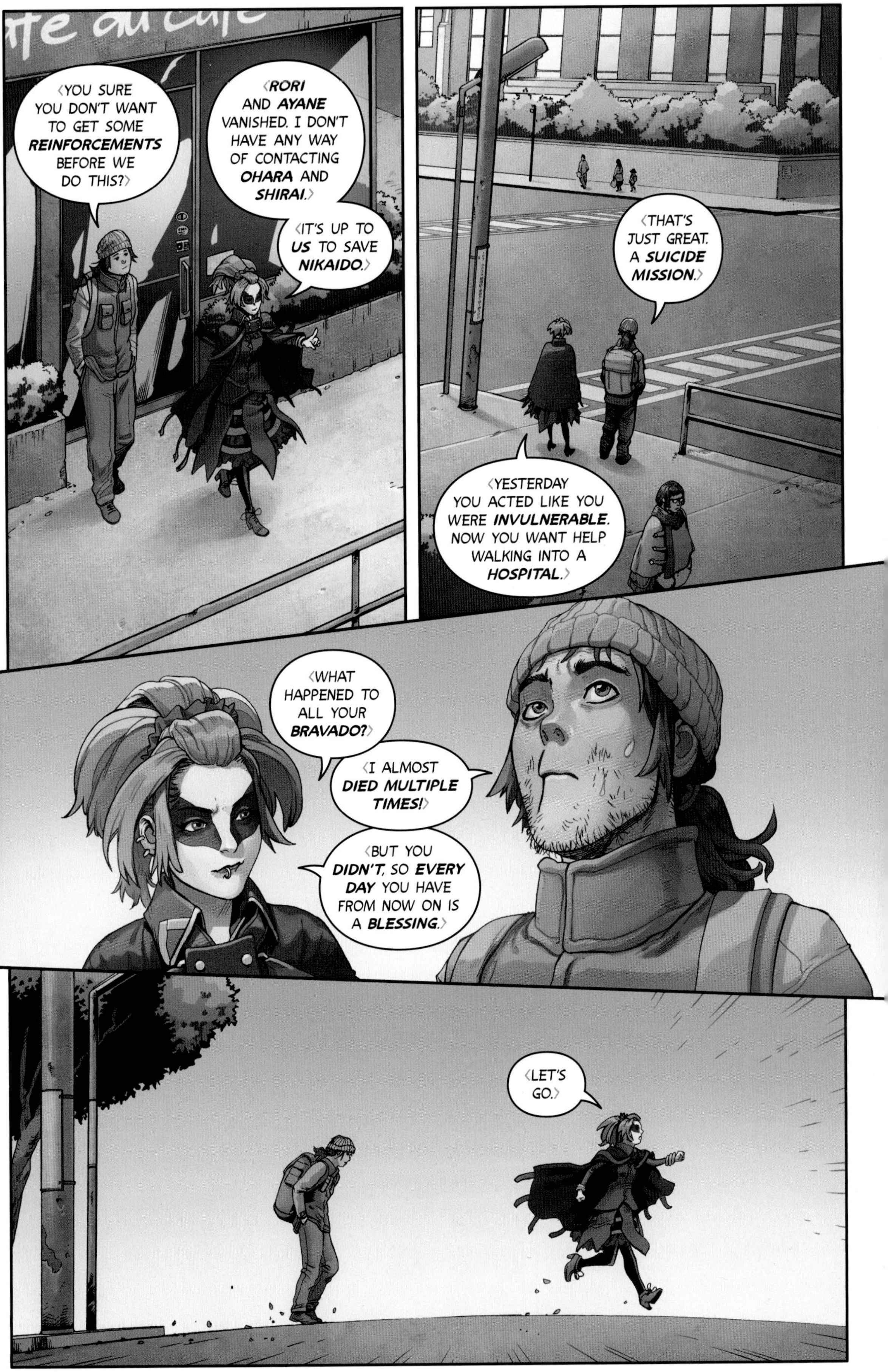

‹YOU SURE YOU DON'T WANT TO GET SOME REINFORCEMENTS BEFORE WE DO THIS?›
‹RORI AND AYANE VANISHED. I DON'T HAVE ANY WAY OF CONTACTING OHARA AND SHIRAI.›
‹IT'S UP TO US TO SAVE NIKAIDO.›
‹THAT'S JUST GREAT. A SUICIDE MISSION.›
‹YESTERDAY YOU ACTED LIKE YOU WERE INVULNERABLE. NOW YOU WANT HELP WALKING INTO A HOSPITAL.›
‹WHAT HAPPENED TO ALL YOUR BRAVADO?›
‹I ALMOST DIED MULTIPLE TIMES!›
‹BUT YOU DIDN'T, SO EVERY DAY YOU HAVE FROM NOW ON IS A BLESSING.›
‹LET'S GO.›

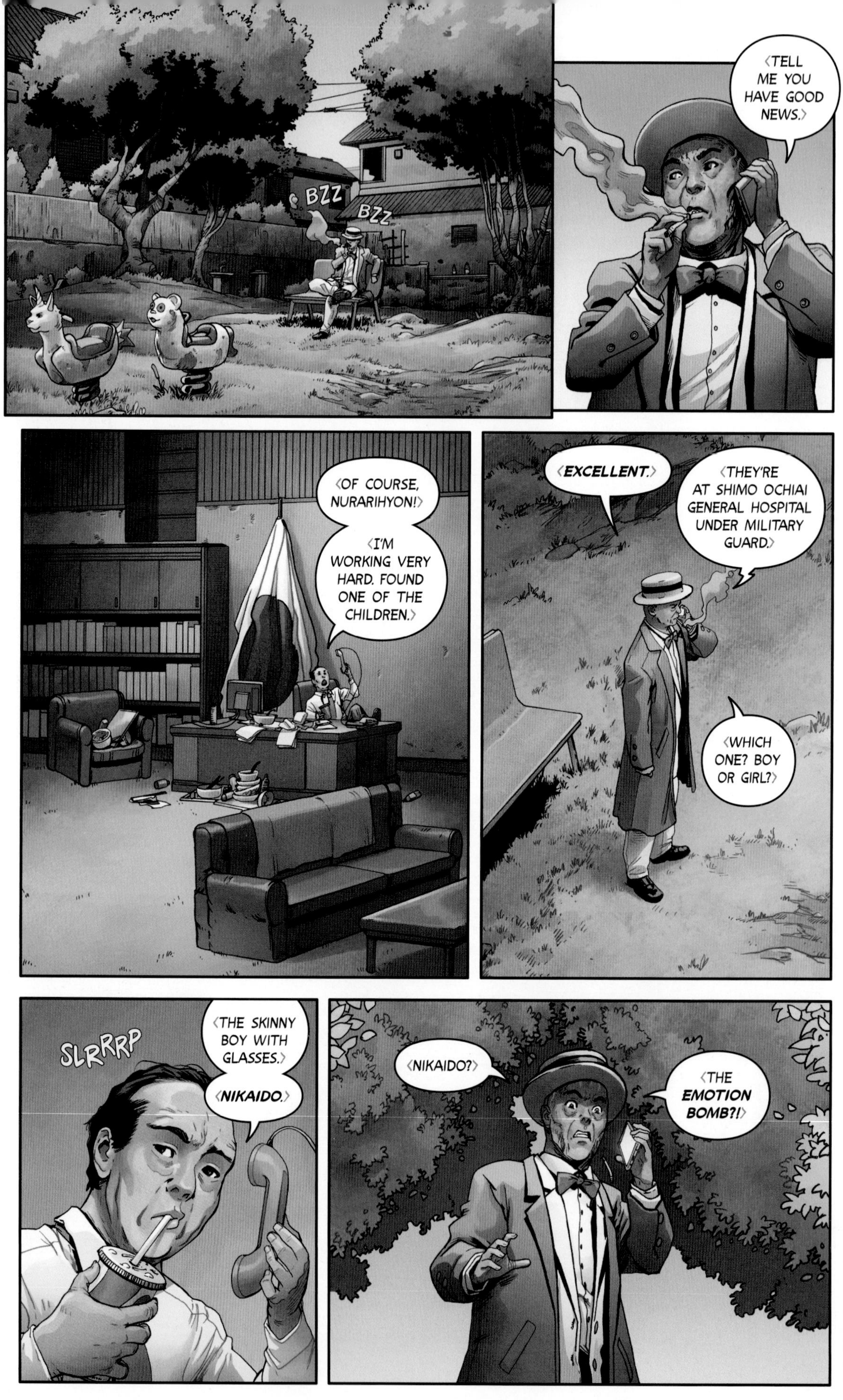
BZZ
BZZ
⟨TELL ME YOU HAVE GOOD NEWS.⟩
⟨OF COURSE, NURARIHYON!⟩
⟨I'M WORKING VERY HARD. FOUND ONE OF THE CHILDREN.⟩
⟨EXCELLENT.⟩
⟨THEY'RE AT SHIMO OCHIAI GENERAL HOSPITAL UNDER MILITARY GUARD.⟩
⟨WHICH ONE? BOY OR GIRL?⟩
SLRRRP
⟨THE SKINNY BOY WITH GLASSES.⟩
⟨NIKAIDO.⟩
⟨NIKAIDO?⟩
⟨THE EMOTION BOMB?!⟩

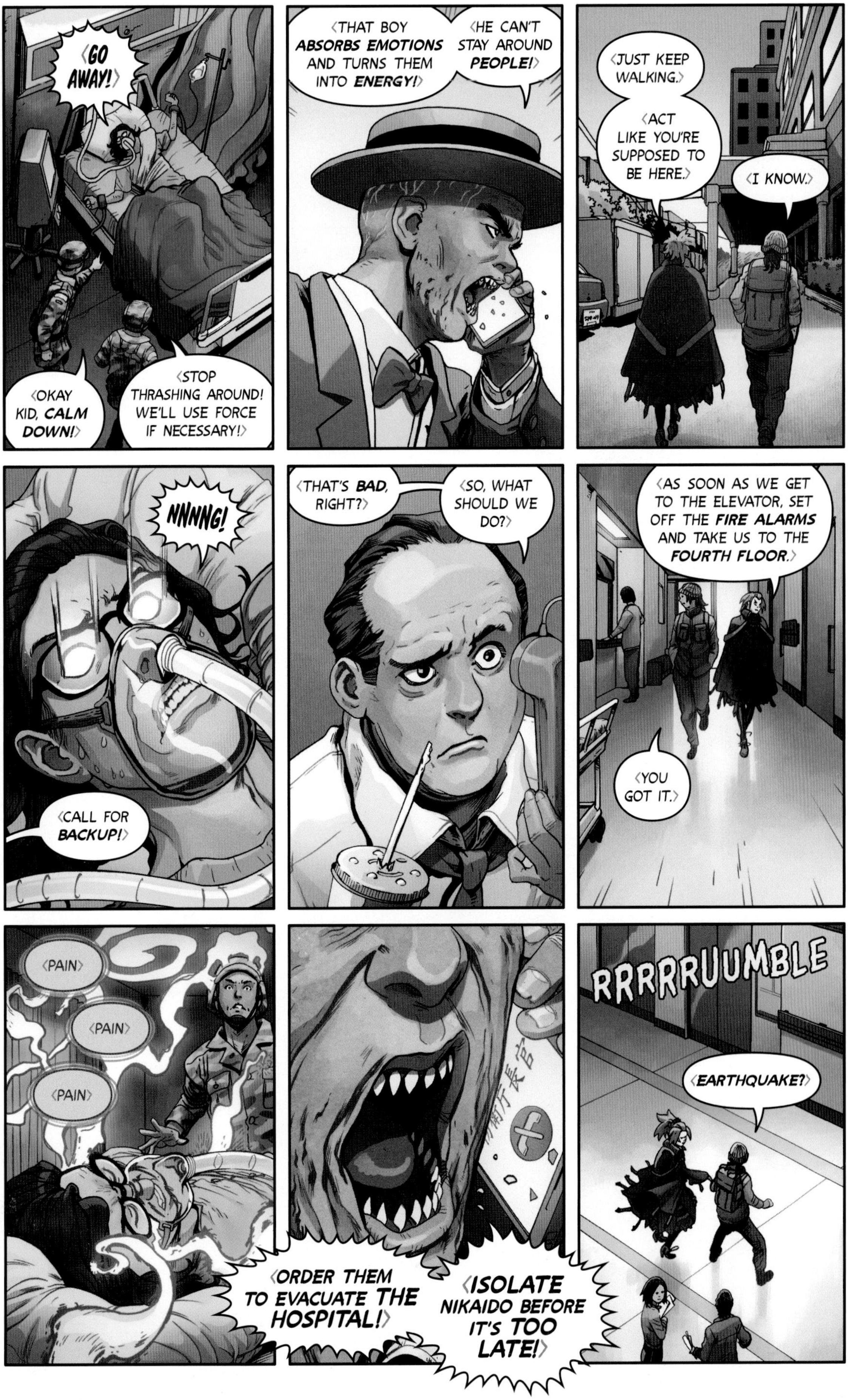

⟨GO AWAY!⟩
⟨OKAY KID, CALM DOWN!⟩
⟨STOP THRASHING AROUND! WE'LL USE FORCE IF NECESSARY!⟩
⟨THAT BOY ABSORBS EMOTIONS AND TURNS THEM INTO ENERGY!⟩
⟨HE CAN'T STAY AROUND PEOPLE!⟩
⟨JUST KEEP WALKING.⟩
⟨ACT LIKE YOU'RE SUPPOSED TO BE HERE.⟩
⟨I KNOW.⟩
NNNNG!
⟨CALL FOR BACKUP!⟩
⟨THAT'S BAD, RIGHT?⟩
⟨SO, WHAT SHOULD WE DO?⟩
⟨AS SOON AS WE GET TO THE ELEVATOR, SET OFF THE FIRE ALARMS AND TAKE US TO THE FOURTH FLOOR.⟩
⟨YOU GOT IT.⟩
⟨PAIN⟩
⟨PAIN⟩
⟨PAIN⟩
⟨ORDER THEM TO EVACUATE THE HOSPITAL!⟩
⟨ISOLATE NIKAIDO BEFORE IT'S TOO LATE!⟩
RRRRRUUMBLE
⟨EARTHQUAKE?⟩

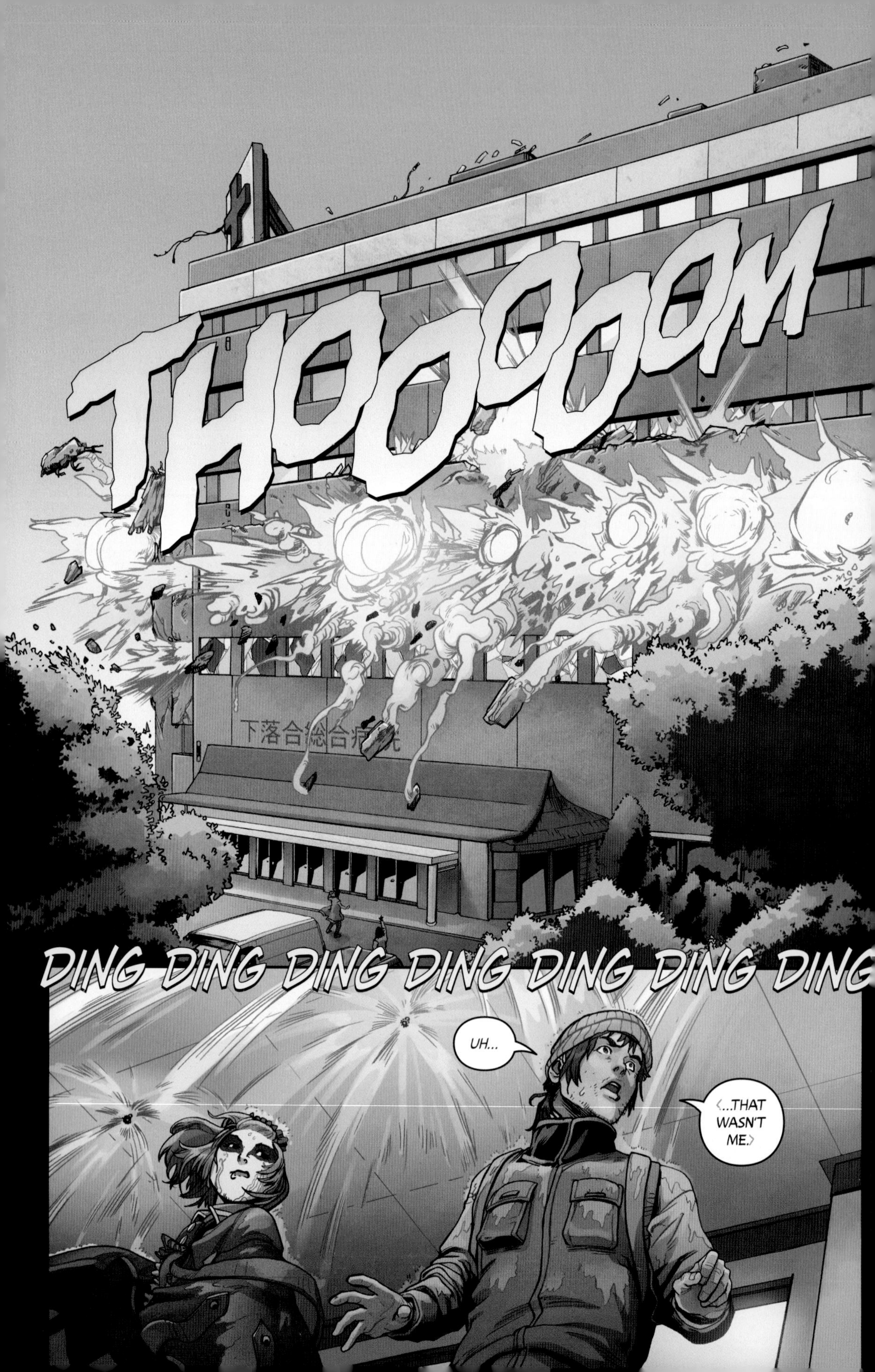
THOOOOOM
下落合総合病院
DING DING DING DING DING DING DING
UH...
<...THAT WASN'T ME.>

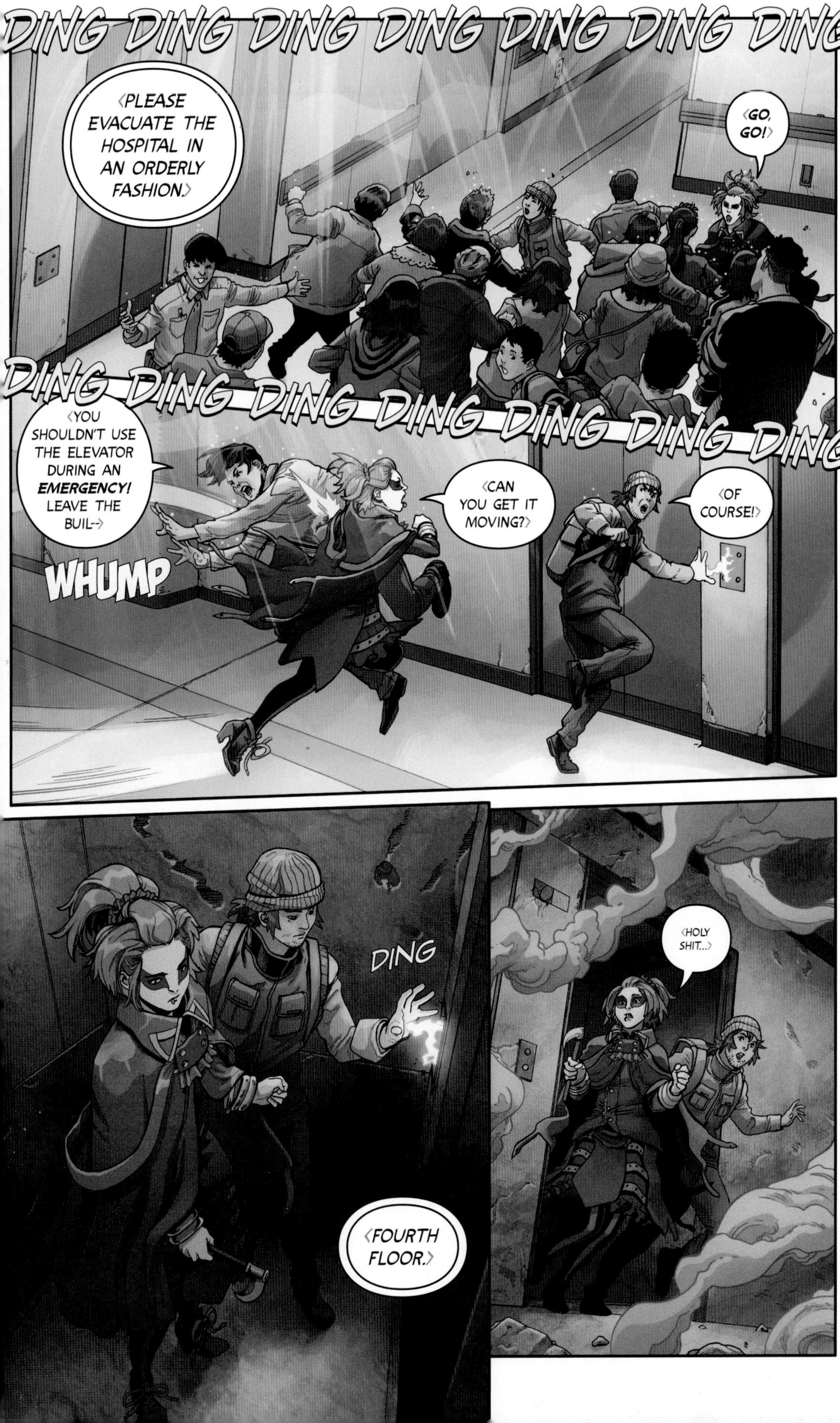
DING DING DING DING DING DING DING
‹PLEASE EVACUATE THE HOSPITAL IN AN ORDERLY FASHION.›
‹GO, GO!›
DING DING DING DING DING DING DING
‹YOU SHOULDN'T USE THE ELEVATOR DURING AN **EMERGENCY!** LEAVE THE BUIL--›
WHUMP
‹CAN YOU GET IT MOVING?›
‹OF COURSE!›
DING
‹FOURTH FLOOR.›
‹HOLY SHIT...›

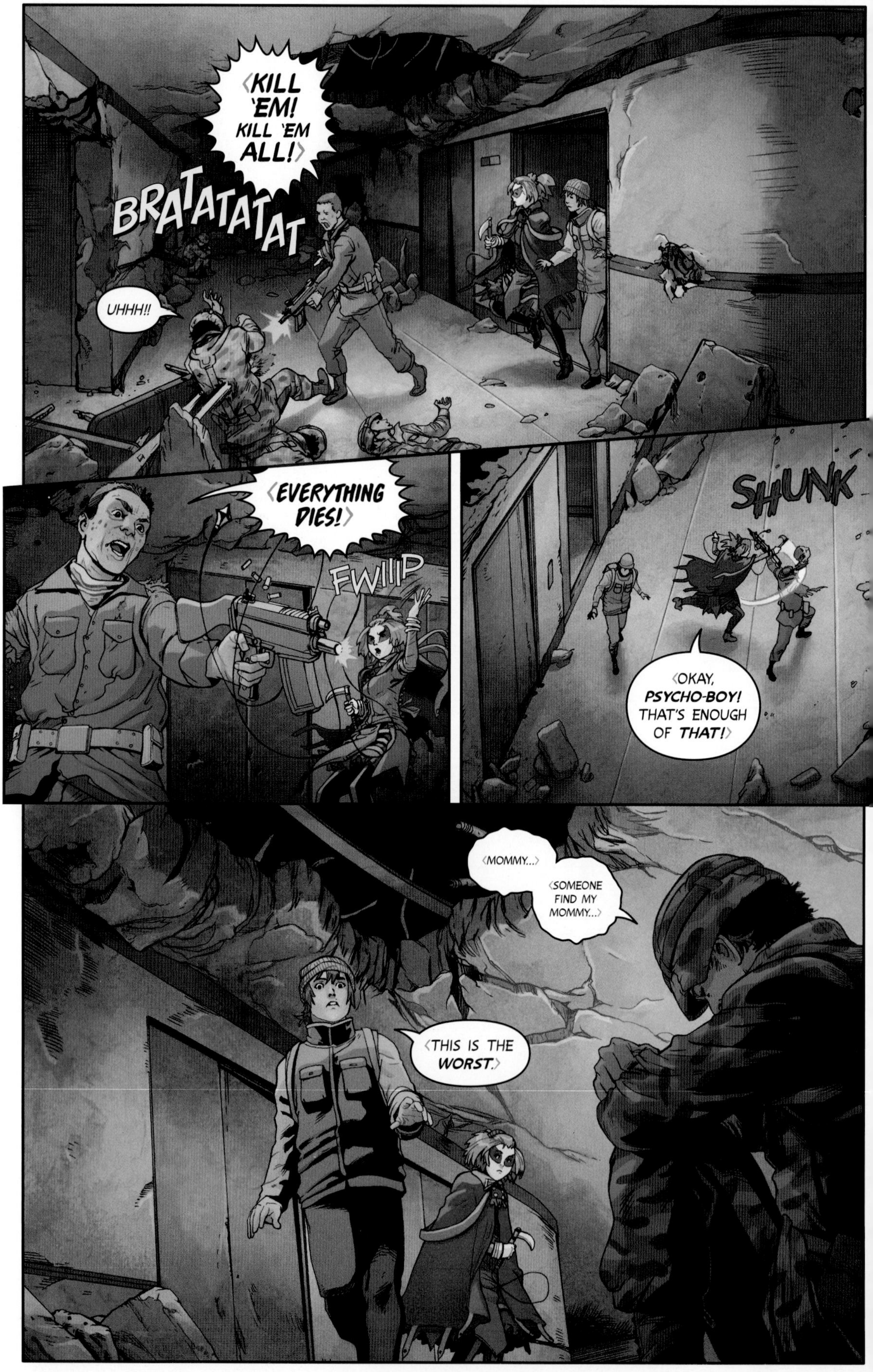

⟨KILL 'EM! KILL 'EM ALL!⟩
BRATATATAT
UHHH!!
⟨EVERYTHING DIES!⟩
FWIIIP
SHUNK
⟨OKAY, PSYCHO-BOY! THAT'S ENOUGH OF THAT!⟩
⟨MOMMY...⟩
⟨SOMEONE FIND MY MOMMY...⟩
⟨THIS IS THE WORST.⟩

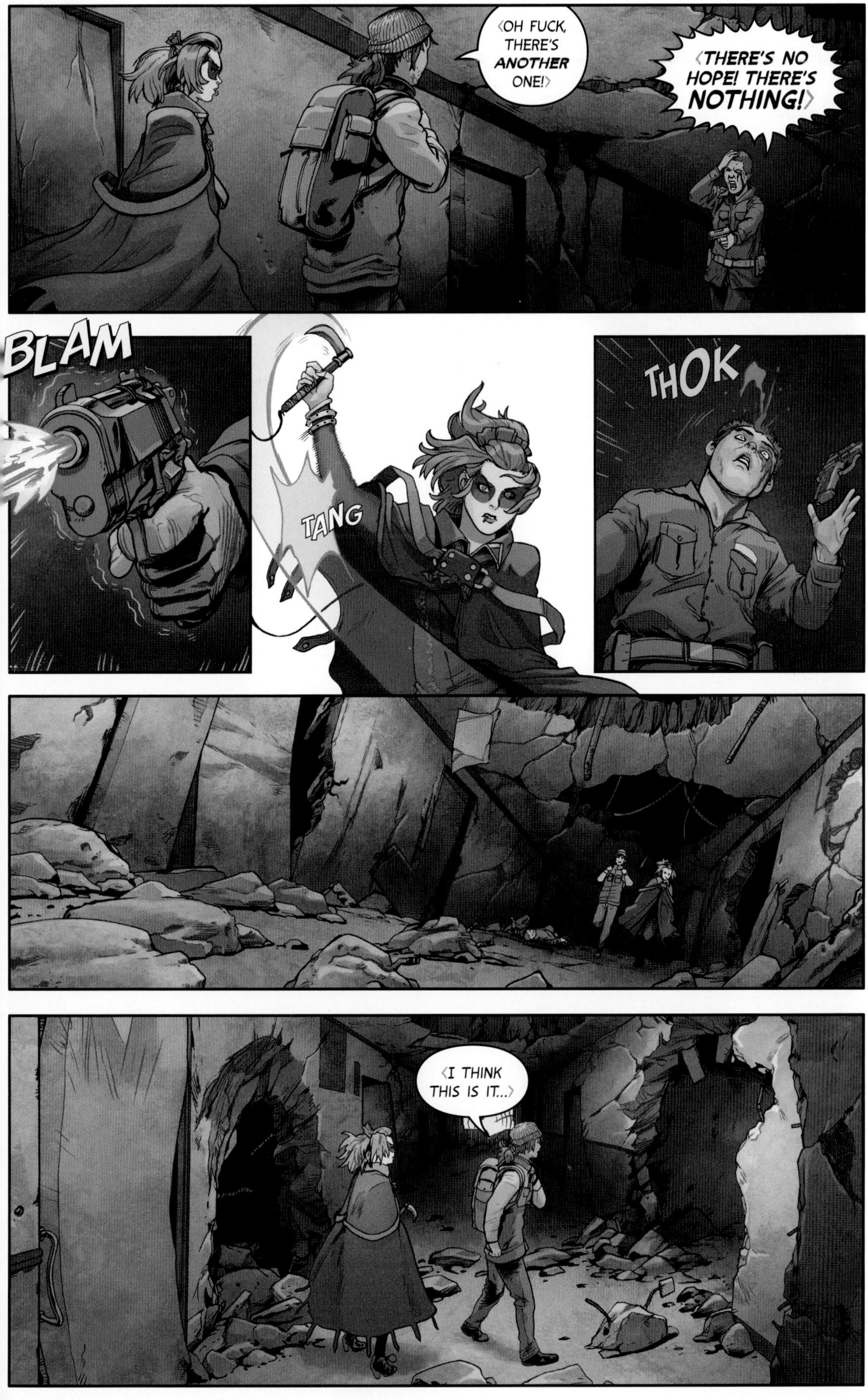

‹OH FUCK, THERE'S ANOTHER ONE!›
‹THERE'S NO HOPE! THERE'S NOTHING!›
BLAM
TANG
THOK
‹I THINK THIS IS IT...›

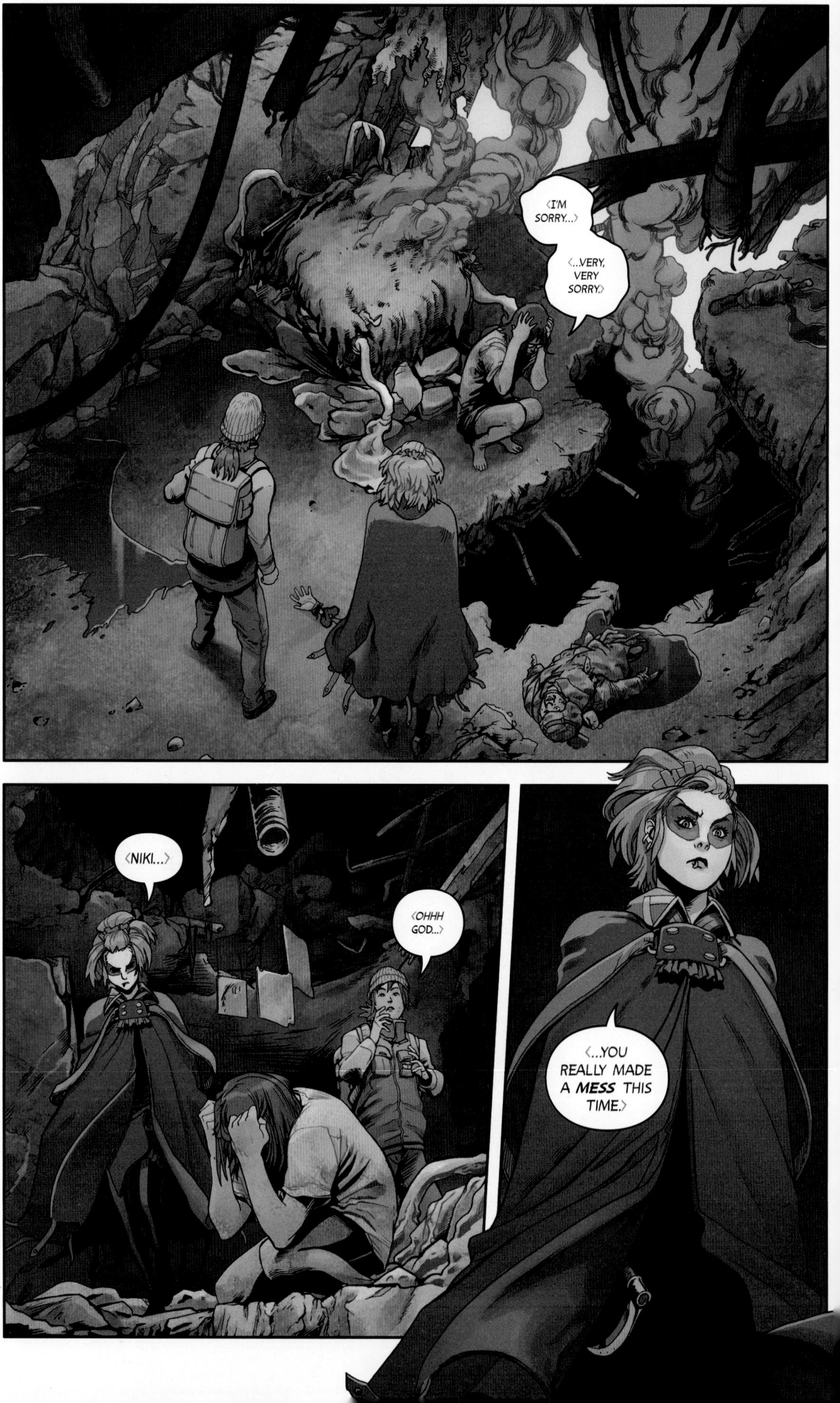
‹I'M SORRY...›
‹...VERY, VERY SORRY.›
‹NIKI...›
‹OHHH GOD...›
‹...YOU REALLY MADE A ***MESS*** THIS TIME.›

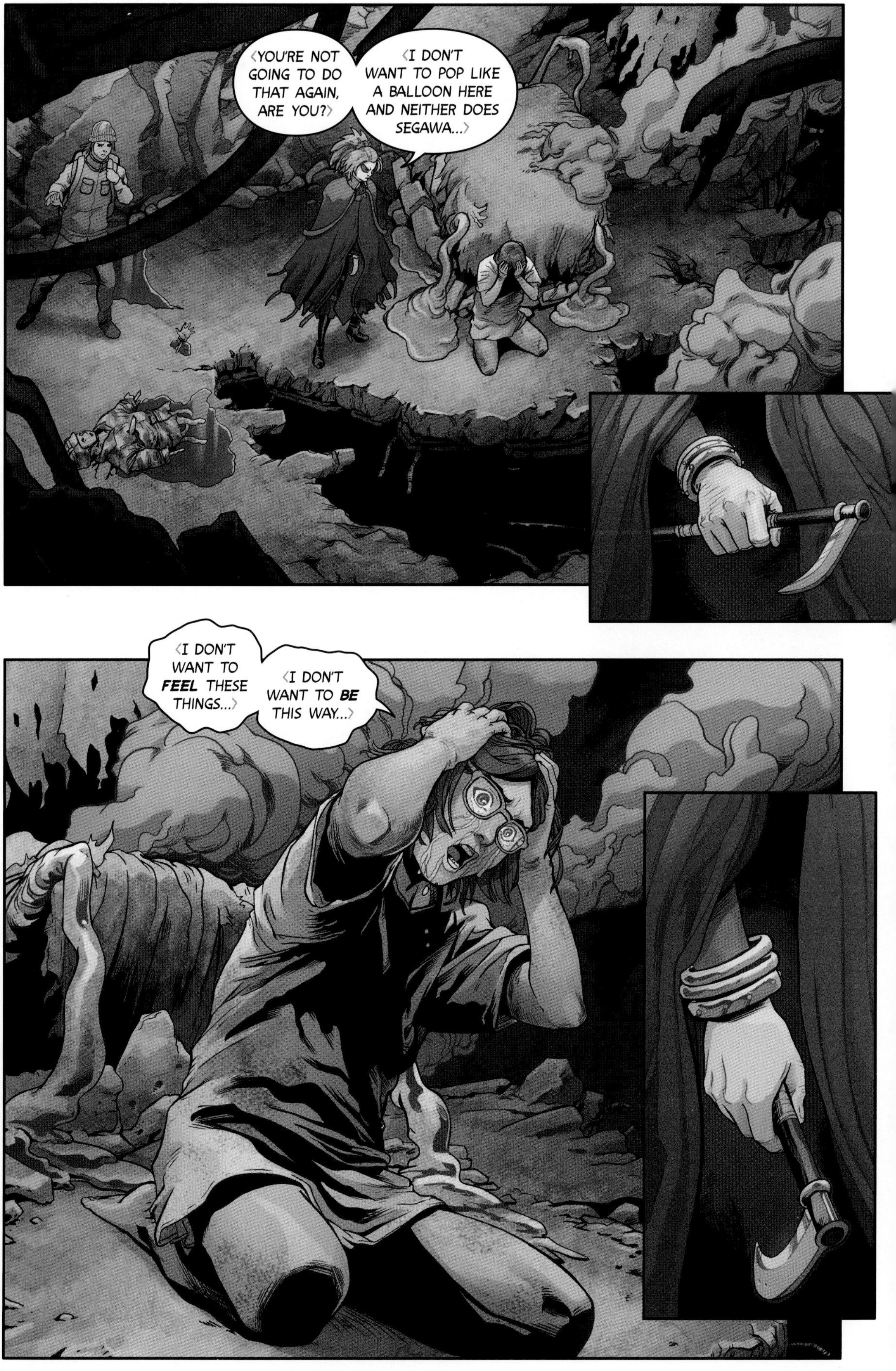
‹YOU'RE NOT GOING TO DO THAT AGAIN, ARE YOU?›
‹I DON'T WANT TO POP LIKE A BALLOON HERE AND NEITHER DOES SEGAWA...›
‹I DON'T WANT TO FEEL THESE THINGS...›
‹I DON'T WANT TO BE THIS WAY...›

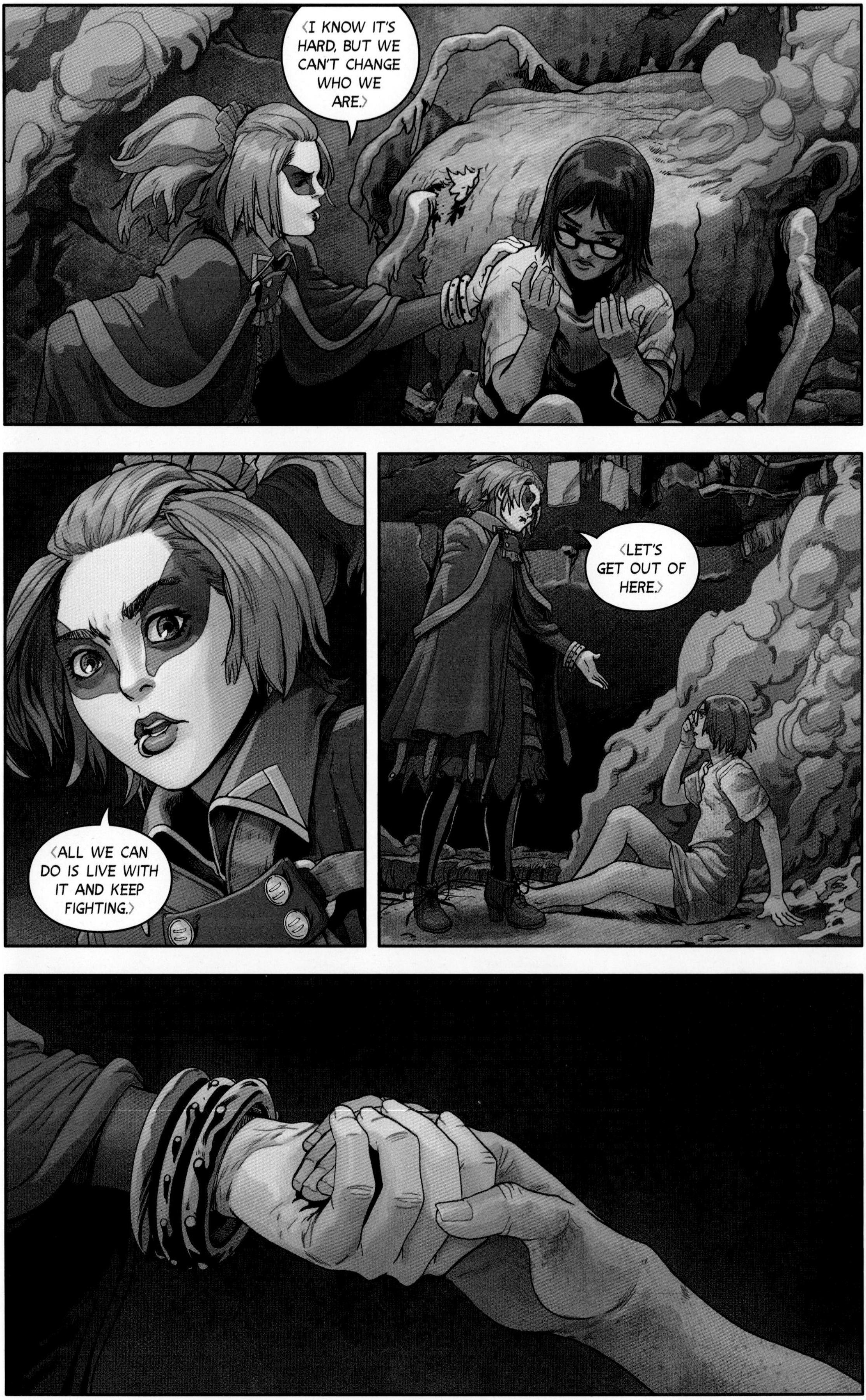

<I KNOW IT'S HARD, BUT WE CAN'T CHANGE WHO WE ARE.>
<ALL WE CAN DO IS LIVE WITH IT AND KEEP FIGHTING.>
<LET'S GET OUT OF HERE.>

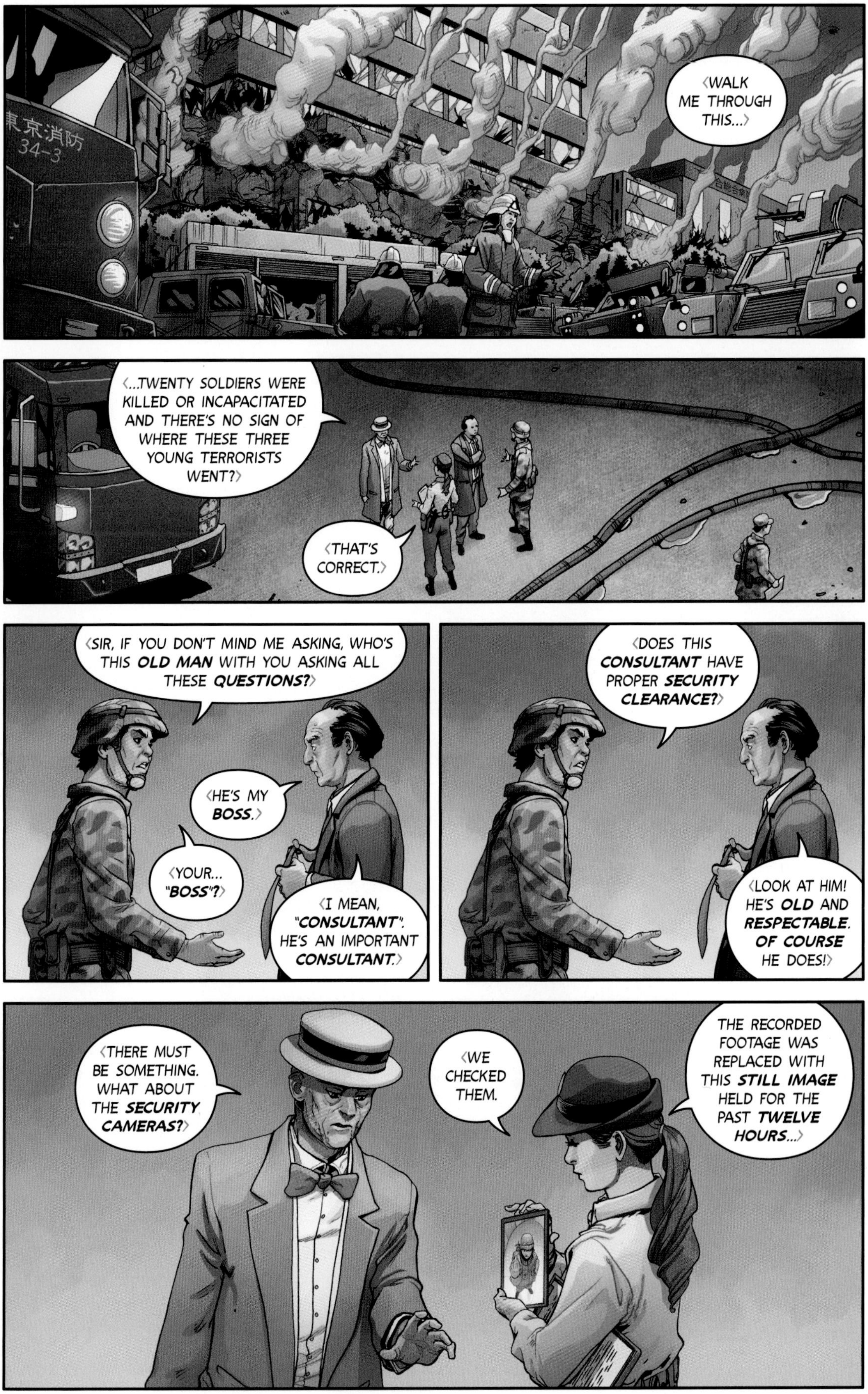

東京消防
34-3
‹WALK ME THROUGH THIS...›
‹...TWENTY SOLDIERS WERE KILLED OR INCAPACITATED AND THERE'S NO SIGN OF WHERE THESE THREE YOUNG TERRORISTS WENT?›
‹THAT'S CORRECT.›
‹SIR, IF YOU DON'T MIND ME ASKING, WHO'S THIS OLD MAN WITH YOU ASKING ALL THESE QUESTIONS?›
‹HE'S MY BOSS.›
‹YOUR... "BOSS"?›
‹I MEAN, "CONSULTANT". HE'S AN IMPORTANT CONSULTANT.›
‹DOES THIS CONSULTANT HAVE PROPER SECURITY CLEARANCE?›
‹LOOK AT HIM! HE'S OLD AND RESPECTABLE. OF COURSE HE DOES!›
‹THERE MUST BE SOMETHING. WHAT ABOUT THE SECURITY CAMERAS?›
‹WE CHECKED THEM.
THE RECORDED FOOTAGE WAS REPLACED WITH THIS STILL IMAGE HELD FOR THE PAST TWELVE HOURS...›

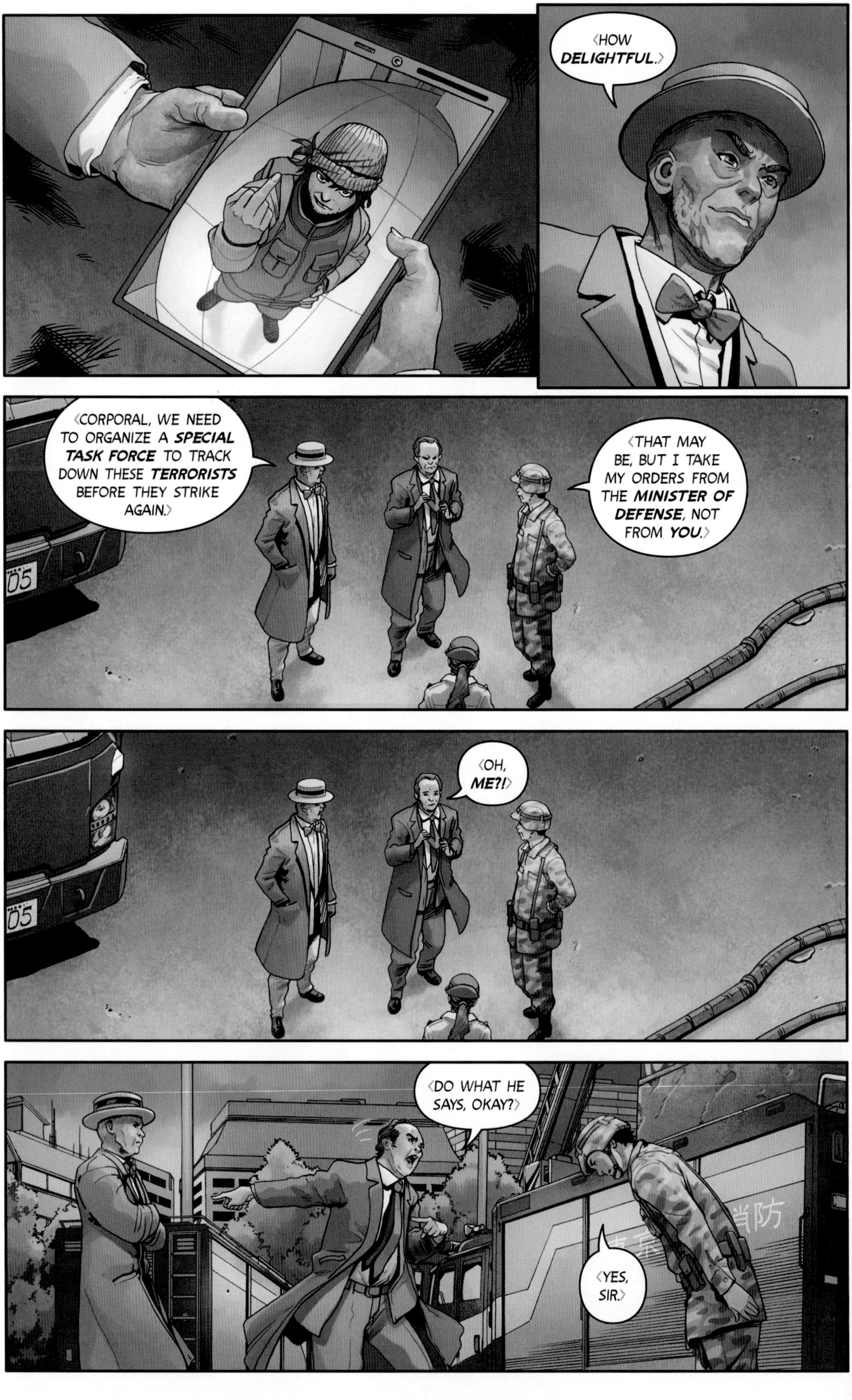
‹HOW DELIGHTFUL.›
‹CORPORAL, WE NEED TO ORGANIZE A SPECIAL TASK FORCE TO TRACK DOWN THESE TERRORISTS BEFORE THEY STRIKE AGAIN.›
‹THAT MAY BE, BUT I TAKE MY ORDERS FROM THE MINISTER OF DEFENSE, NOT FROM YOU.›
‹OH, ME?!›
‹DO WHAT HE SAYS, OKAY?›
‹YES, SIR.›

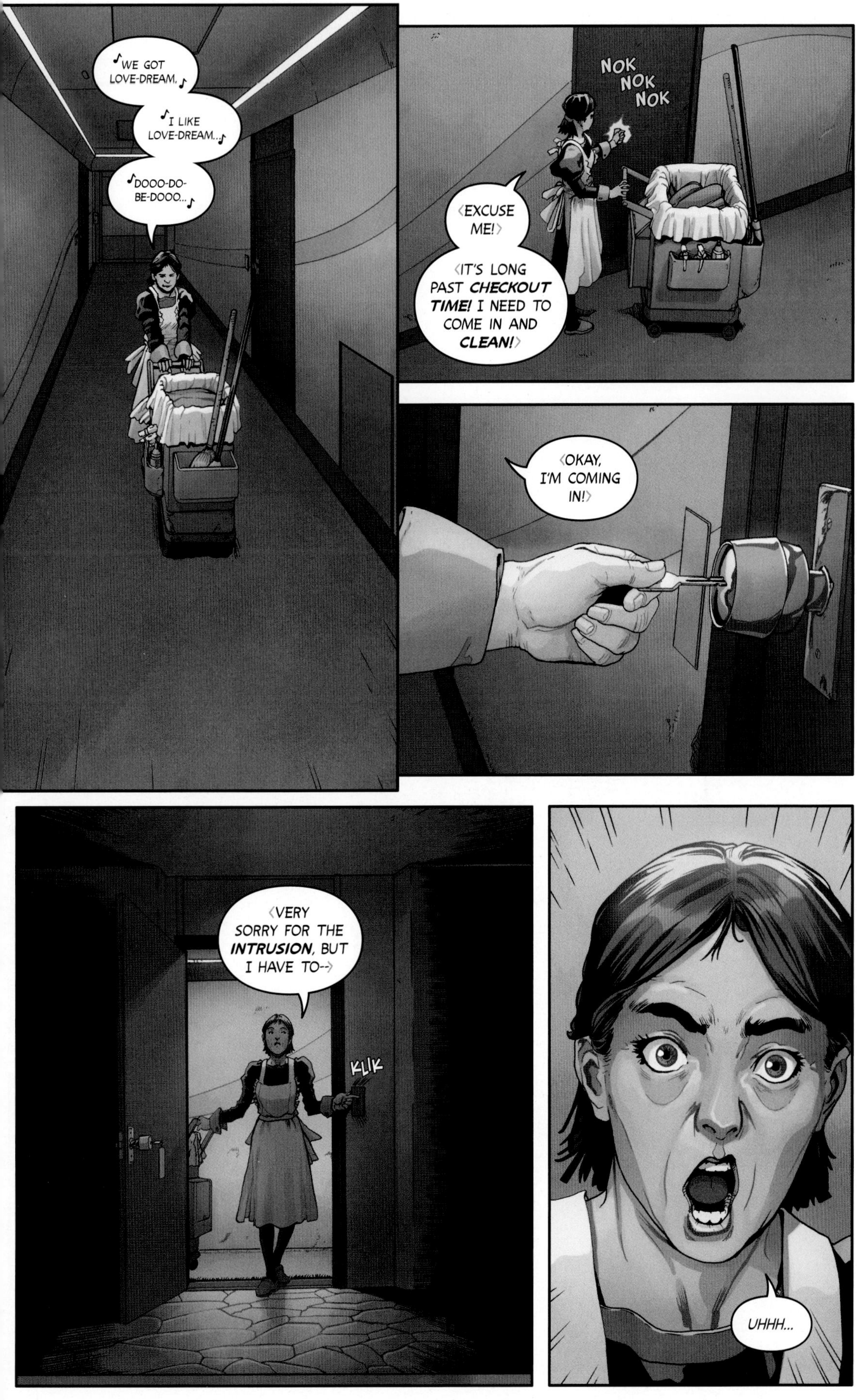

♪WE GOT LOVE-DREAM.♪
♪I LIKE LOVE-DREAM...♪
♪DOOO-DO-BE-DOOO...♪
NOK NOK NOK
‹EXCUSE ME!›
‹IT'S LONG PAST CHECKOUT TIME! I NEED TO COME IN AND CLEAN!›
‹OKAY, I'M COMING IN!›
‹VERY SORRY FOR THE INTRUSION, BUT I HAVE TO--›
KLIK
UHHH...

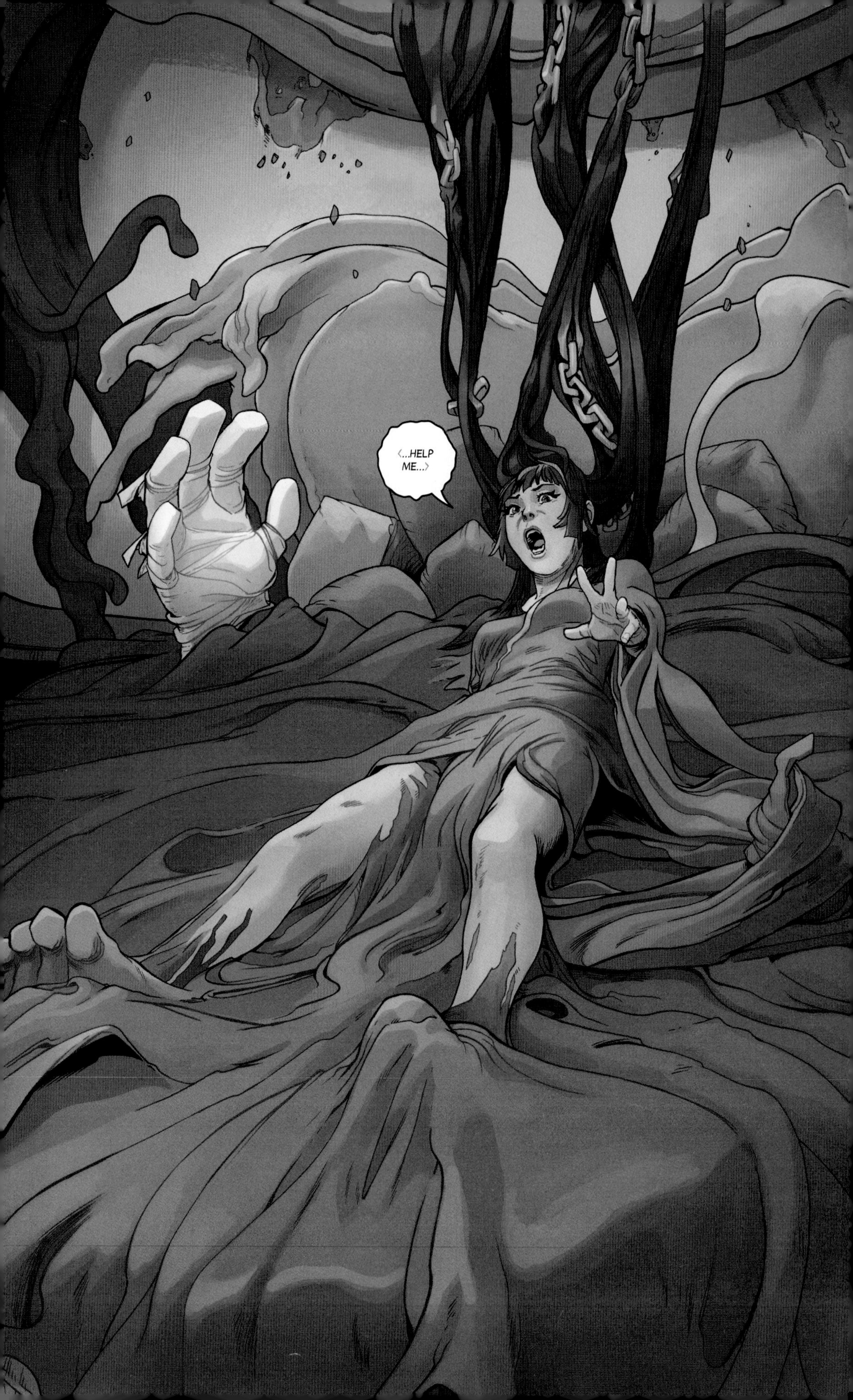
<...HELP ME...>

Chapter Twenty-Two

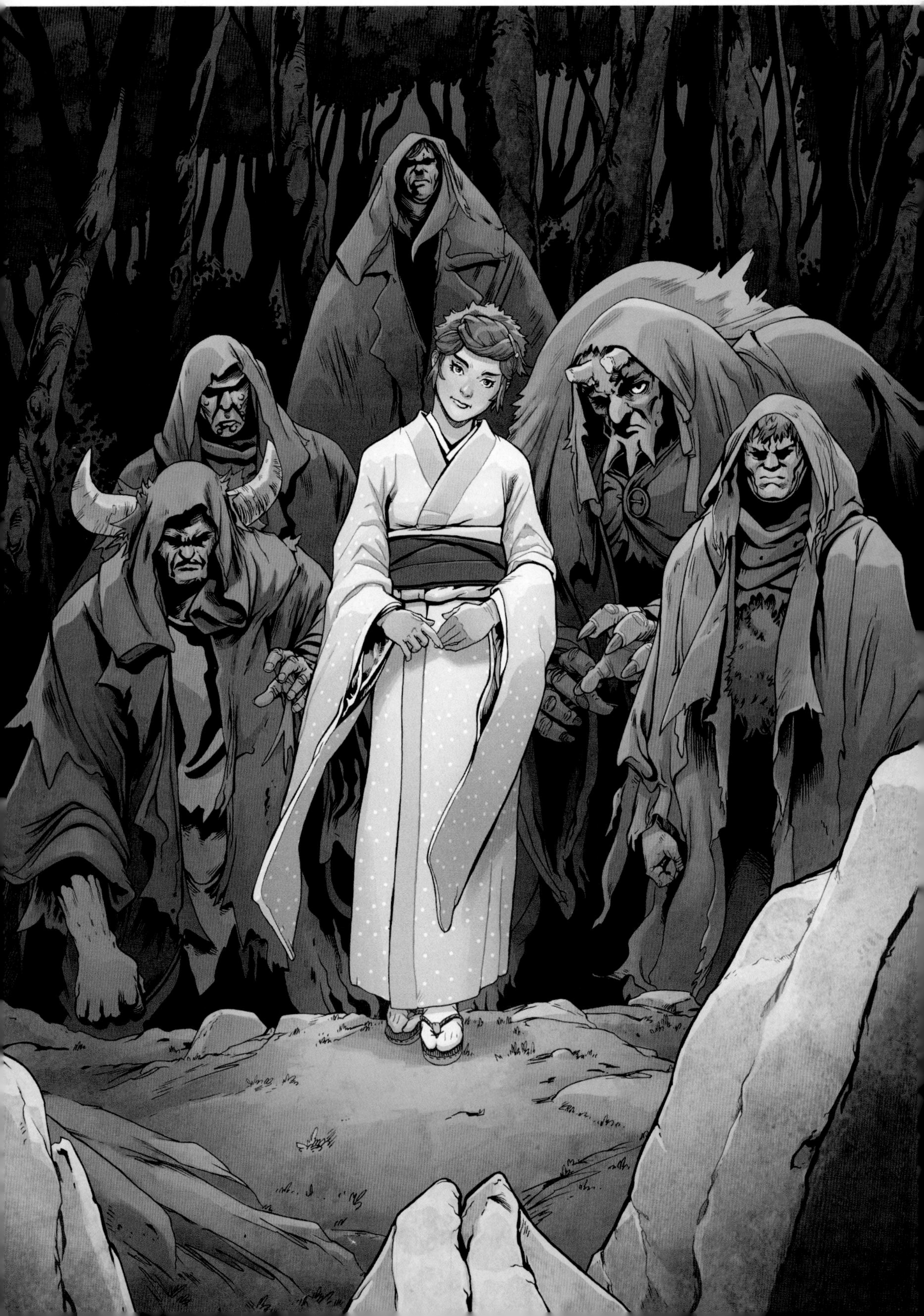

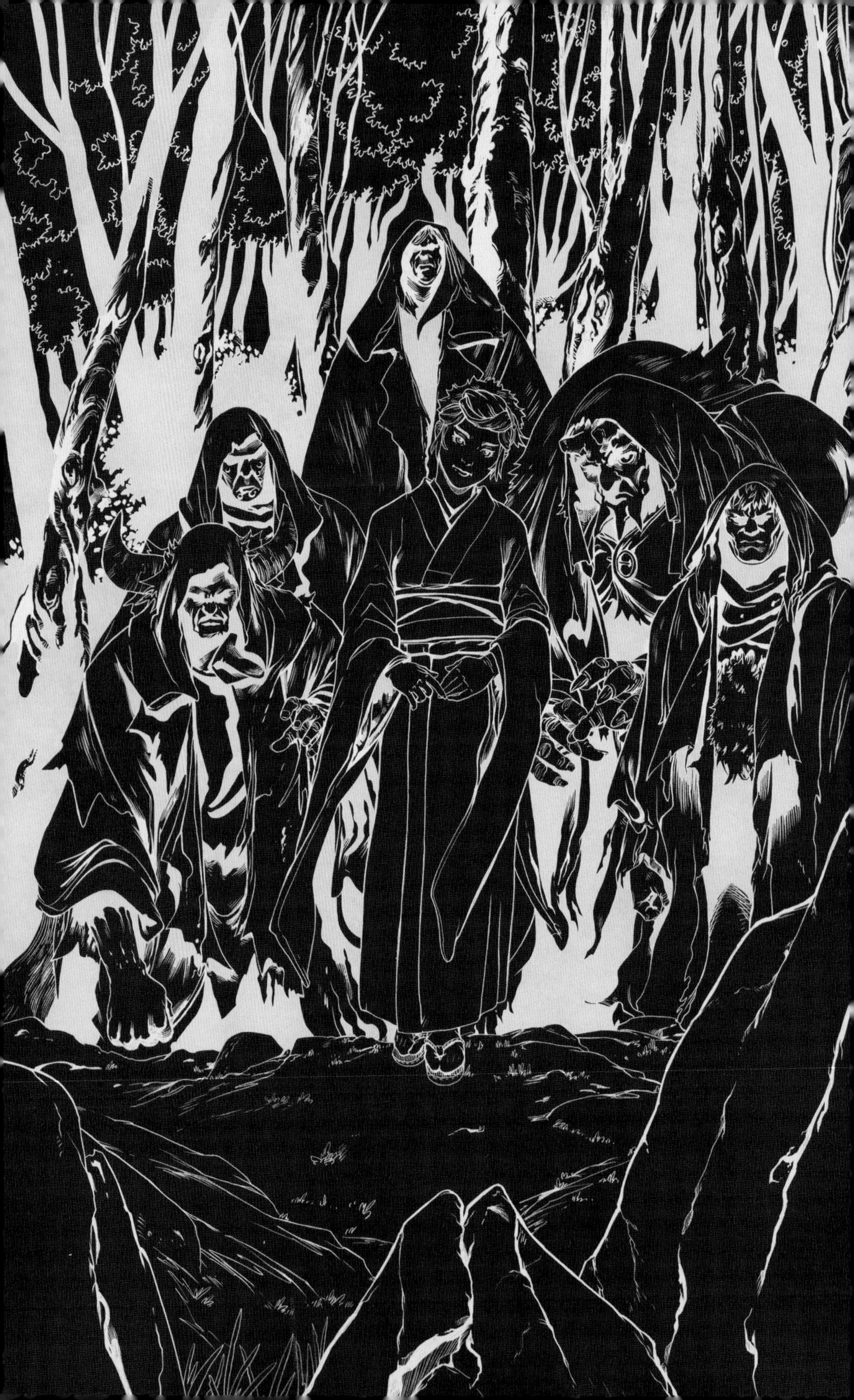

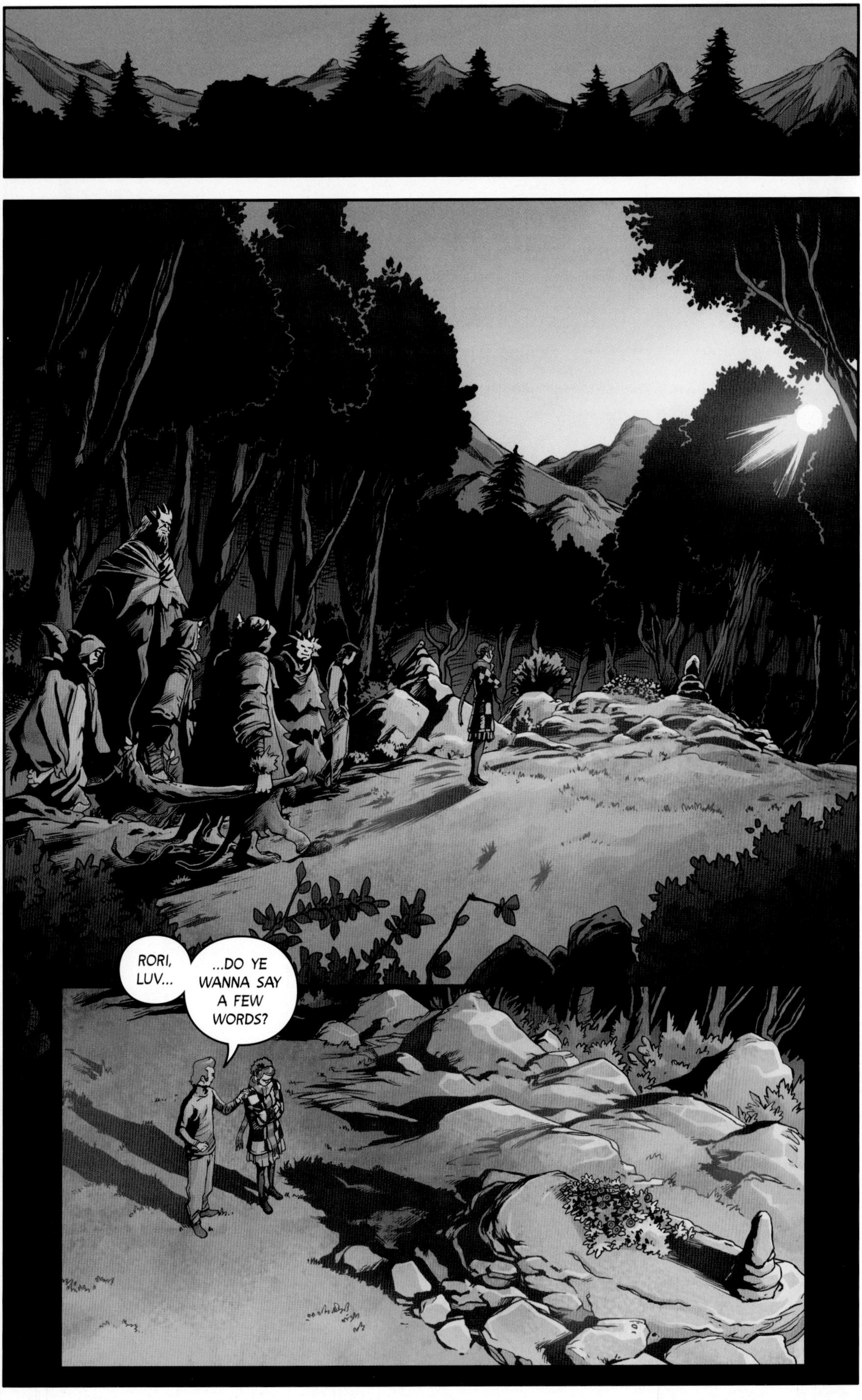
RORI, LUV...
...DO YE WANNA SAY A FEW WORDS?

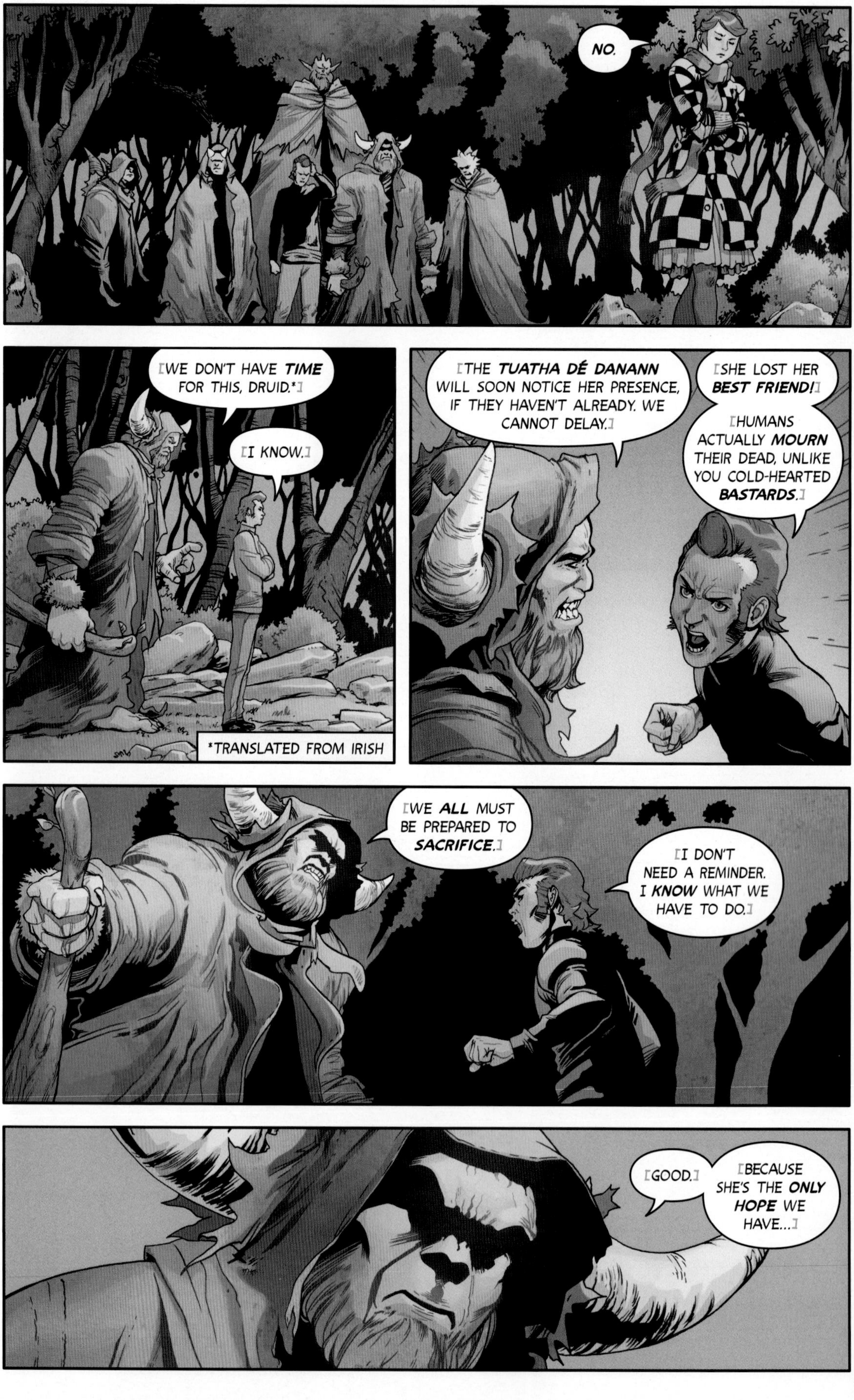
NO.
[WE DON'T HAVE TIME FOR THIS, DRUID.*]
[I KNOW.]
*TRANSLATED FROM IRISH
[THE TUATHA DÉ DANANN WILL SOON NOTICE HER PRESENCE, IF THEY HAVEN'T ALREADY. WE CANNOT DELAY.]
[SHE LOST HER BEST FRIEND!]
[HUMANS ACTUALLY MOURN THEIR DEAD, UNLIKE YOU COLD-HEARTED BASTARDS.]
[WE ALL MUST BE PREPARED TO SACRIFICE.]
[I DON'T NEED A REMINDER. I KNOW WHAT WE HAVE TO DO.]
[GOOD.]
[BECAUSE SHE'S THE ONLY HOPE WE HAVE...]

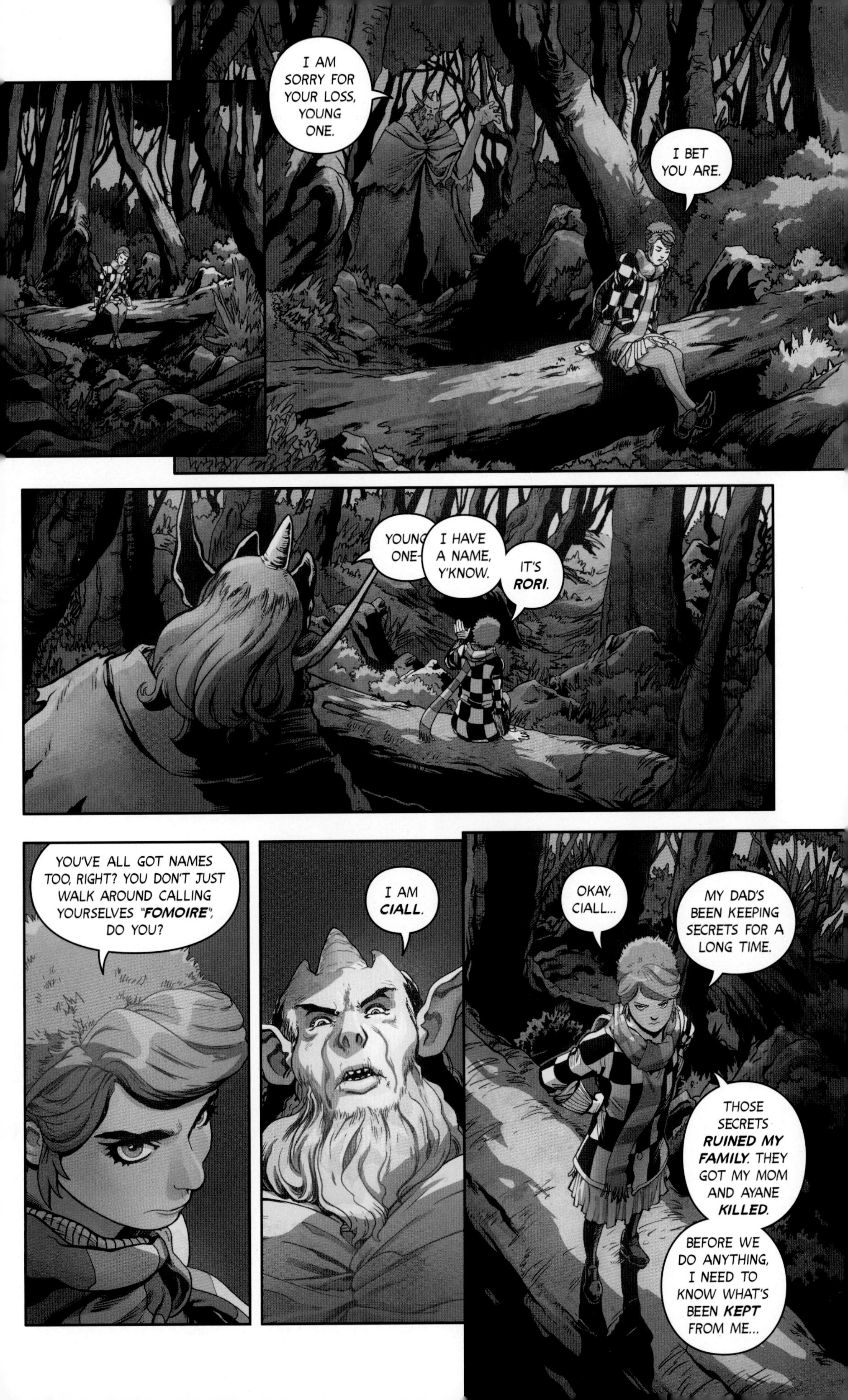
I AM SORRY FOR YOUR LOSS, YOUNG ONE.
I BET YOU ARE.
YOUNG ONE--
I HAVE A NAME, Y'KNOW.
IT'S RORI.
YOU'VE ALL GOT NAMES TOO, RIGHT? YOU DON'T JUST WALK AROUND CALLING YOURSELVES "FOMOIRE", DO YOU?
I AM CIALL.
OKAY, CIALL...
MY DAD'S BEEN KEEPING SECRETS FOR A LONG TIME.
THOSE SECRETS RUINED MY FAMILY. THEY GOT MY MOM AND AYANE KILLED.
BEFORE WE DO ANYTHING, I NEED TO KNOW WHAT'S BEEN KEPT FROM ME...

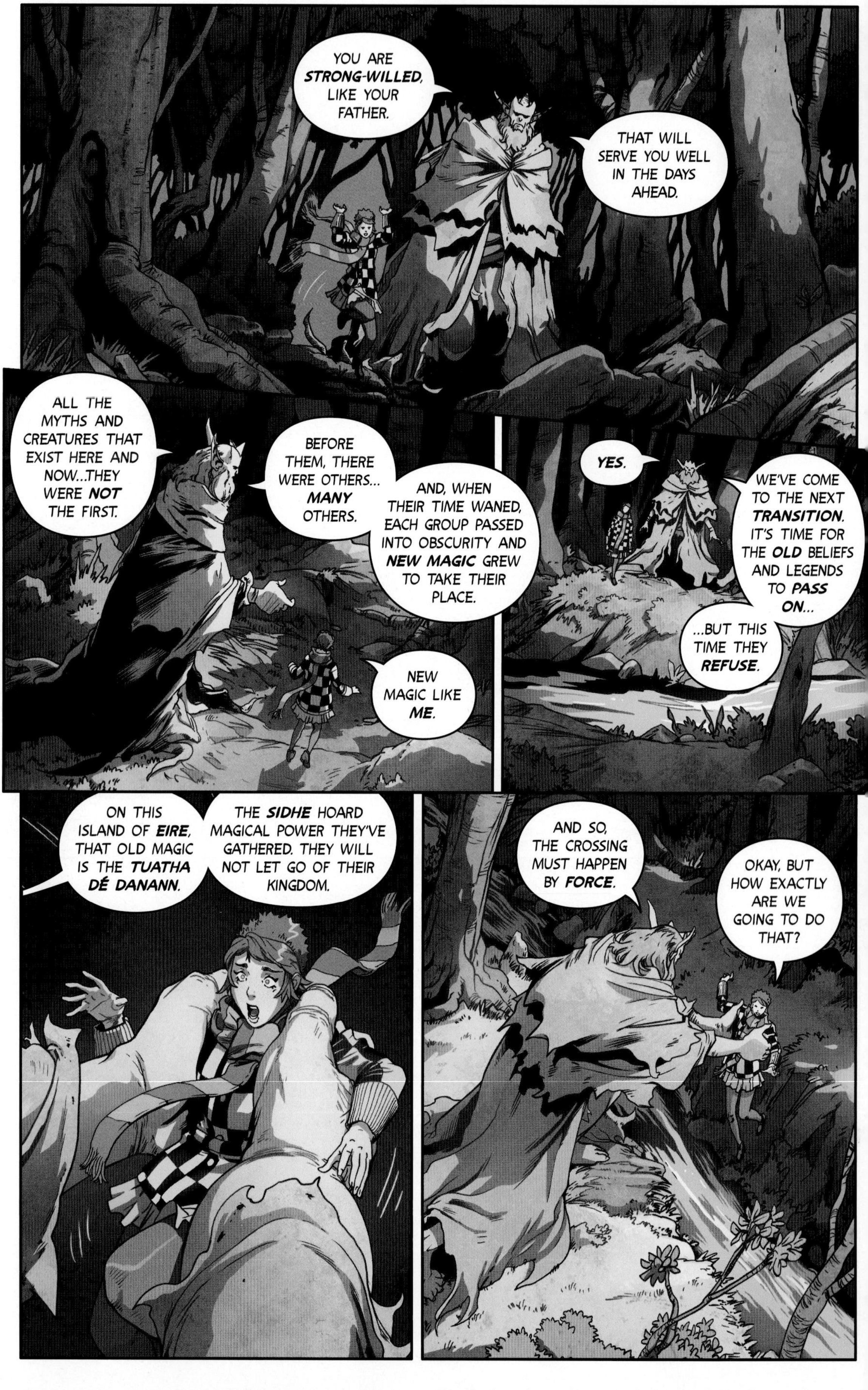
YOU ARE STRONG-WILLED, LIKE YOUR FATHER.
THAT WILL SERVE YOU WELL IN THE DAYS AHEAD.
ALL THE MYTHS AND CREATURES THAT EXIST HERE AND NOW...THEY WERE NOT THE FIRST.
BEFORE THEM, THERE WERE OTHERS... MANY OTHERS.
AND, WHEN THEIR TIME WANED, EACH GROUP PASSED INTO OBSCURITY AND NEW MAGIC GREW TO TAKE THEIR PLACE.
NEW MAGIC LIKE ME.
YES.
WE'VE COME TO THE NEXT TRANSITION. IT'S TIME FOR THE OLD BELIEFS AND LEGENDS TO PASS ON...
...BUT THIS TIME THEY REFUSE.
ON THIS ISLAND OF EIRE, THAT OLD MAGIC IS THE TUATHA DÉ DANANN.
THE SIDHE HOARD MAGICAL POWER THEY'VE GATHERED. THEY WILL NOT LET GO OF THEIR KINGDOM.
AND SO, THE CROSSING MUST HAPPEN BY FORCE.
OKAY, BUT HOW EXACTLY ARE WE GOING TO DO THAT?

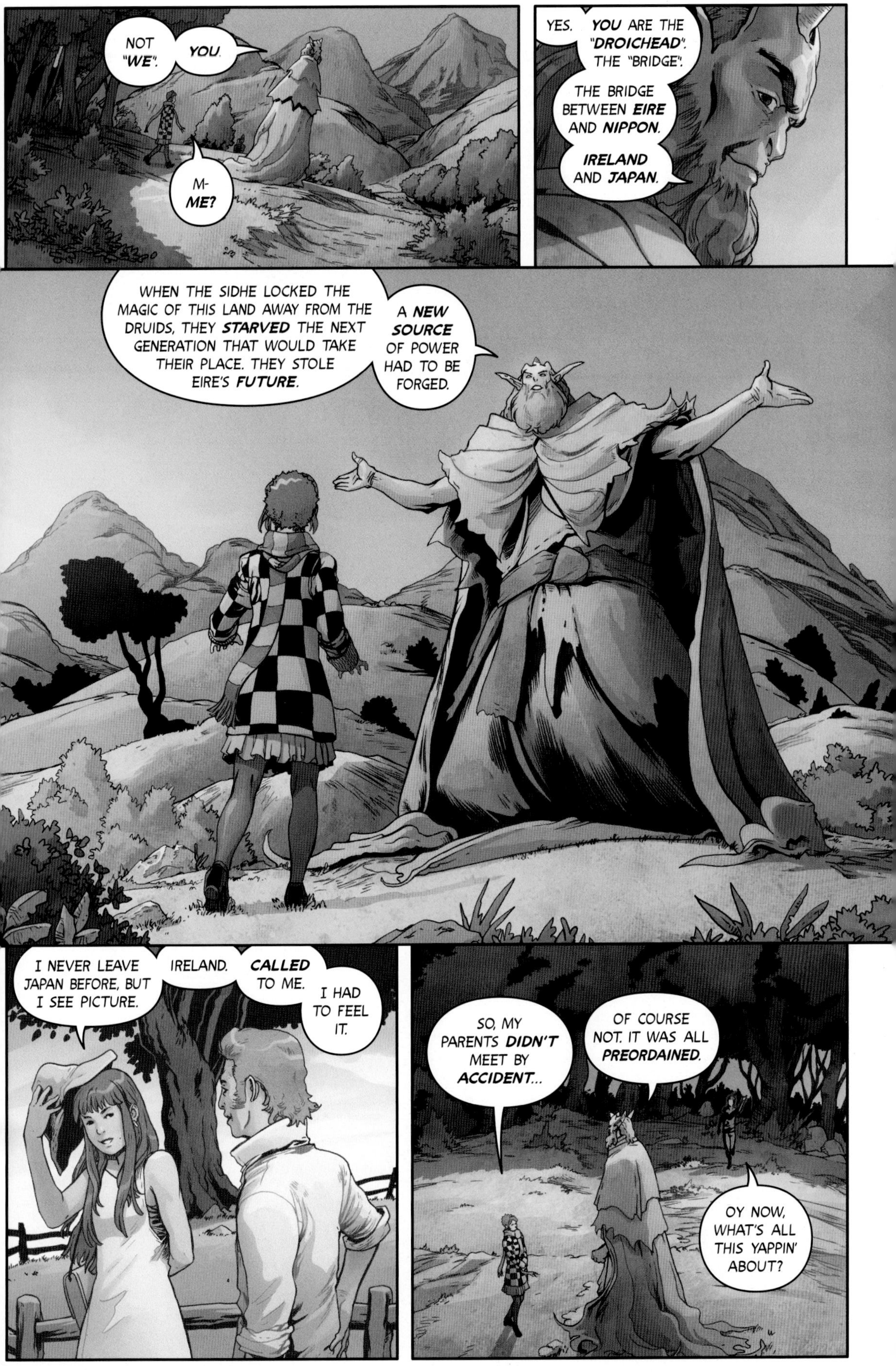
NOT "WE".
YOU.
M-ME?
YES.
YOU ARE THE "DROICHEAD". THE "BRIDGE".
THE BRIDGE BETWEEN EIRE AND NIPPON.
IRELAND AND JAPAN.
WHEN THE SIDHE LOCKED THE MAGIC OF THIS LAND AWAY FROM THE DRUIDS, THEY STARVED THE NEXT GENERATION THAT WOULD TAKE THEIR PLACE. THEY STOLE EIRE'S FUTURE.
A NEW SOURCE OF POWER HAD TO BE FORGED.
I NEVER LEAVE JAPAN BEFORE, BUT I SEE PICTURE.
IRELAND.
CALLED TO ME.
I HAD TO FEEL IT.
SO, MY PARENTS DIDN'T MEET BY ACCIDENT...
OF COURSE NOT. IT WAS ALL PREORDAINED.
OY NOW, WHAT'S ALL THIS YAPPIN' ABOUT?

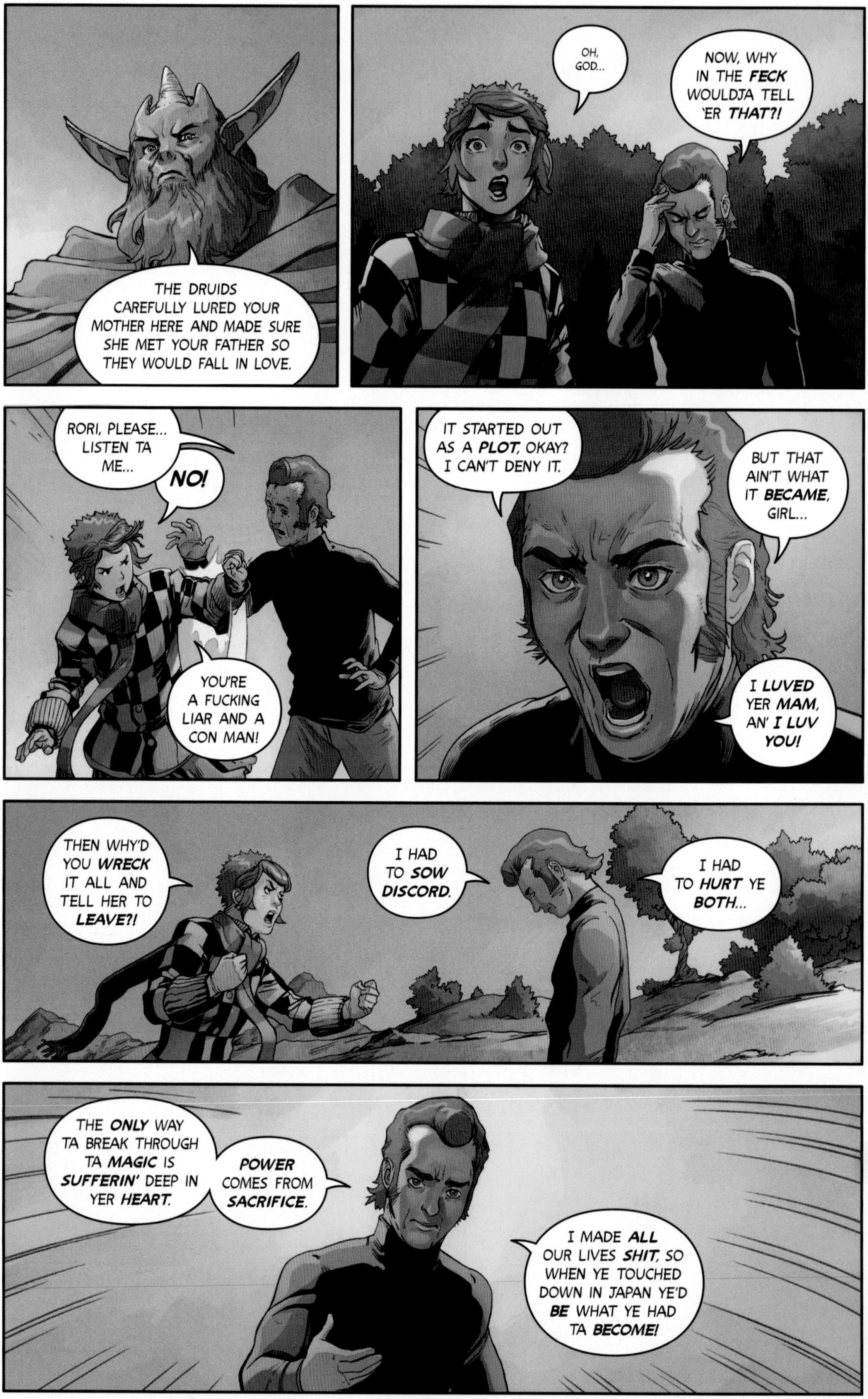
THE DRUIDS CAREFULLY LURED YOUR MOTHER HERE AND MADE SURE SHE MET YOUR FATHER SO THEY WOULD FALL IN LOVE.
OH, GOD...
NOW, WHY IN THE FECK WOULDJA TELL 'ER THAT?!
RORI, PLEASE... LISTEN TA ME...
NO!
YOU'RE A FUCKING LIAR AND A CON MAN!
IT STARTED OUT AS A PLOT, OKAY? I CAN'T DENY IT.
BUT THAT AIN'T WHAT IT BECAME, GIRL...
I LUVED YER MAM, AN' I LUV YOU!
THEN WHY'D YOU WRECK IT ALL AND TELL HER TO LEAVE?!
I HAD TO SOW DISCORD.
I HAD TO HURT YE BOTH...
THE ONLY WAY TA BREAK THROUGH TA MAGIC IS SUFFERIN' DEEP IN YER HEART.
POWER COMES FROM SACRIFICE.
I MADE ALL OUR LIVES SHIT, SO WHEN YE TOUCHED DOWN IN JAPAN YE'D BE WHAT YE HAD TA BECOME!

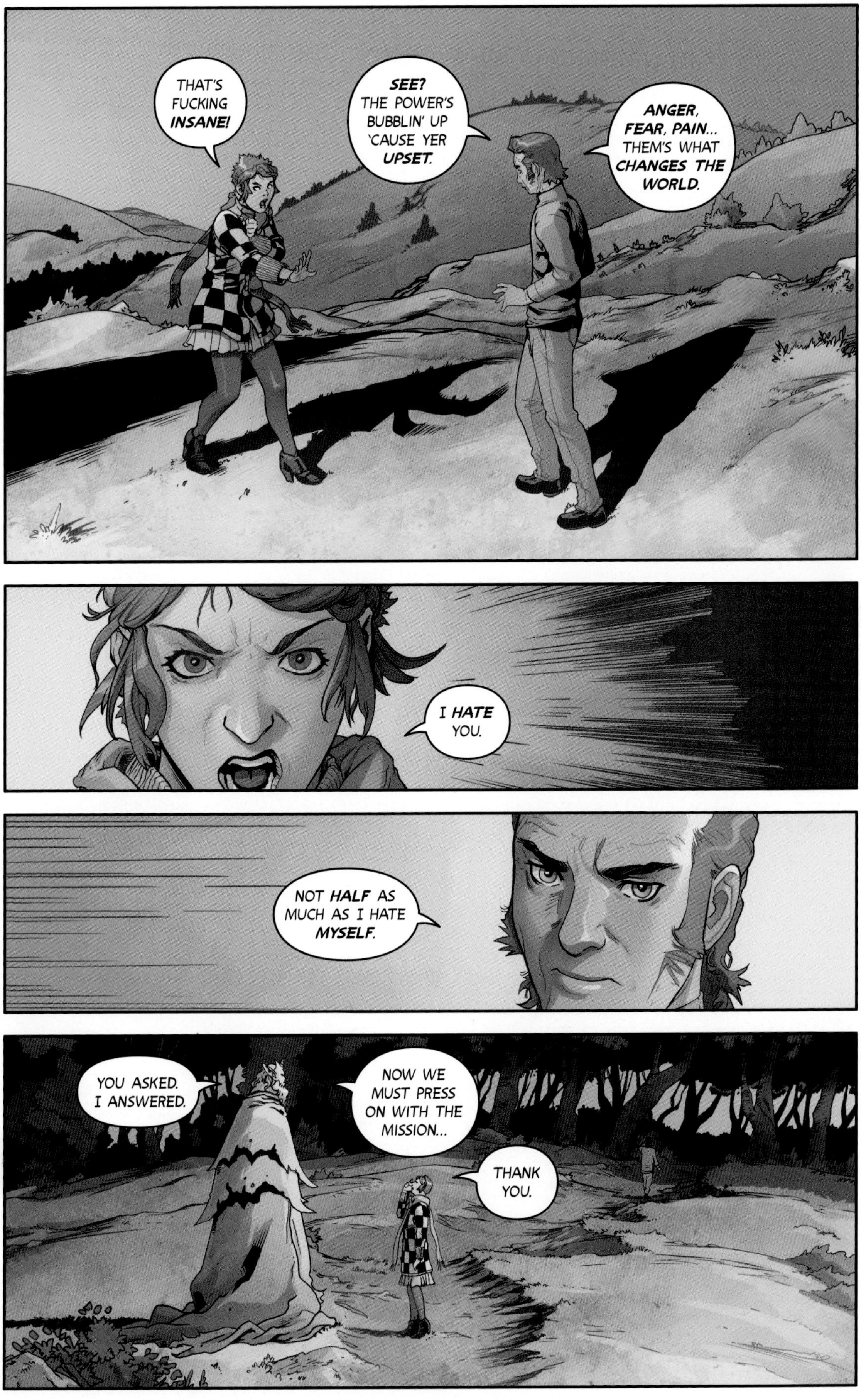
THAT'S FUCKING INSANE!
SEE? THE POWER'S BUBBLIN' UP 'CAUSE YER UPSET.
ANGER, FEAR, PAIN... THEM'S WHAT CHANGES THE WORLD.
I HATE YOU.
NOT HALF AS MUCH AS I HATE MYSELF.
YOU ASKED. I ANSWERED.
NOW WE MUST PRESS ON WITH THE MISSION...
THANK YOU.

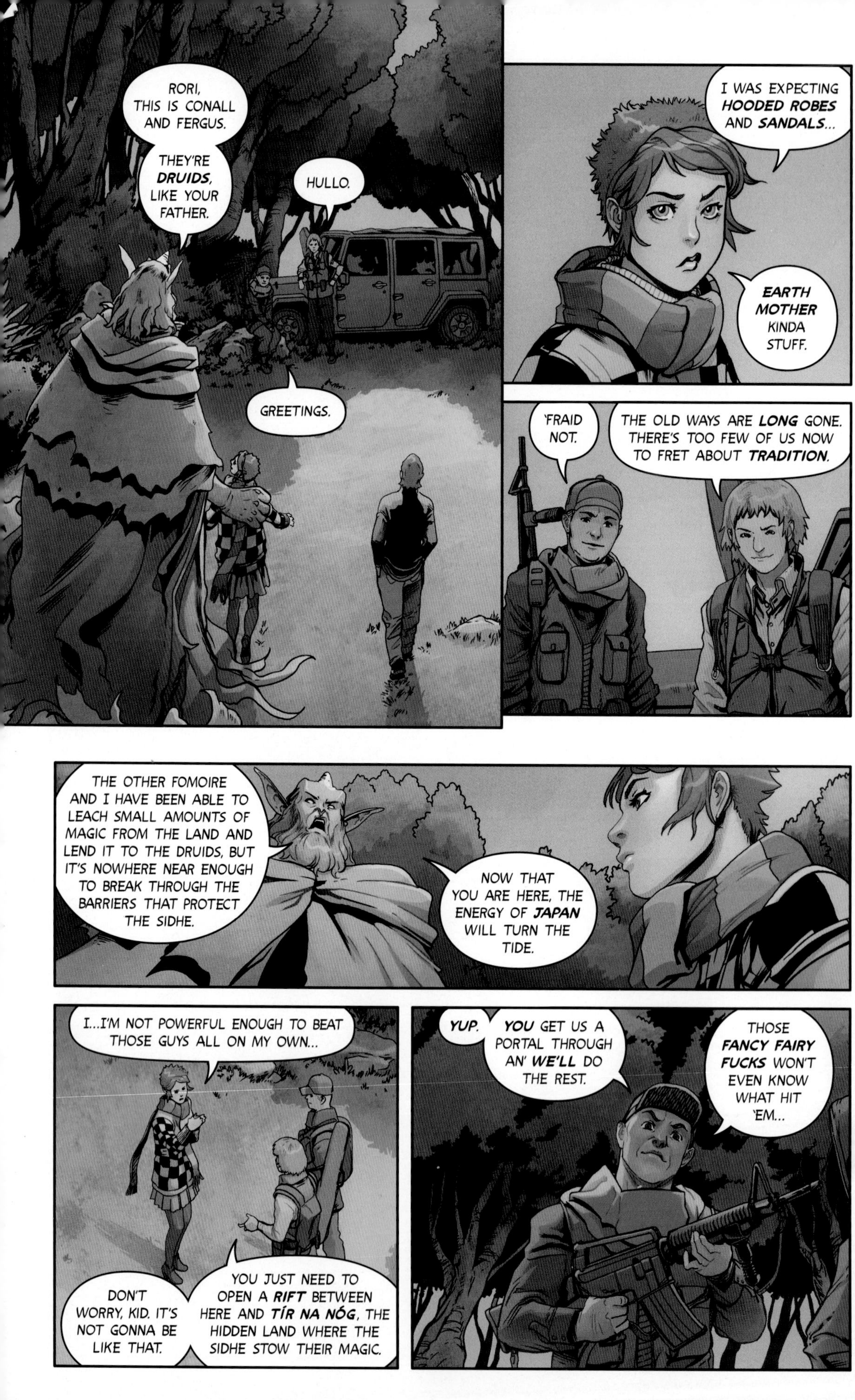
RORI, THIS IS CONALL AND FERGUS.
THEY'RE DRUIDS, LIKE YOUR FATHER.
HULLO.
GREETINGS.
I WAS EXPECTING HOODED ROBES AND SANDALS...
EARTH MOTHER KINDA STUFF.
'FRAID NOT.
THE OLD WAYS ARE LONG GONE. THERE'S TOO FEW OF US NOW TO FRET ABOUT TRADITION.
THE OTHER FOMOIRE AND I HAVE BEEN ABLE TO LEACH SMALL AMOUNTS OF MAGIC FROM THE LAND AND LEND IT TO THE DRUIDS, BUT IT'S NOWHERE NEAR ENOUGH TO BREAK THROUGH THE BARRIERS THAT PROTECT THE SIDHE.
NOW THAT YOU ARE HERE, THE ENERGY OF JAPAN WILL TURN THE TIDE.
I...I'M NOT POWERFUL ENOUGH TO BEAT THOSE GUYS ALL ON MY OWN...
DON'T WORRY, KID. IT'S NOT GONNA BE LIKE THAT.
YOU JUST NEED TO OPEN A RIFT BETWEEN HERE AND TÍR NA NÓG, THE HIDDEN LAND WHERE THE SIDHE STOW THEIR MAGIC.
YUP.
YOU GET US A PORTAL THROUGH AN' WE'LL DO THE REST.
THOSE FANCY FAIRY FUCKS WON'T EVEN KNOW WHAT HIT 'EM...

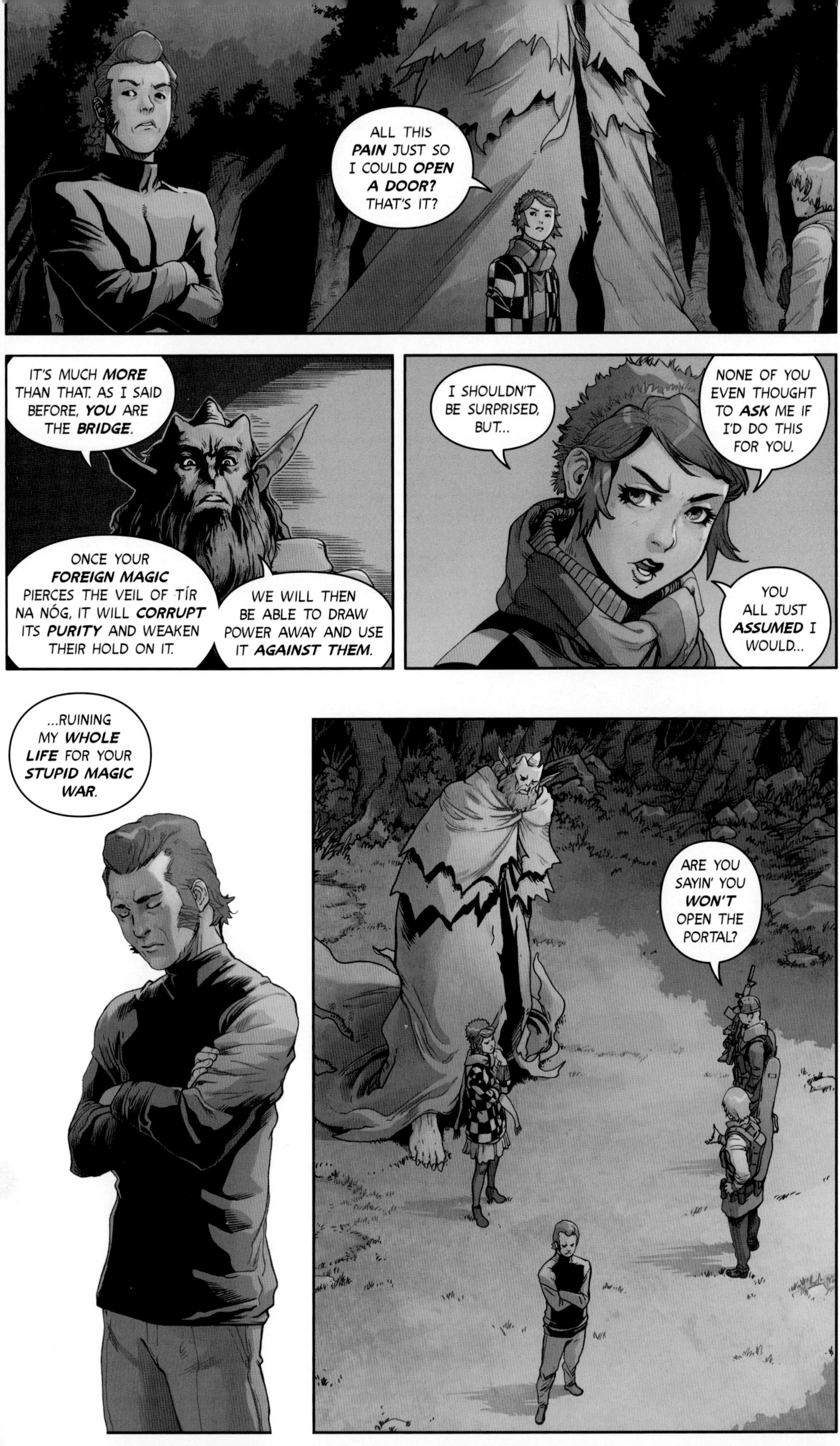
ALL THIS PAIN JUST SO I COULD OPEN A DOOR? THAT'S IT?
IT'S MUCH MORE THAN THAT. AS I SAID BEFORE, YOU ARE THE BRIDGE.
ONCE YOUR FOREIGN MAGIC PIERCES THE VEIL OF TÍR NA NÓG, IT WILL CORRUPT ITS PURITY AND WEAKEN THEIR HOLD ON IT.
WE WILL THEN BE ABLE TO DRAW POWER AWAY AND USE IT AGAINST THEM.
I SHOULDN'T BE SURPRISED, BUT...
NONE OF YOU EVEN THOUGHT TO ASK ME IF I'D DO THIS FOR YOU.
YOU ALL JUST ASSUMED I WOULD...
...RUINING MY WHOLE LIFE FOR YOUR STUPID MAGIC WAR.
ARE YOU SAYIN' YOU WON'T OPEN THE PORTAL?

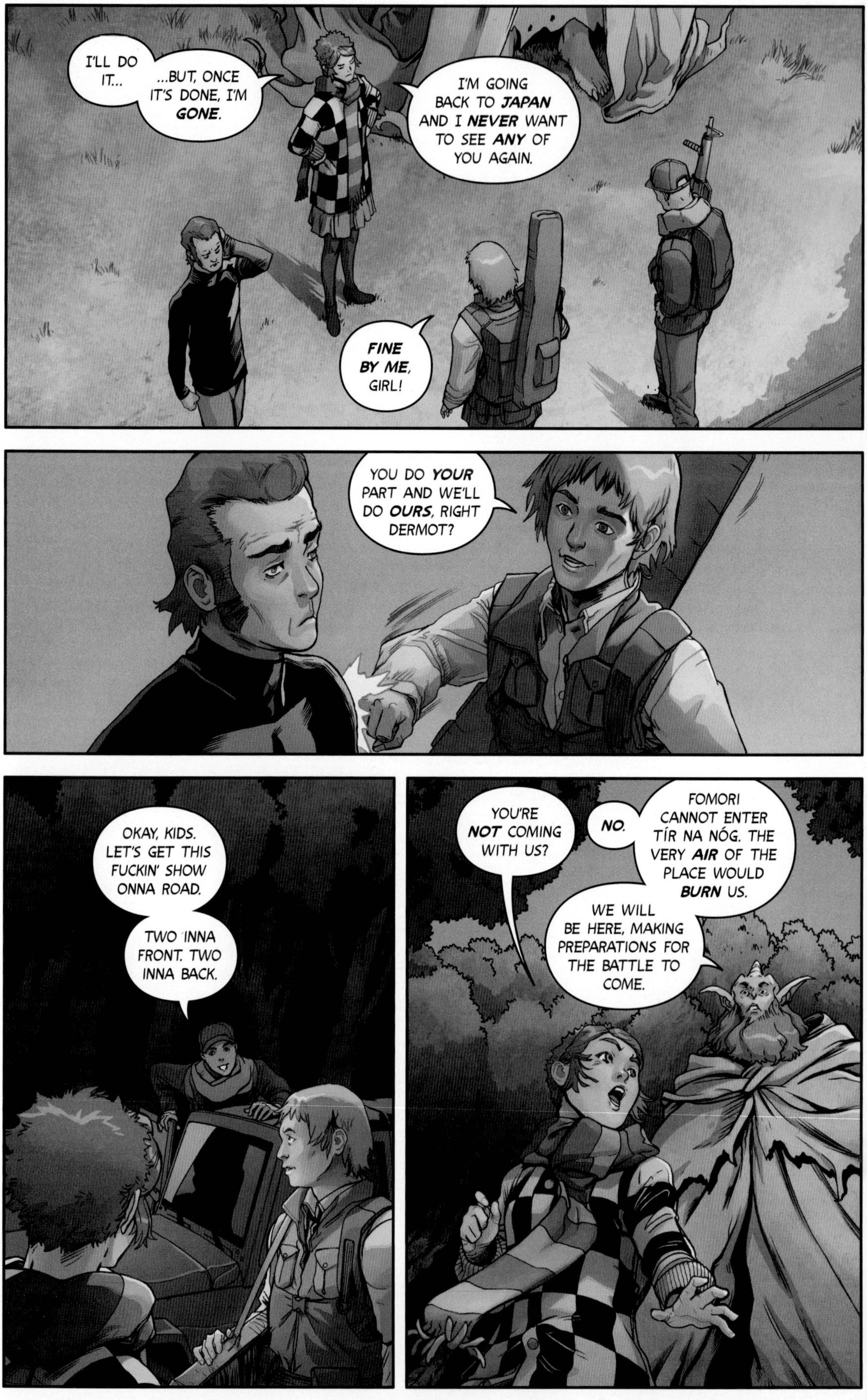
I'LL DO IT...
...BUT, ONCE IT'S DONE, I'M **GONE.**
I'M GOING BACK TO **JAPAN** AND I **NEVER** WANT TO SEE **ANY** OF YOU AGAIN.
FINE BY ME, GIRL!
YOU DO **YOUR** PART AND WE'LL DO **OURS**, RIGHT DERMOT?
OKAY, KIDS. LET'S GET THIS FUCKIN' SHOW ONNA ROAD.
TWO INNA FRONT. TWO INNA BACK.
YOU'RE **NOT** COMING WITH US?
NO.
FOMORI CANNOT ENTER TÍR NA NÓG. THE VERY **AIR** OF THE PLACE WOULD **BURN** US.
WE WILL BE HERE, MAKING PREPARATIONS FOR THE BATTLE TO COME.

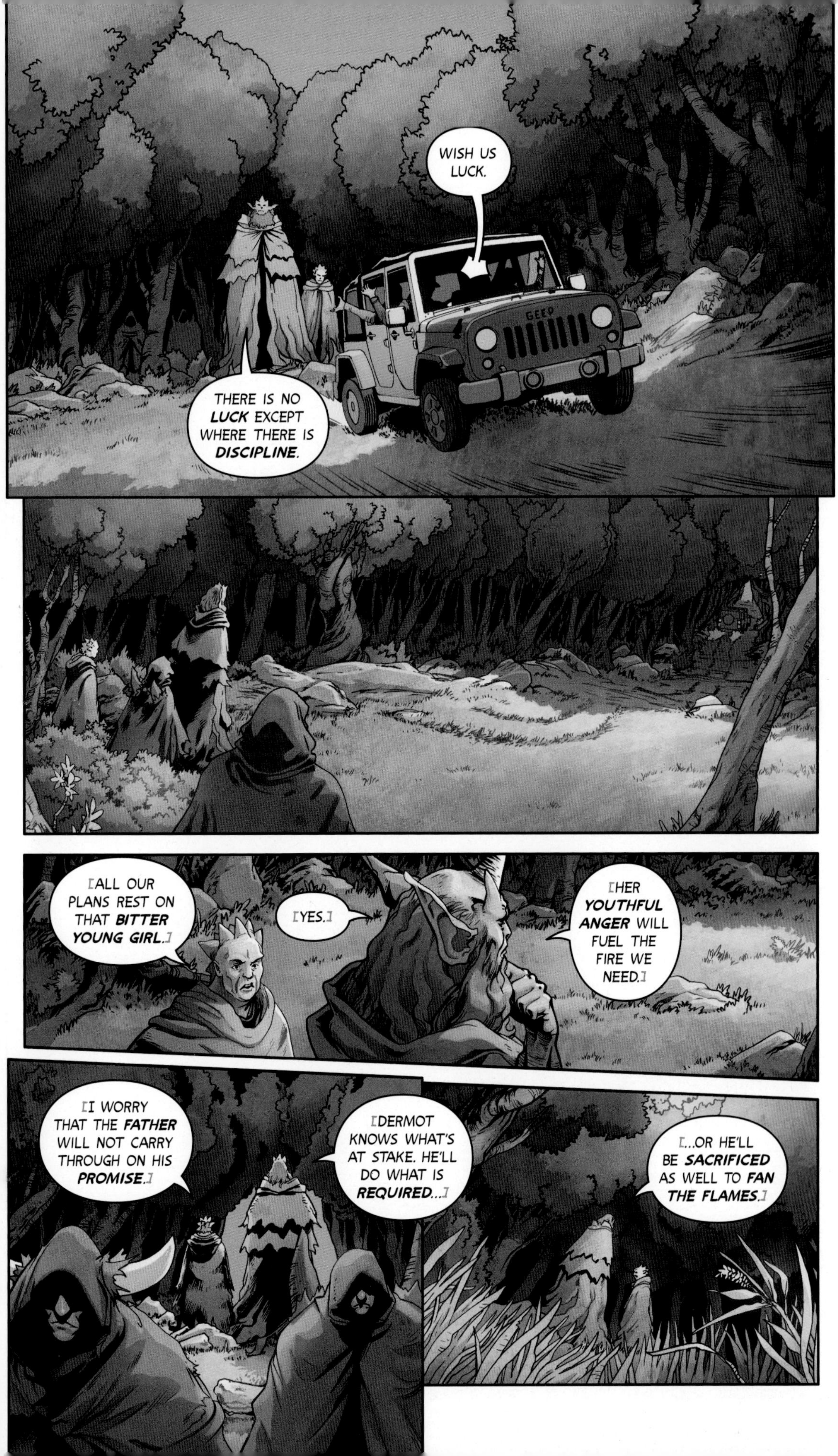
WISH US LUCK.
THERE IS NO LUCK EXCEPT WHERE THERE IS DISCIPLINE.
GEEP
[ALL OUR PLANS REST ON THAT BITTER YOUNG GIRL.]
[YES.]
[HER YOUTHFUL ANGER WILL FUEL THE FIRE WE NEED.]
[I WORRY THAT THE FATHER WILL NOT CARRY THROUGH ON HIS PROMISE.]
[DERMOT KNOWS WHAT'S AT STAKE. HE'LL DO WHAT IS REQUIRED...]
[...OR HE'LL BE SACRIFICED AS WELL TO FAN THE FLAMES.]

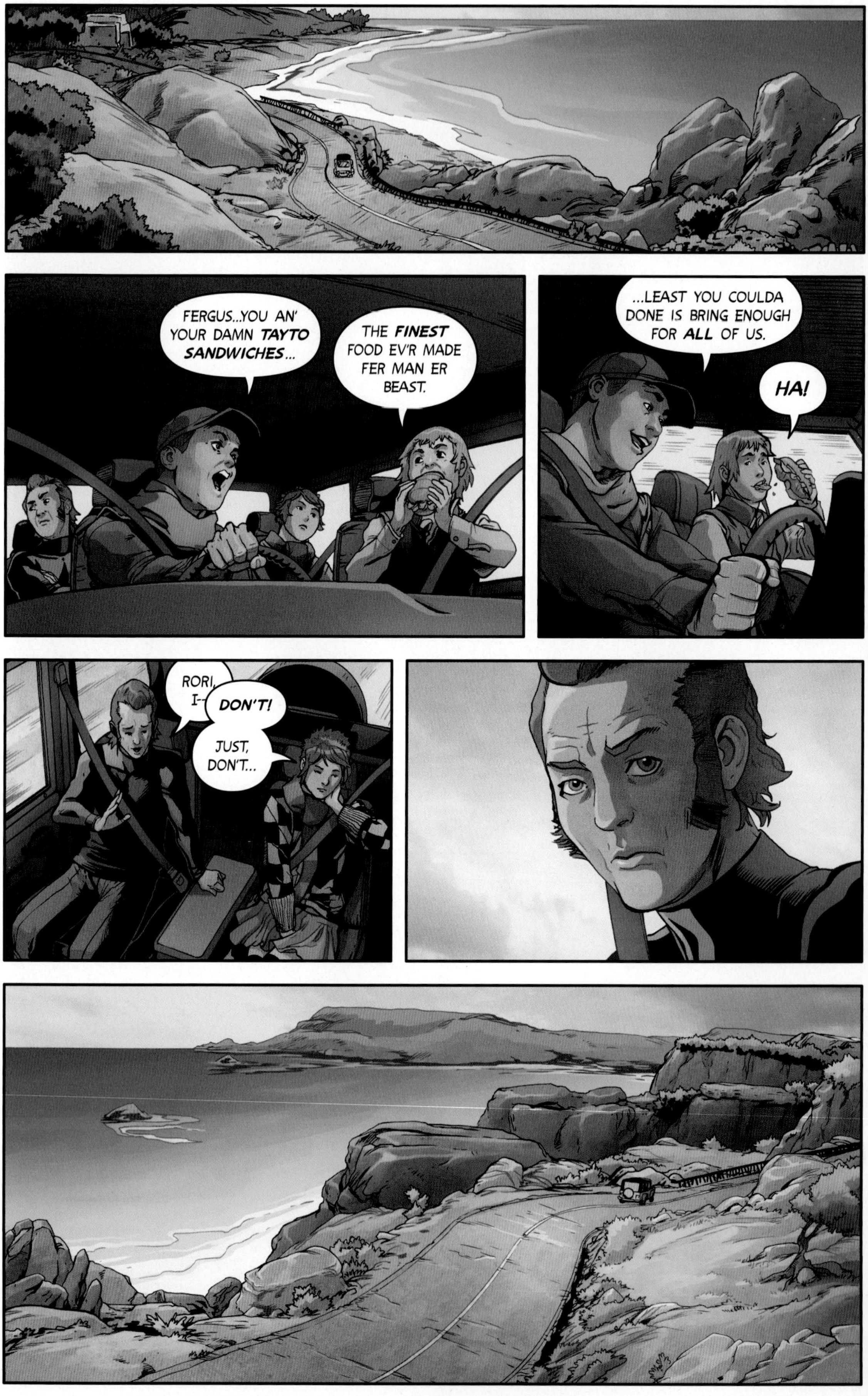
FERGUS...YOU AN' YOUR DAMN TAYTO SANDWICHES...
THE FINEST FOOD EV'R MADE FER MAN ER BEAST.
...LEAST YOU COULDA DONE IS BRING ENOUGH FOR ALL OF US.
HA!
RORI, I--
DON'T!
JUST, DON'T...

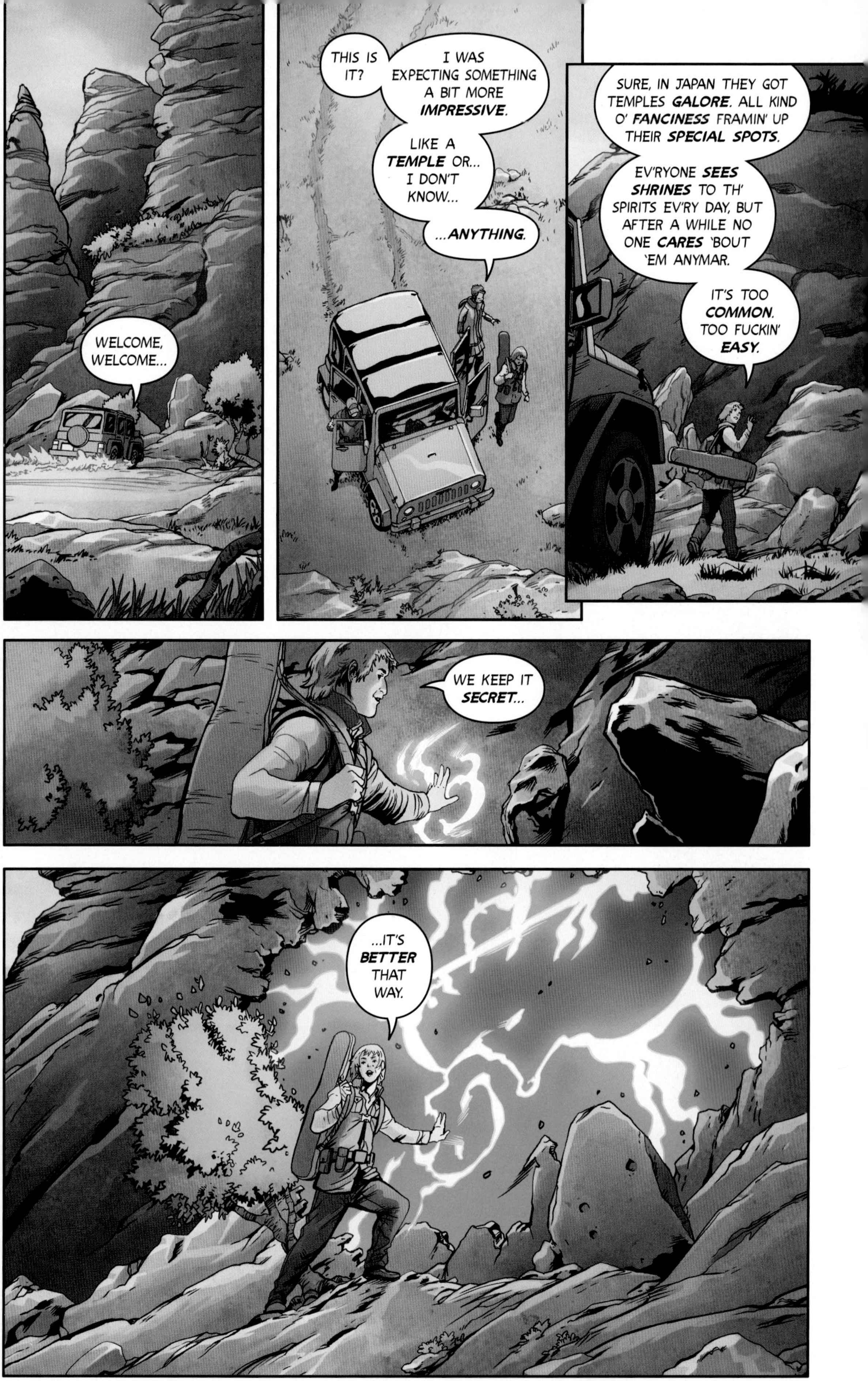
WELCOME, WELCOME...
THIS IS IT?
I WAS EXPECTING SOMETHING A BIT MORE IMPRESSIVE.
LIKE A TEMPLE OR... I DON'T KNOW...
...ANYTHING.
SURE, IN JAPAN THEY GOT TEMPLES GALORE. ALL KIND O' FANCINESS FRAMIN' UP THEIR SPECIAL SPOTS.
EV'RYONE SEES SHRINES TO TH' SPIRITS EV'RY DAY, BUT AFTER A WHILE NO ONE CARES 'BOUT 'EM ANYMAR.
IT'S TOO COMMON. TOO FUCKIN' EASY.
WE KEEP IT SECRET...
...IT'S BETTER THAT WAY.

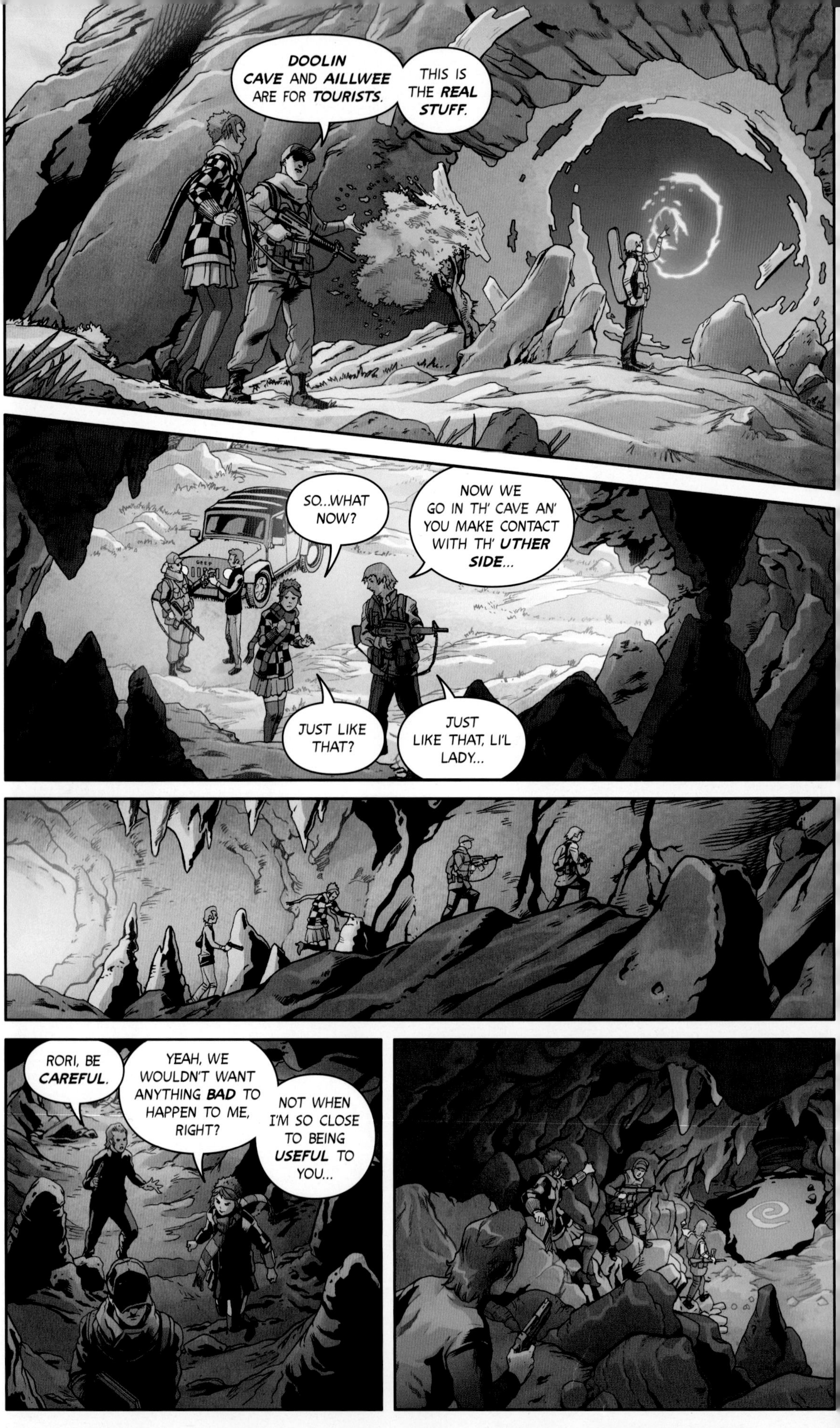
DOOLIN CAVE AND AILLWEE ARE FOR TOURISTS.
THIS IS THE REAL STUFF.
SO...WHAT NOW?
NOW WE GO IN TH' CAVE AN' YOU MAKE CONTACT WITH TH' UTHER SIDE...
JUST LIKE THAT?
JUST LIKE THAT, LI'L LADY...
RORI, BE CAREFUL.
YEAH, WE WOULDN'T WANT ANYTHING BAD TO HAPPEN TO ME, RIGHT?
NOT WHEN I'M SO CLOSE TO BEING USEFUL TO YOU...

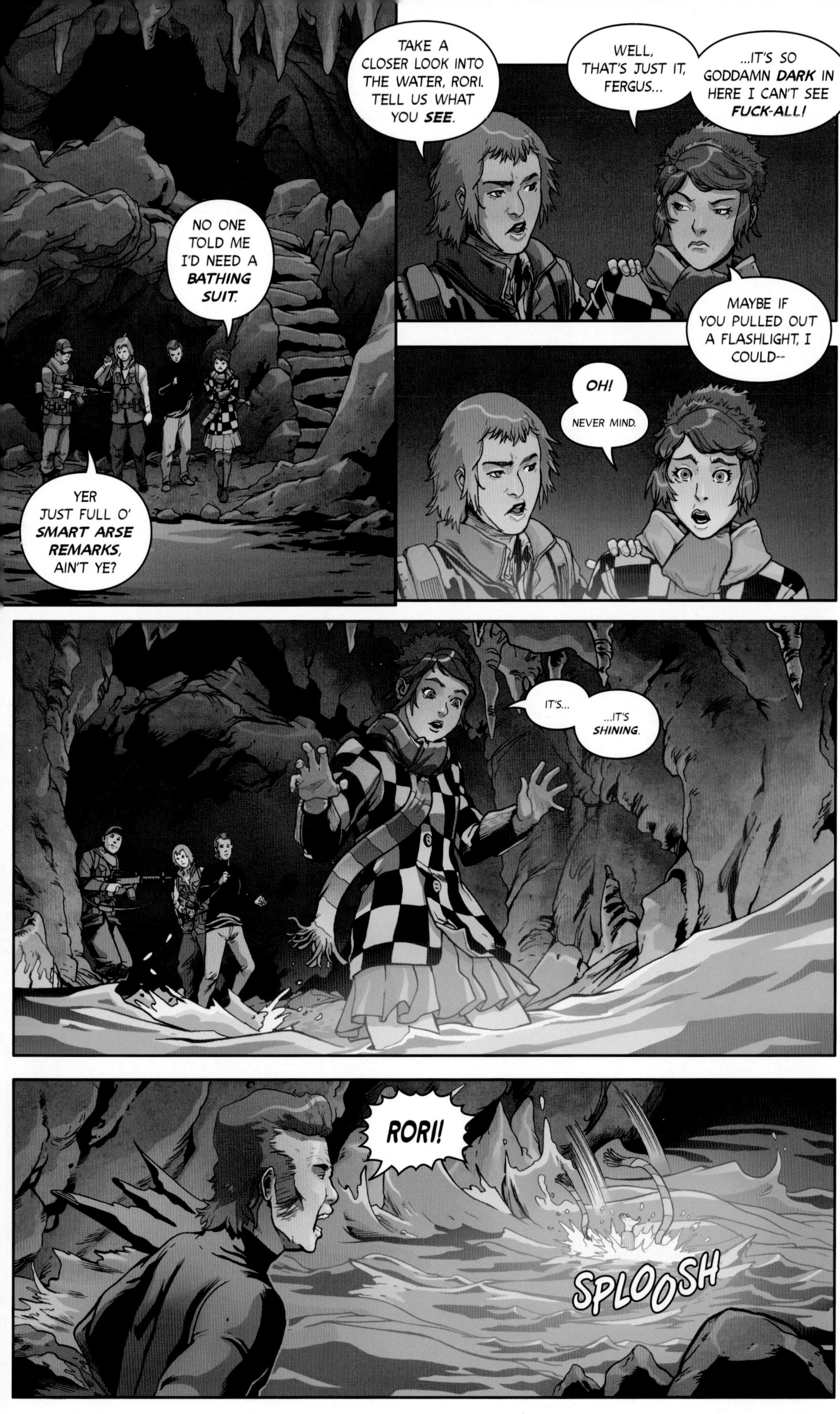
NO ONE TOLD ME I'D NEED A **BATHING SUIT**.
YER JUST FULL O' **SMART ARSE REMARKS**, AIN'T YE?
TAKE A CLOSER LOOK INTO THE WATER, RORI. TELL US WHAT YOU **SEE**.
WELL, THAT'S JUST IT, FERGUS...
...IT'S SO GODDAMN **DARK** IN HERE I CAN'T SEE **FUCK-ALL!**
MAYBE IF YOU PULLED OUT A FLASHLIGHT, I COULD--
OH!
NEVER MIND.
IT'S...
...IT'S **SHINING**.
RORI!
SPLOOSH

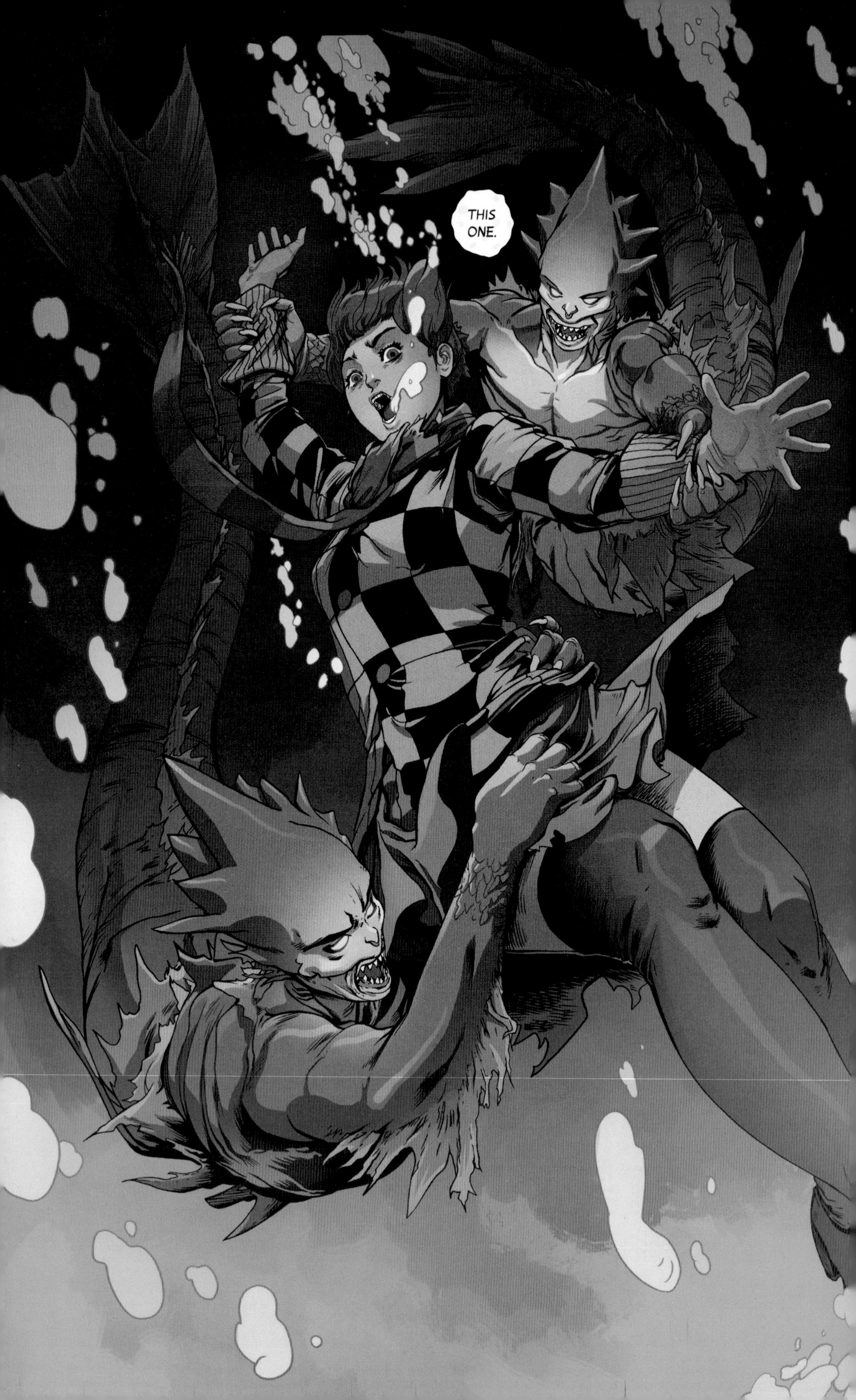
THIS ONE.

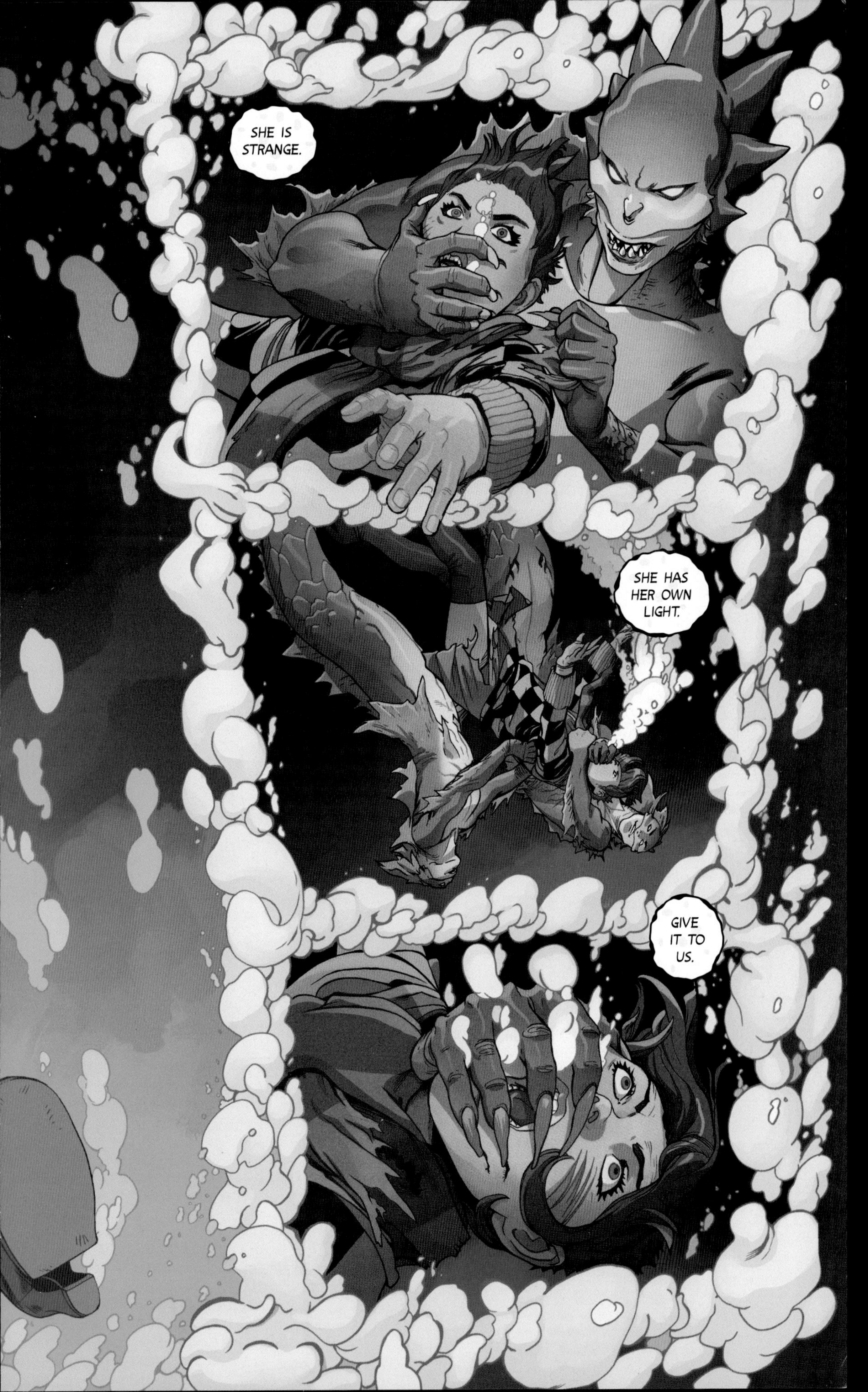
SHE IS STRANGE.
SHE HAS HER OWN LIGHT.
GIVE IT TO US.

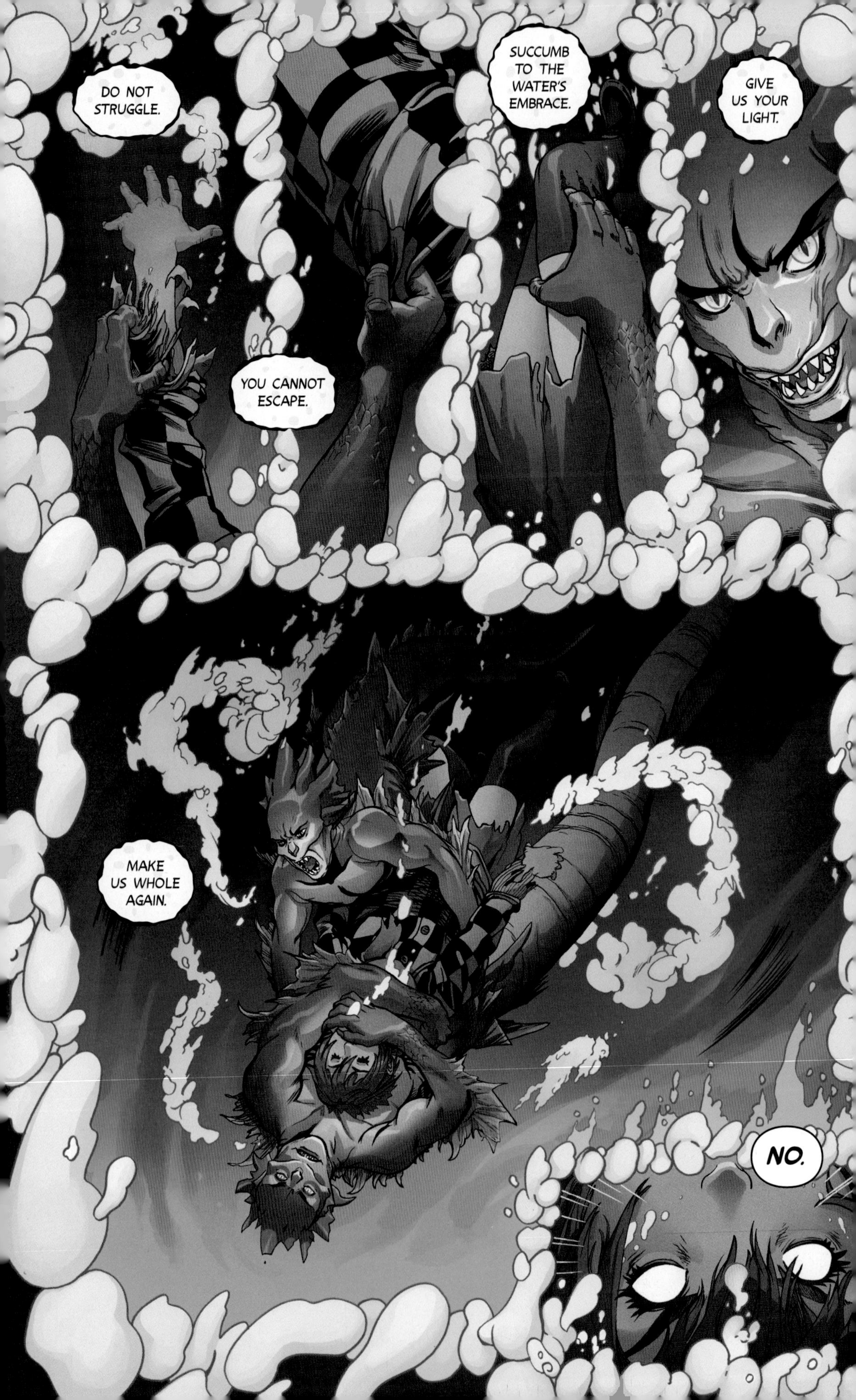
DO NOT STRUGGLE.
YOU CANNOT ESCAPE.
SUCCUMB TO THE WATER'S EMBRACE.
GIVE US YOUR LIGHT.
MAKE US WHOLE AGAIN.
NO.

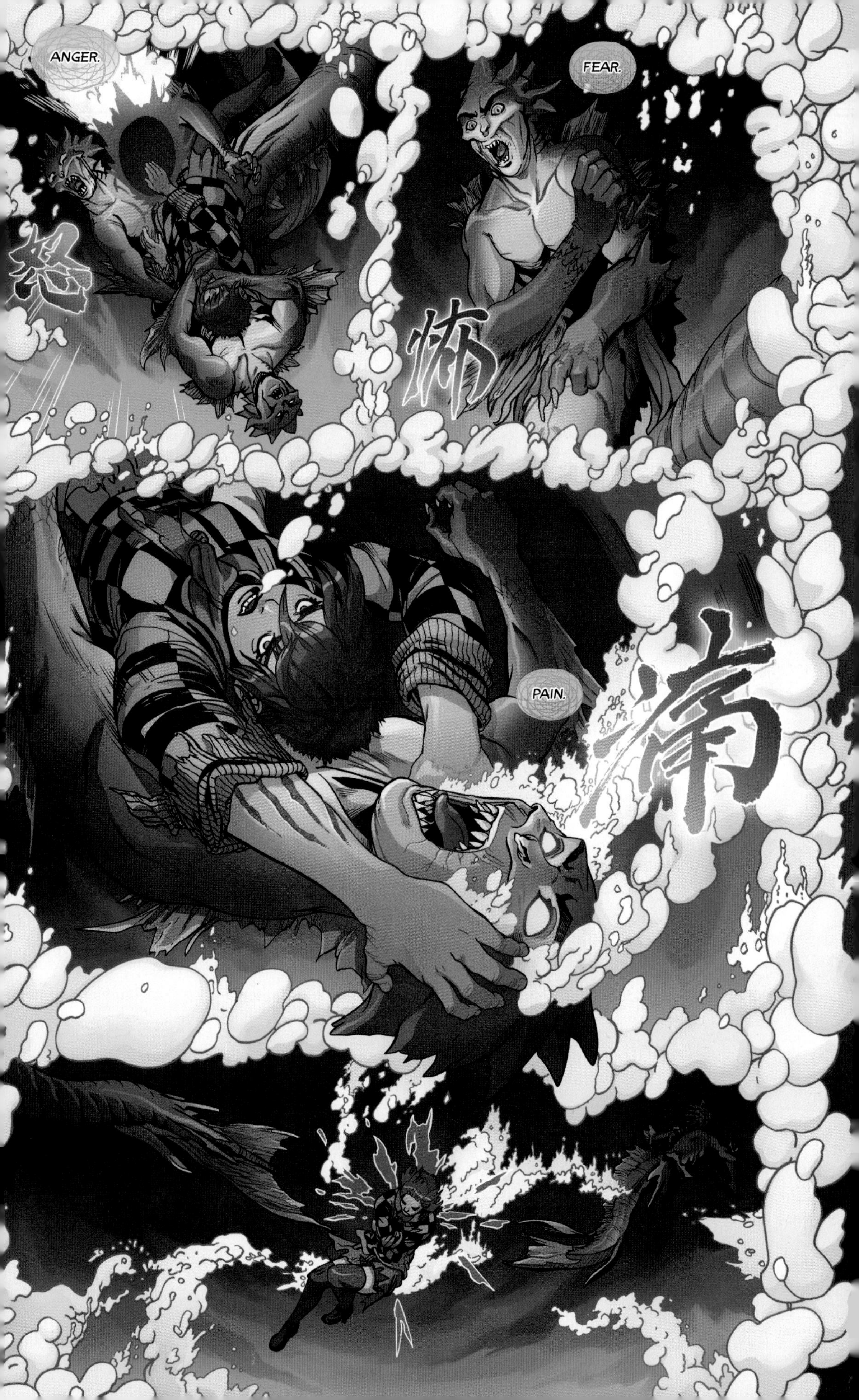
ANGER.
怒
FEAR.
怖
PAIN.
痛

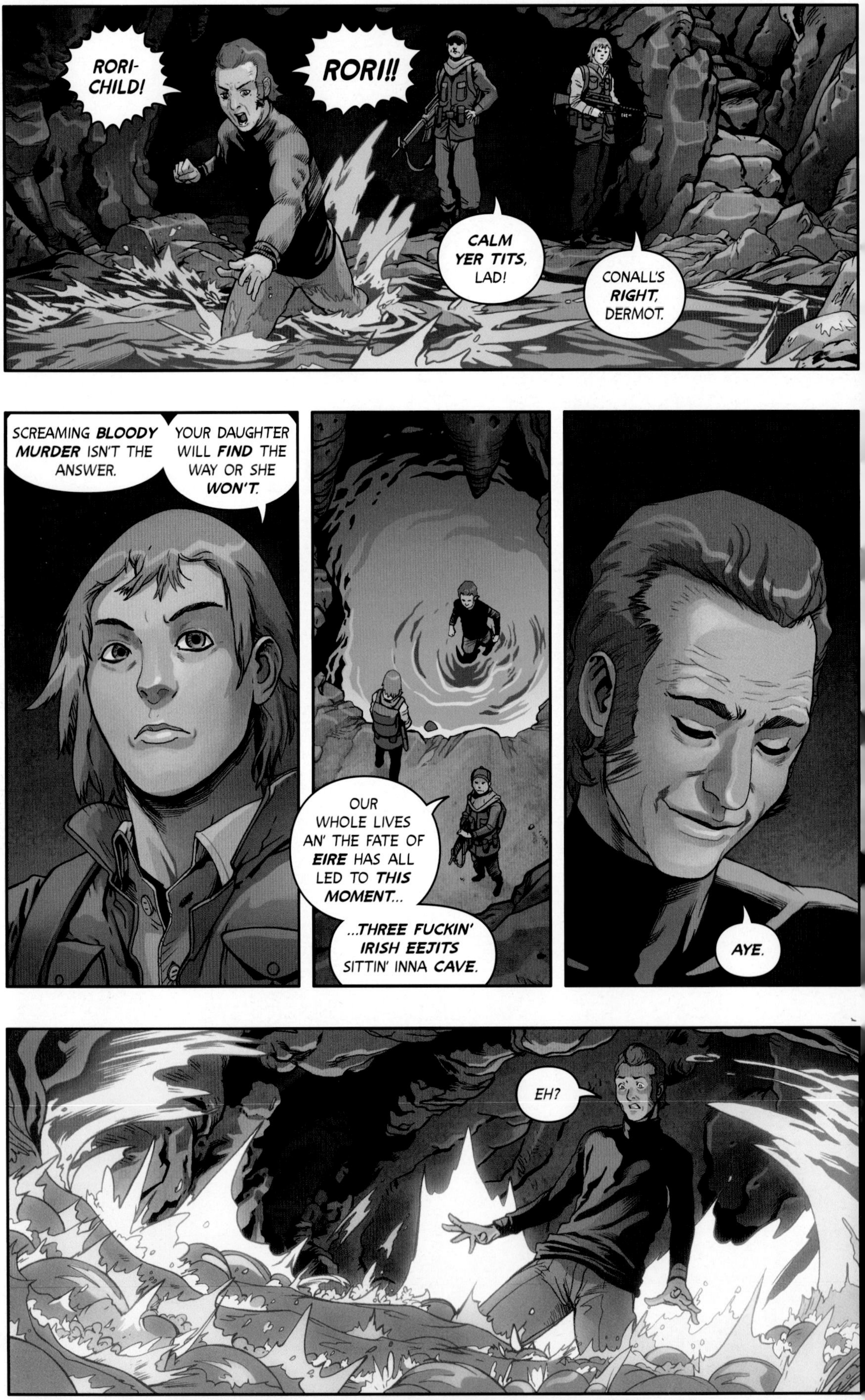
RORI-
CHILD!
RORI!!
CALM
YER TITS,
LAD!
CONALL'S
RIGHT,
DERMOT.
SCREAMING BLOODY MURDER ISN'T THE ANSWER.
YOUR DAUGHTER WILL FIND THE WAY OR SHE WON'T.
OUR WHOLE LIVES AN' THE FATE OF EIRE HAS ALL LED TO THIS MOMENT...
...THREE FUCKIN' IRISH EEJITS SITTIN' INNA CAVE.
AYE.
EH?

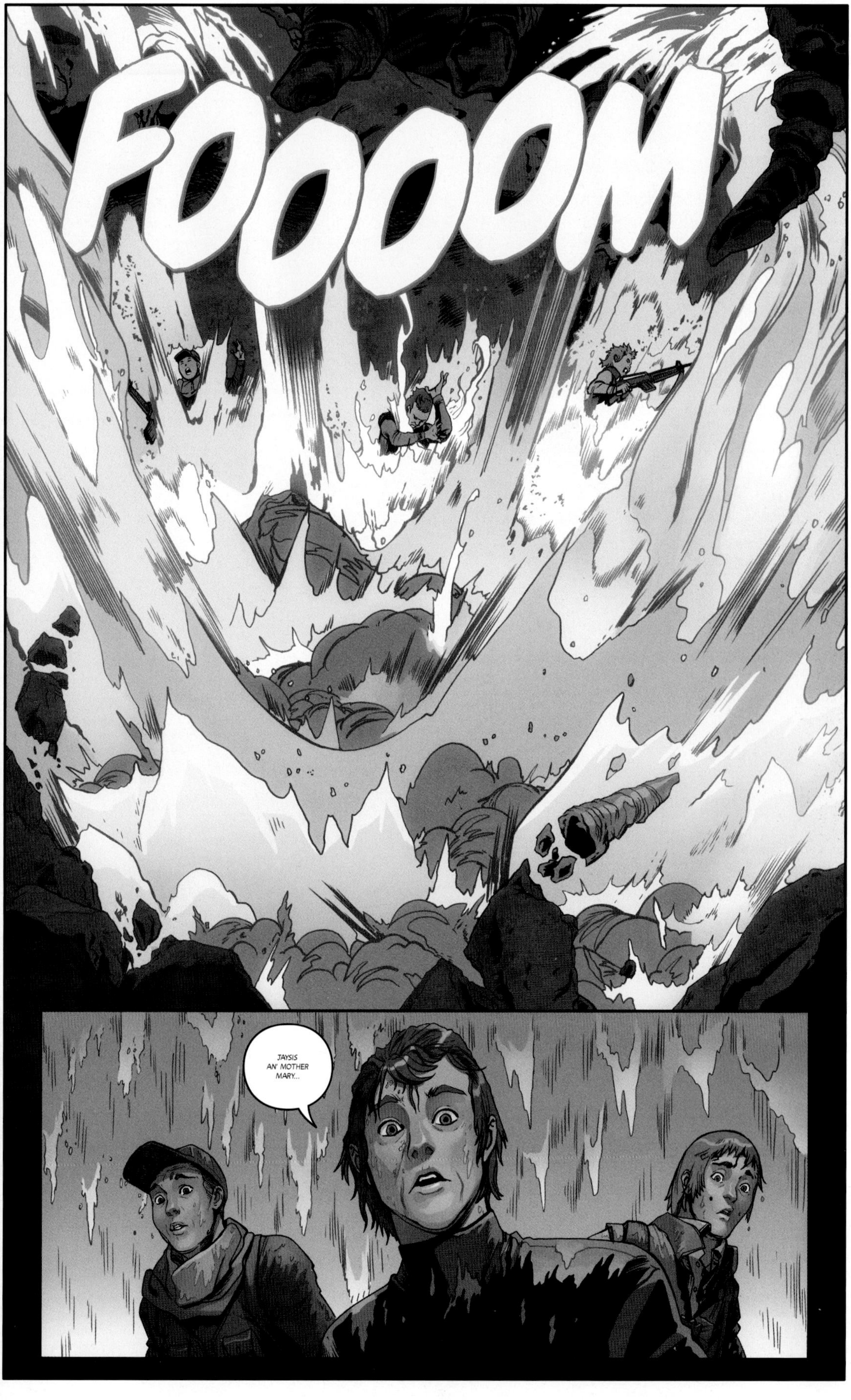
FOOOOM
JAYSIS AN' MOTHER MARY...

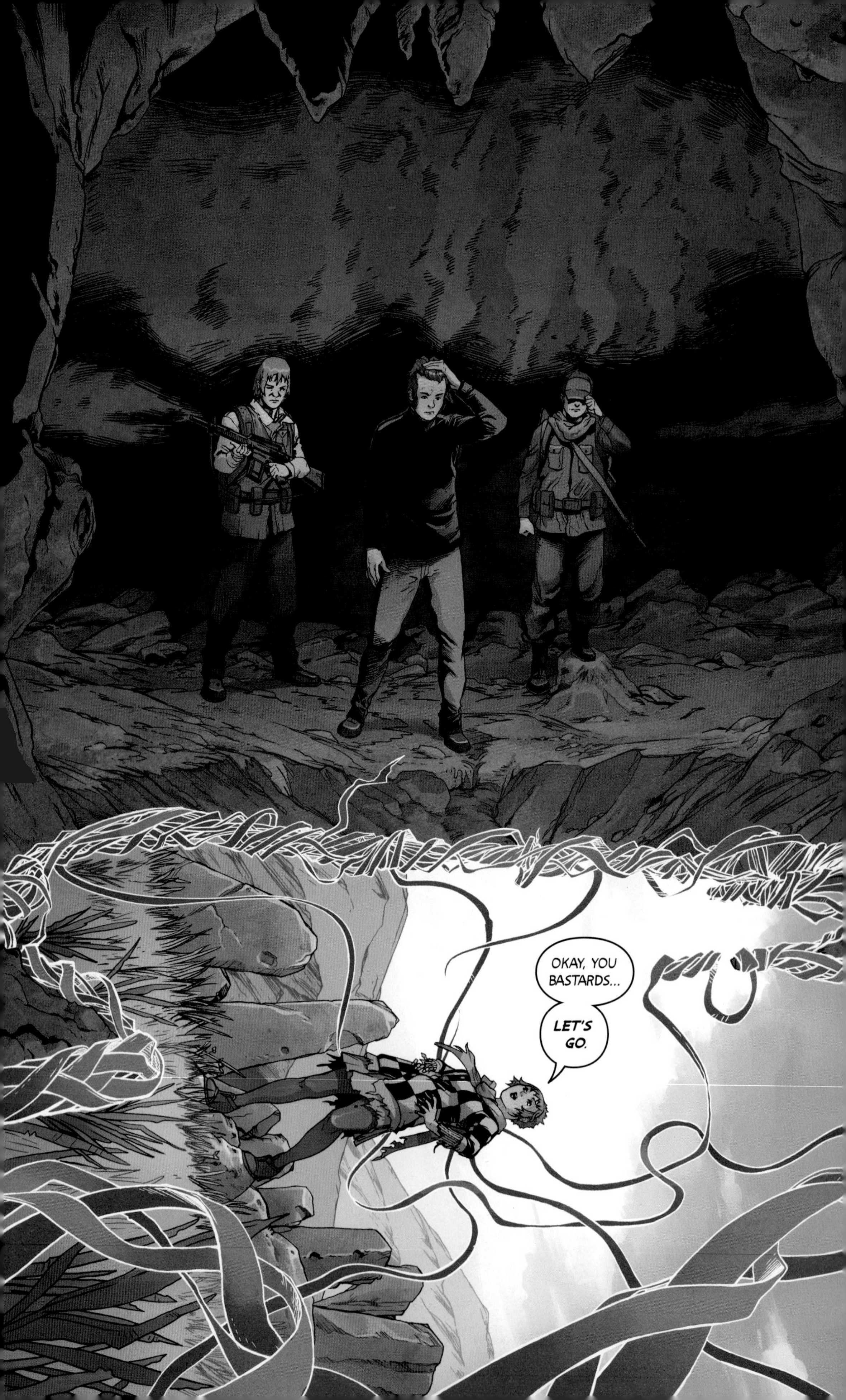
OKAY, YOU BASTARDS...
LET'S GO.

Chapter Twenty-Three

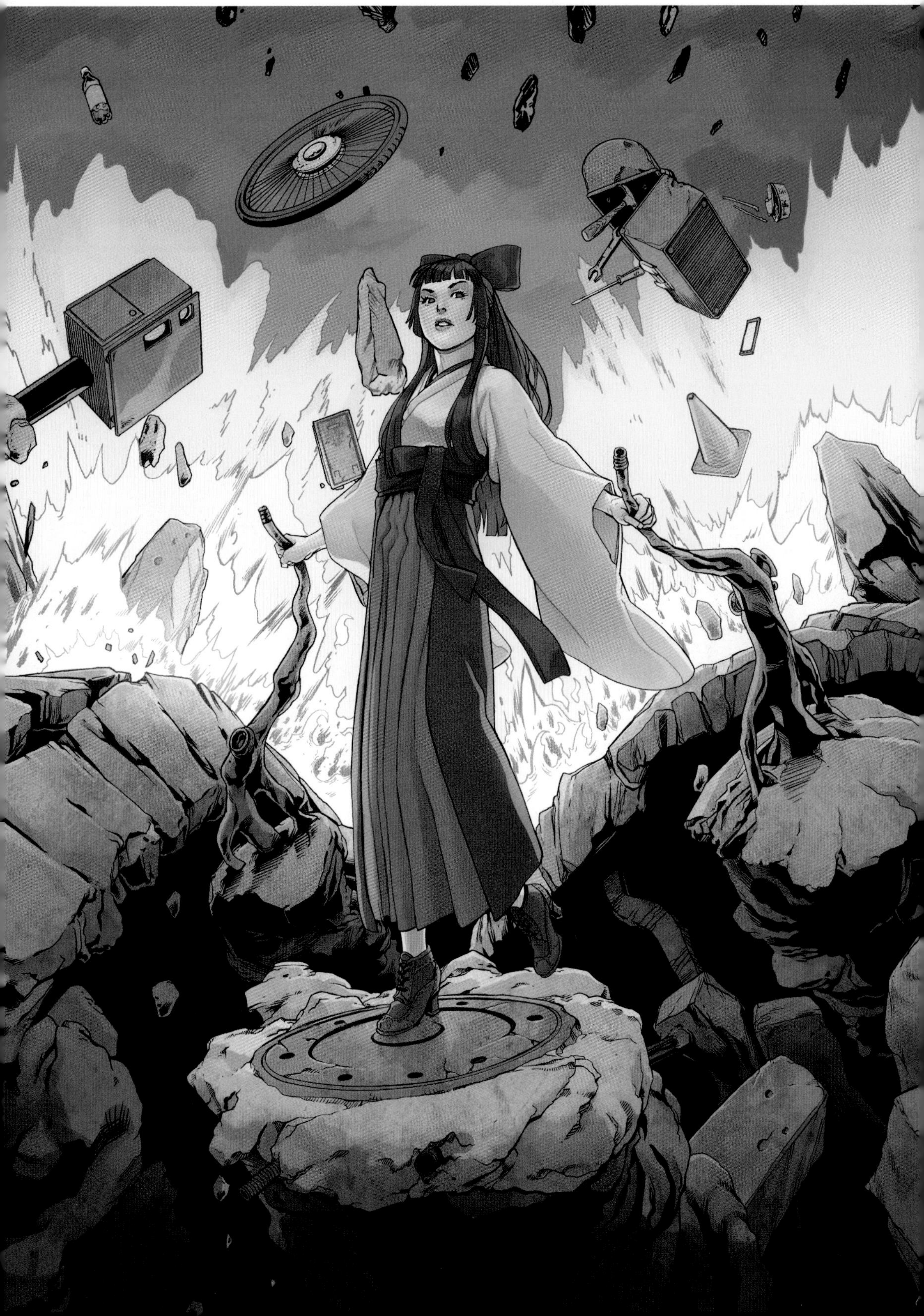

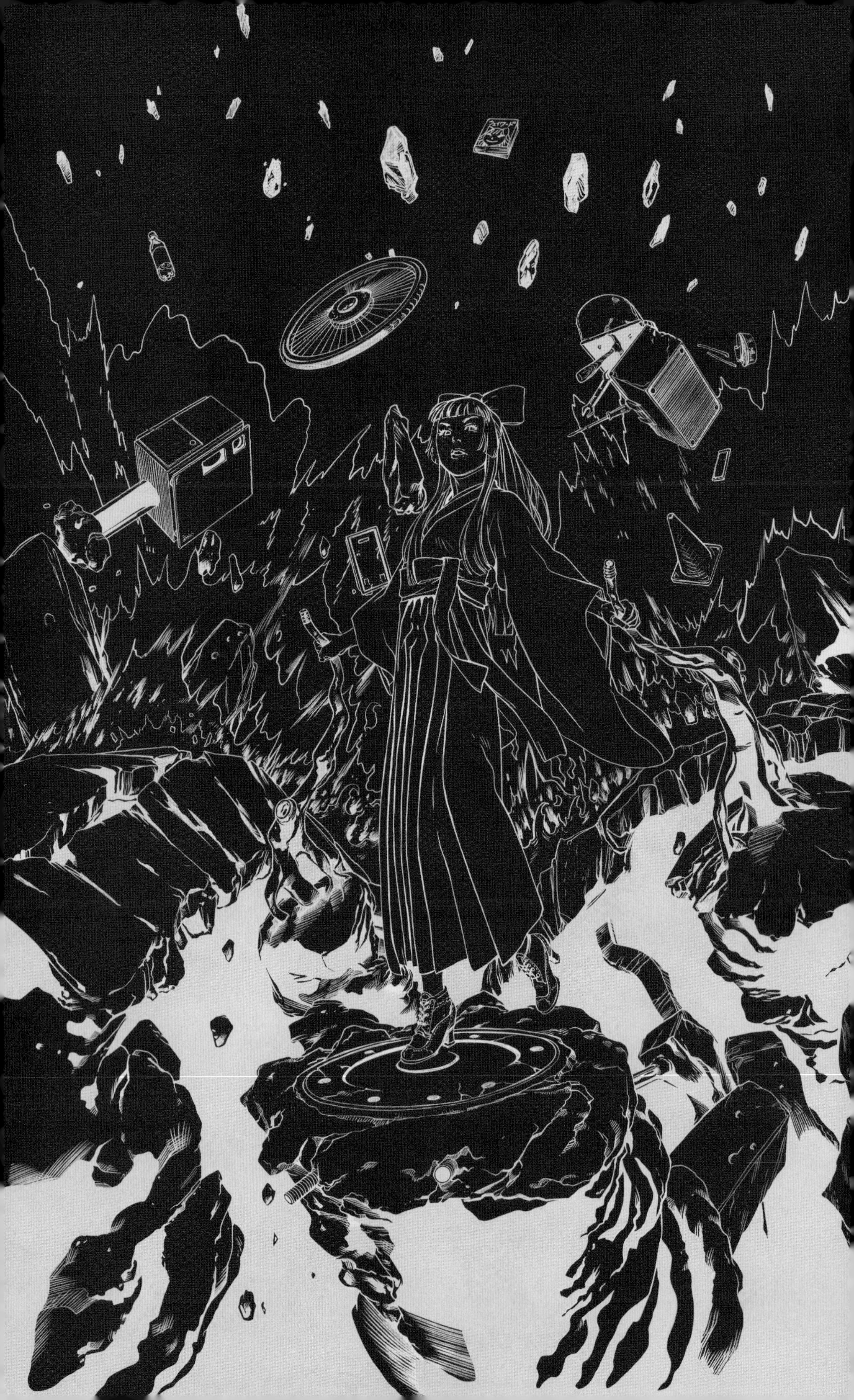
ウェイワード

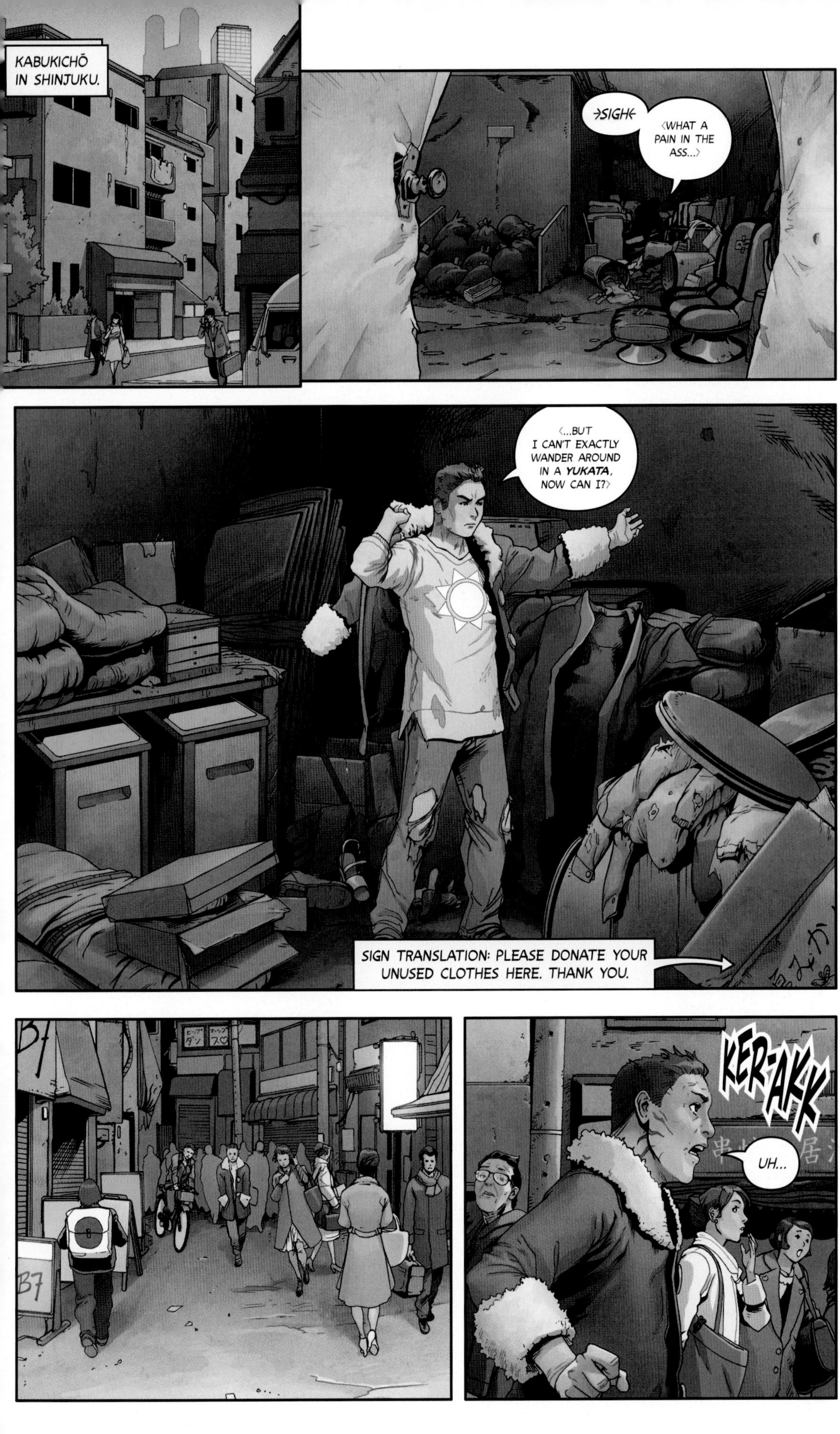
KABUKICHŌ IN SHINJUKU.
→SIGH←
‹WHAT A PAIN IN THE ASS...›
‹...BUT I CAN'T EXACTLY WANDER AROUND IN A *YUKATA*, NOW CAN I?›
SIGN TRANSLATION: PLEASE DONATE YOUR UNUSED CLOTHES HERE. THANK YOU.
B7
B7
KER-AKK
UH...

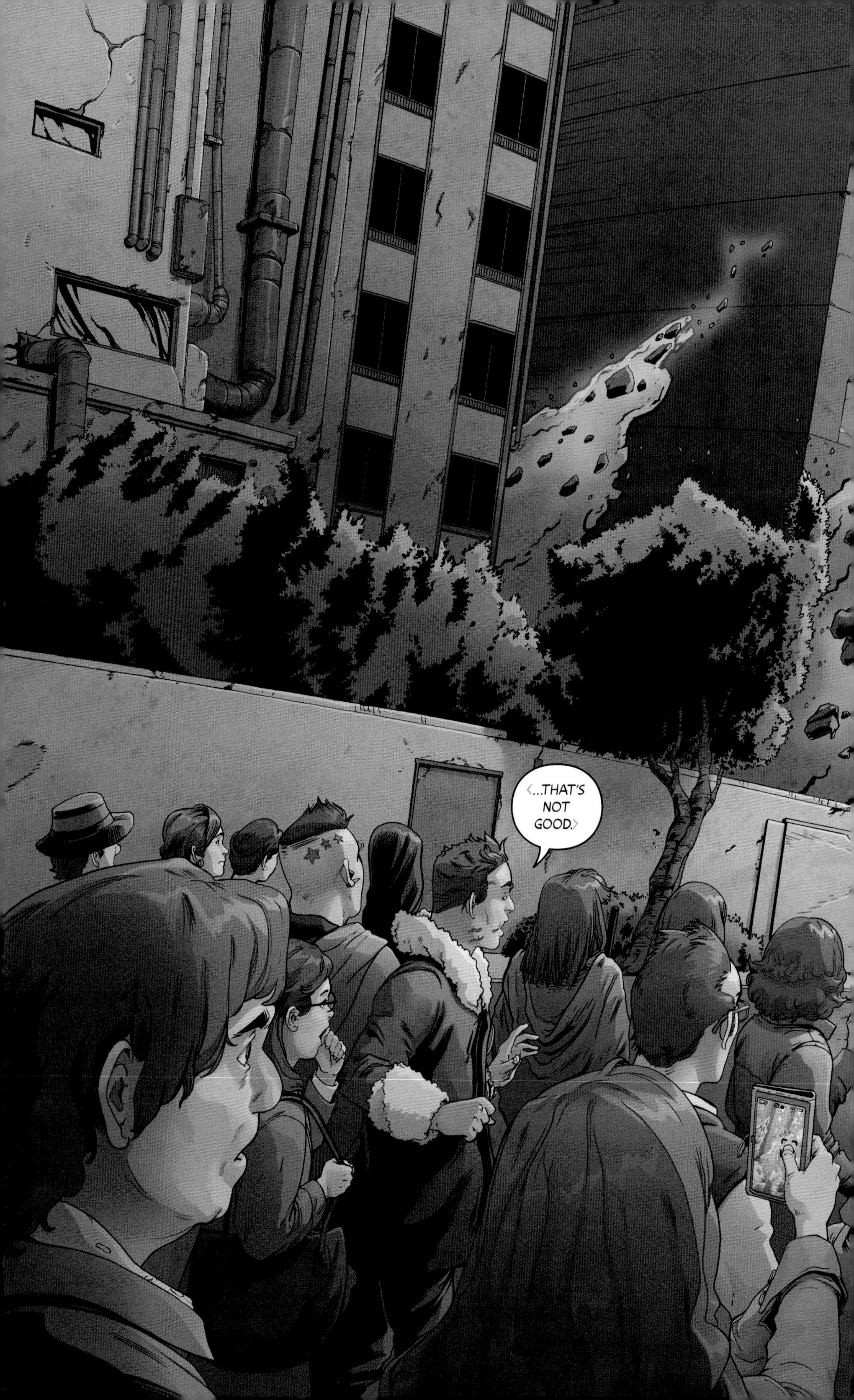
⟨...THAT'S NOT GOOD.⟩

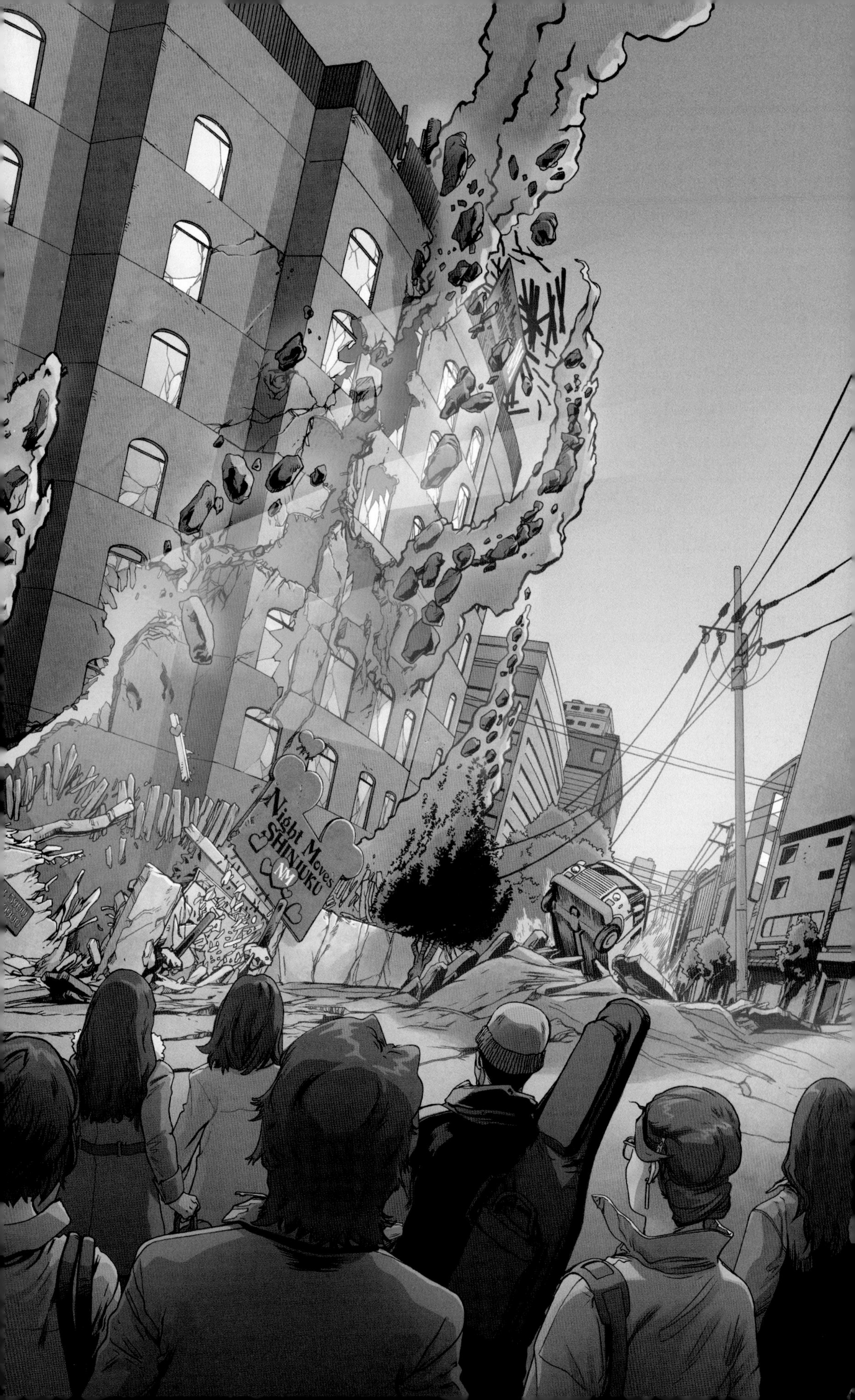
Night Moves
SHINJUKU
NM

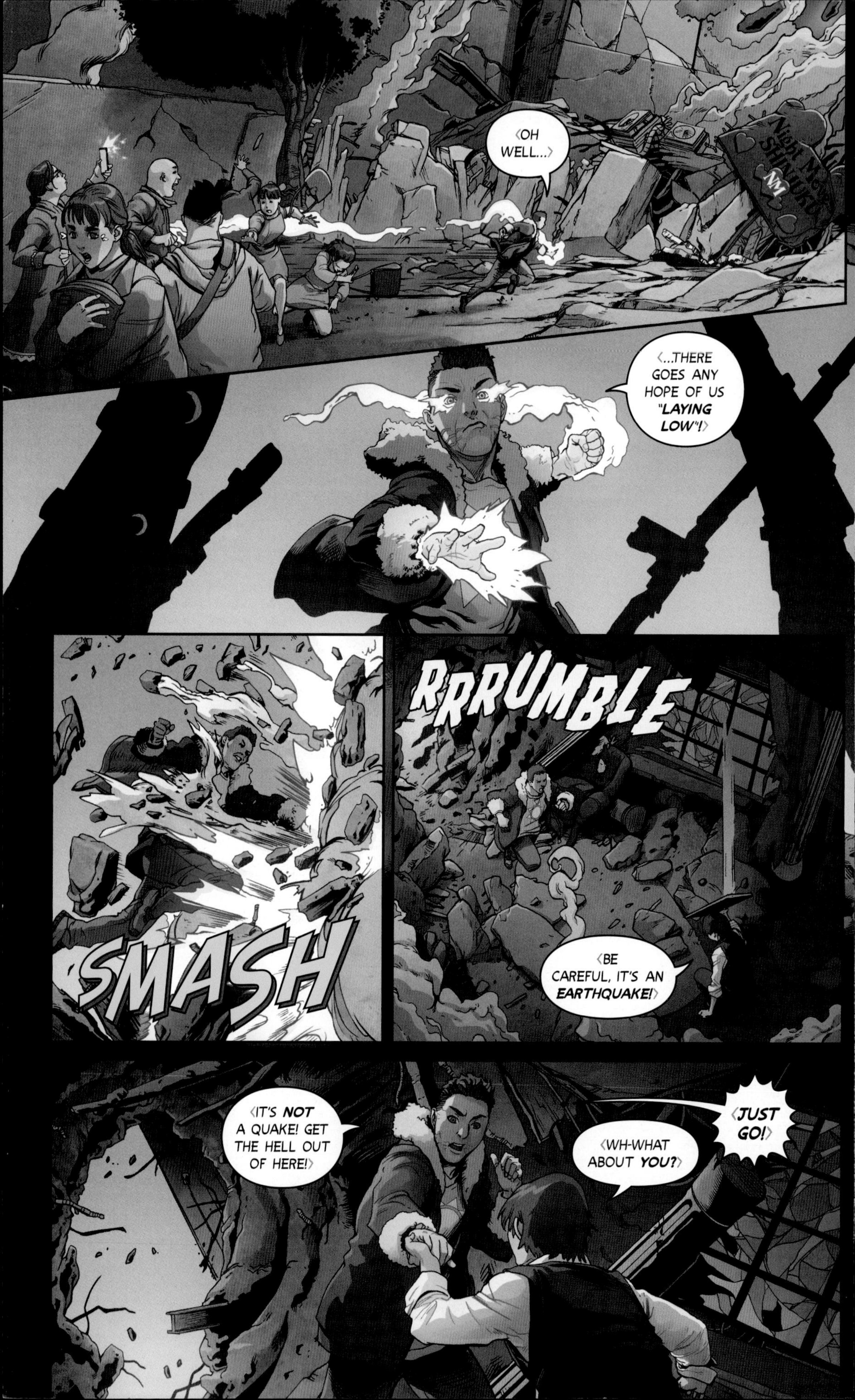
‹OH WELL...›
‹...THERE GOES ANY HOPE OF US "LAYING LOW"!›
SMASH
RRRUMBLE
‹BE CAREFUL, IT'S AN EARTHQUAKE!›
‹IT'S NOT A QUAKE! GET THE HELL OUT OF HERE!›
‹WH-WHAT ABOUT YOU?›
‹JUST GO!›

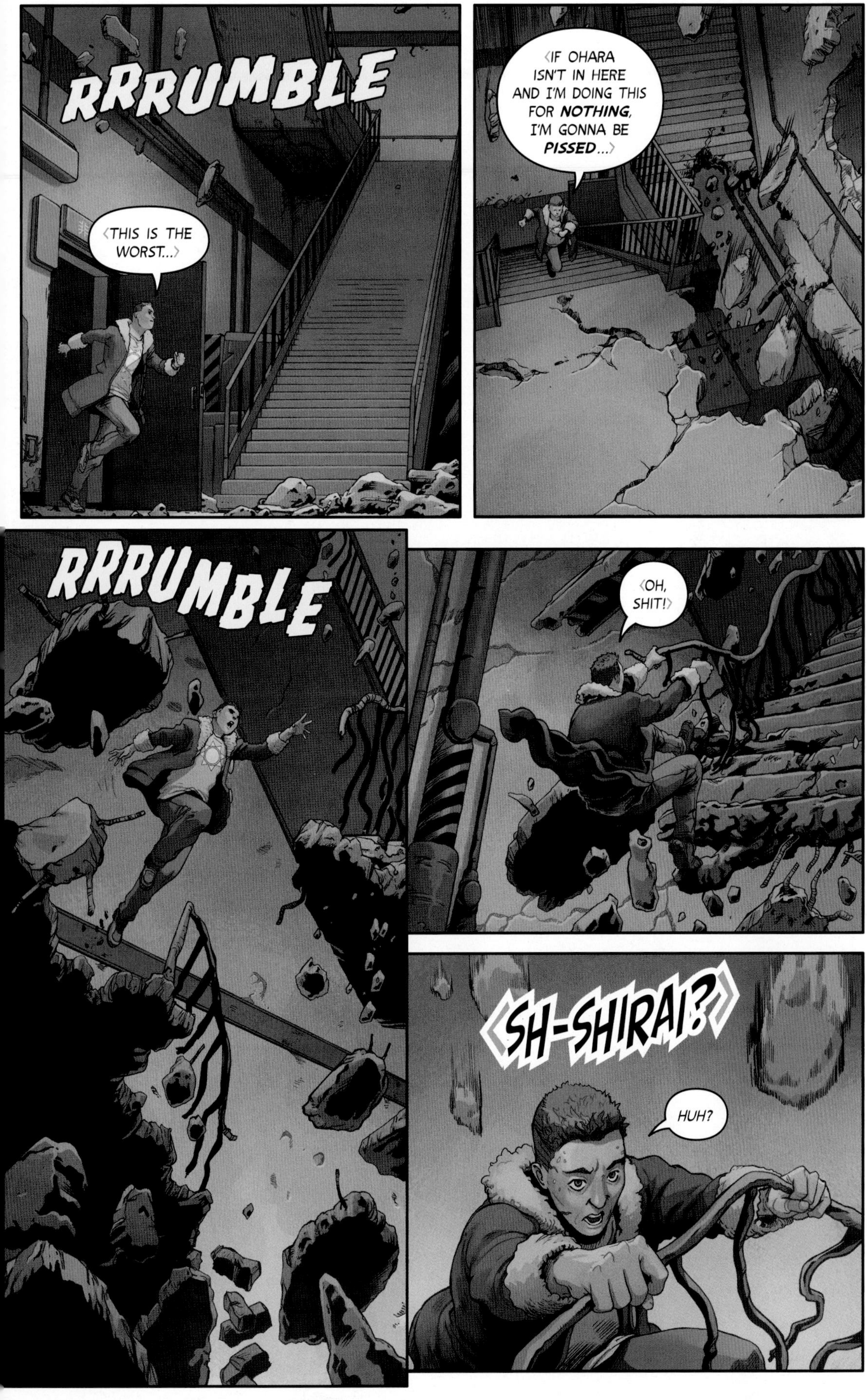
RRRUMBLE
⟨THIS IS THE WORST...⟩
⟨IF OHARA ISN'T IN HERE AND I'M DOING THIS FOR **NOTHING**, I'M GONNA BE **PISSED**...⟩
RRRUMBLE
⟨OH, SHIT!⟩
⟨SH-SHIRAI?⟩
HUH?

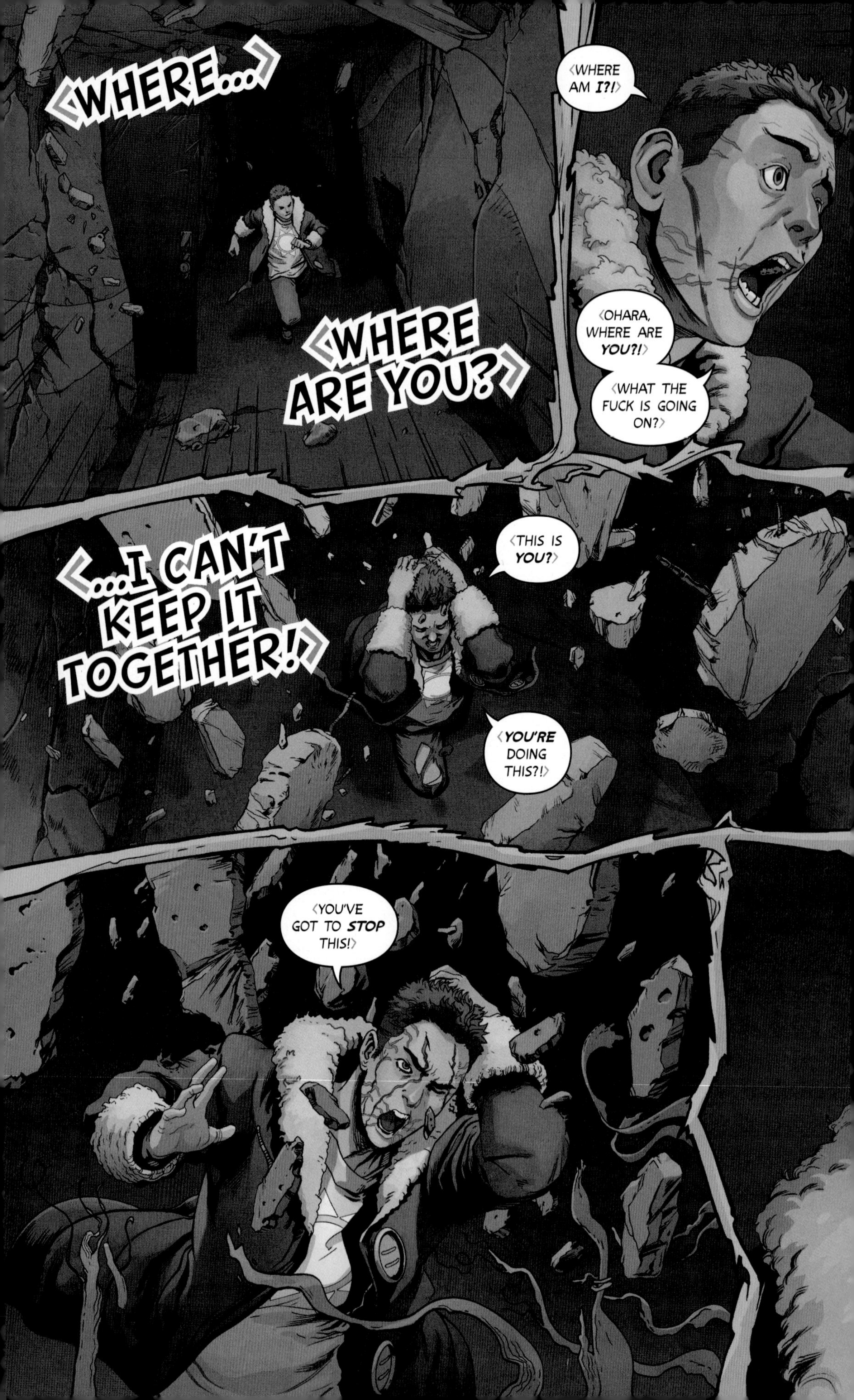
‹WHERE...›
‹WHERE AM I?!›
‹WHERE ARE YOU?›
‹OHARA, WHERE ARE YOU?!›
‹WHAT THE FUCK IS GOING ON?›
‹...I CAN'T KEEP IT TOGETHER!›
‹THIS IS YOU?›
‹YOU'RE DOING THIS?!›
‹YOU'VE GOT TO STOP THIS!›

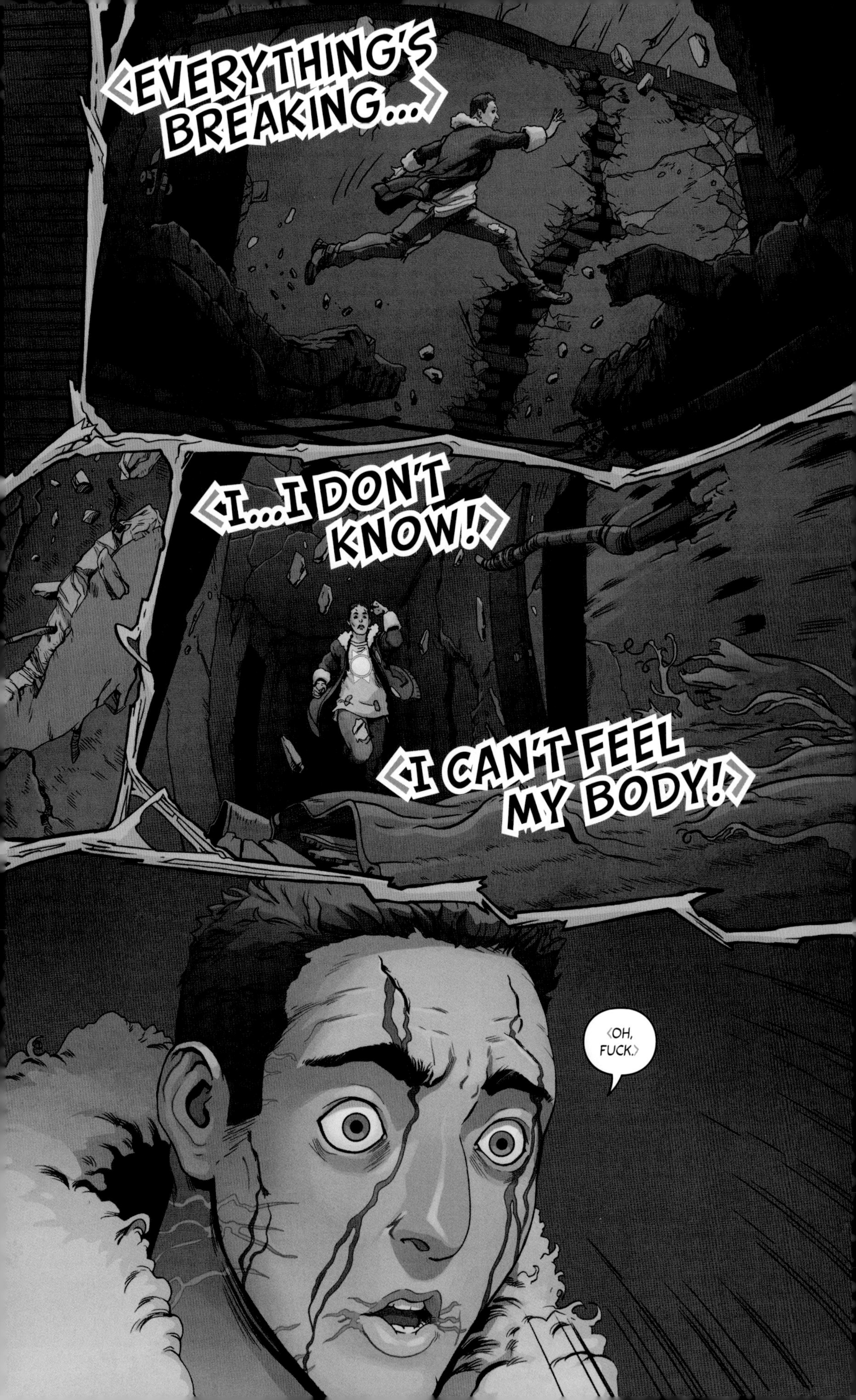
‹EVERYTHING'S BREAKING...›
‹I...I DON'T KNOW!›
‹I CAN'T FEEL MY BODY!›
‹OH, FUCK.›

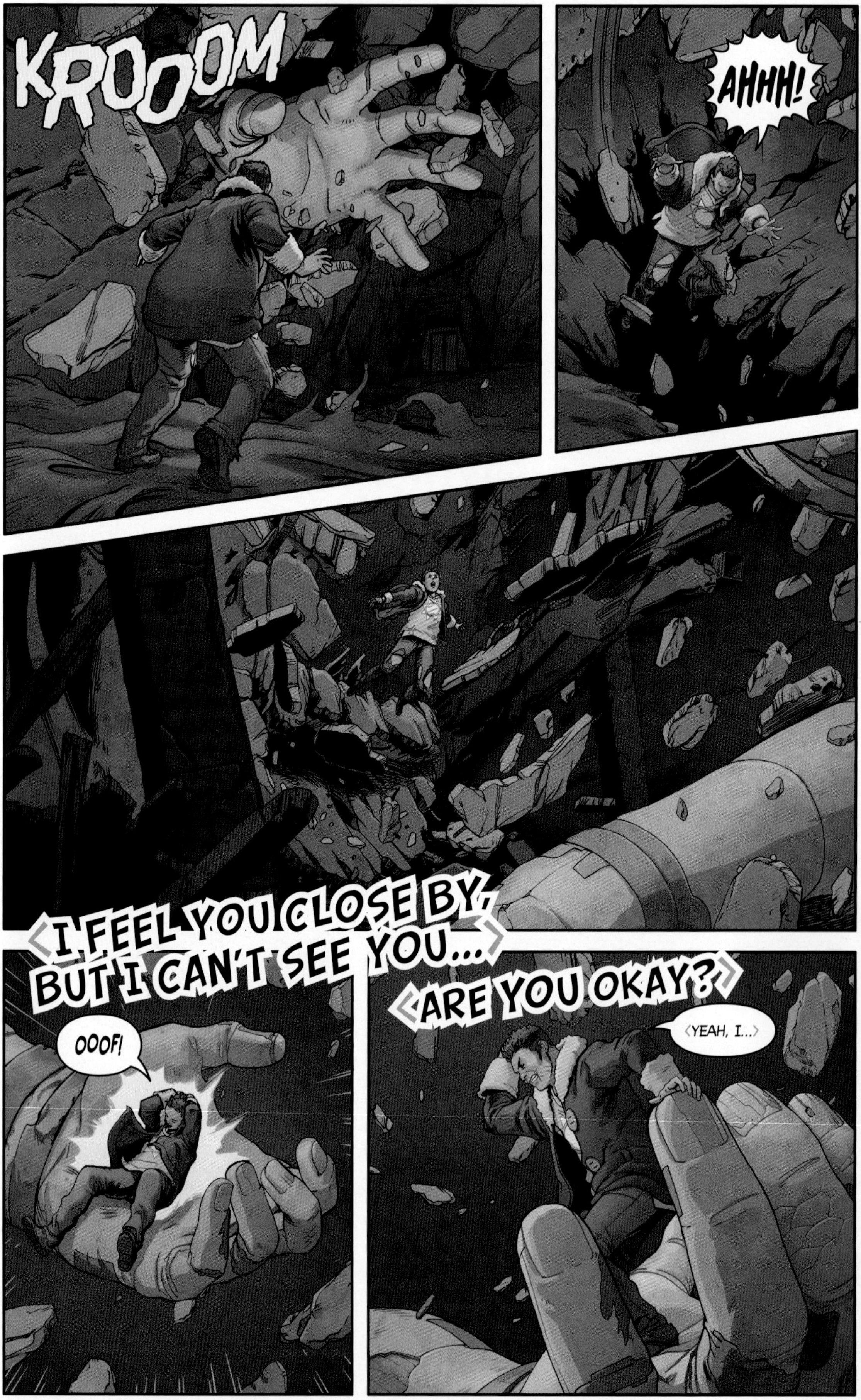
KROOOM
AHHH!
I FEEL YOU CLOSE BY, BUT I CAN'T SEE YOU...
ARE YOU OKAY?
OOOF!
YEAH, I...

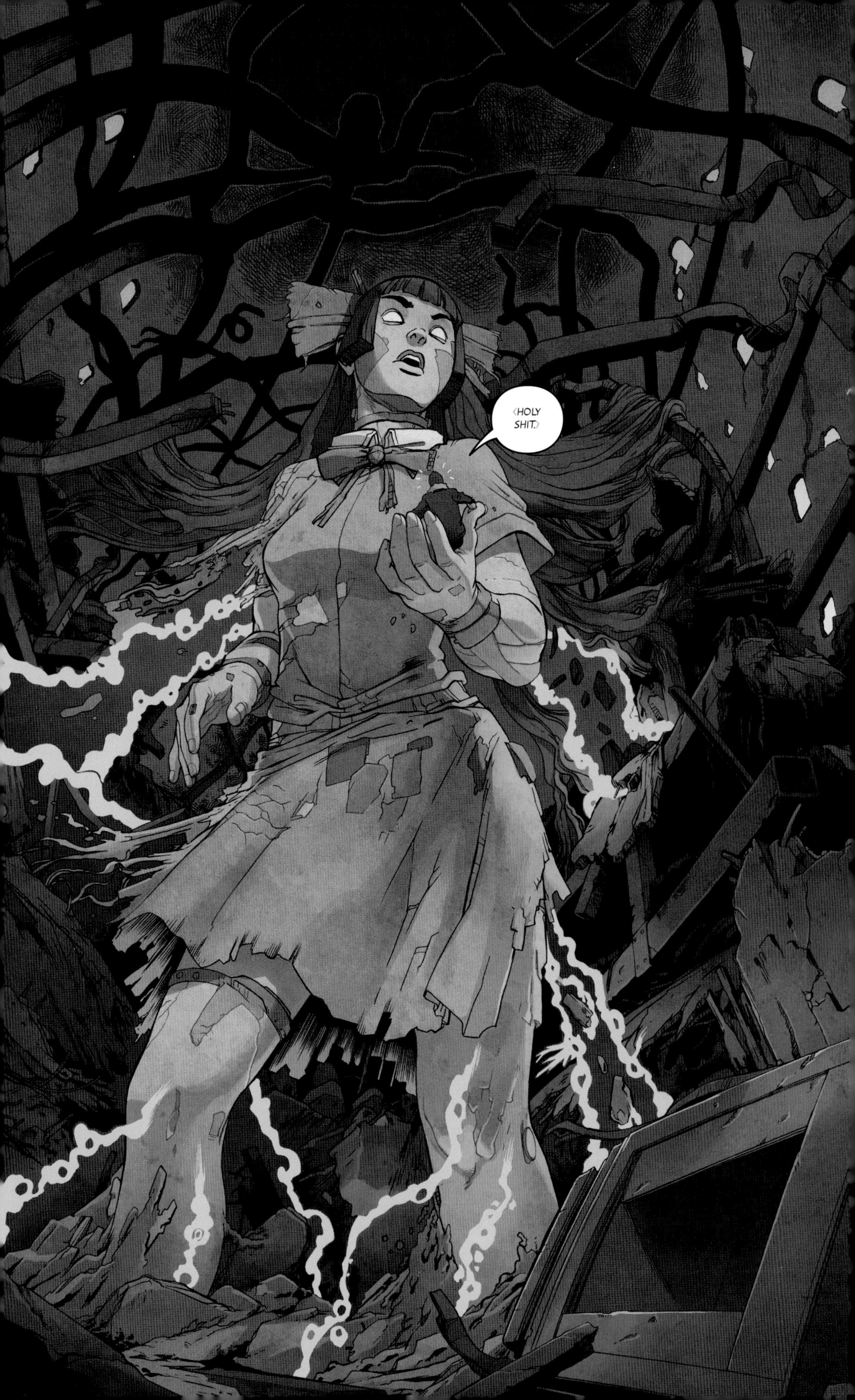
‹HOLY SHIT.›

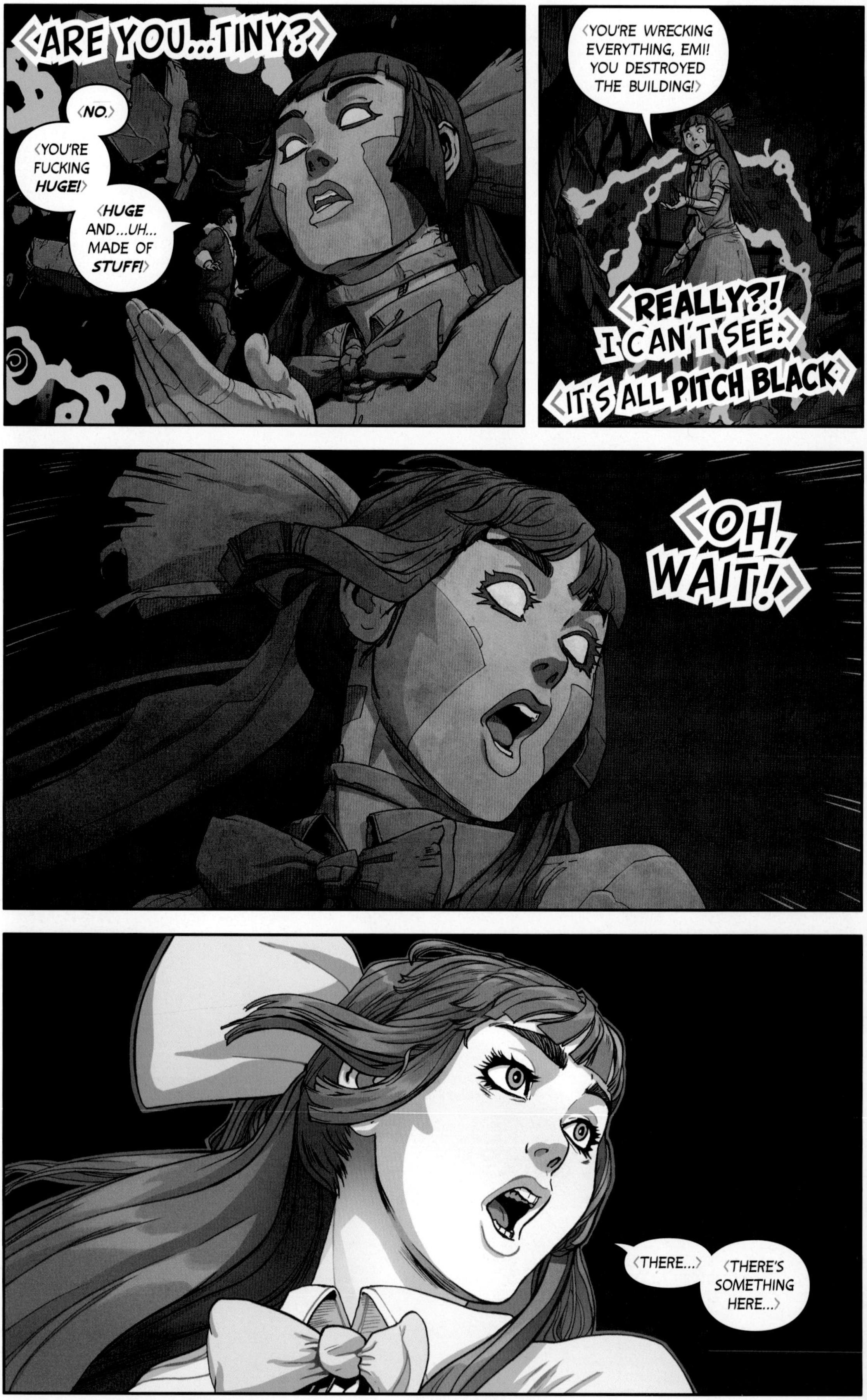
‹ARE YOU...TINY?›
‹NO.›
‹YOU'RE FUCKING HUGE!›
‹HUGE AND...UH... MADE OF STUFF!›
‹YOU'RE WRECKING EVERYTHING, EMI! YOU DESTROYED THE BUILDING!›
‹REALLY?! I CAN'T SEE.›
‹IT'S ALL PITCH BLACK.›
‹OH, WAIT!›
‹THERE...›
‹THERE'S SOMETHING HERE...›

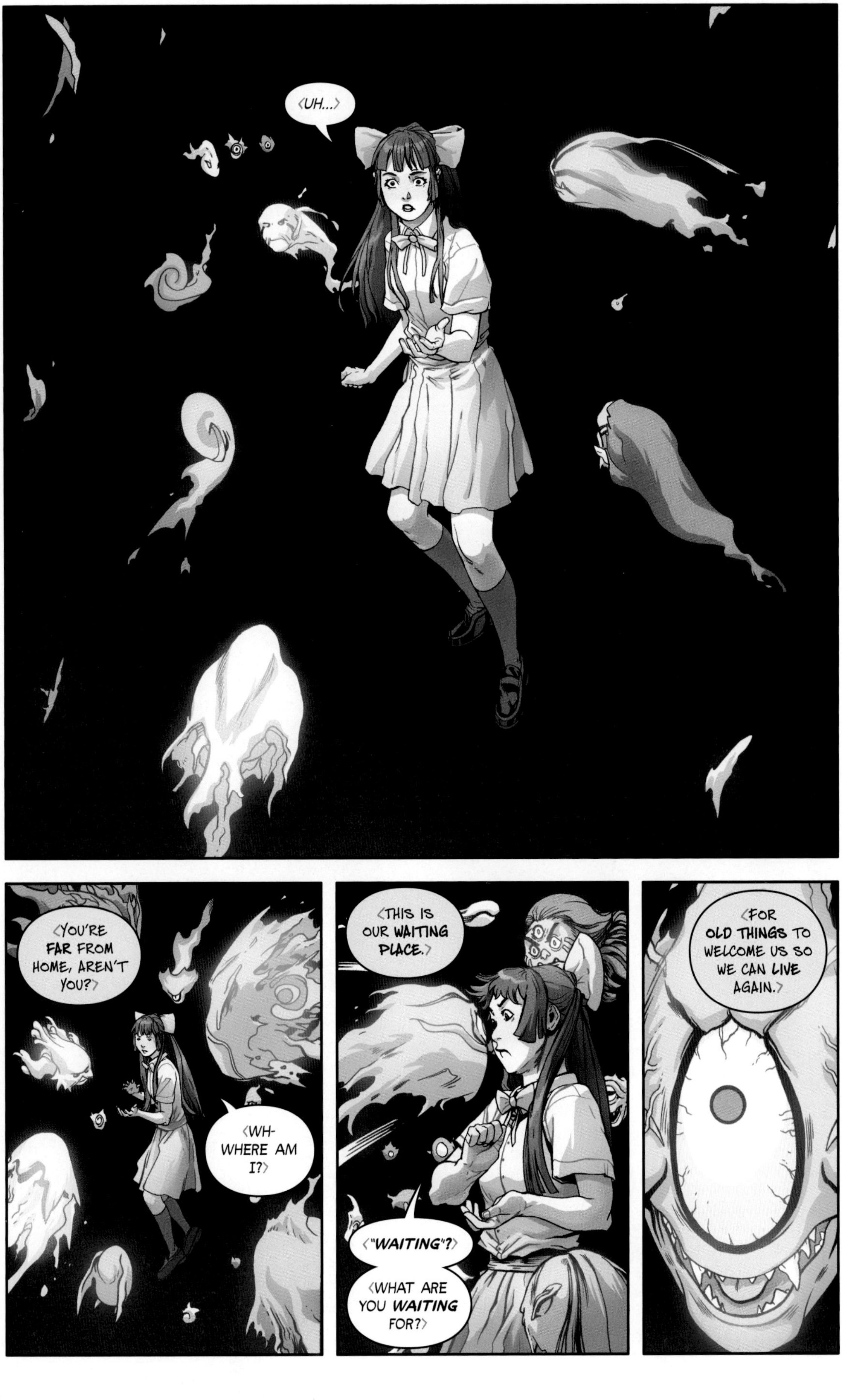
‹UH...›
‹YOU'RE FAR FROM HOME, AREN'T YOU?›
‹WH- WHERE AM I?›
‹THIS IS OUR WAITING PLACE.›
‹"WAITING"?›
‹WHAT ARE YOU WAITING FOR?›
‹FOR OLD THINGS TO WELCOME US SO WE CAN LIVE AGAIN.›

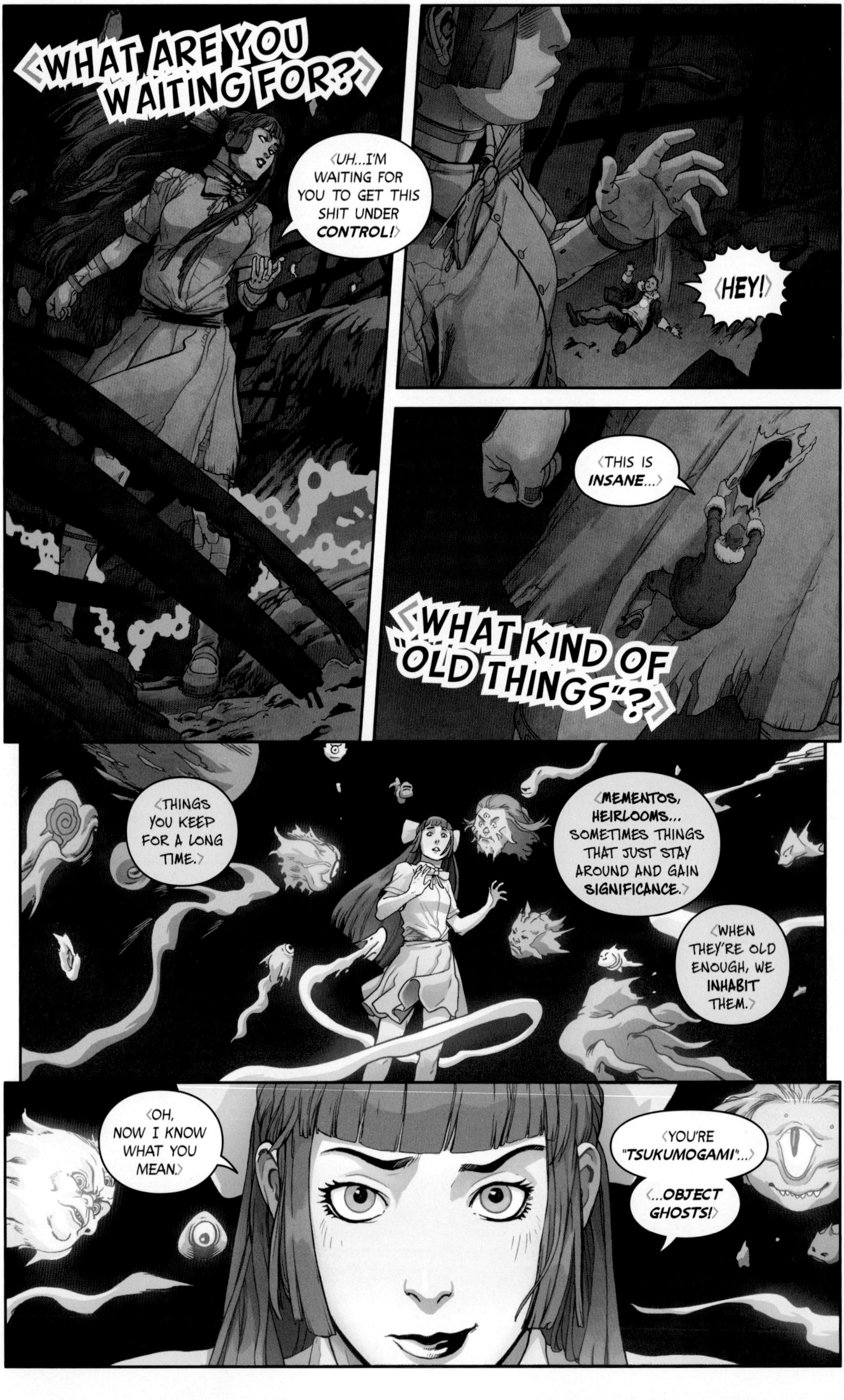

⟨WHAT ARE YOU WAITING FOR?⟩
⟨UH...I'M WAITING FOR YOU TO GET THIS SHIT UNDER CONTROL!⟩
⟨HEY!⟩
⟨THIS IS INSANE...⟩
⟨WHAT KIND OF "OLD THINGS"?⟩
⟨THINGS YOU KEEP FOR A LONG TIME.⟩
⟨MEMENTOS, HEIRLOOMS... SOMETIMES THINGS THAT JUST STAY AROUND AND GAIN SIGNIFICANCE.⟩
⟨WHEN THEY'RE OLD ENOUGH, WE INHABIT THEM.⟩
⟨OH, NOW I KNOW WHAT YOU MEAN.⟩
⟨YOU'RE "TSUKUMOGAMI"...⟩
⟨...OBJECT GHOSTS!⟩

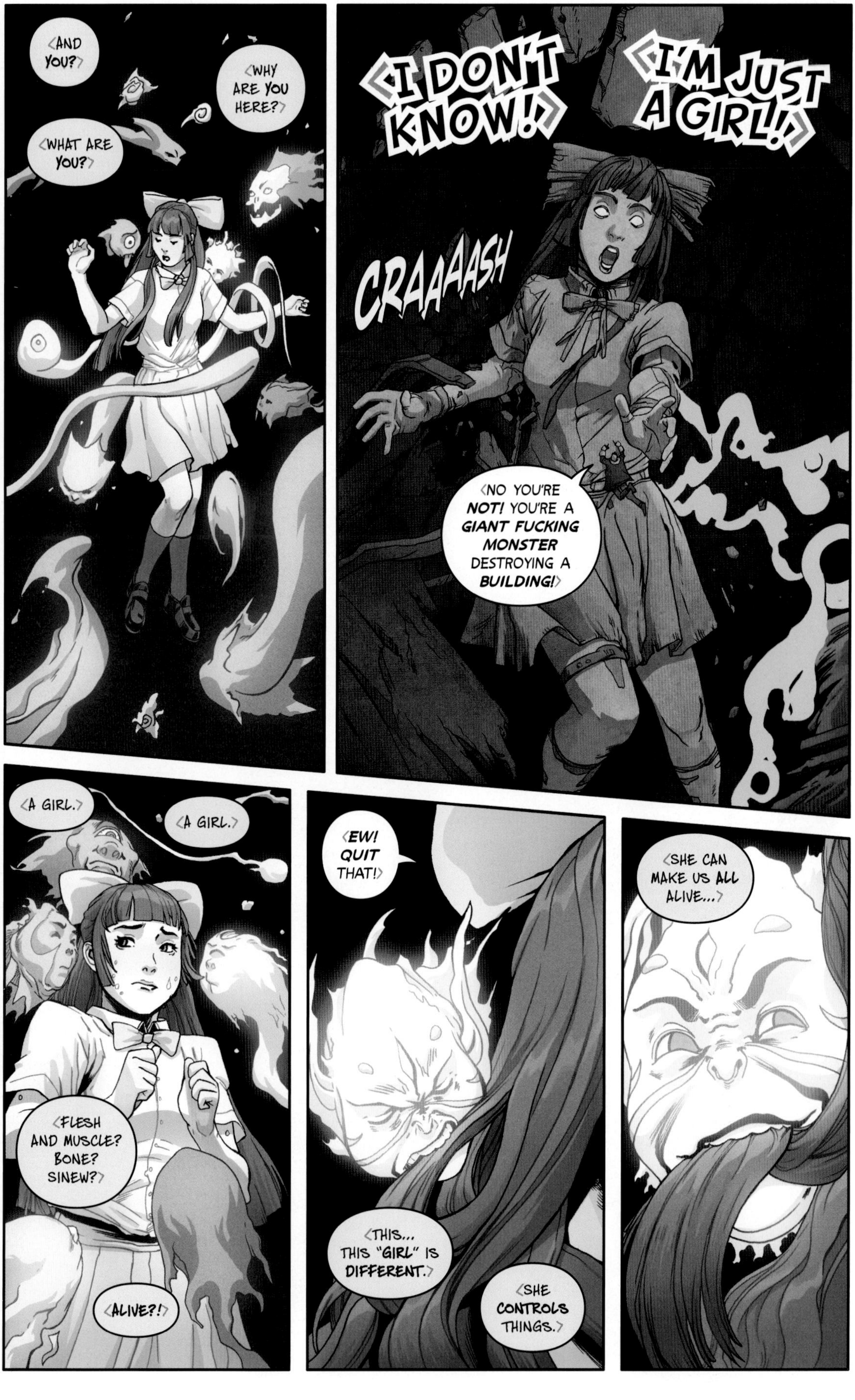
<AND YOU?>
<WHY ARE YOU HERE?>
<WHAT ARE YOU?>
<I DON'T KNOW!>
<I'M JUST A GIRL!>
CRAAAASH
<NO YOU'RE NOT! YOU'RE A GIANT FUCKING MONSTER DESTROYING A BUILDING!>
<A GIRL.>
<A GIRL.>
<FLESH AND MUSCLE? BONE? SINEW?>
<ALIVE?!>
<EW! QUIT THAT!>
<THIS... THIS "GIRL" IS DIFFERENT.>
<SHE CONTROLS THINGS.>
<SHE CAN MAKE US ALL ALIVE...>

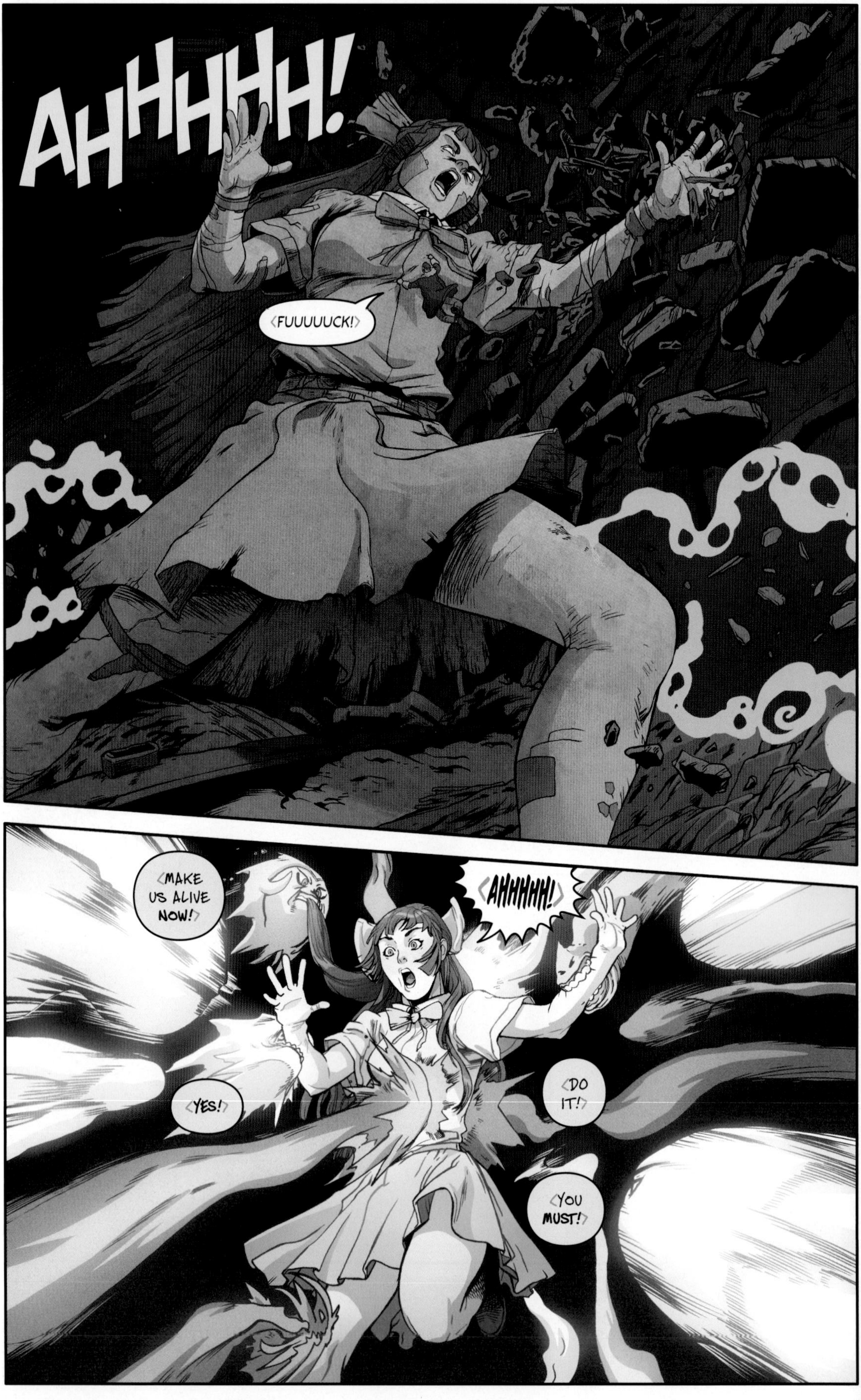
AHHHHH!
<FUUUUUCK!>
<MAKE US ALIVE NOW!>
<AHHHHH!>
<YES!>
<DO IT!>
<YOU MUST!>

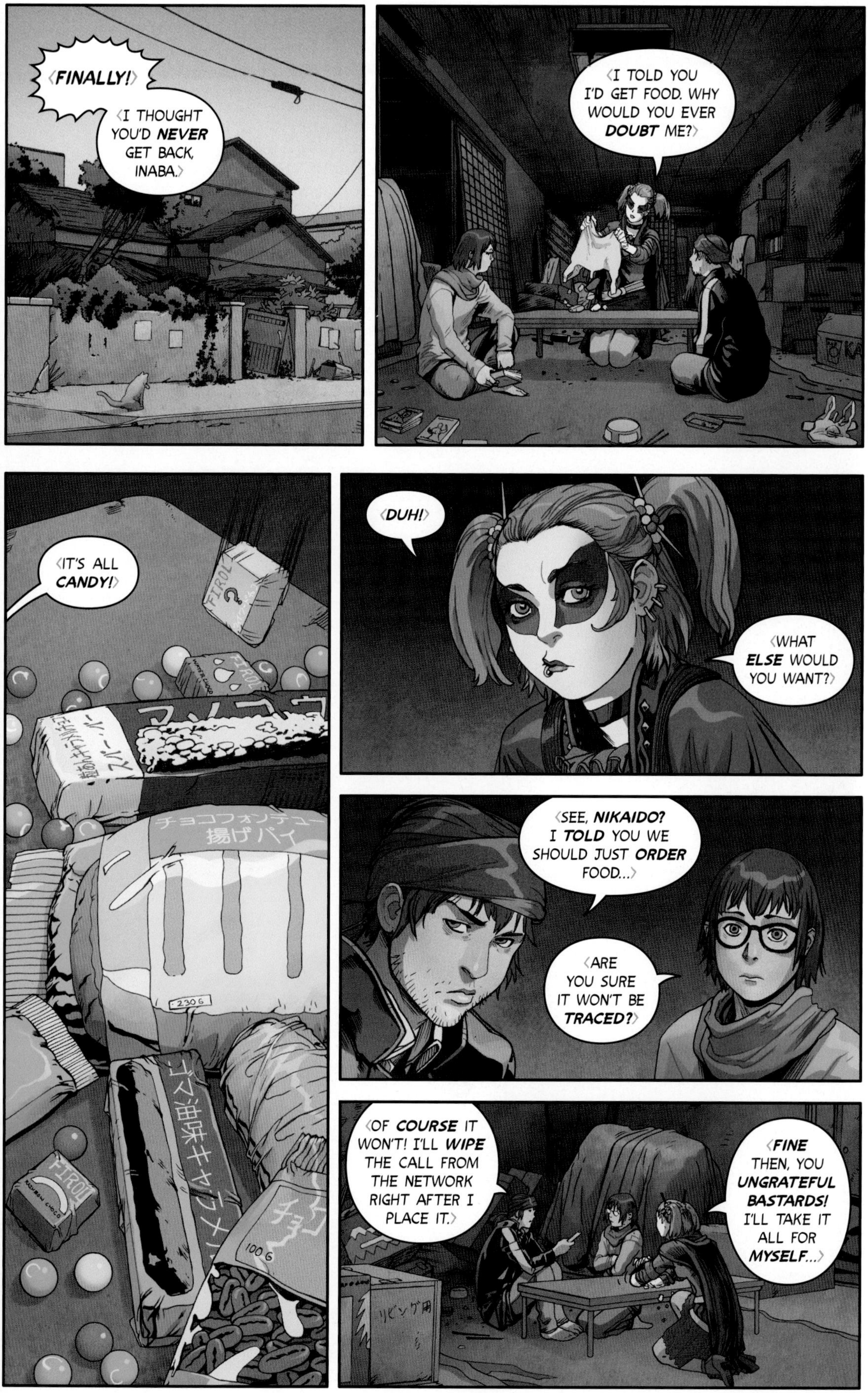
〈FINALLY!〉
〈I THOUGHT YOU'D NEVER GET BACK, INABA.〉
〈I TOLD YOU I'D GET FOOD. WHY WOULD YOU EVER DOUBT ME?〉
〈IT'S ALL CANDY!〉
FIROL
チョコフォンデュー
揚げパイ
〈DUH!〉
〈WHAT ELSE WOULD YOU WANT?〉
〈SEE, NIKAIDO? I TOLD YOU WE SHOULD JUST ORDER FOOD...〉
〈ARE YOU SURE IT WON'T BE TRACED?〉
〈OF COURSE IT WON'T! I'LL WIPE THE CALL FROM THE NETWORK RIGHT AFTER I PLACE IT.〉
〈FINE THEN, YOU UNGRATEFUL BASTARDS! I'LL TAKE IT ALL FOR MYSELF...〉

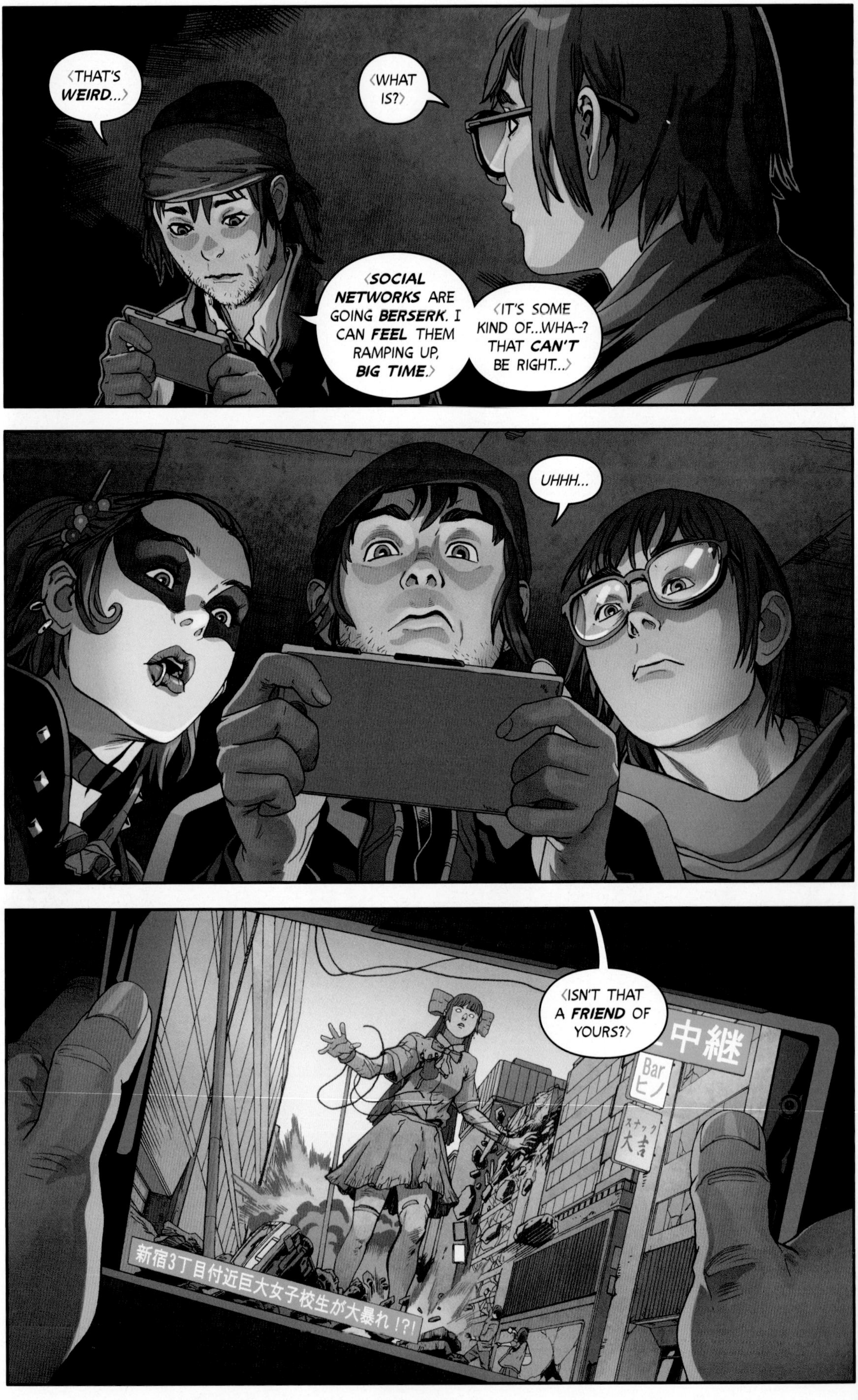
⟨THAT'S WEIRD...⟩
⟨WHAT IS?⟩
⟨SOCIAL NETWORKS ARE GOING BERSERK. I CAN FEEL THEM RAMPING UP, BIG TIME.⟩
⟨IT'S SOME KIND OF...WHA--? THAT CAN'T BE RIGHT...⟩
UHHH...
⟨ISN'T THAT A FRIEND OF YOURS?⟩
中継
Bar
ヒノ
スナック
大吉
新宿3丁目付近巨大女子校生が大暴れ !?!

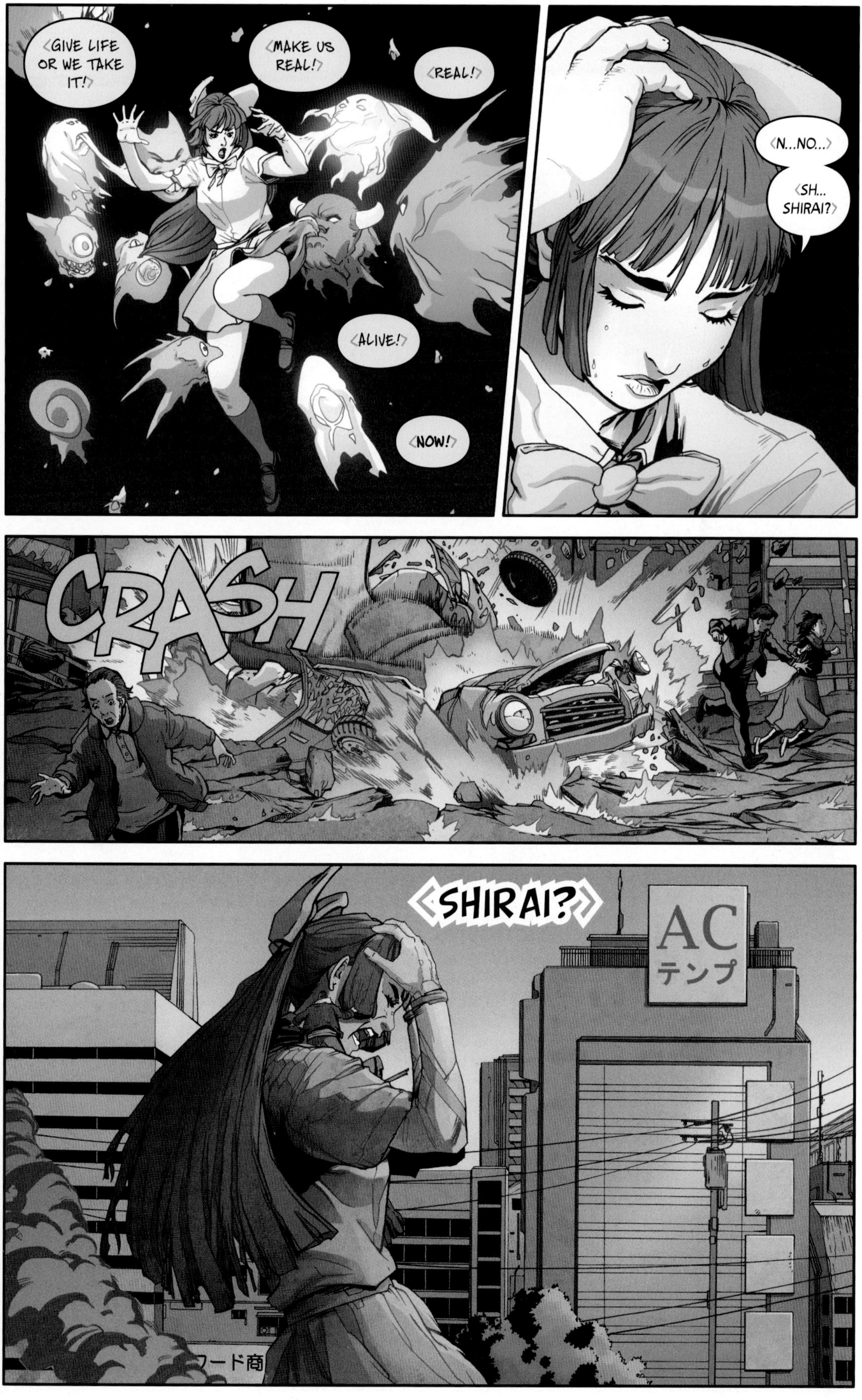

‹GIVE LIFE OR WE TAKE IT!›
‹MAKE US REAL!›
‹REAL!›
‹ALIVE!›
‹NOW!›
‹N...NO...›
‹SH... SHIRAI?›
CRASH
‹SHIRAI?›
AC
テンプ
フード商

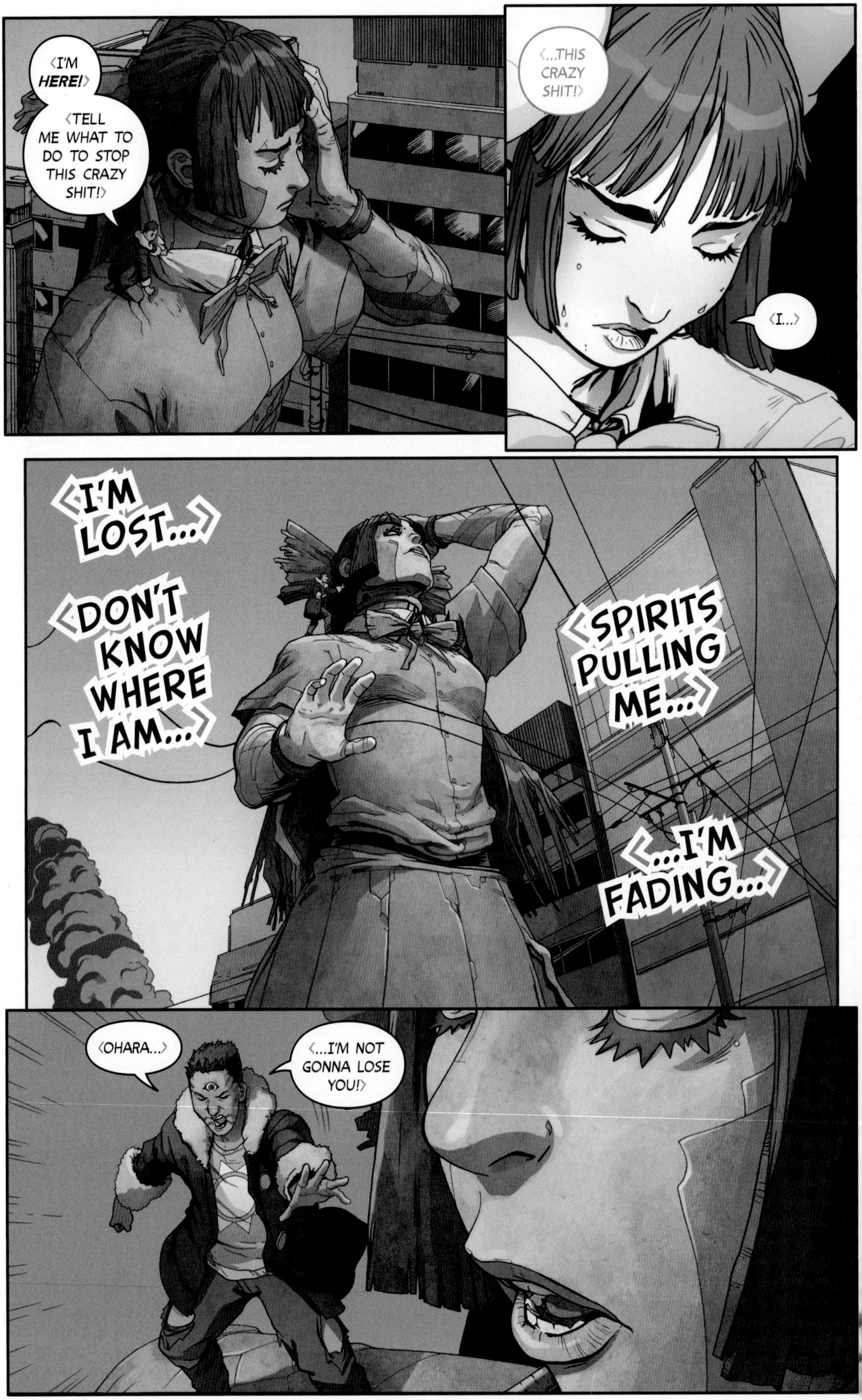

‹I'M *HERE!*›
‹TELL ME WHAT TO DO TO STOP THIS CRAZY SHIT!›
‹...THIS CRAZY SHIT!›
‹I...›
‹I'M LOST...›
‹DON'T KNOW WHERE I AM...›
‹SPIRITS PULLING ME...›
‹...I'M FADING...›
‹OHARA...›
‹...I'M NOT GONNA LOSE YOU!›

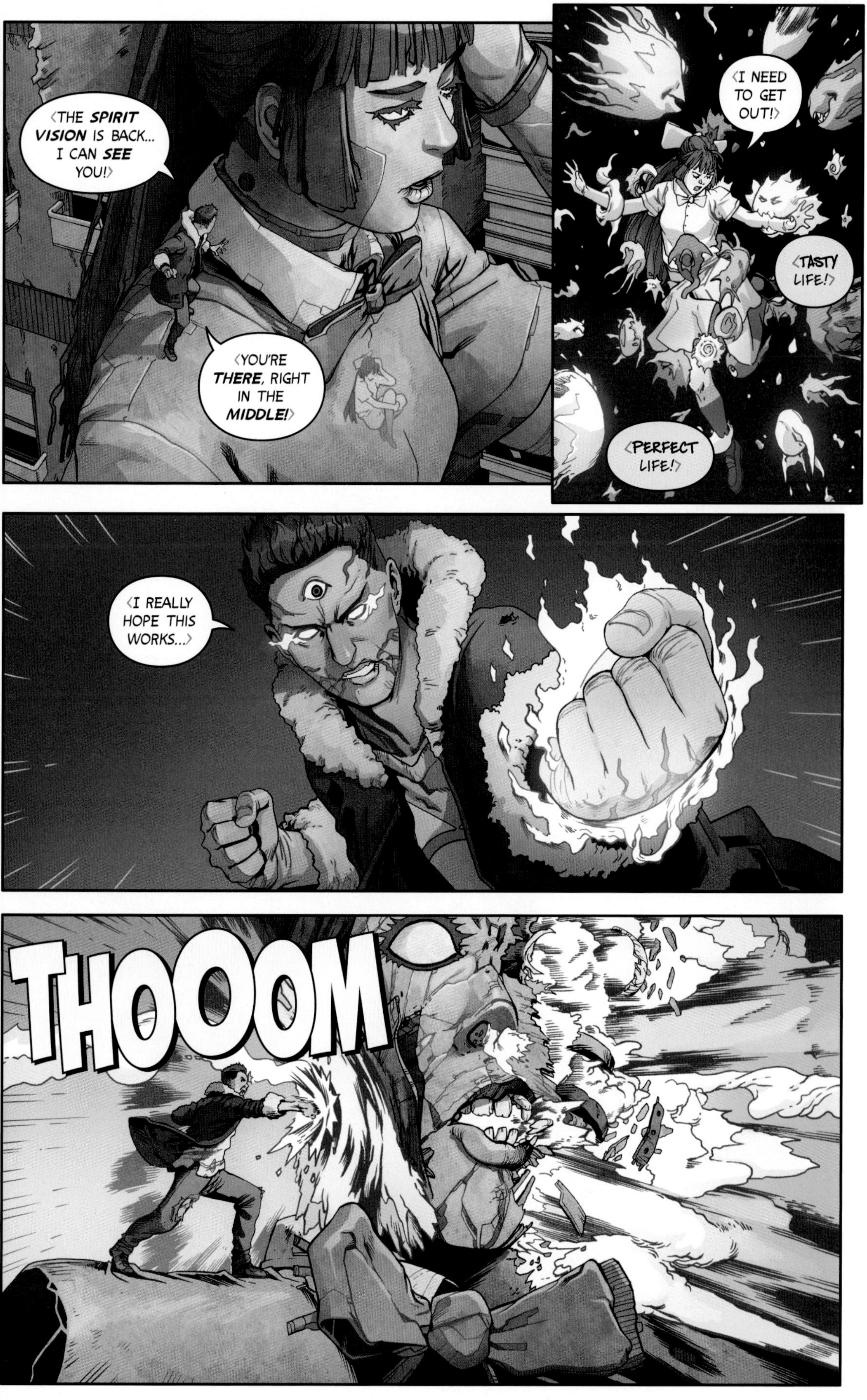

‹THE SPIRIT VISION IS BACK... I CAN SEE YOU!›
‹YOU'RE THERE, RIGHT IN THE MIDDLE!›
‹I NEED TO GET OUT!›
‹TASTY LIFE!›
‹PERFECT LIFE!›
‹I REALLY HOPE THIS WORKS...›
THOOOM

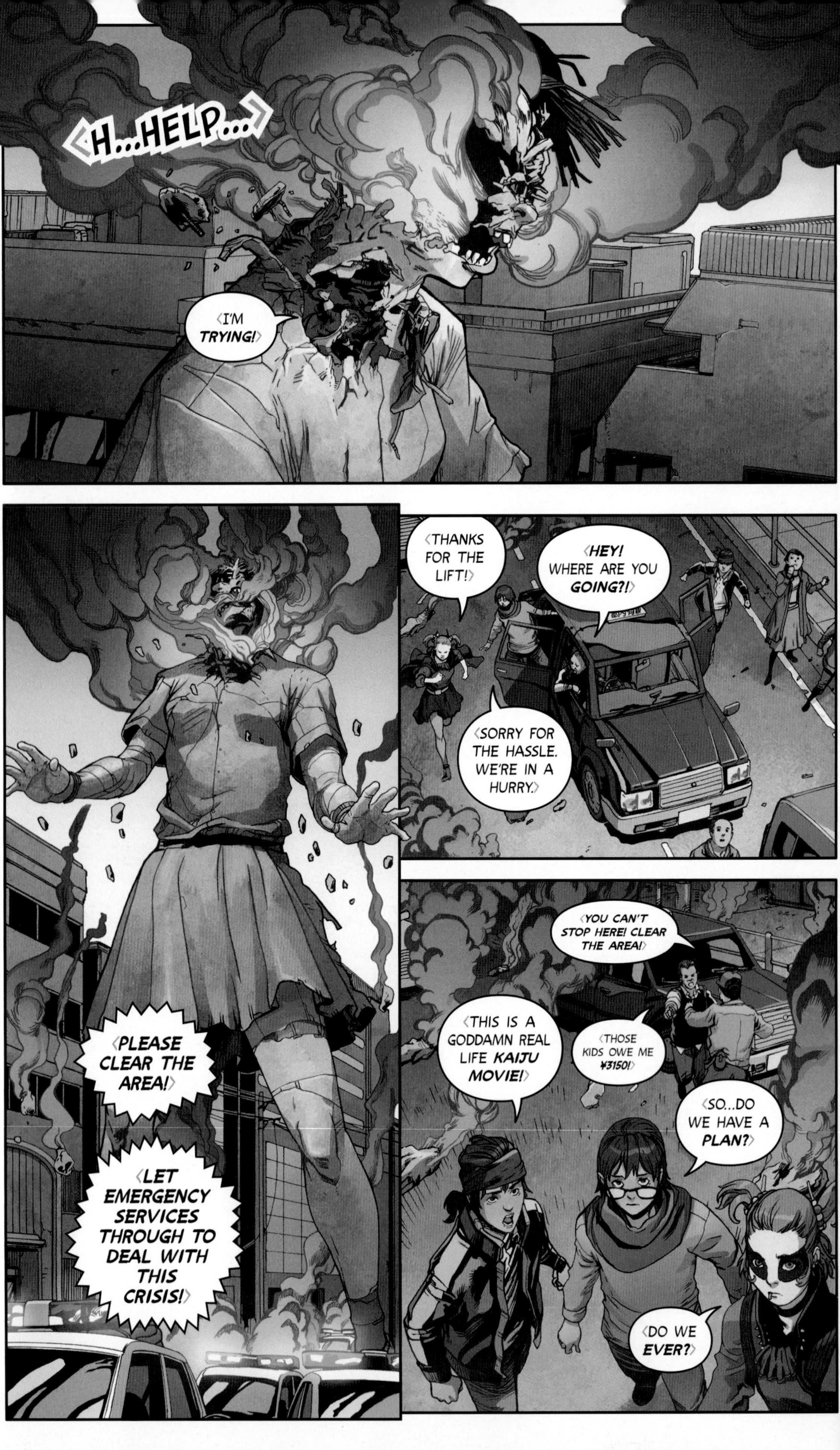
<H...HELP...>
<I'M TRYING!>
<THANKS FOR THE LIFT!>
<HEY! WHERE ARE YOU GOING?!>
<SORRY FOR THE HASSLE. WE'RE IN A HURRY.>
<PLEASE CLEAR THE AREA!>
<LET EMERGENCY SERVICES THROUGH TO DEAL WITH THIS CRISIS!>
<YOU CAN'T STOP HERE! CLEAR THE AREA!>
<THIS IS A GODDAMN REAL LIFE KAIJU MOVIE!>
<THOSE KIDS OWE ME ¥3150!>
<SO...DO WE HAVE A PLAN?>
<DO WE EVER?>

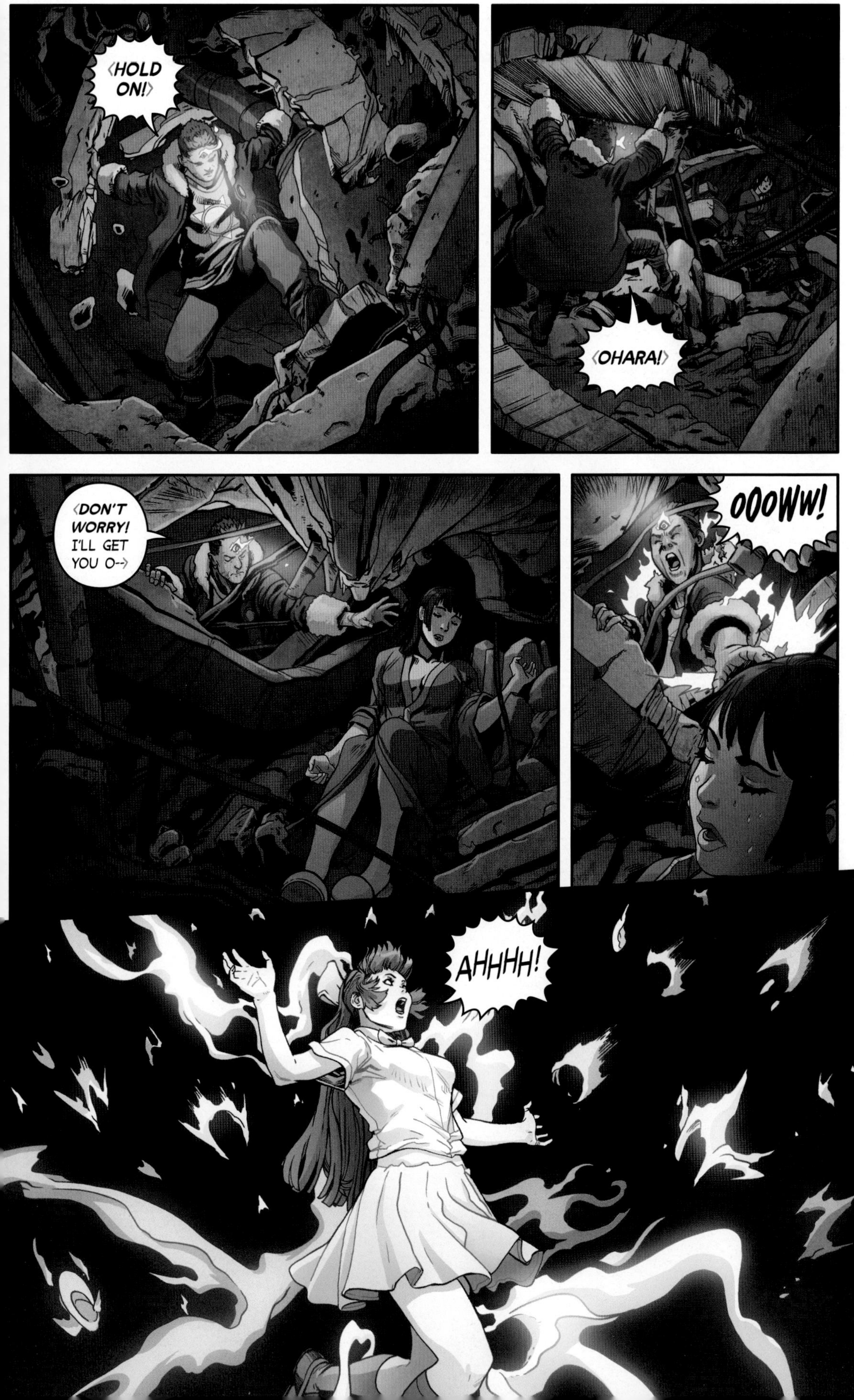

⟨HOLD ON!⟩
⟨OHARA!⟩
⟨DON'T WORRY! I'LL GET YOU O--⟩
OOOWW!
AHHHH!

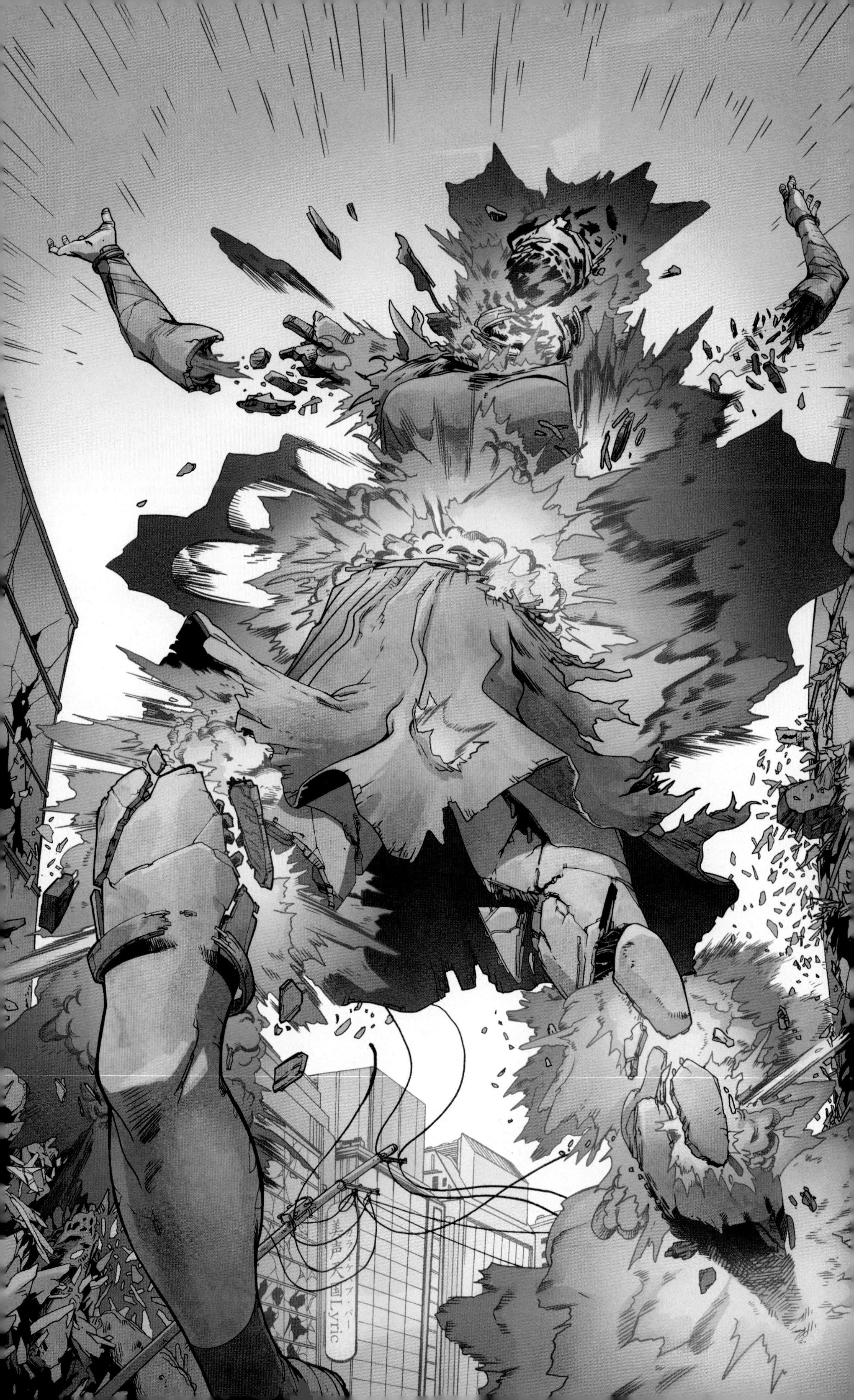
カラオケ・パブ・バー
美声天国Lyric

Chapter Twenty-Four

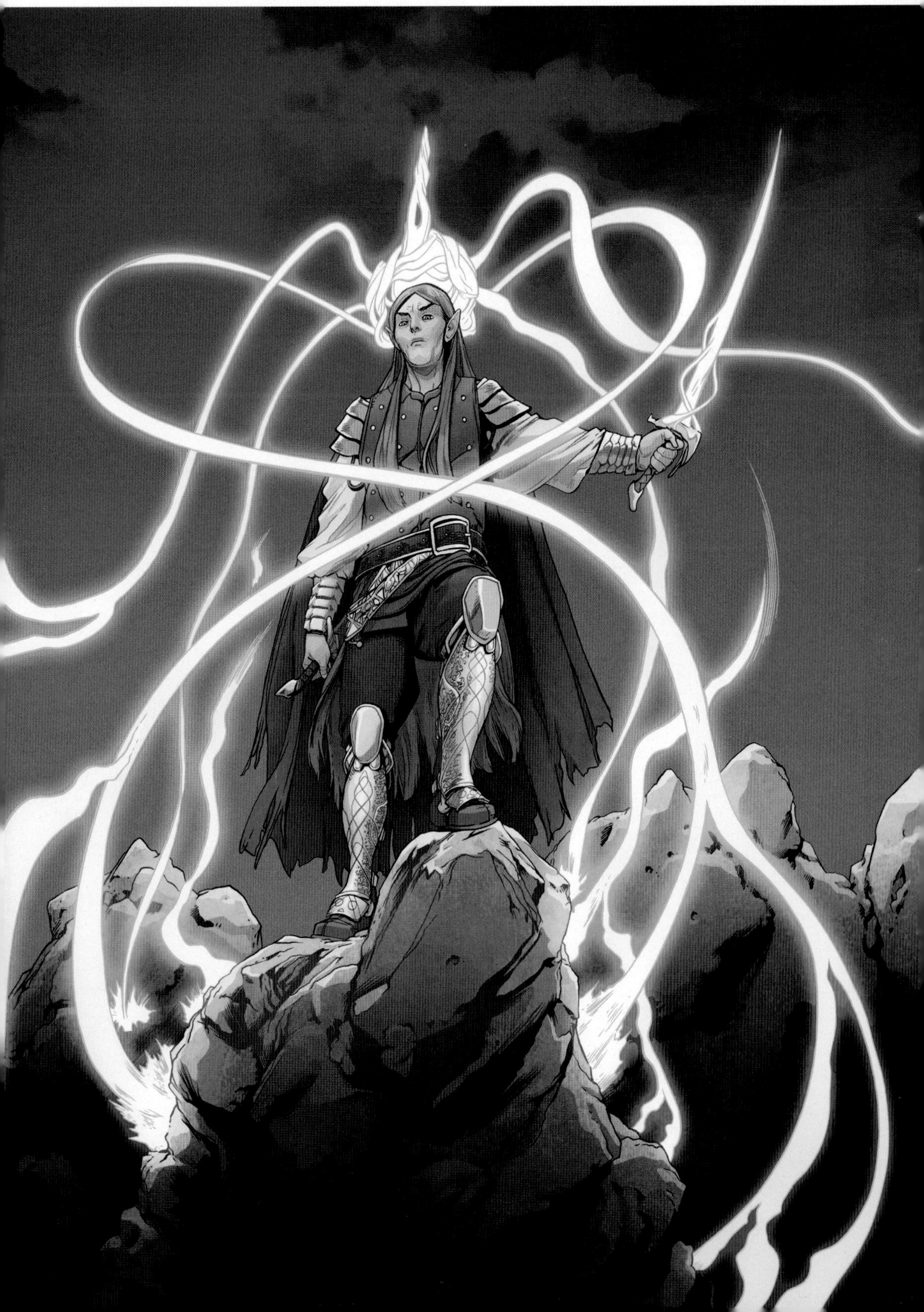

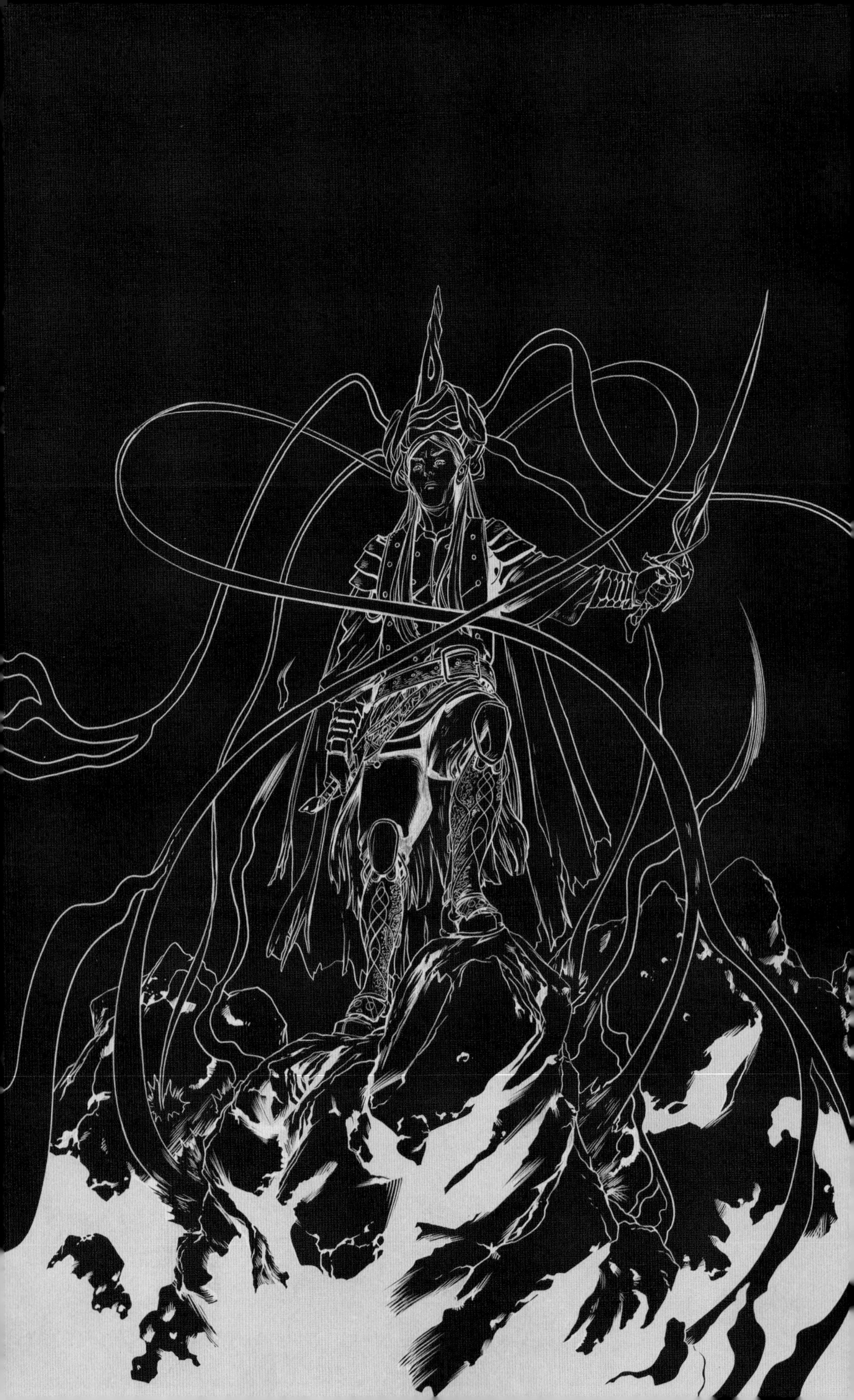

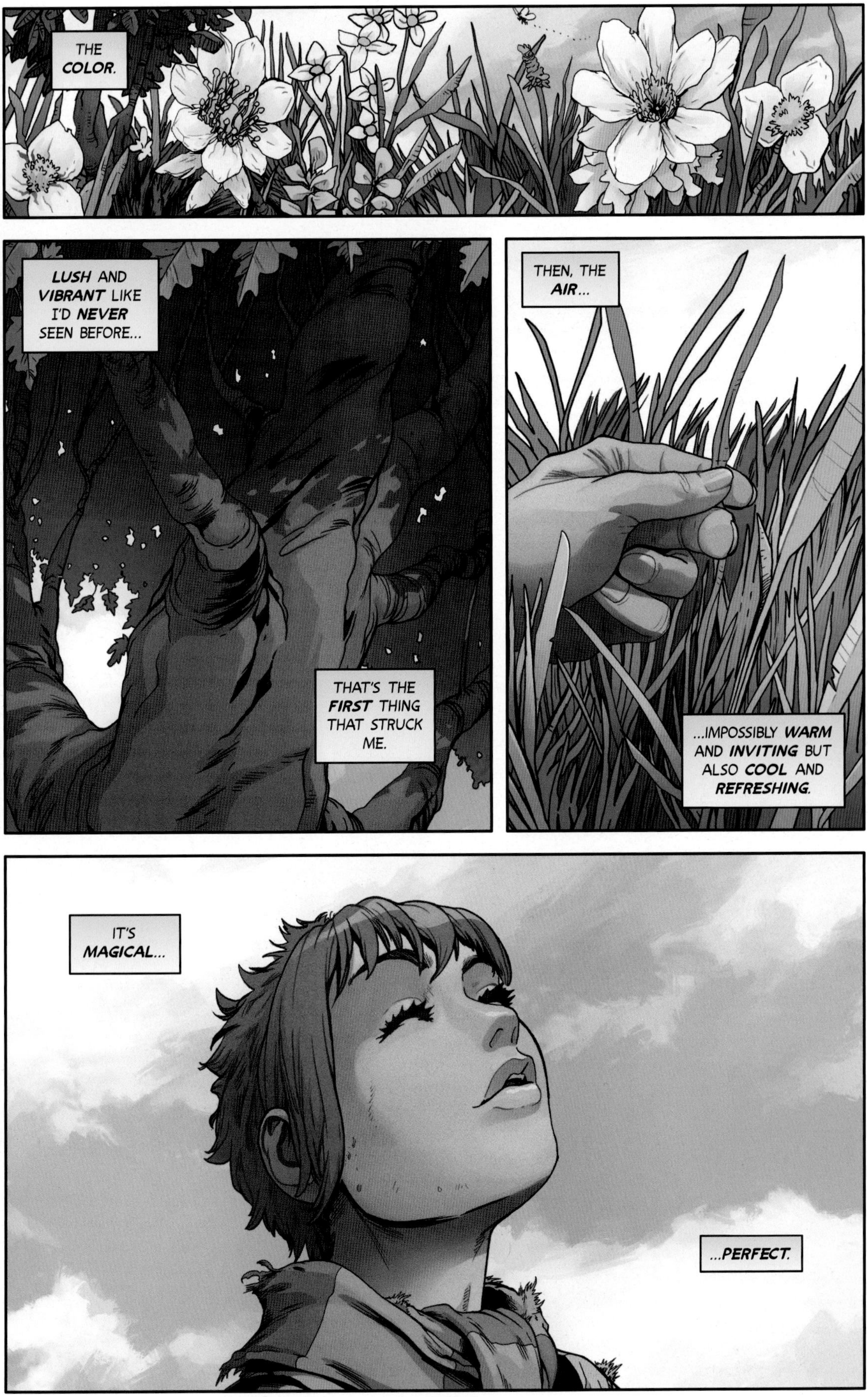
THE COLOR.
LUSH AND VIBRANT LIKE I'D NEVER SEEN BEFORE...
THAT'S THE FIRST THING THAT STRUCK ME.
THEN, THE AIR...
...IMPOSSIBLY WARM AND INVITING BUT ALSO COOL AND REFRESHING.
IT'S MAGICAL...
...PERFECT.

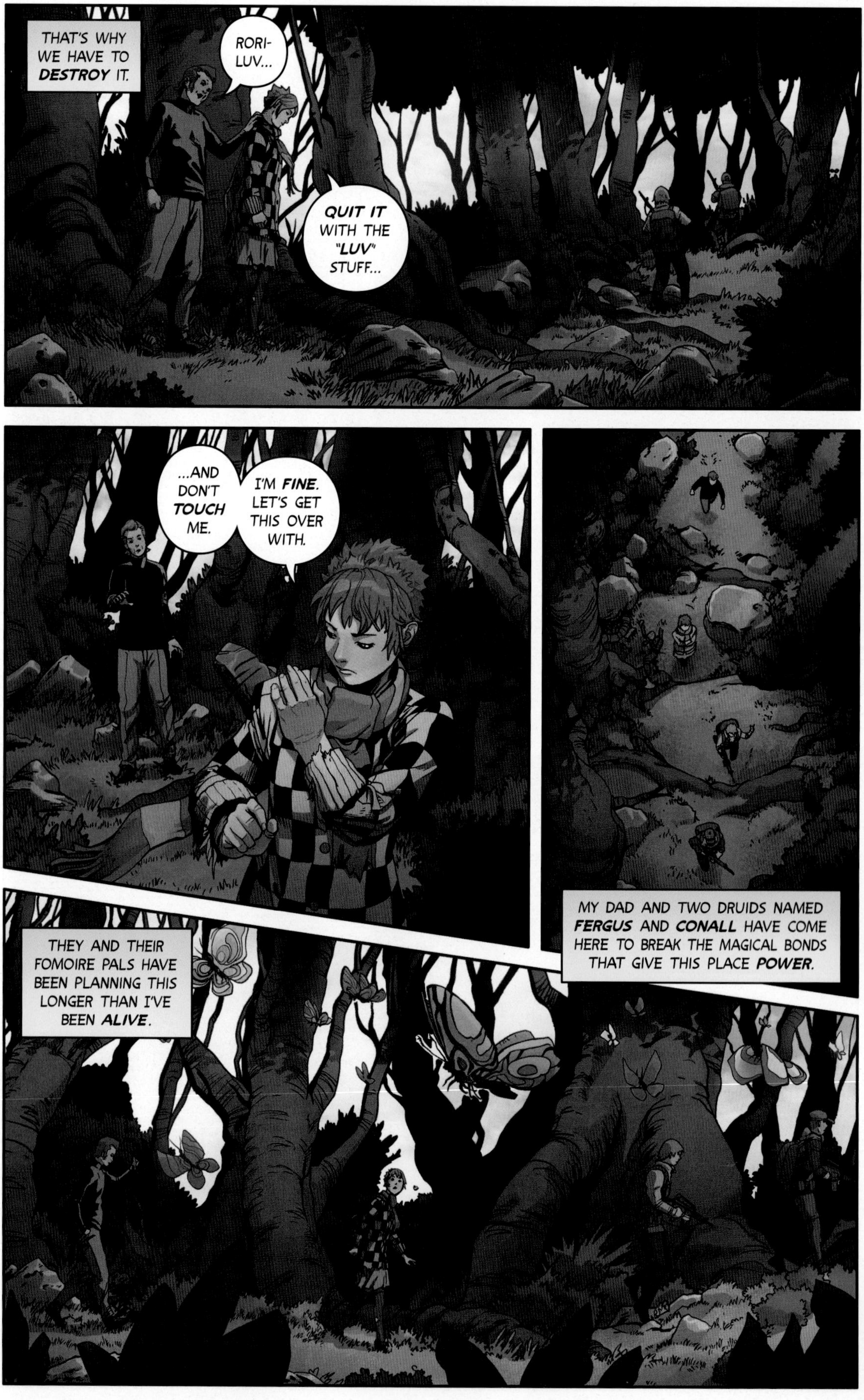
THAT'S WHY WE HAVE TO DESTROY IT.
RORI-LUV...
QUIT IT WITH THE "LUV" STUFF...
...AND DON'T TOUCH ME.
I'M FINE. LET'S GET THIS OVER WITH.
MY DAD AND TWO DRUIDS NAMED FERGUS AND CONALL HAVE COME HERE TO BREAK THE MAGICAL BONDS THAT GIVE THIS PLACE POWER.
THEY AND THEIR FOMOIRE PALS HAVE BEEN PLANNING THIS LONGER THAN I'VE BEEN ALIVE.

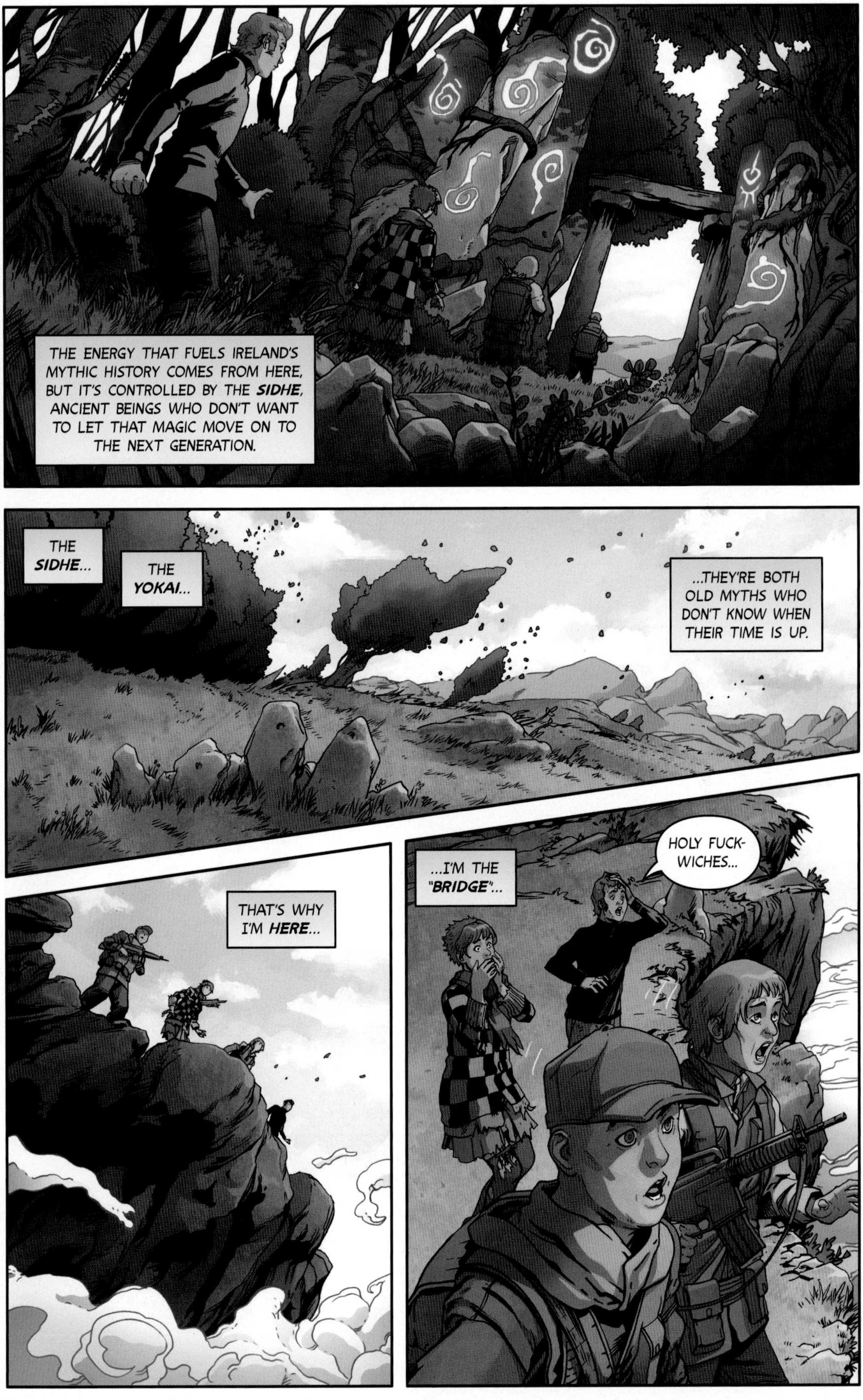
THE ENERGY THAT FUELS IRELAND'S MYTHIC HISTORY COMES FROM HERE, BUT IT'S CONTROLLED BY THE *SIDHE*, ANCIENT BEINGS WHO DON'T WANT TO LET THAT MAGIC MOVE ON TO THE NEXT GENERATION.
THE *SIDHE*...
THE *YOKAI*...
...THEY'RE BOTH OLD MYTHS WHO DON'T KNOW WHEN THEIR TIME IS UP.
THAT'S WHY I'M *HERE*...
...I'M THE "*BRIDGE*"...
HOLY FUCK-WICHES...

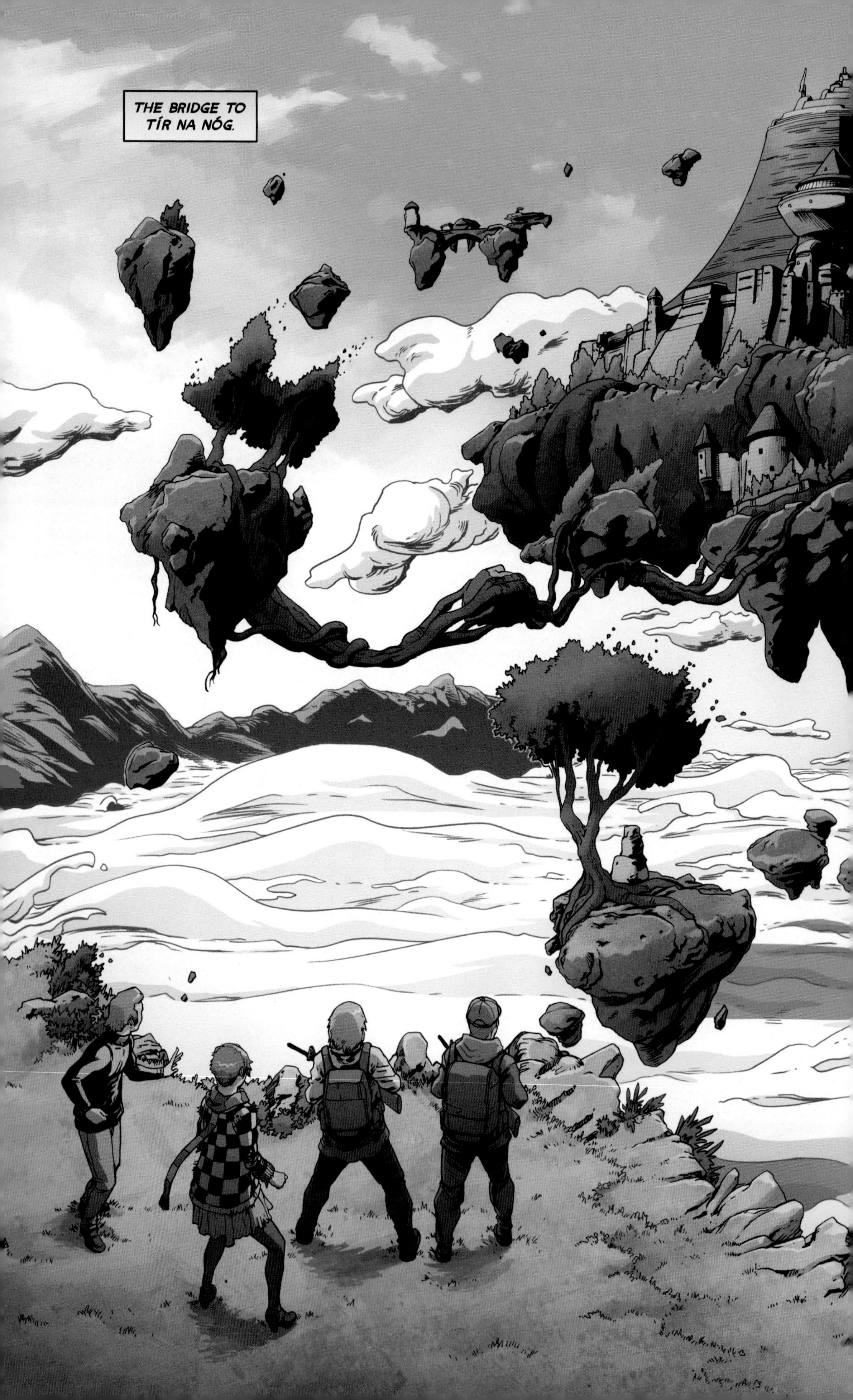
THE BRIDGE TO TÍR NA NÓG.

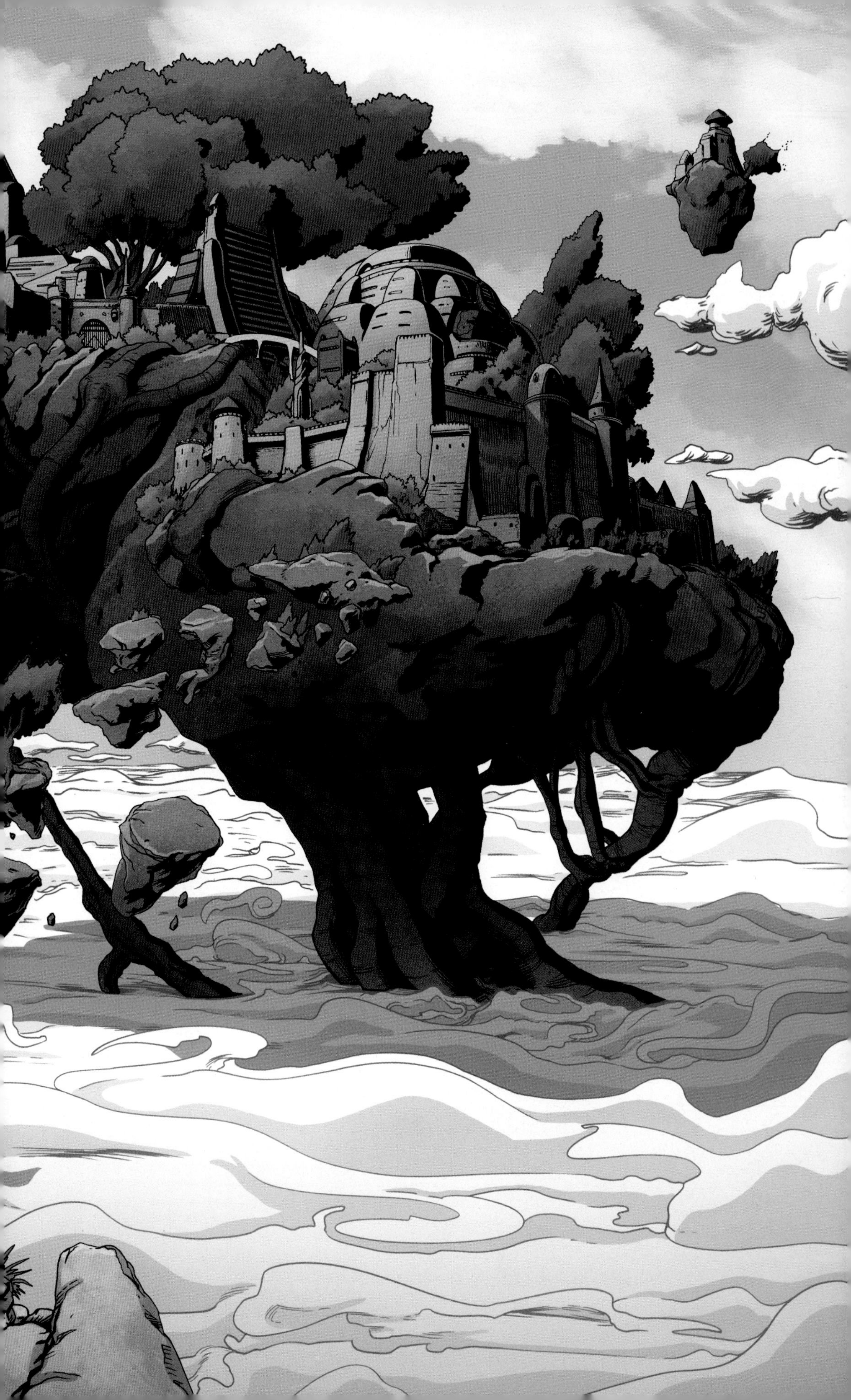

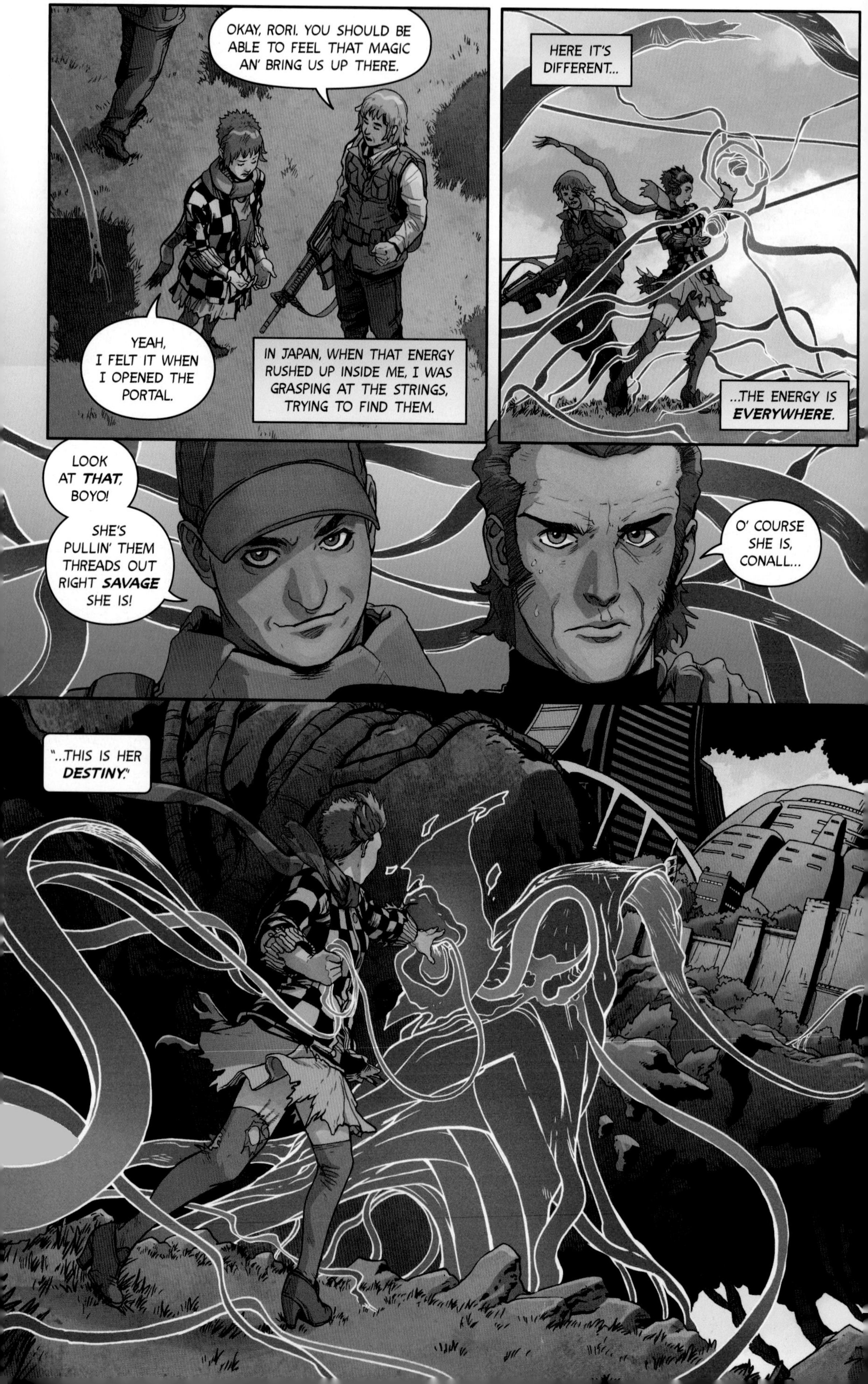
OKAY, RORI. YOU SHOULD BE ABLE TO FEEL THAT MAGIC AN' BRING US UP THERE.
YEAH, I FELT IT WHEN I OPENED THE PORTAL.
IN JAPAN, WHEN THAT ENERGY RUSHED UP INSIDE ME, I WAS GRASPING AT THE STRINGS, TRYING TO FIND THEM.
HERE IT'S DIFFERENT...
...THE ENERGY IS **EVERYWHERE**.
LOOK AT **THAT**, BOYO!
SHE'S PULLIN' THEM THREADS OUT RIGHT **SAVAGE** SHE IS!
O' COURSE SHE IS, CONALL...
"...THIS IS HER **DESTINY**."

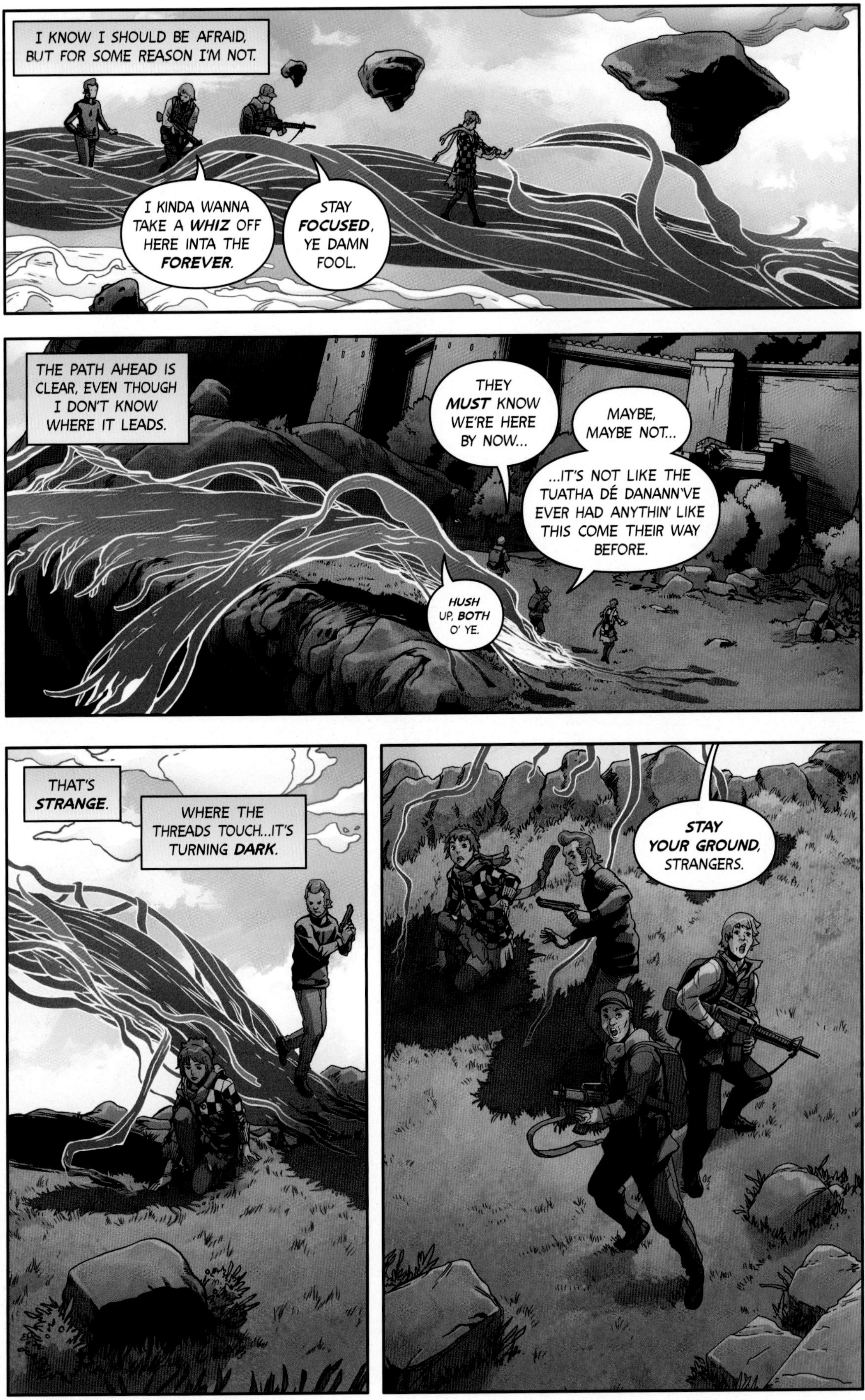
I KNOW I SHOULD BE AFRAID, BUT FOR SOME REASON I'M NOT.
I KINDA WANNA TAKE A *WHIZ* OFF HERE INTA THE *FOREVER*.
STAY *FOCUSED*, YE DAMN FOOL.
THE PATH AHEAD IS CLEAR, EVEN THOUGH I DON'T KNOW WHERE IT LEADS.
THEY *MUST* KNOW WE'RE HERE BY NOW...
MAYBE, MAYBE NOT...
...IT'S NOT LIKE THE TUATHA DÉ DANANN'VE EVER HAD ANYTHIN' LIKE THIS COME THEIR WAY BEFORE.
HUSH UP, *BOTH* O' YE.
THAT'S *STRANGE*.
WHERE THE THREADS TOUCH...IT'S TURNING *DARK*.
STAY YOUR GROUND, STRANGERS.

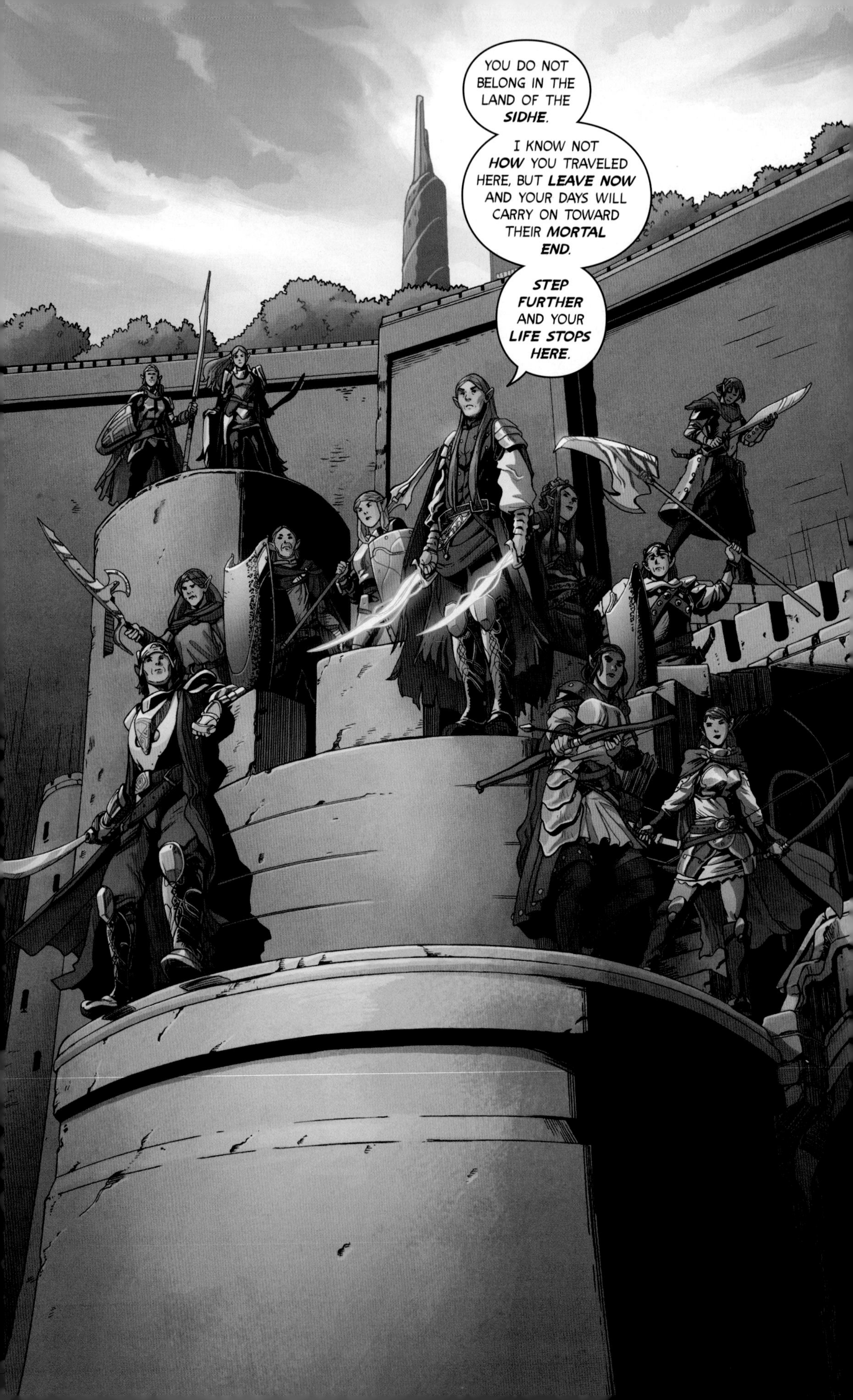
YOU DO NOT BELONG IN THE LAND OF THE SIDHE.
I KNOW NOT HOW YOU TRAVELED HERE, BUT LEAVE NOW AND YOUR DAYS WILL CARRY ON TOWARD THEIR MORTAL END.
STEP FURTHER AND YOUR LIFE STOPS HERE.

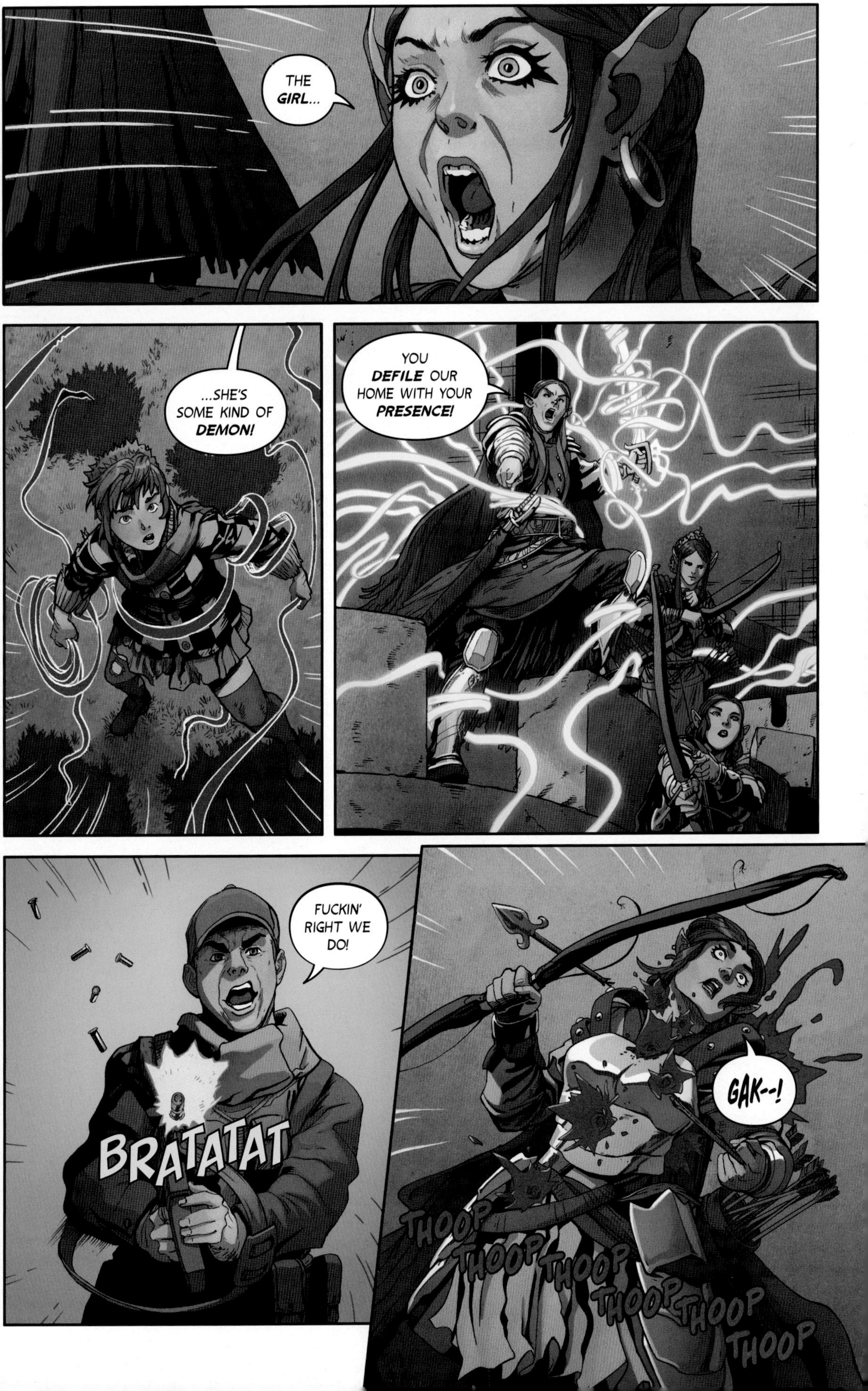
THE GIRL...
...SHE'S SOME KIND OF DEMON!
YOU DEFILE OUR HOME WITH YOUR PRESENCE!
FUCKIN' RIGHT WE DO!
BRATATAT
GAK--!
THOOP
THOOP
THOOP
THOOP
THOOP
THOOP

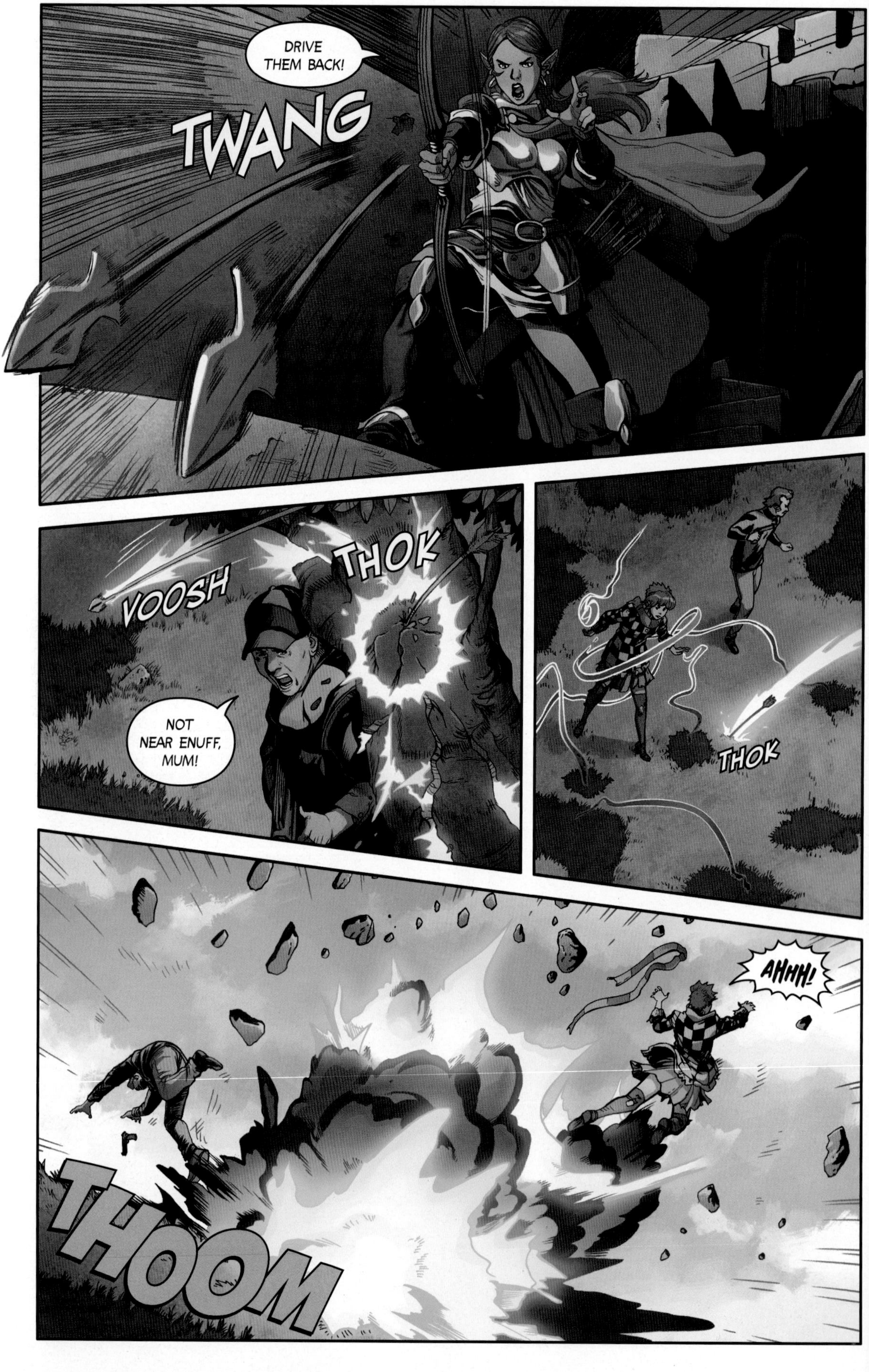
DRIVE THEM BACK!
TWANG
VOOSH
THOK
NOT NEAR ENUFF, MUM!
THOK
AHHH!
THOOM

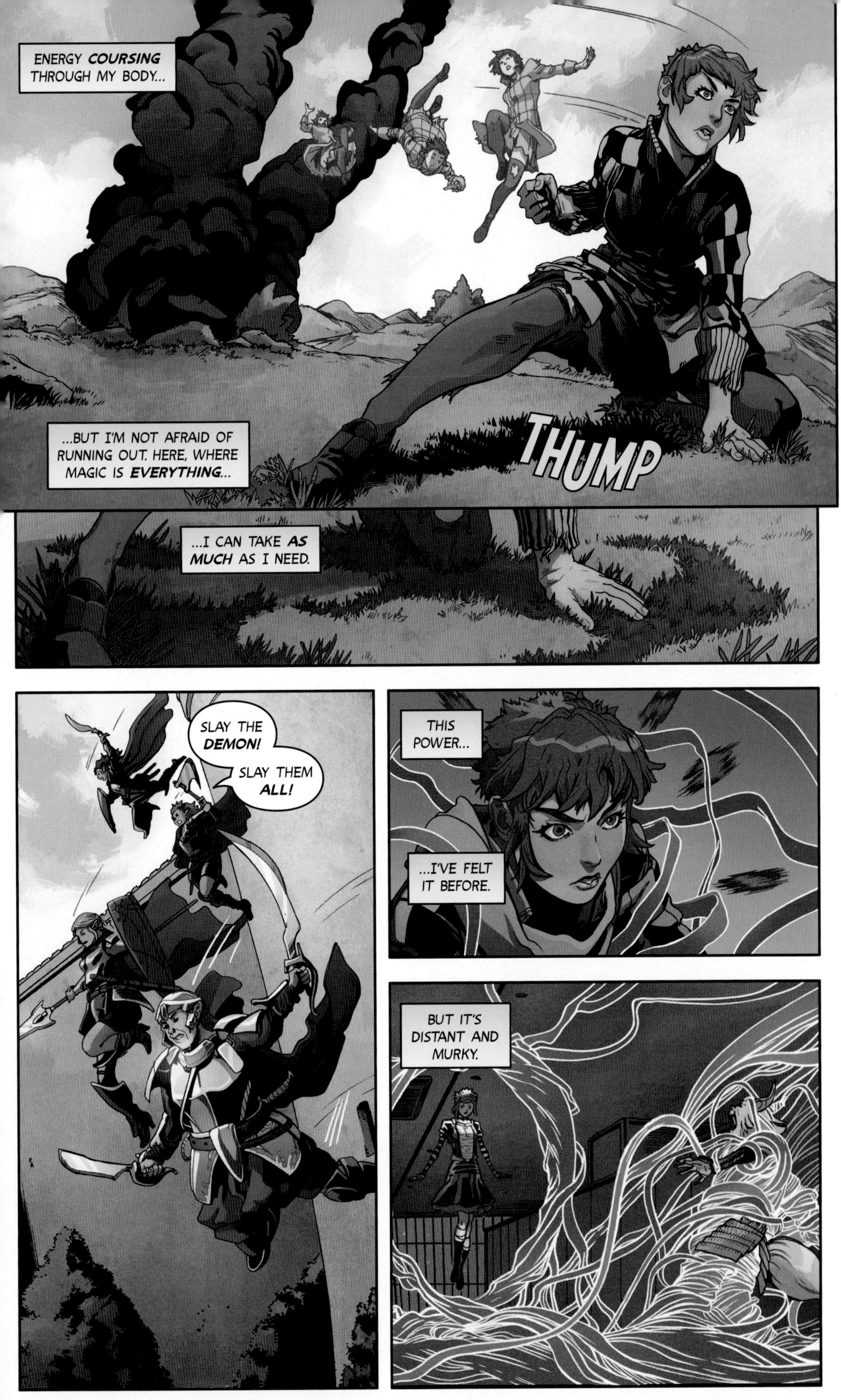
ENERGY COURSING THROUGH MY BODY...
...BUT I'M NOT AFRAID OF RUNNING OUT. HERE, WHERE MAGIC IS EVERYTHING...
THUMP
...I CAN TAKE AS MUCH AS I NEED.
SLAY THE DEMON!
SLAY THEM ALL!
THIS POWER...
...I'VE FELT IT BEFORE.
BUT IT'S DISTANT AND MURKY.

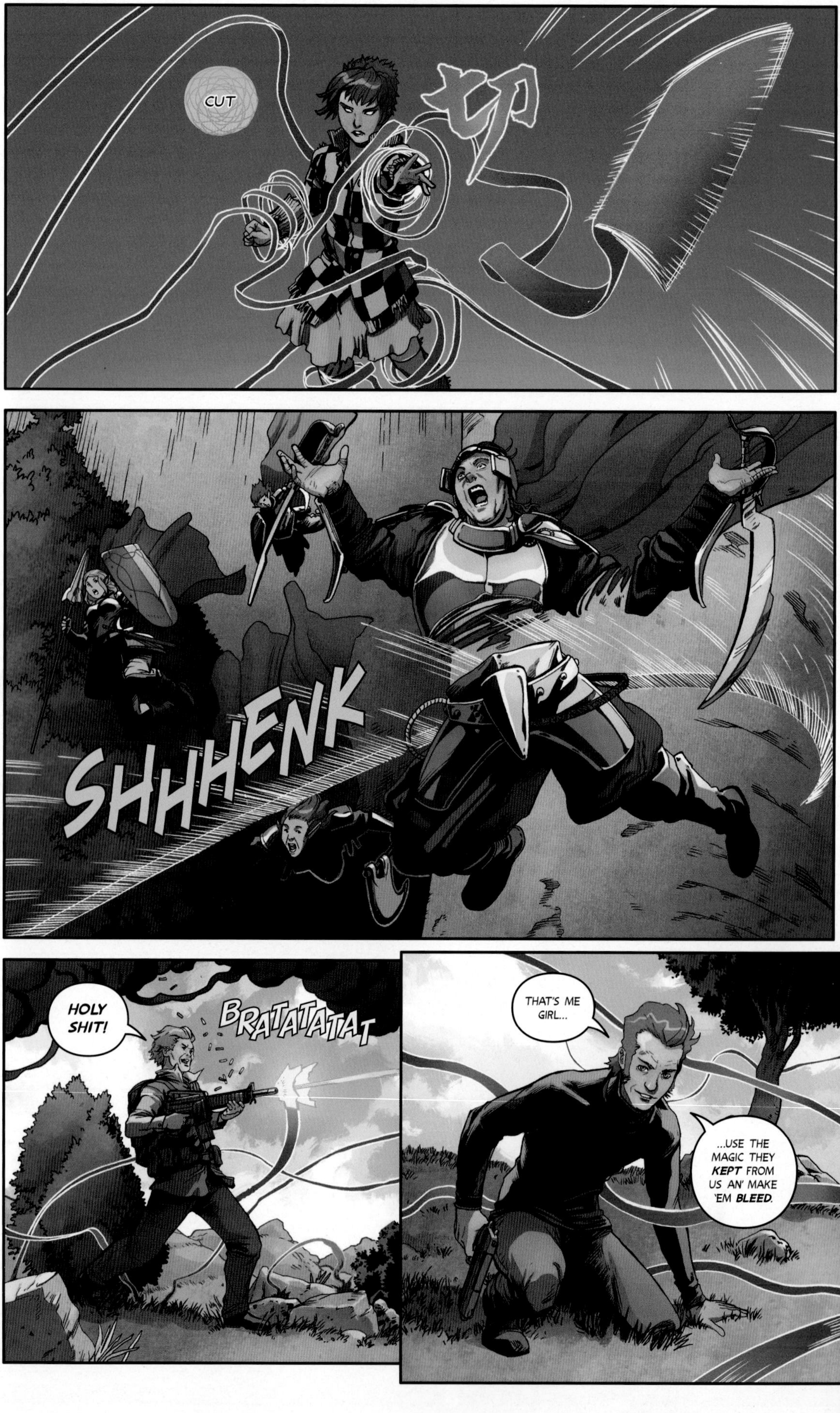
CUT
切
SHHHENK
HOLY SHIT!
BRATATATAT
THAT'S ME GIRL...
...USE THE MAGIC THEY KEPT FROM US AN' MAKE 'EM BLEED.

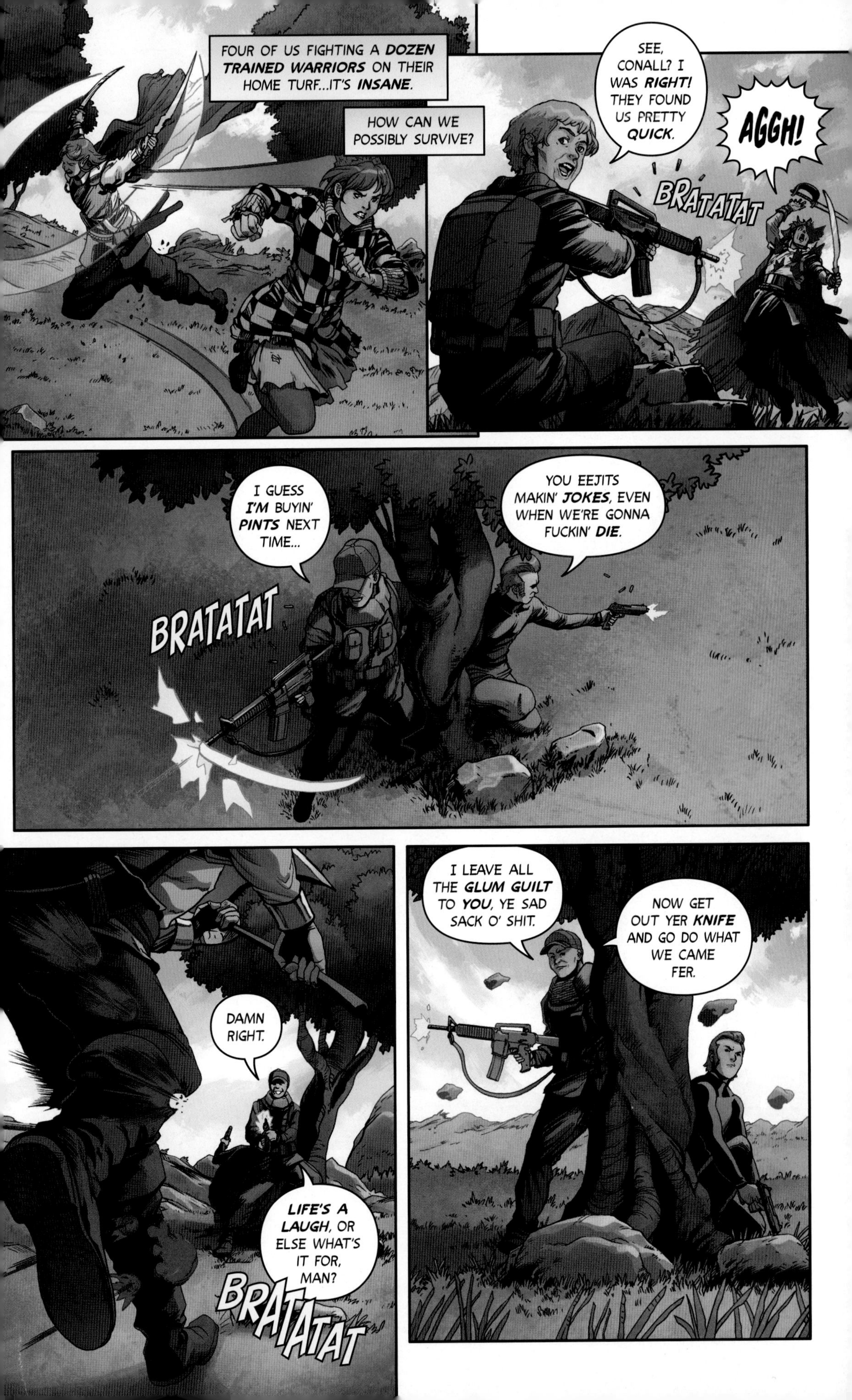
FOUR OF US FIGHTING A DOZEN TRAINED WARRIORS ON THEIR HOME TURF...IT'S INSANE.
HOW CAN WE POSSIBLY SURVIVE?
SEE, CONALL? I WAS RIGHT! THEY FOUND US PRETTY QUICK.
AGGH!
BRATATAT
I GUESS I'M BUYIN' PINTS NEXT TIME...
YOU EEJITS MAKIN' JOKES, EVEN WHEN WE'RE GONNA FUCKIN' DIE.
BRATATAT
DAMN RIGHT.
LIFE'S A LAUGH, OR ELSE WHAT'S IT FOR, MAN?
BRATATAT
I LEAVE ALL THE GLUM GUILT TO YOU, YE SAD SACK O' SHIT.
NOW GET OUT YER KNIFE AND GO DO WHAT WE CAME FER.

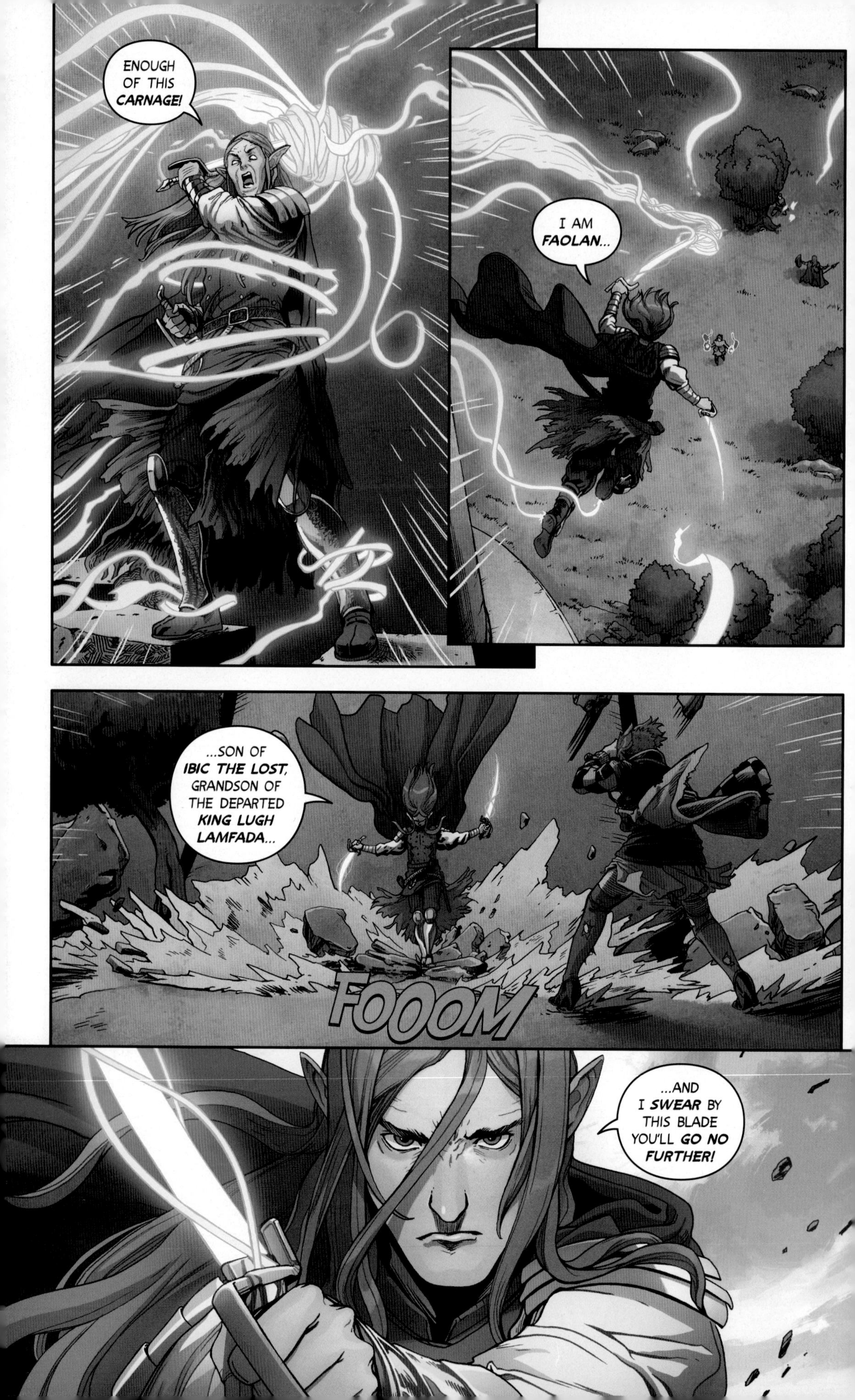
ENOUGH OF THIS CARNAGE!
I AM FAOLAN...
...SON OF IBIC THE LOST, GRANDSON OF THE DEPARTED KING LUGH LAMFADA...
FOOOM
...AND I SWEAR BY THIS BLADE YOU'LL GO NO FURTHER!

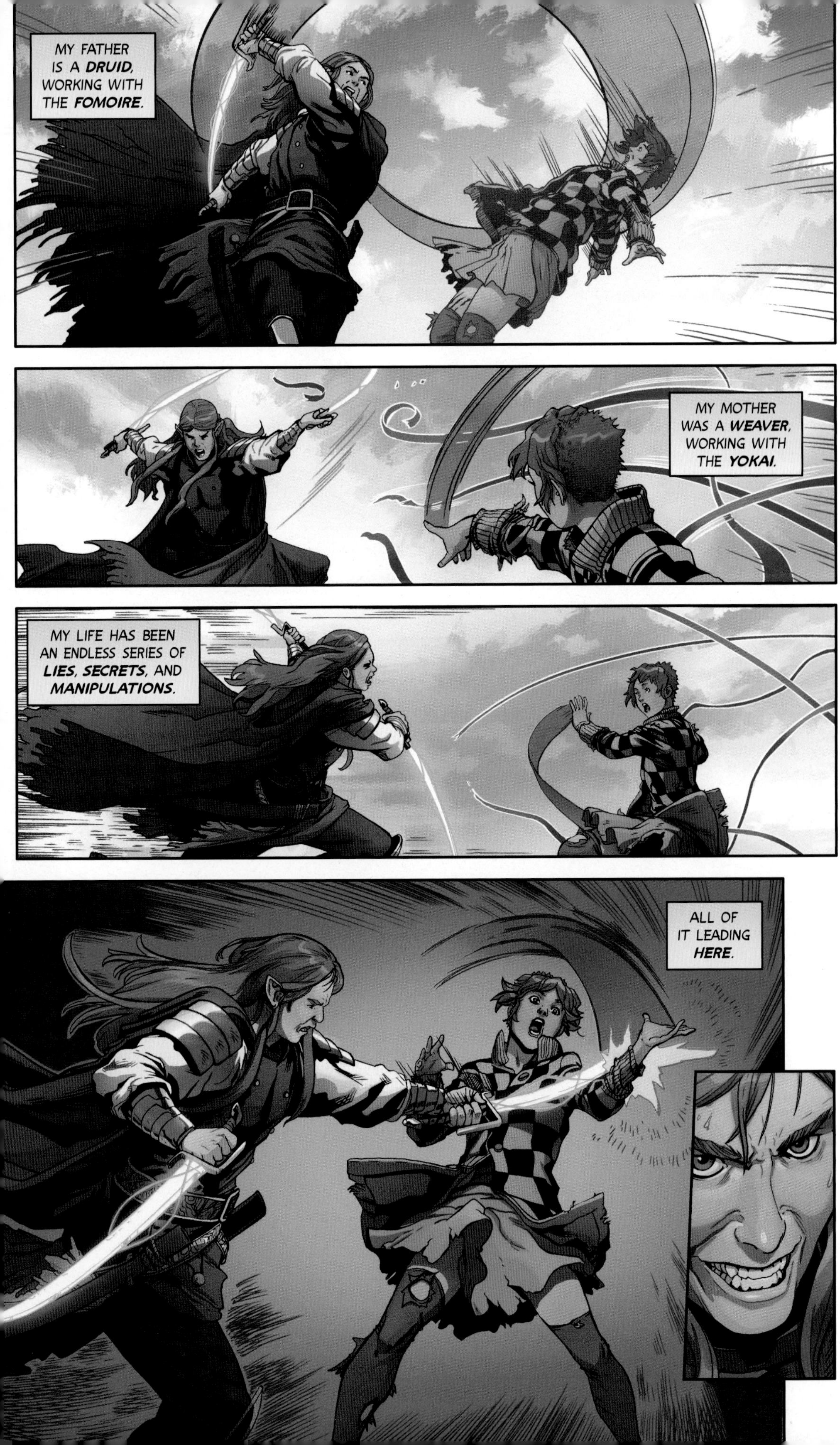
MY FATHER IS A *DRUID*, WORKING WITH THE *FOMOIRE*.
MY MOTHER WAS A *WEAVER*, WORKING WITH THE *YOKAI*.
MY LIFE HAS BEEN AN ENDLESS SERIES OF *LIES*, *SECRETS*, AND *MANIPULATIONS*.
ALL OF IT LEADING *HERE*.

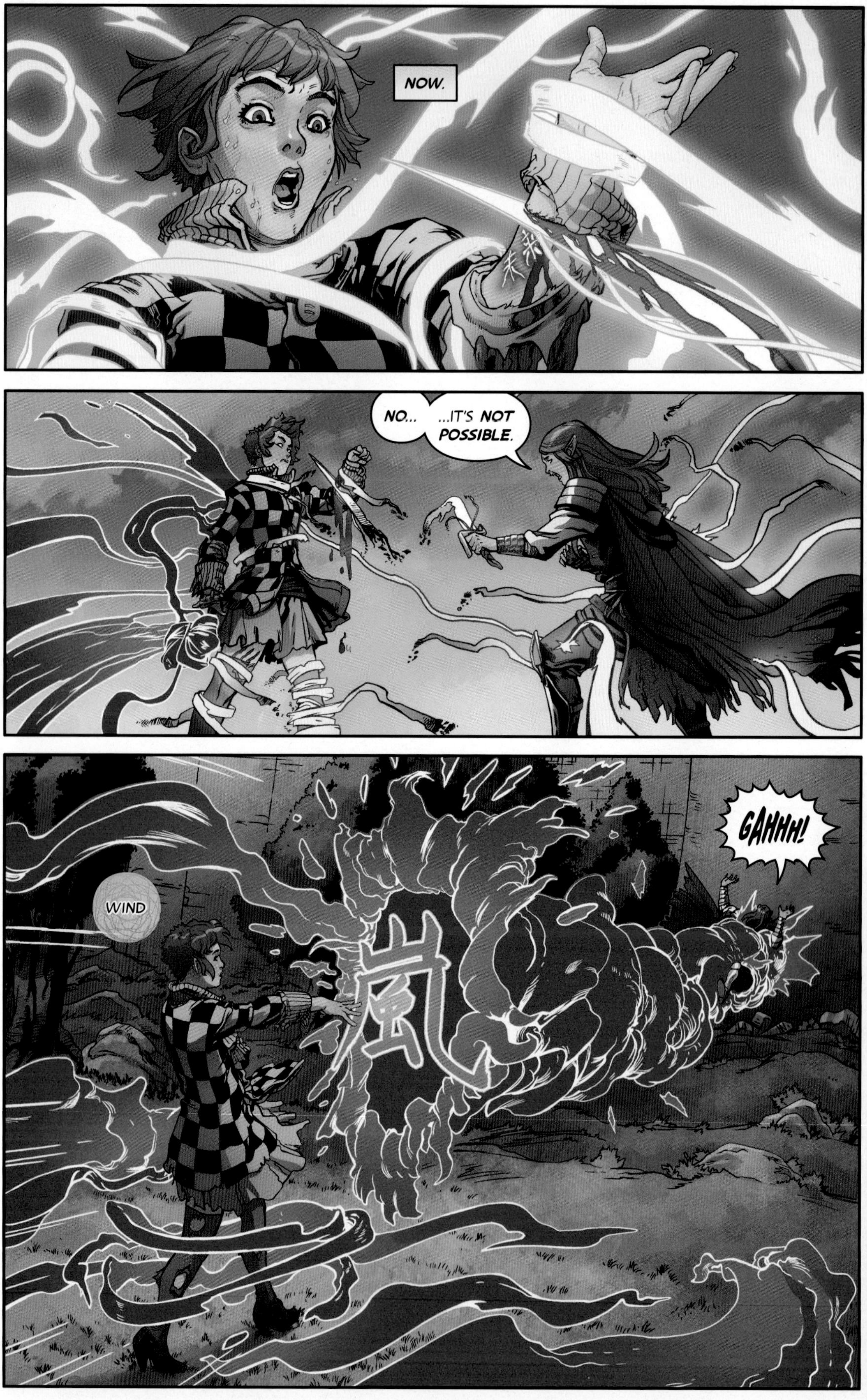
NOW.
NO...
...IT'S NOT POSSIBLE.
WIND
嵐
GAHHH!

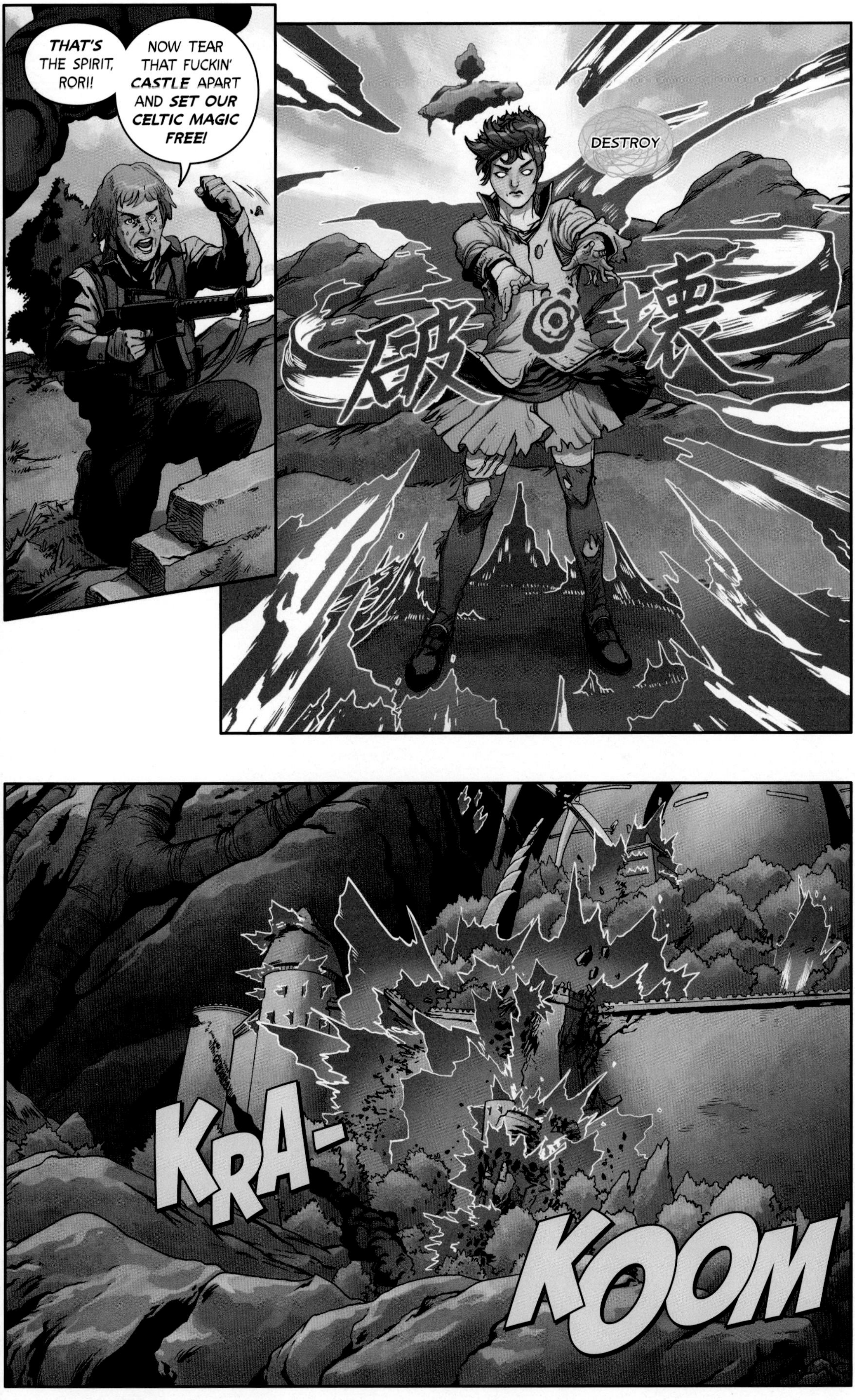
THAT'S THE SPIRIT, RORI!
NOW TEAR THAT FUCKIN' CASTLE APART AND SET OUR CELTIC MAGIC FREE!
DESTROY
破壊
KRA-
KOOM

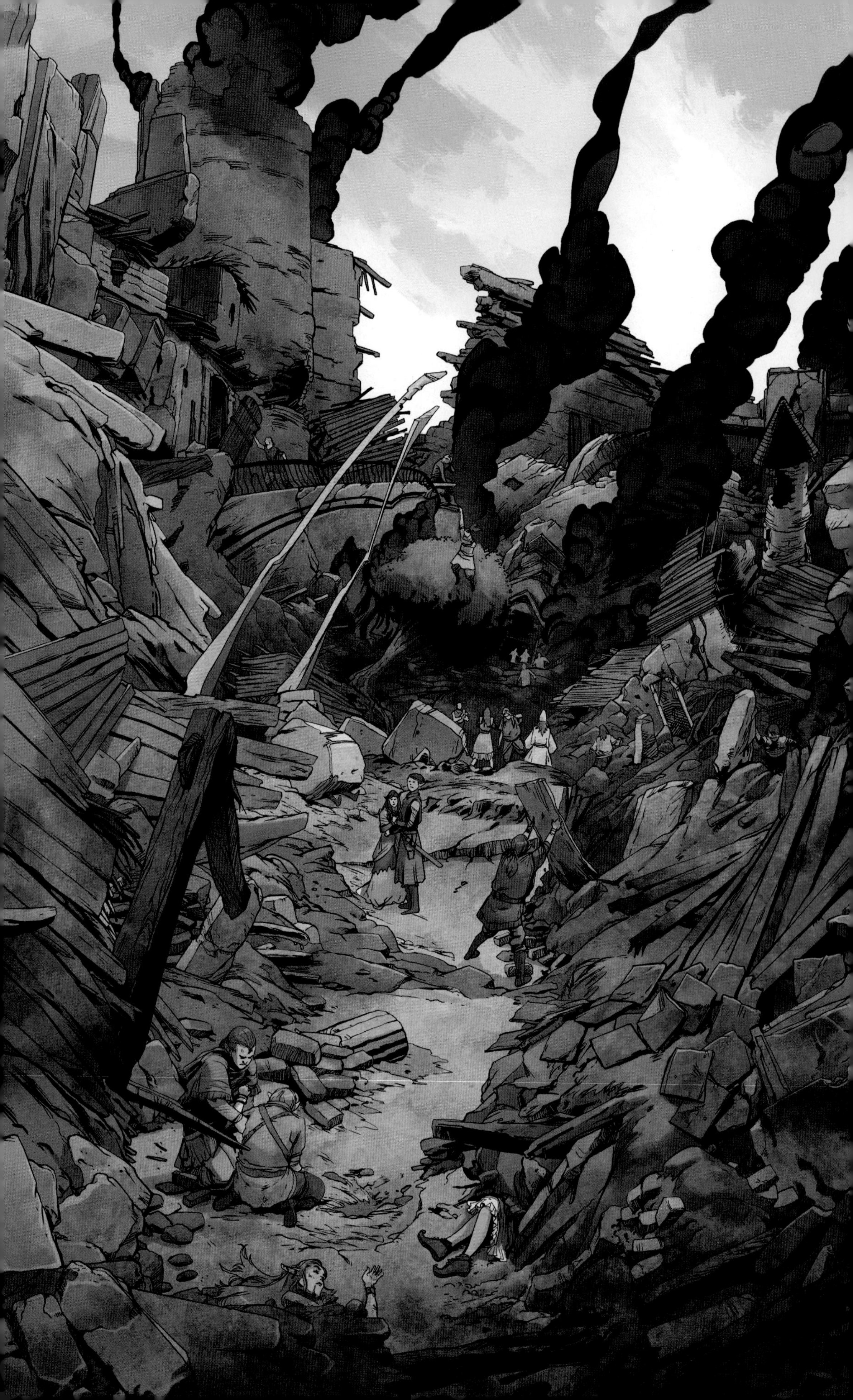

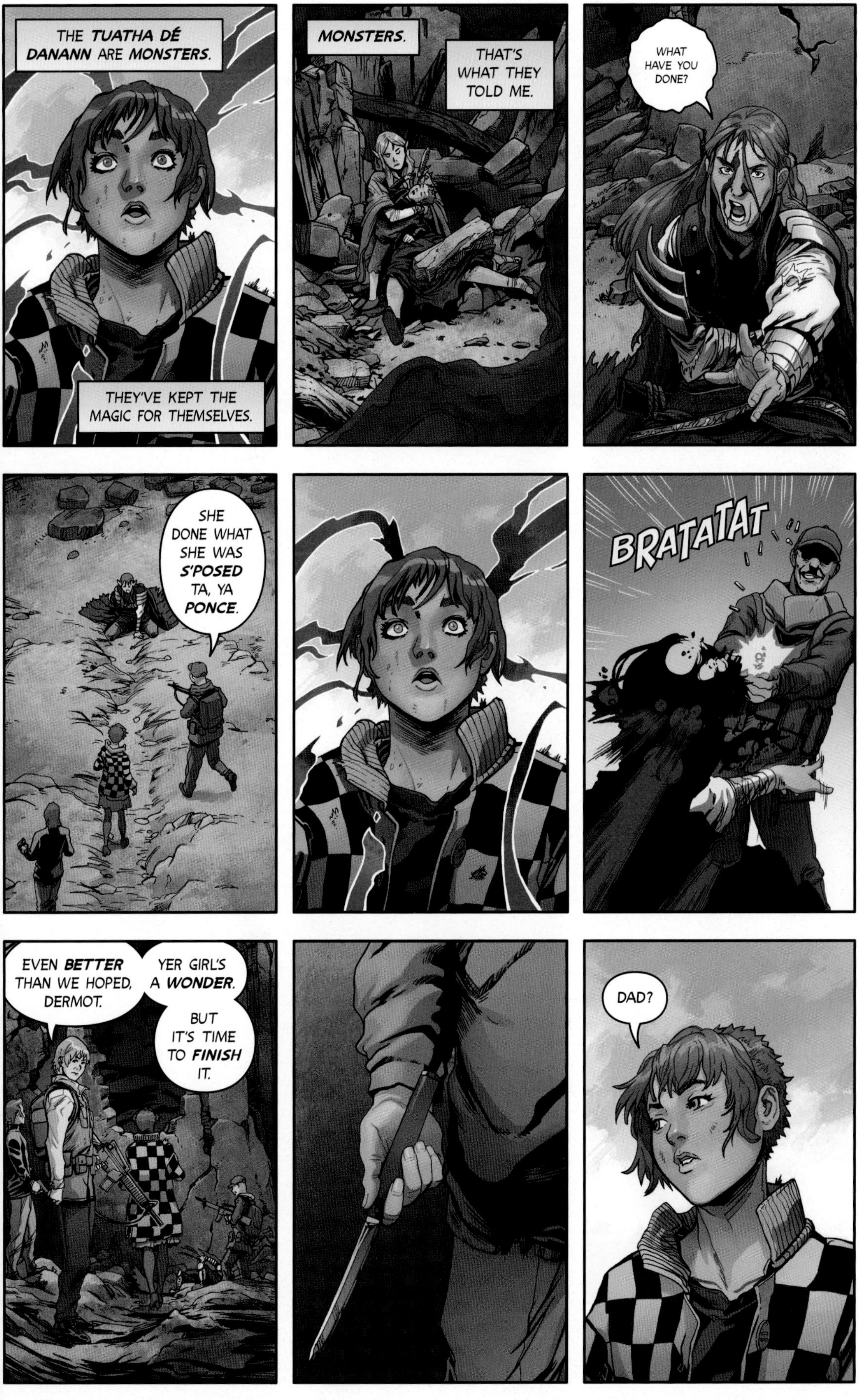

THE TUATHA DÉ DANANN ARE MONSTERS.
THEY'VE KEPT THE MAGIC FOR THEMSELVES.
MONSTERS.
THAT'S WHAT THEY TOLD ME.
WHAT HAVE YOU DONE?
SHE DONE WHAT SHE WAS S'POSED TA, YA PONCE.
BRATATAT
EVEN BETTER THAN WE HOPED, DERMOT.
YER GIRL'S A WONDER.
BUT IT'S TIME TO FINISH IT.
DAD?

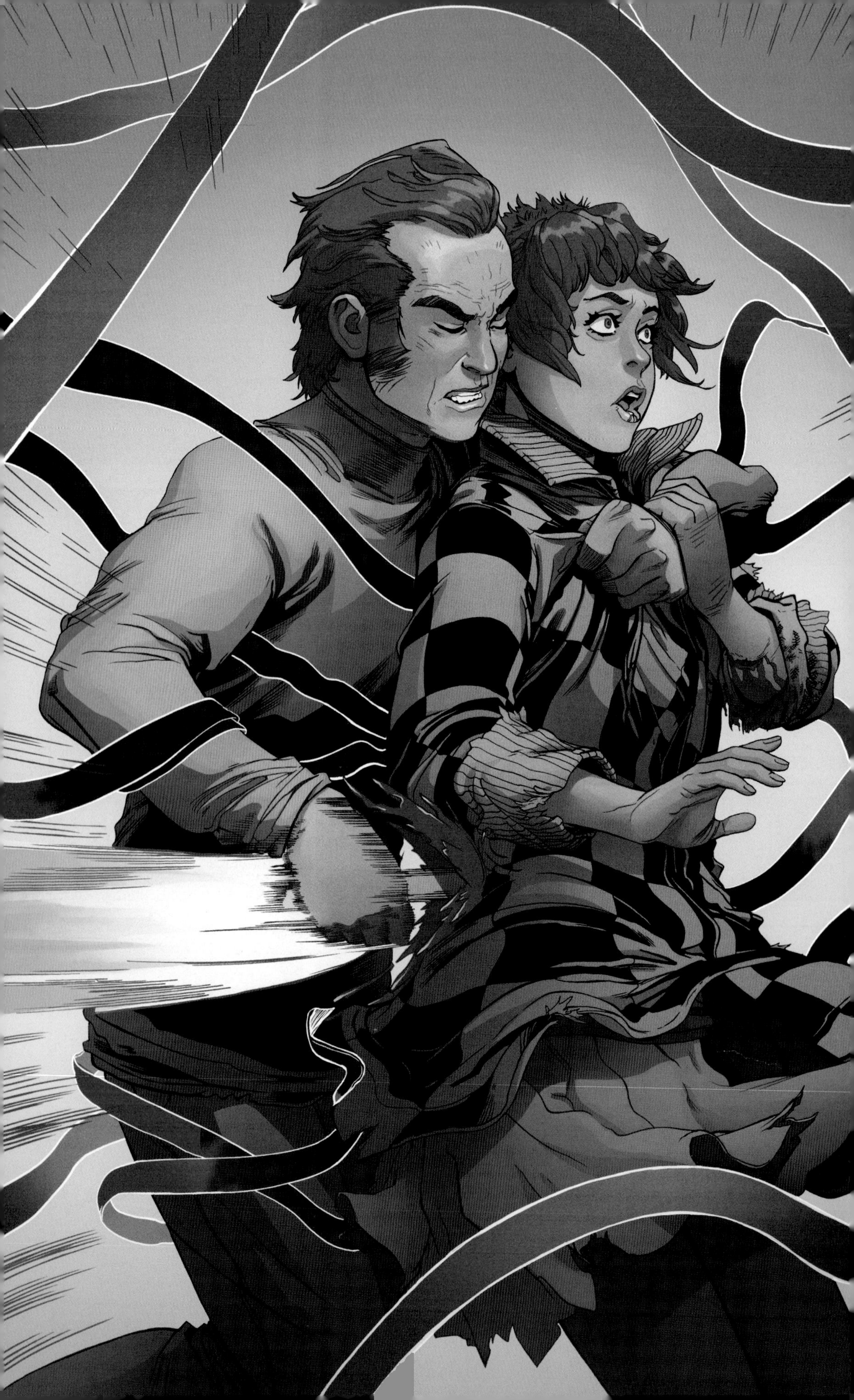

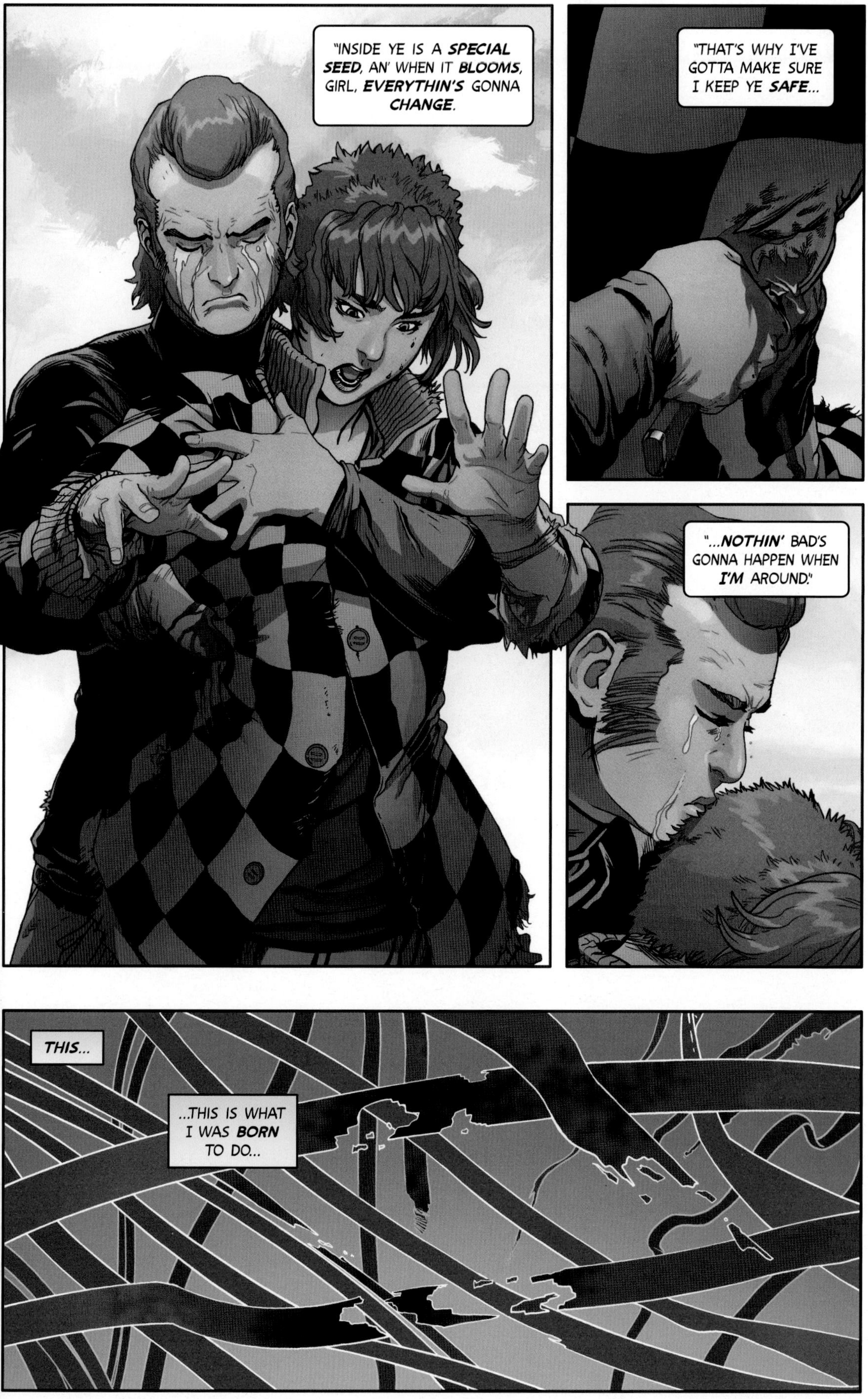
"INSIDE YE IS A **SPECIAL SEED**, AN' WHEN IT **BLOOMS**, GIRL, **EVERYTHIN'S** GONNA **CHANGE**.
"THAT'S WHY I'VE GOTTA MAKE SURE I KEEP YE **SAFE**...
"...**NOTHIN'** BAD'S GONNA HAPPEN WHEN **I'M** AROUND."
THIS...
...THIS IS WHAT I WAS **BORN** TO DO...

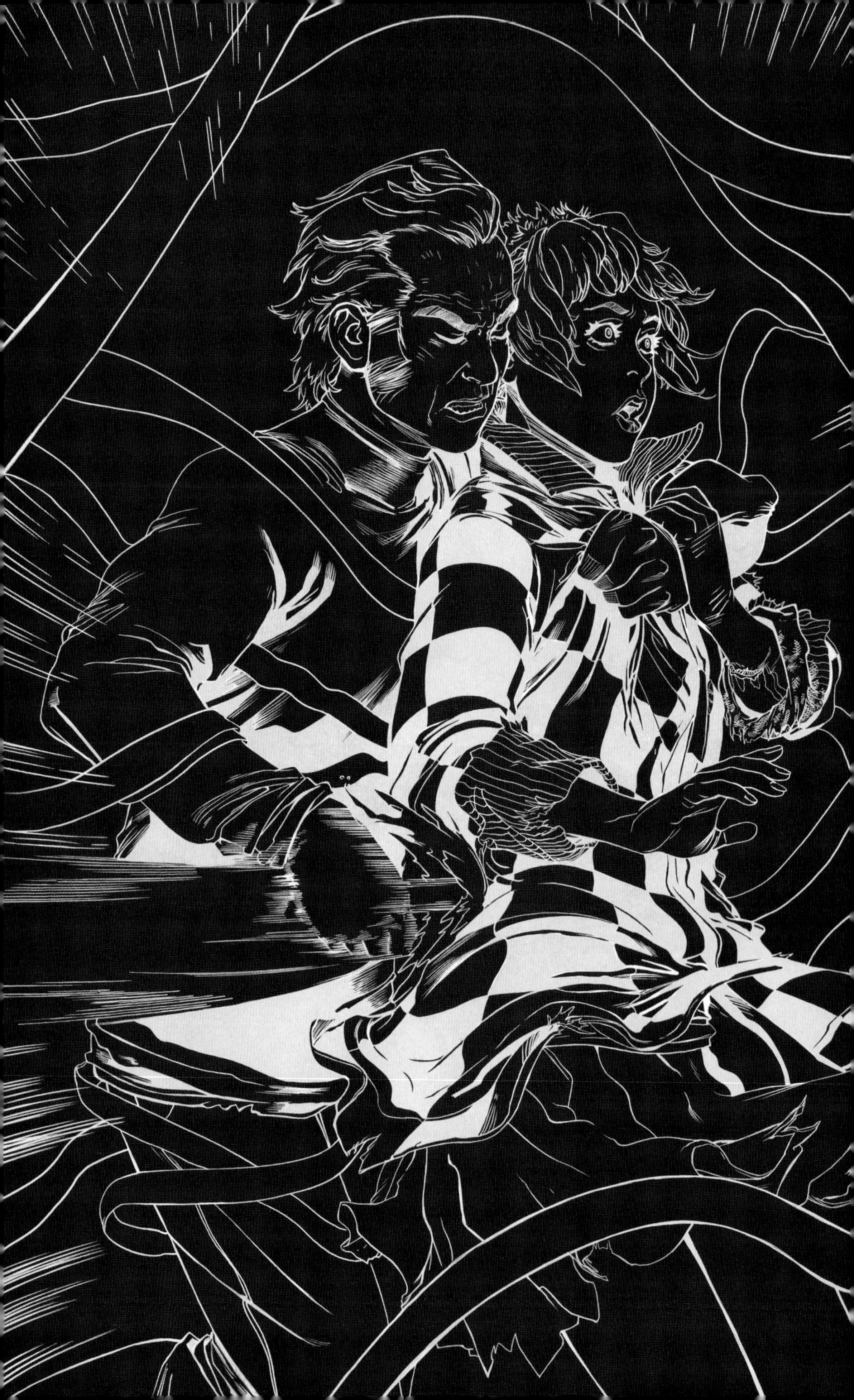

Chapter Twenty-Five

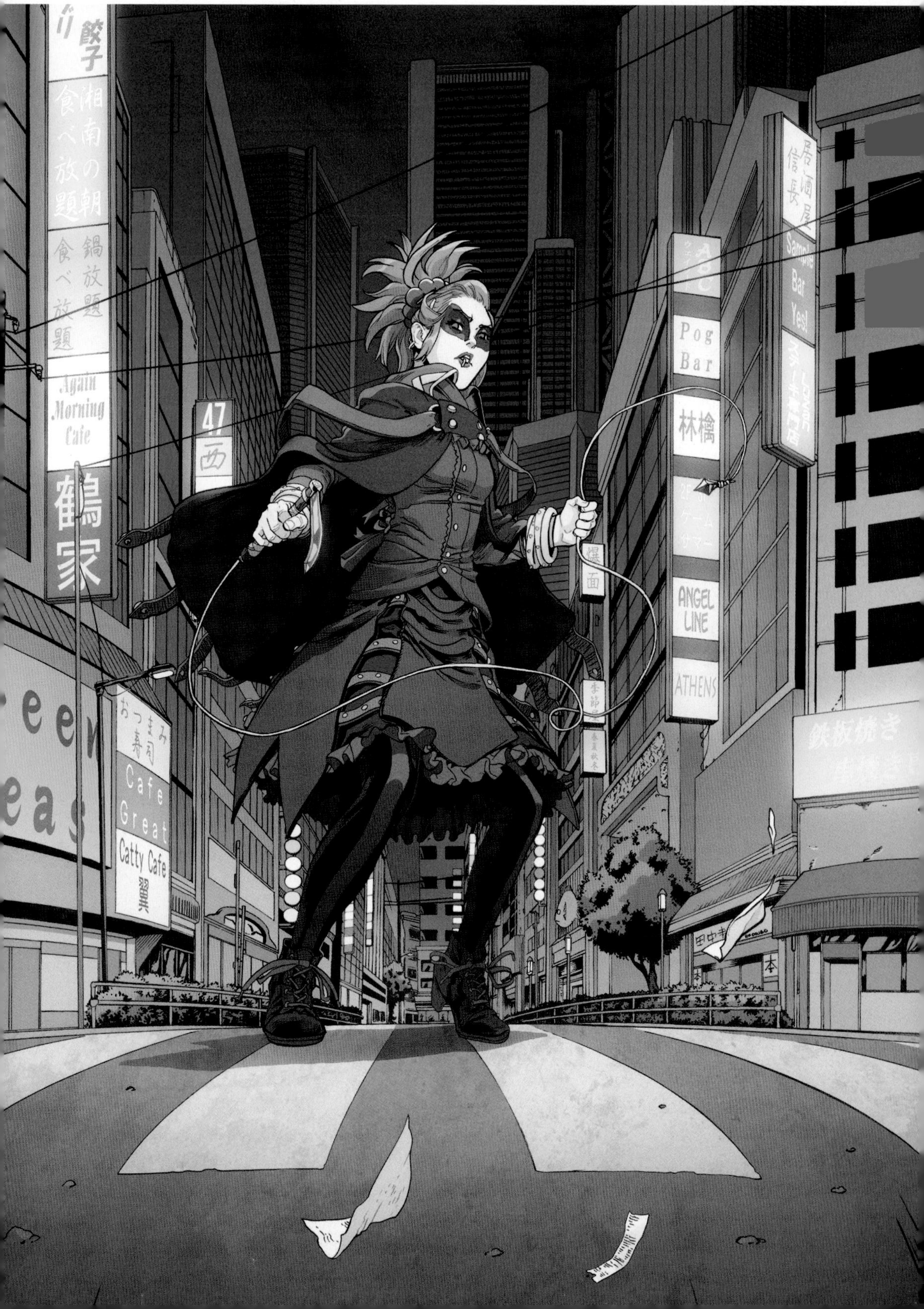

餃子
湘南の朝
食べ放題
鍋放題
食べ放題
Again Morning Cafe
鶴家
47
西
居酒屋
信長
Sample Bar Yes!
Pog Bar
林檎
ANGEL LINE
ATHENS
鉄板焼き
おつまみ寿司
Cafe Great
Catty Cafe
翼

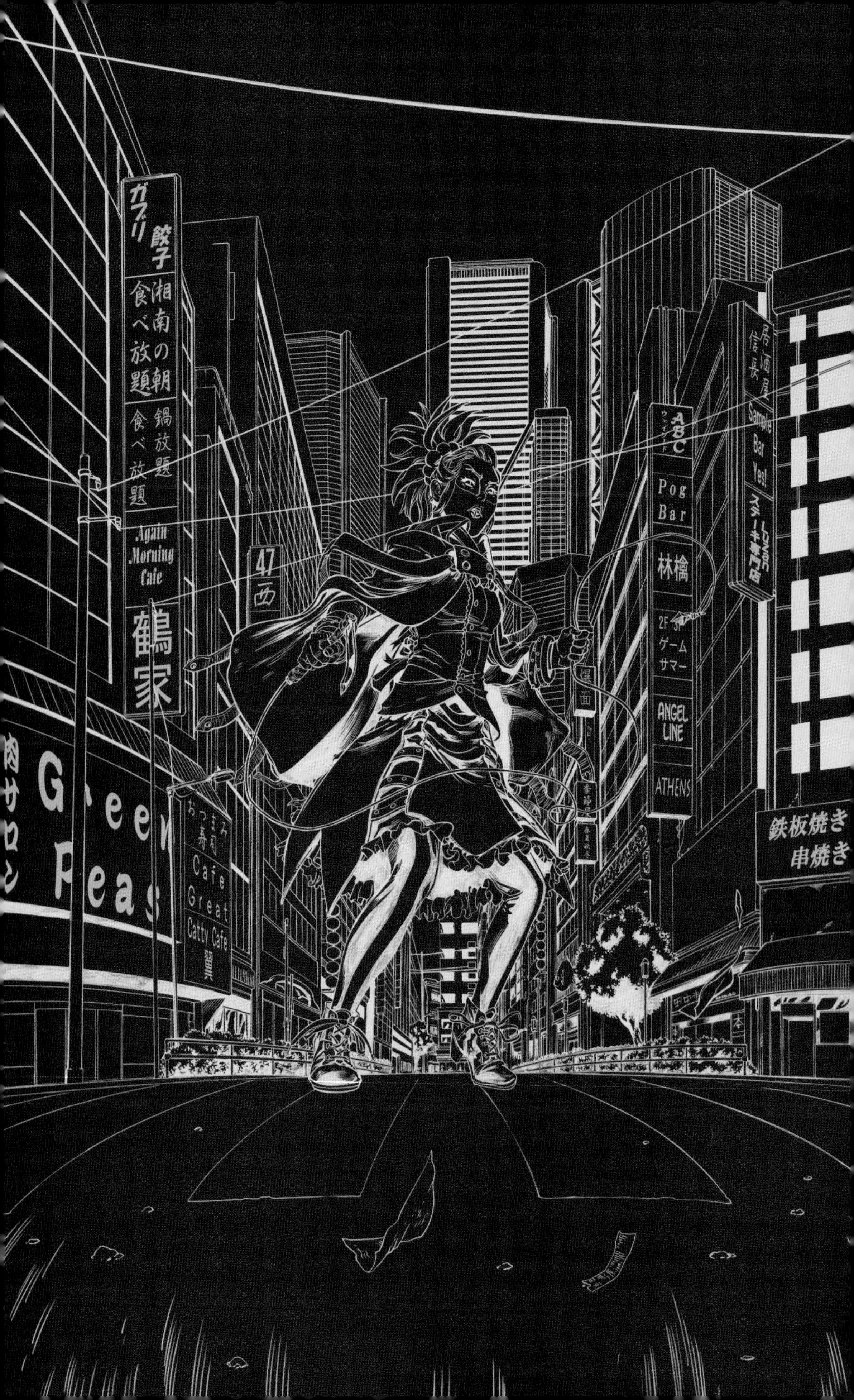
ガブリ
餃子
湘南の朝
食べ放題
鍋放題
食べ放題
Again Morning Cafe
鶴家
47
西
肉サロン
Green Peas
おつまみ
寿司
Cafe
Great
Catty Cafe
翼
ABC
Pog Bar
林檎
ゲーム
サマー
ANGEL LINE
ATHENS
居酒屋
信長
Sample Bar Yes!
ステーキ専門店
鉄板焼き
串焼き

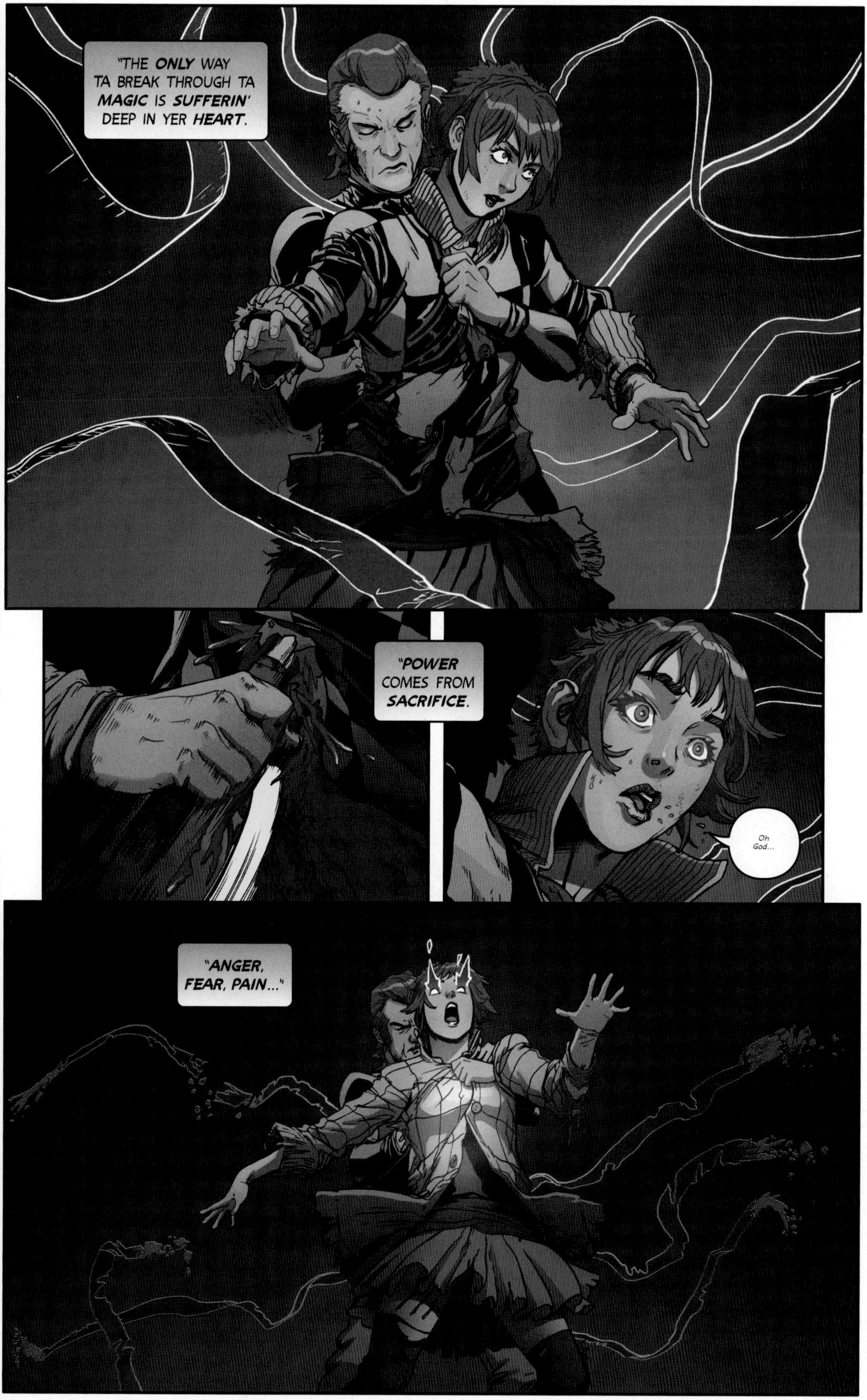
"THE ONLY WAY TA BREAK THROUGH TA MAGIC IS SUFFERIN' DEEP IN YER HEART.
"POWER COMES FROM SACRIFICE.
Oh God...
"ANGER, FEAR, PAIN..."

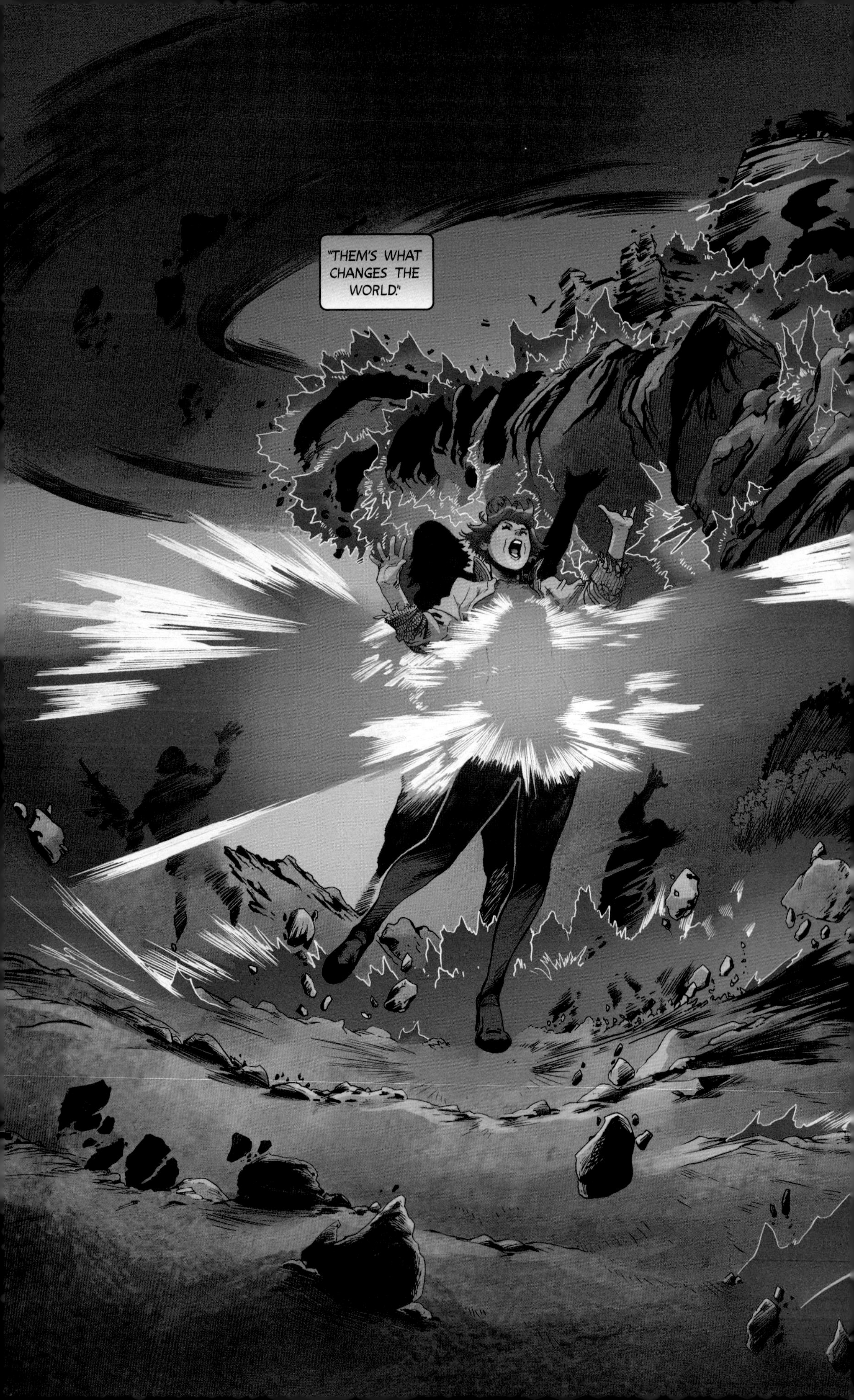
"THEM'S WHAT CHANGES THE WORLD."

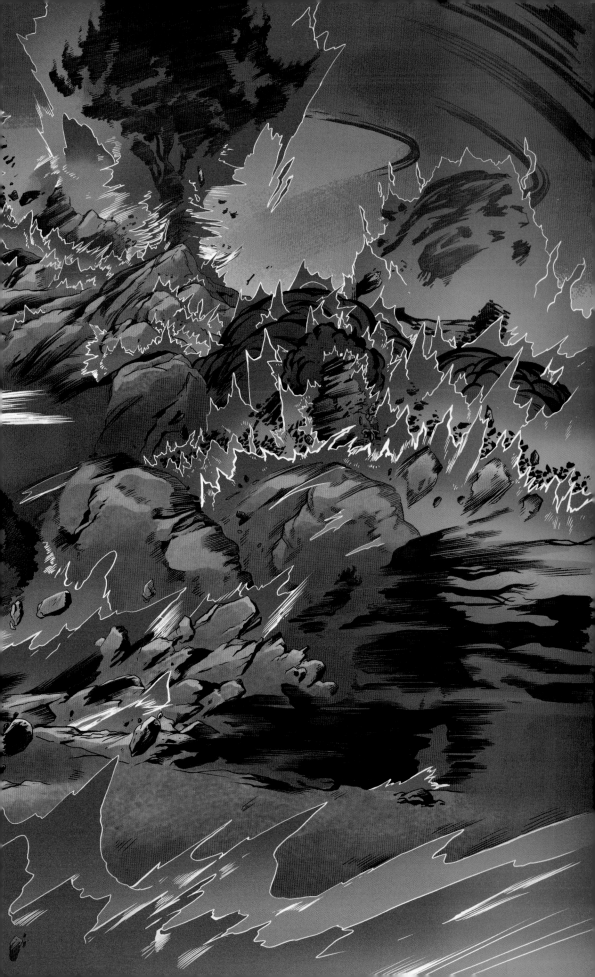

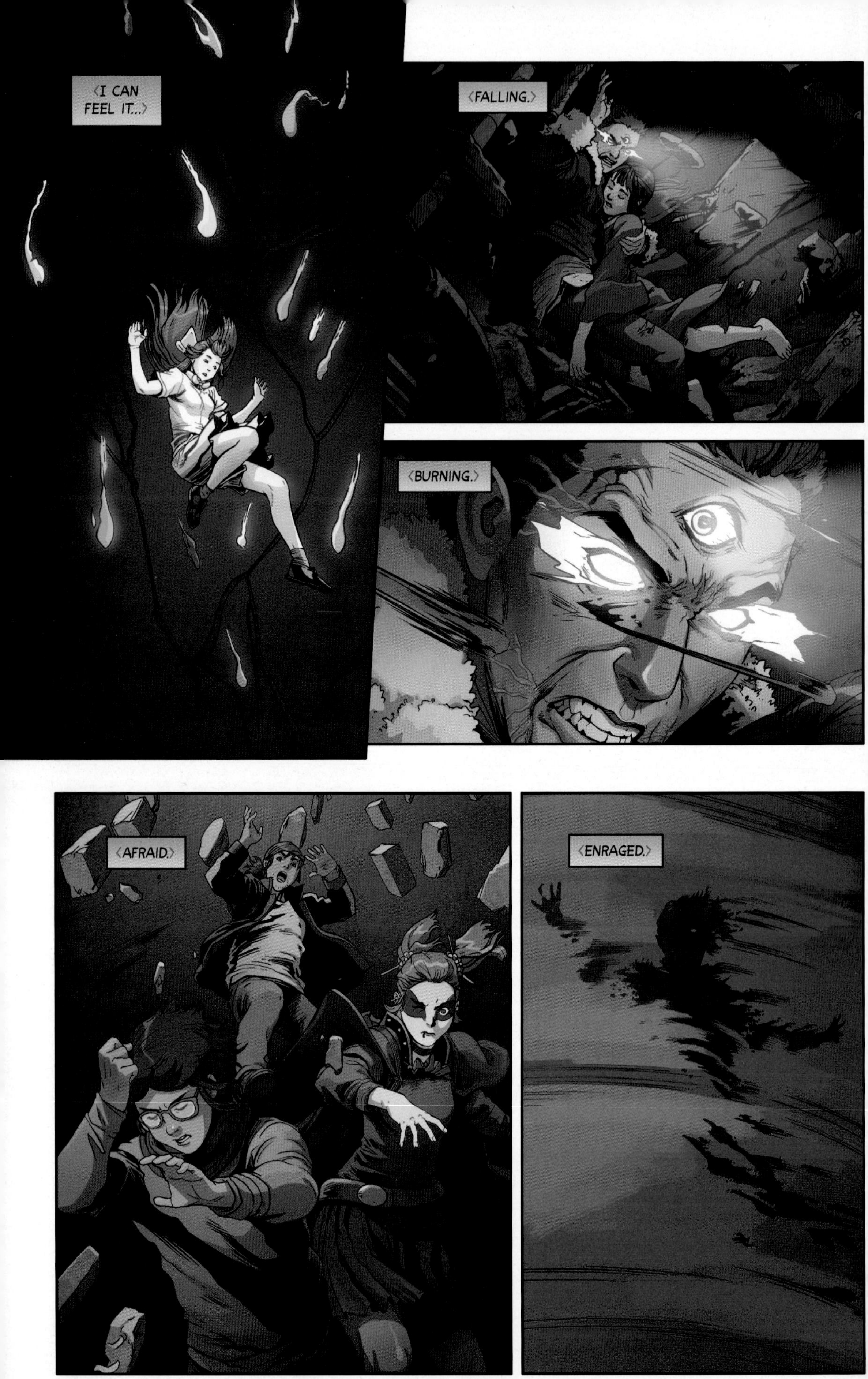

⟨I CAN FEEL IT...⟩
⟨FALLING.⟩
⟨BURNING.⟩
⟨AFRAID.⟩
⟨ENRAGED.⟩

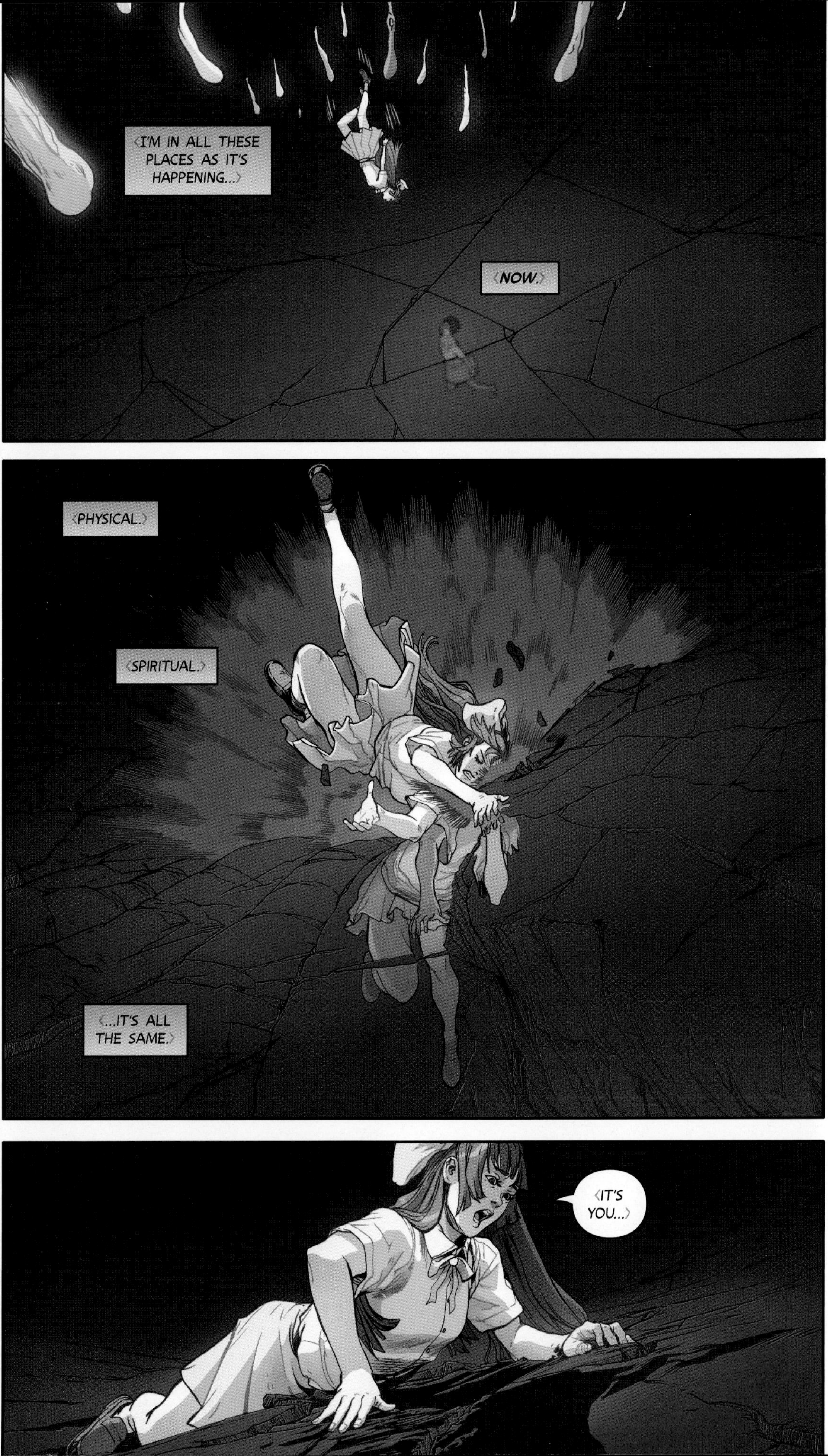
‹I'M IN ALL THESE PLACES AS IT'S HAPPENING...›
‹NOW.›
‹PHYSICAL.›
‹SPIRITUAL.›
‹...IT'S ALL THE SAME.›
‹IT'S YOU...›

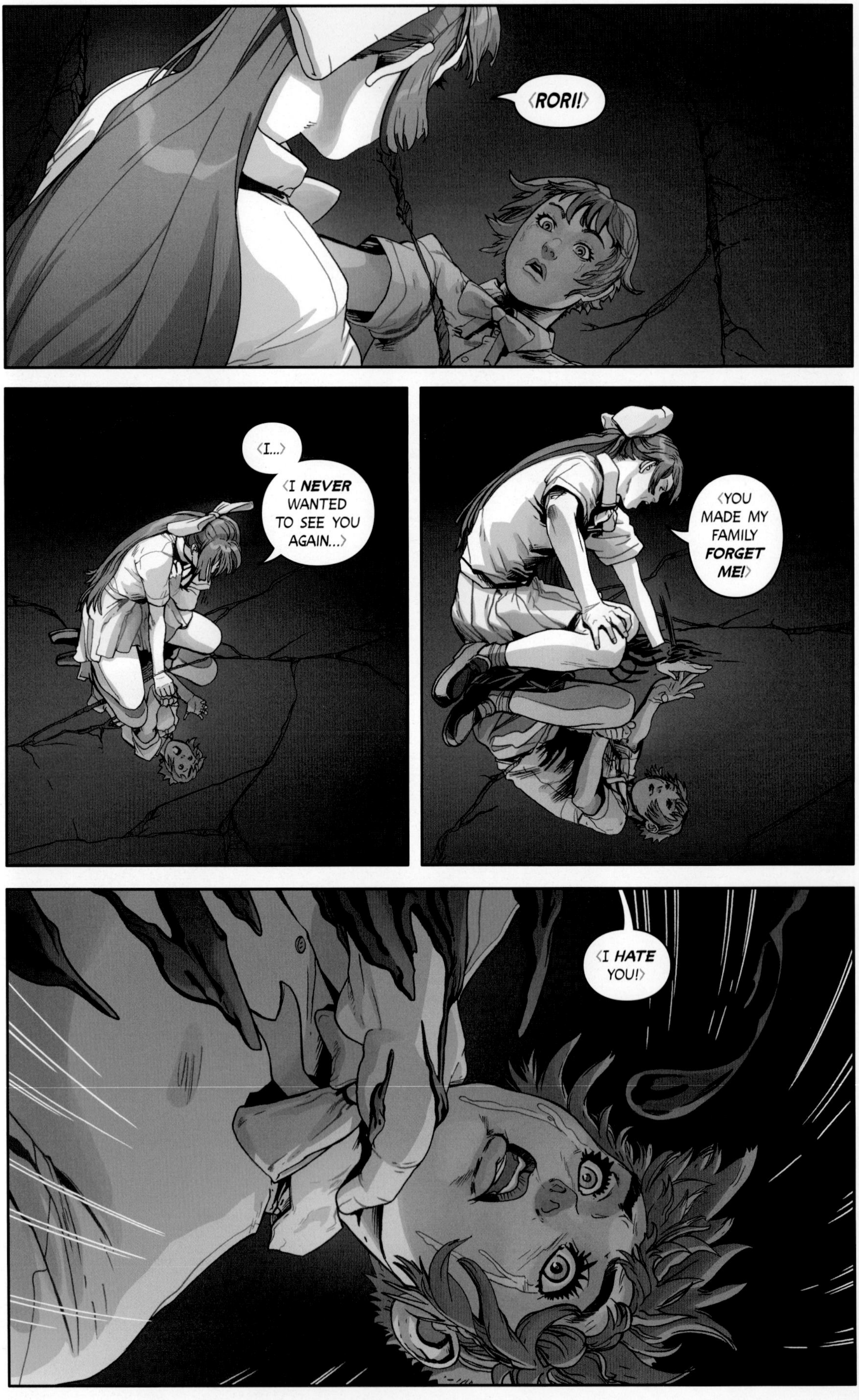
⟨RORI!⟩
⟨I...⟩
⟨I NEVER WANTED TO SEE YOU AGAIN...⟩
⟨YOU MADE MY FAMILY FORGET ME!⟩
⟨I HATE YOU!⟩

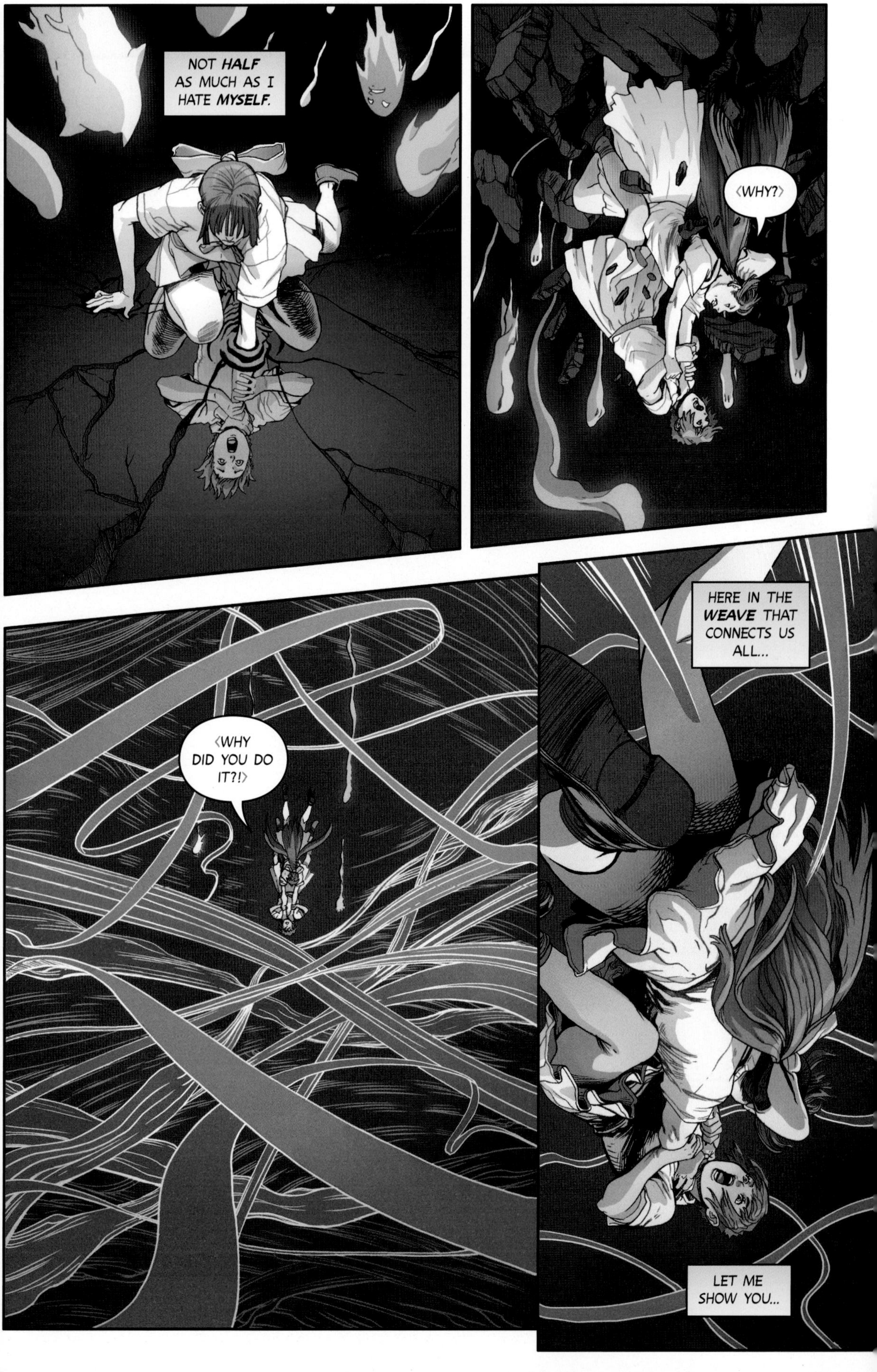
NOT HALF AS MUCH AS I HATE MYSELF.
<WHY?>
<WHY DID YOU DO IT?!>
HERE IN THE WEAVE THAT CONNECTS US ALL...
LET ME SHOW YOU...

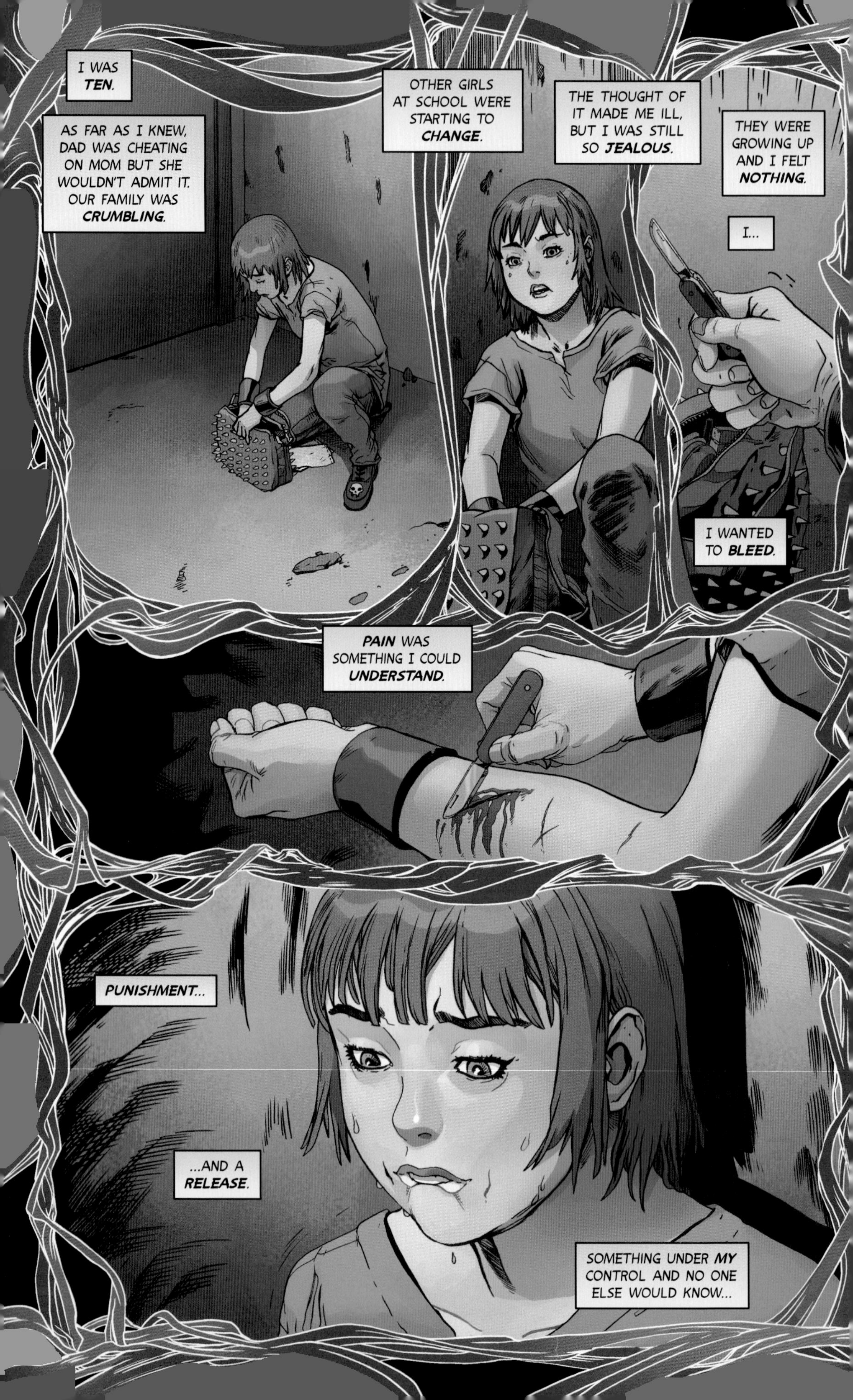
I WAS *TEN*.
AS FAR AS I KNEW, DAD WAS CHEATING ON MOM BUT SHE WOULDN'T ADMIT IT. OUR FAMILY WAS *CRUMBLING*.
OTHER GIRLS AT SCHOOL WERE STARTING TO *CHANGE*.
THE THOUGHT OF IT MADE ME ILL, BUT I WAS STILL SO *JEALOUS*.
THEY WERE GROWING UP AND I FELT *NOTHING*.
I...
I WANTED TO *BLEED*.
PAIN WAS SOMETHING I COULD *UNDERSTAND*.
PUNISHMENT...
...AND A *RELEASE*.
SOMETHING UNDER *MY* CONTROL AND NO ONE ELSE WOULD KNOW...

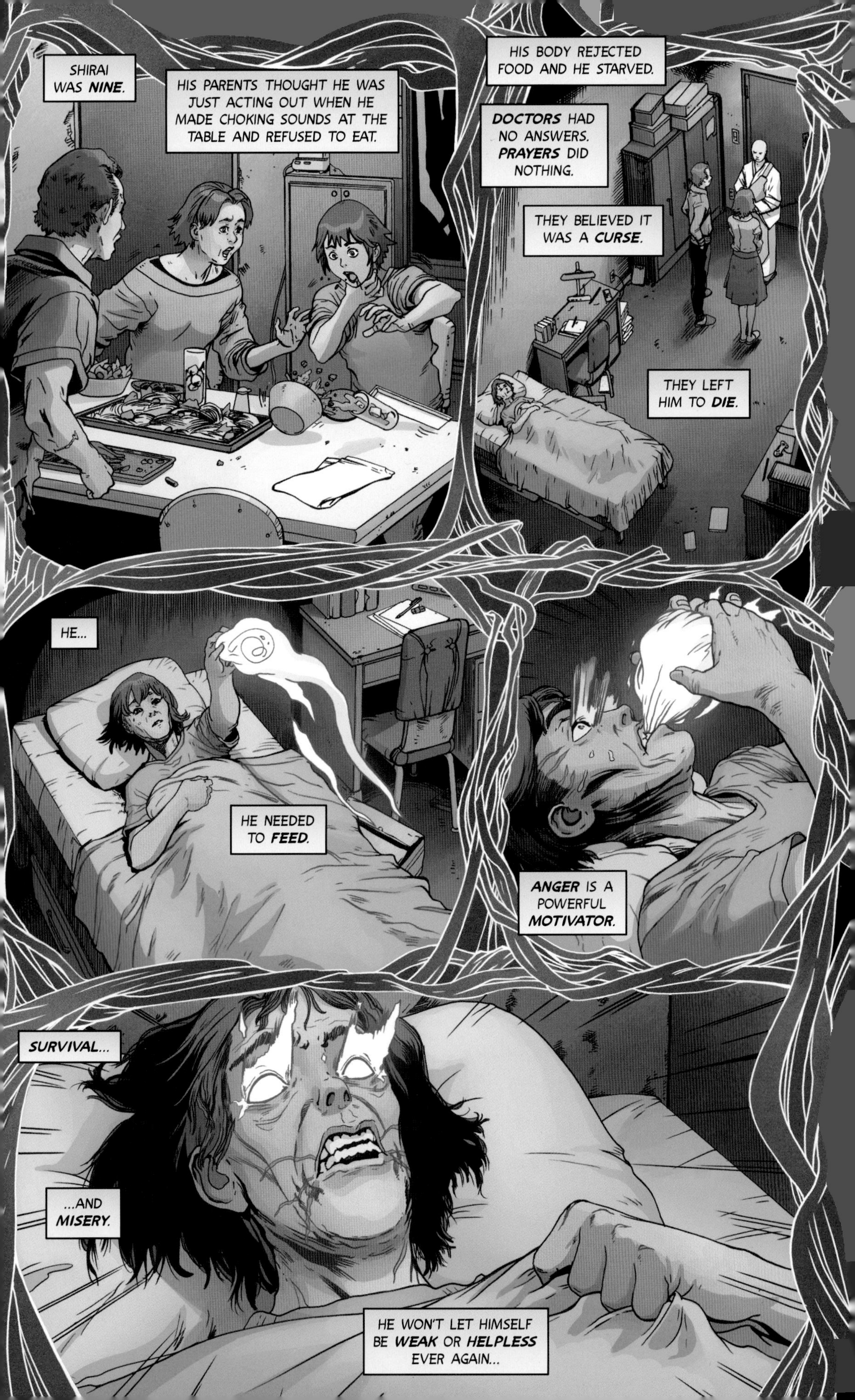
SHIRAI WAS NINE.
HIS PARENTS THOUGHT HE WAS JUST ACTING OUT WHEN HE MADE CHOKING SOUNDS AT THE TABLE AND REFUSED TO EAT.
HIS BODY REJECTED FOOD AND HE STARVED.
DOCTORS HAD NO ANSWERS. PRAYERS DID NOTHING.
THEY BELIEVED IT WAS A CURSE.
THEY LEFT HIM TO DIE.
HE...
HE NEEDED TO FEED.
ANGER IS A POWERFUL MOTIVATOR.
SURVIVAL...
...AND MISERY.
HE WON'T LET HIMSELF BE WEAK OR HELPLESS EVER AGAIN...

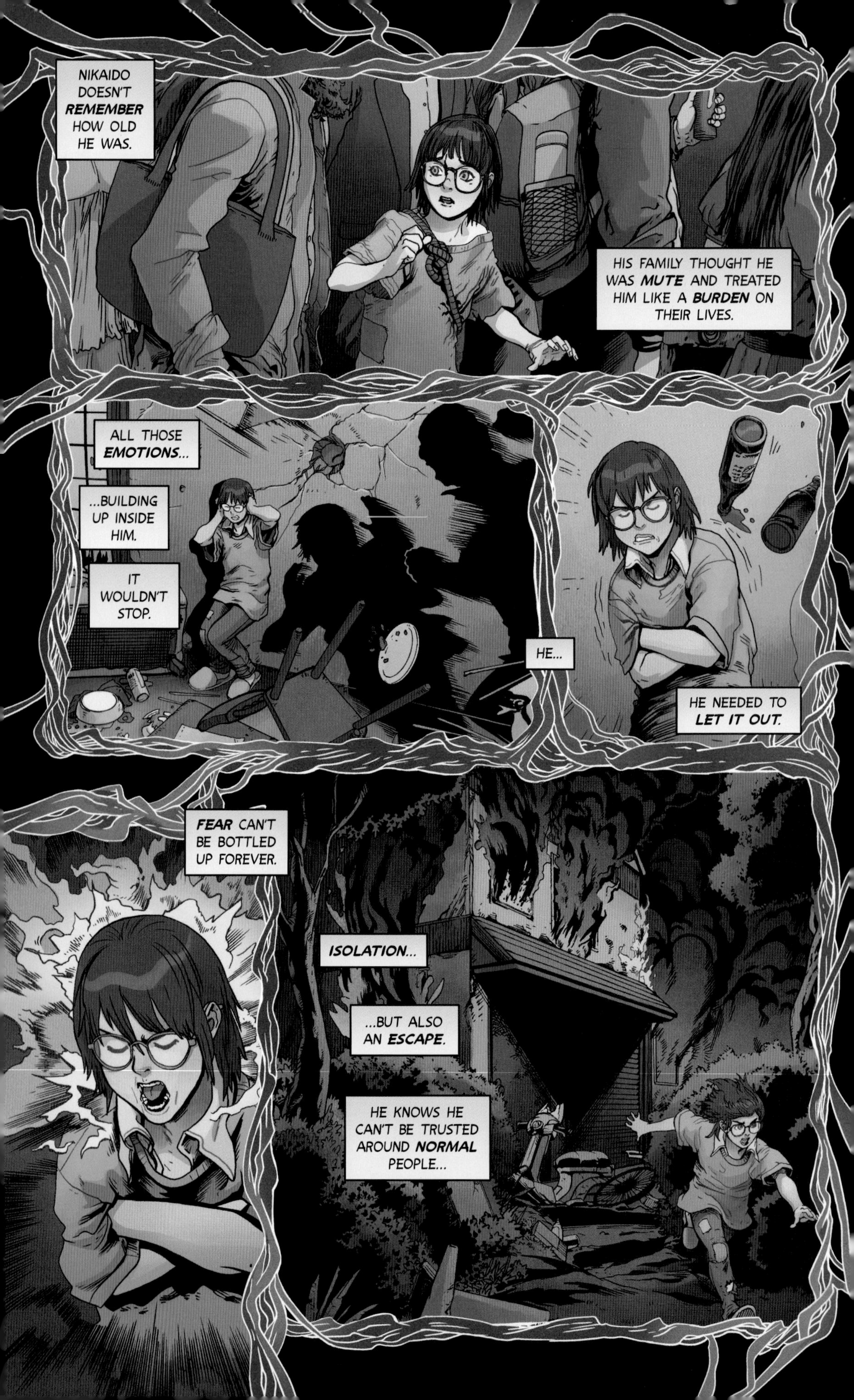
NIKAIDO DOESN'T REMEMBER HOW OLD HE WAS.
HIS FAMILY THOUGHT HE WAS MUTE AND TREATED HIM LIKE A BURDEN ON THEIR LIVES.
ALL THOSE EMOTIONS...
...BUILDING UP INSIDE HIM.
IT WOULDN'T STOP.
HE...
HE NEEDED TO LET IT OUT.
FEAR CAN'T BE BOTTLED UP FOREVER.
ISOLATION...
...BUT ALSO AN ESCAPE.
HE KNOWS HE CAN'T BE TRUSTED AROUND NORMAL PEOPLE...

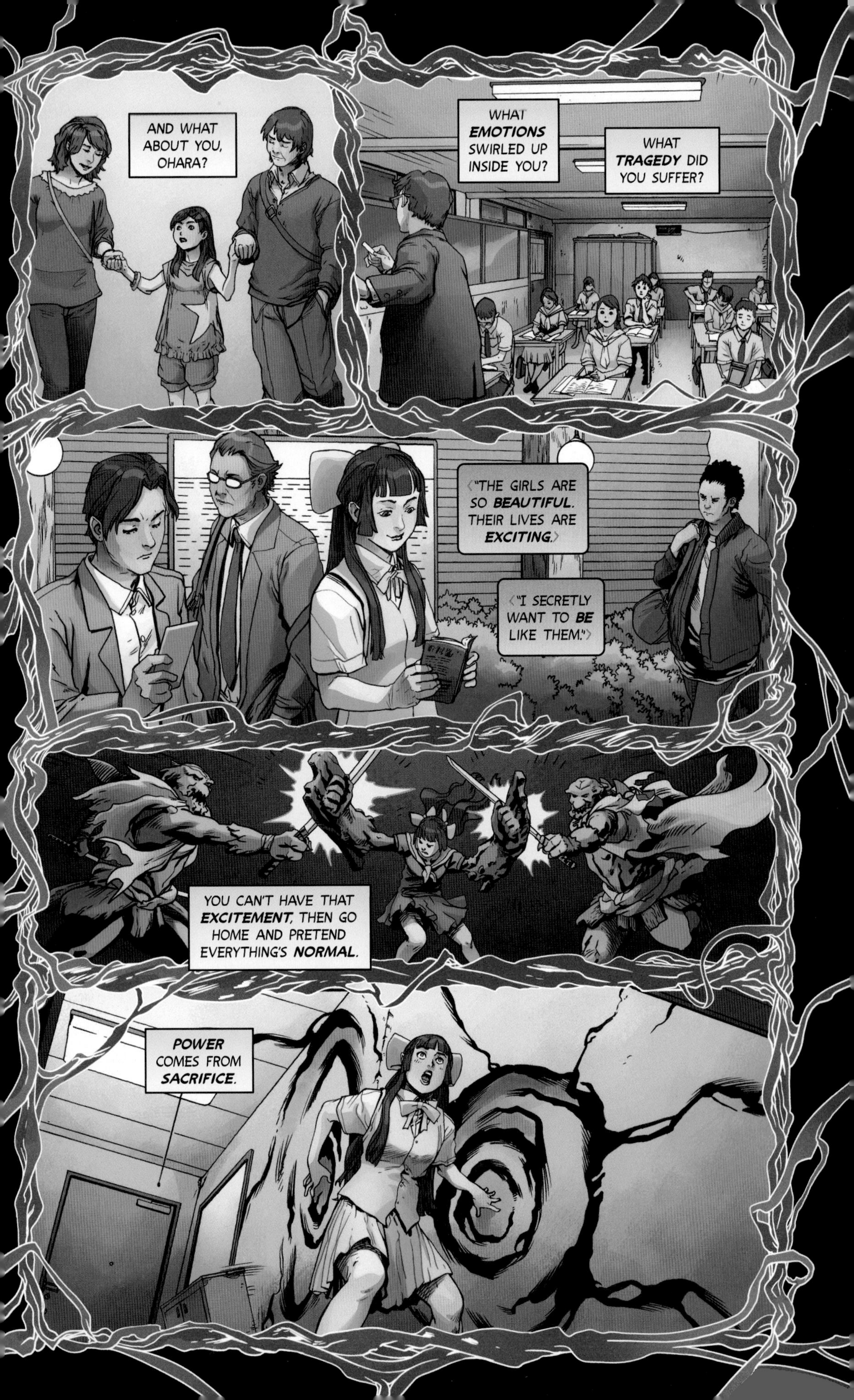

AND WHAT ABOUT YOU, OHARA?
WHAT EMOTIONS SWIRLED UP INSIDE YOU?
WHAT TRAGEDY DID YOU SUFFER?
‹"THE GIRLS ARE SO BEAUTIFUL. THEIR LIVES ARE EXCITING.›
‹"I SECRETLY WANT TO BE LIKE THEM."›
YOU CAN'T HAVE THAT EXCITEMENT, THEN GO HOME AND PRETEND EVERYTHING'S NORMAL.
POWER COMES FROM SACRIFICE.

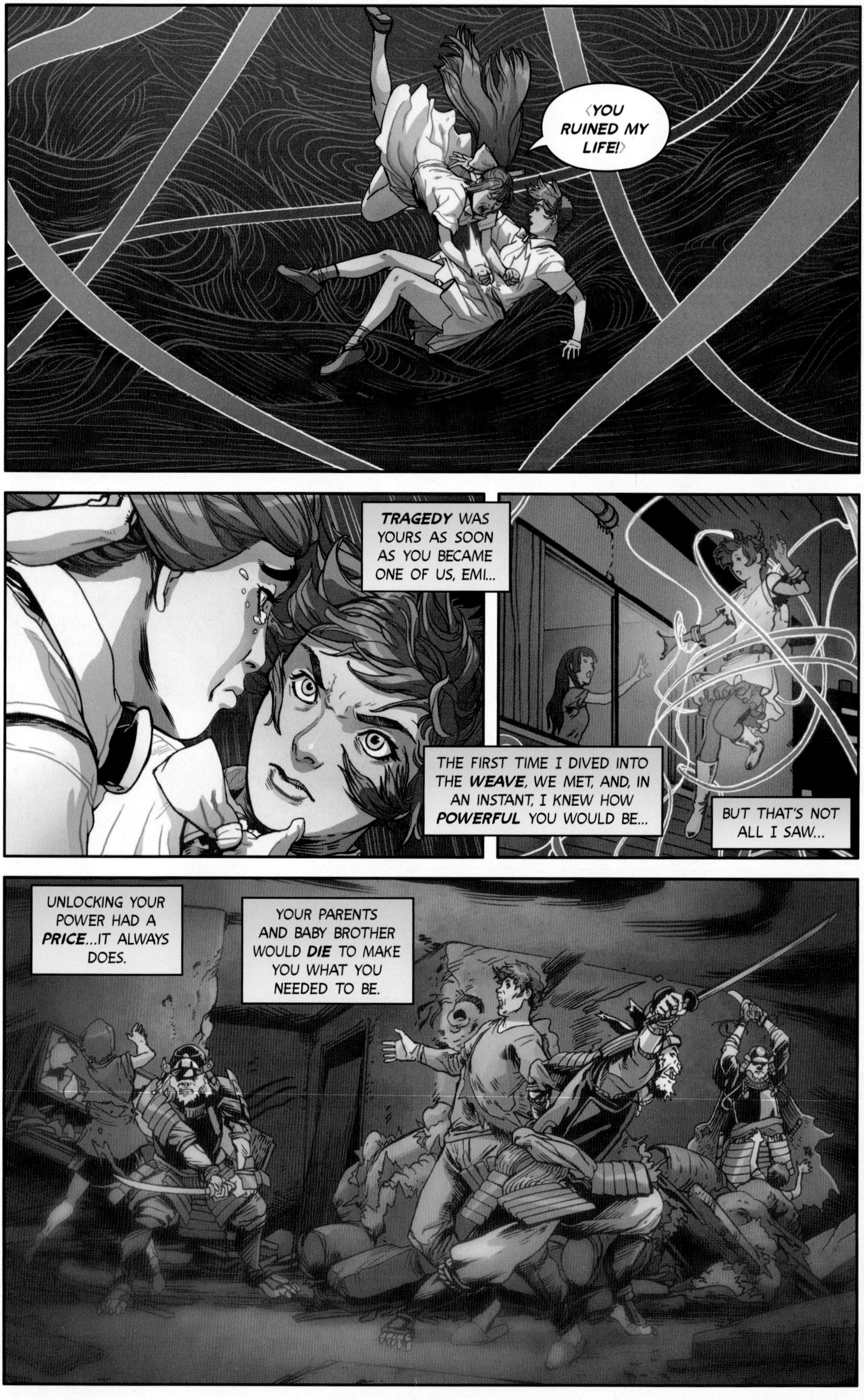

<YOU RUINED MY LIFE!>
TRAGEDY WAS YOURS AS SOON AS YOU BECAME ONE OF US, EMI...
THE FIRST TIME I DIVED INTO THE WEAVE, WE MET, AND, IN AN INSTANT, I KNEW HOW POWERFUL YOU WOULD BE...
BUT THAT'S NOT ALL I SAW...
UNLOCKING YOUR POWER HAD A PRICE...IT ALWAYS DOES.
YOUR PARENTS AND BABY BROTHER WOULD DIE TO MAKE YOU WHAT YOU NEEDED TO BE.

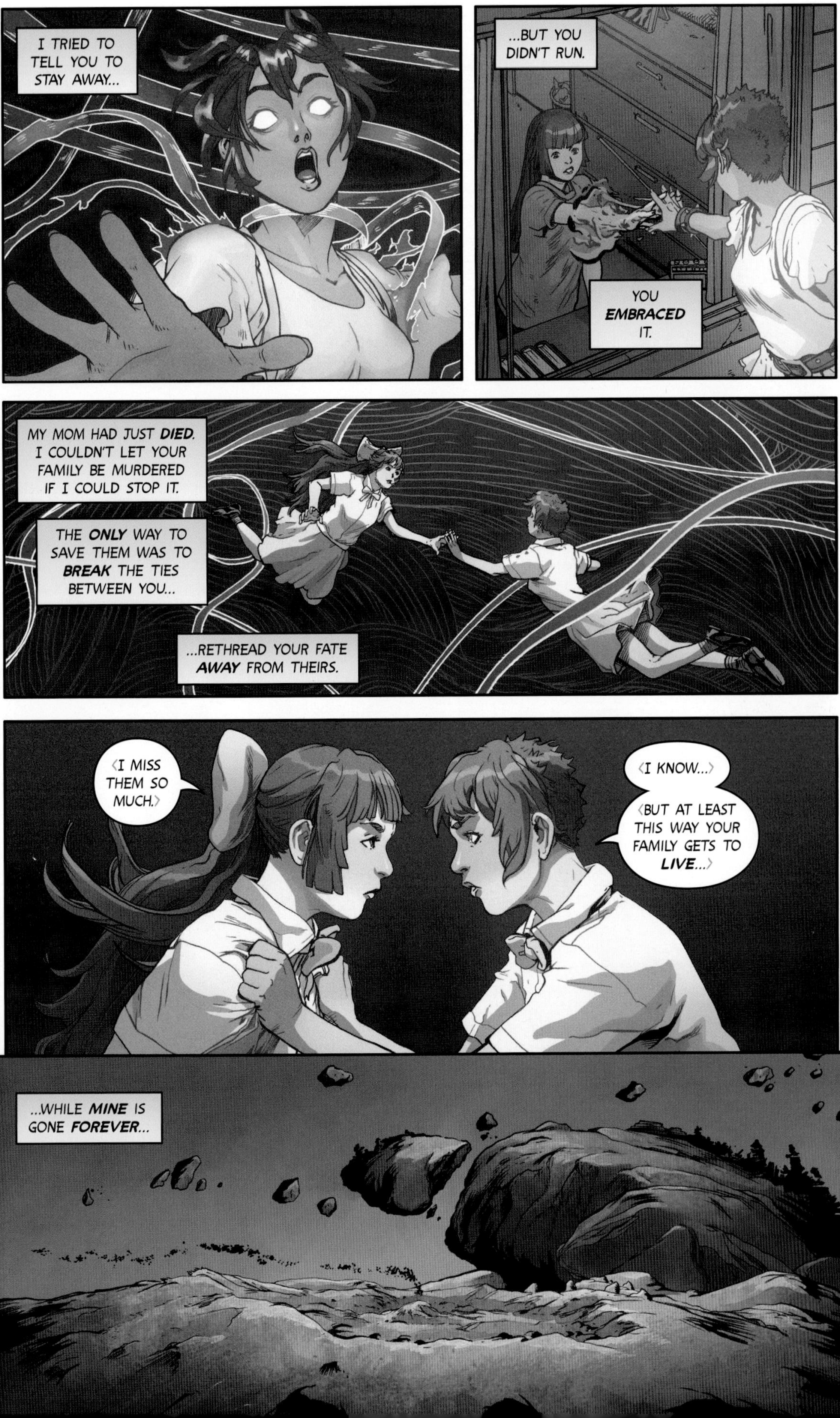
I TRIED TO TELL YOU TO STAY AWAY...
...BUT YOU DIDN'T RUN.
YOU **EMBRACED** IT.
MY MOM HAD JUST **DIED**. I COULDN'T LET YOUR FAMILY BE MURDERED IF I COULD STOP IT.
THE **ONLY** WAY TO SAVE THEM WAS TO **BREAK** THE TIES BETWEEN YOU...
...RETHREAD YOUR FATE **AWAY** FROM THEIRS.
〈I MISS THEM SO MUCH.〉
〈I KNOW...〉
〈BUT AT LEAST THIS WAY YOUR FAMILY GETS TO **LIVE**...〉
...WHILE **MINE** IS GONE **FOREVER**...

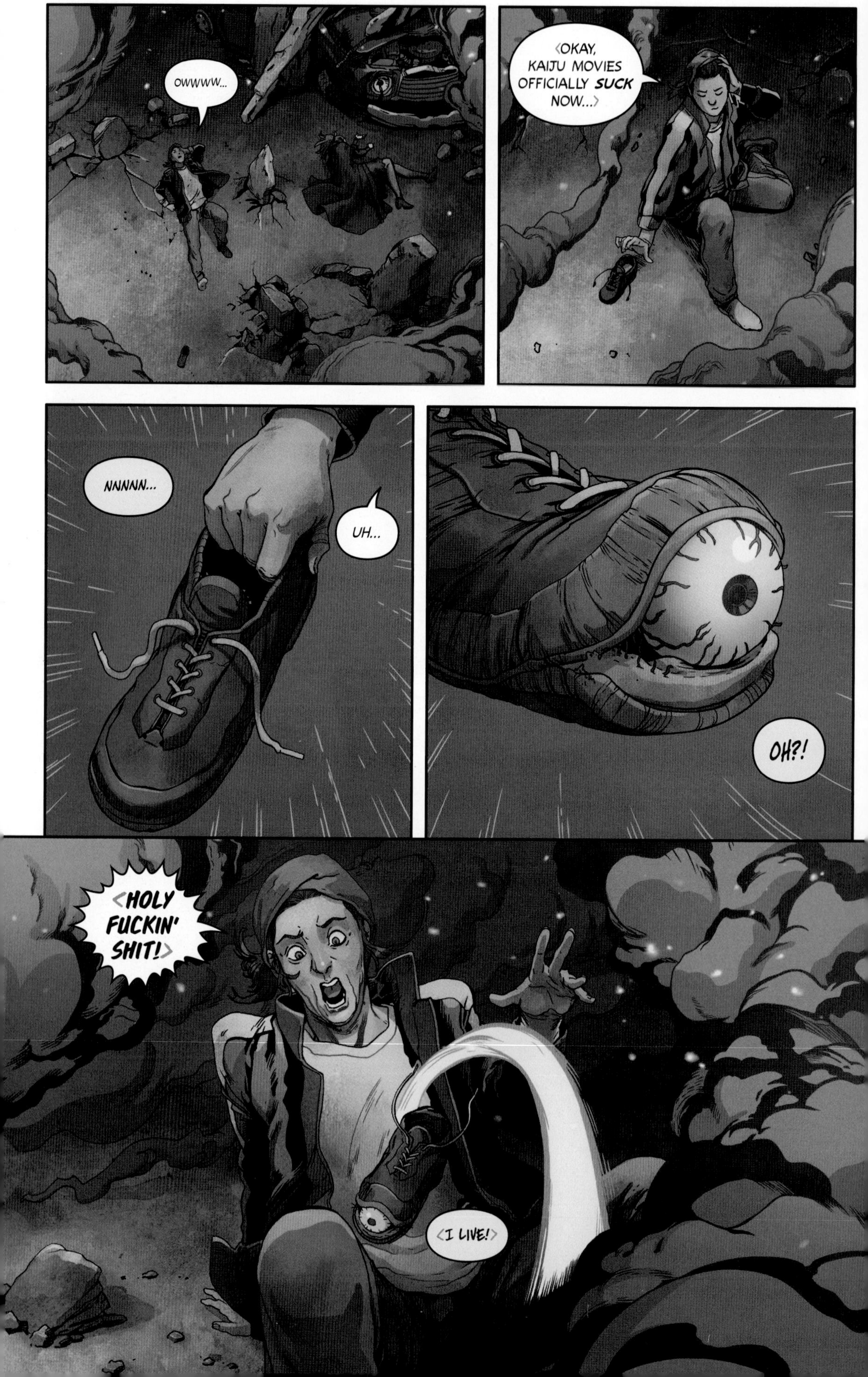
OWWWW...
<OKAY, KAIJU MOVIES OFFICIALLY SUCK NOW...>
NNNNN...
UH...
OH?!
<HOLY FUCKIN' SHIT!>
<I LIVE!>

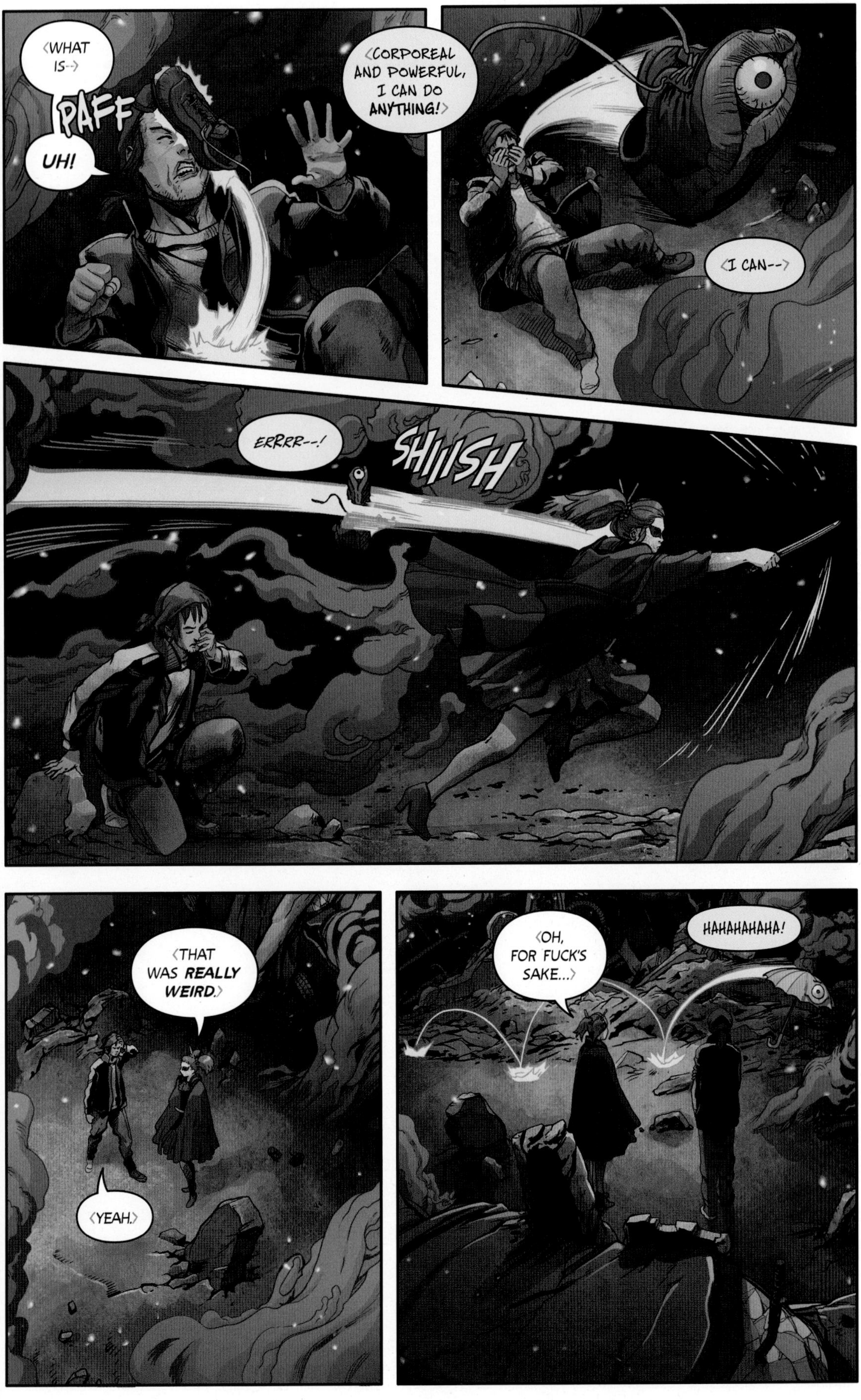
⟨WHAT IS--⟩
PAFF
UH!
⟨CORPOREAL AND POWERFUL, I CAN DO ANYTHING!⟩
⟨I CAN--⟩
ERRRR--!
SHIIISH
⟨THAT WAS REALLY WEIRD.⟩
⟨YEAH.⟩
⟨OH, FOR FUCK'S SAKE...⟩
HAHAHAHAHA!

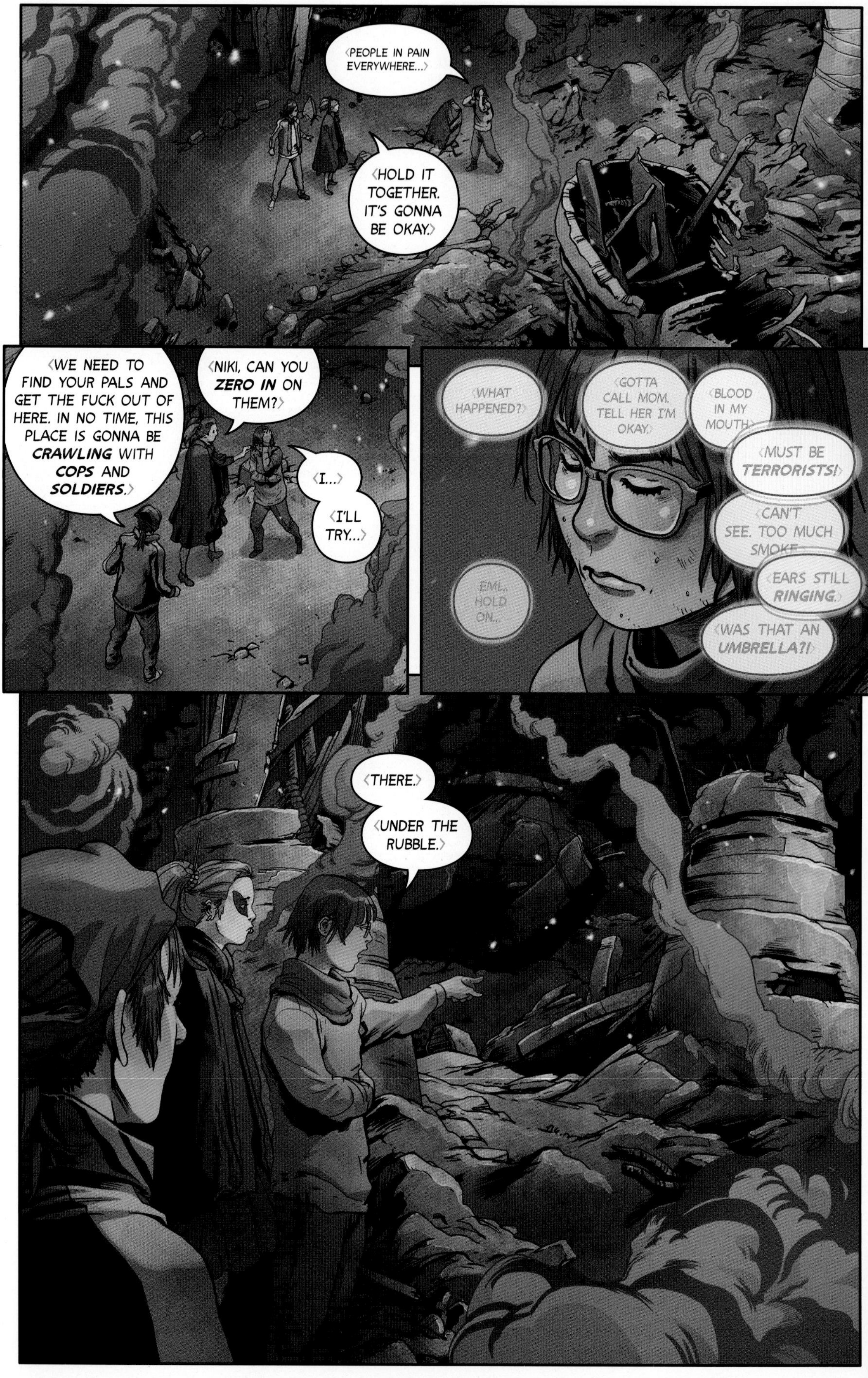

‹PEOPLE IN PAIN EVERYWHERE...›
‹HOLD IT TOGETHER. IT'S GONNA BE OKAY.›
‹WE NEED TO FIND YOUR PALS AND GET THE FUCK OUT OF HERE. IN NO TIME, THIS PLACE IS GONNA BE CRAWLING WITH COPS AND SOLDIERS.›
‹NIKI, CAN YOU ZERO IN ON THEM?›
‹I...›
‹I'LL TRY...›
‹WHAT HAPPENED?›
‹GOTTA CALL MOM. TELL HER I'M OKAY.›
‹BLOOD IN MY MOUTH›
‹MUST BE TERRORISTS!›
‹CAN'T SEE. TOO MUCH SMOKE›
‹EARS STILL RINGING.›
‹WAS THAT AN UMBRELLA?!›
EMI.. HOLD ON...
‹THERE.›
‹UNDER THE RUBBLE.›

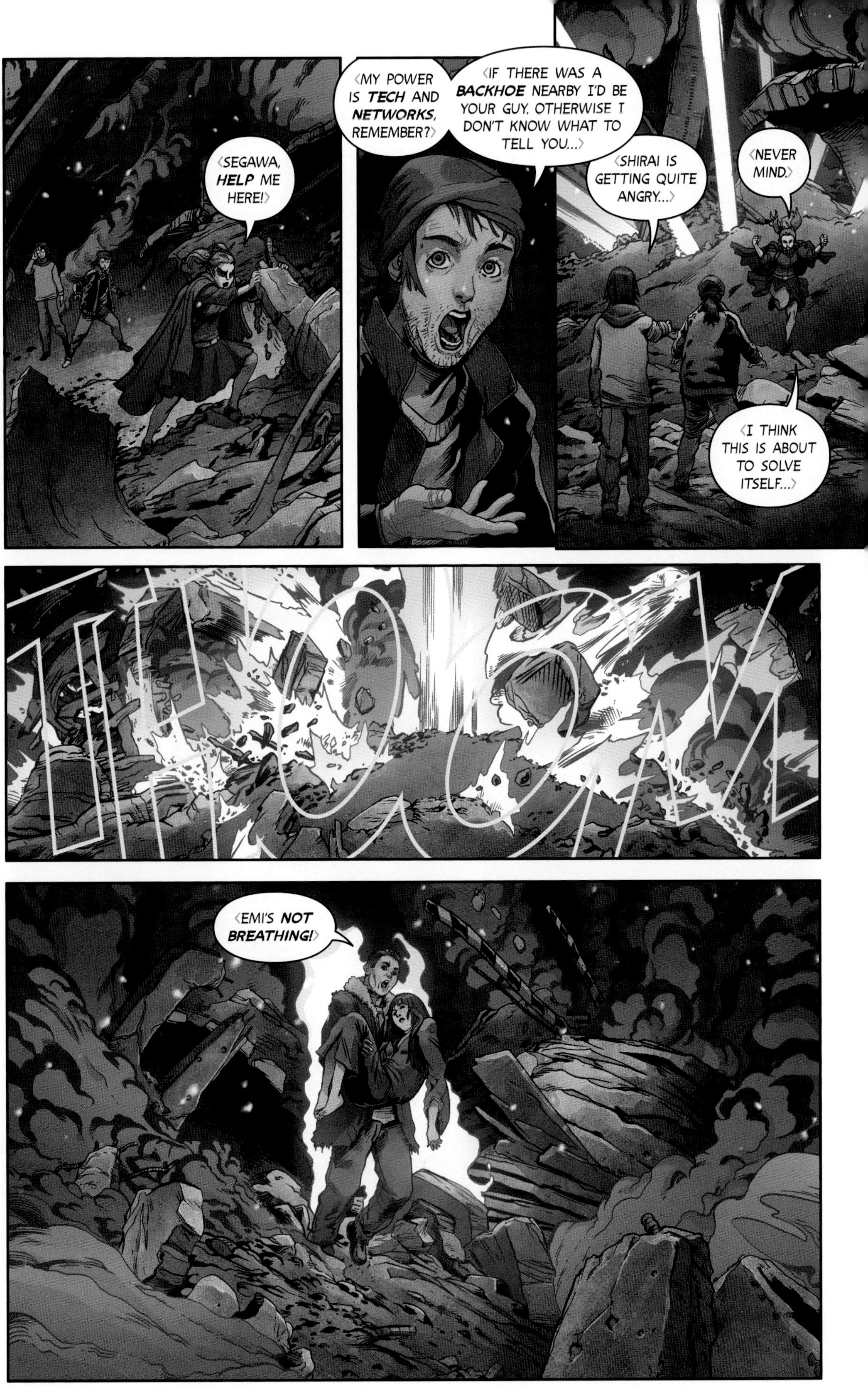

<SEGAWA, HELP ME HERE!>
<MY POWER IS TECH AND NETWORKS, REMEMBER?>
<IF THERE WAS A BACKHOE NEARBY I'D BE YOUR GUY. OTHERWISE I DON'T KNOW WHAT TO TELL YOU...>
<SHIRAI IS GETTING QUITE ANGRY...>
<NEVER MIND.>
<I THINK THIS IS ABOUT TO SOLVE ITSELF...>
THOOM
<EMI'S NOT BREATHING!>

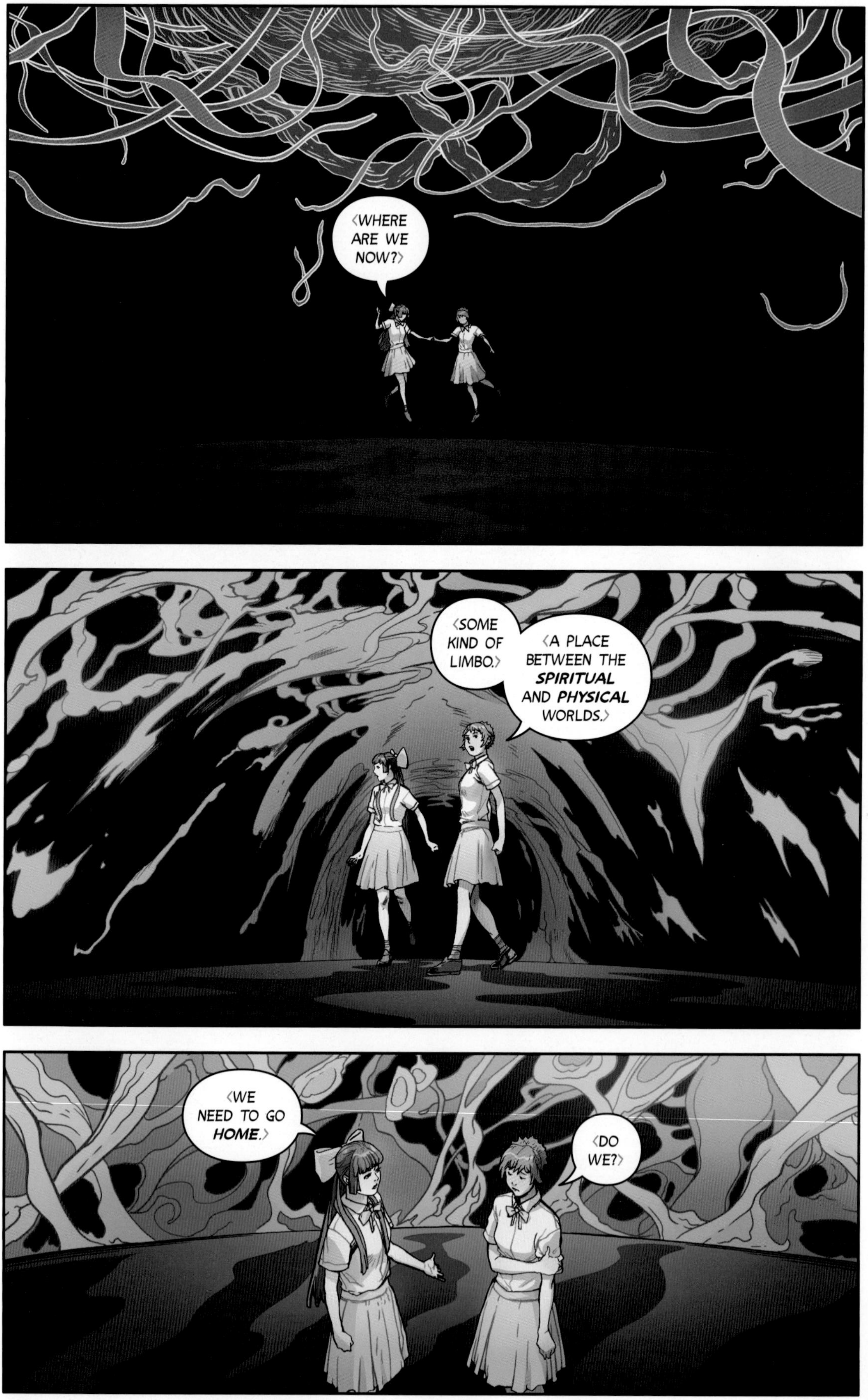
⟨WHERE ARE WE NOW?⟩
⟨SOME KIND OF LIMBO.⟩
⟨A PLACE BETWEEN THE **SPIRITUAL** AND **PHYSICAL** WORLDS.⟩
⟨WE NEED TO GO **HOME**.⟩
⟨DO WE?⟩

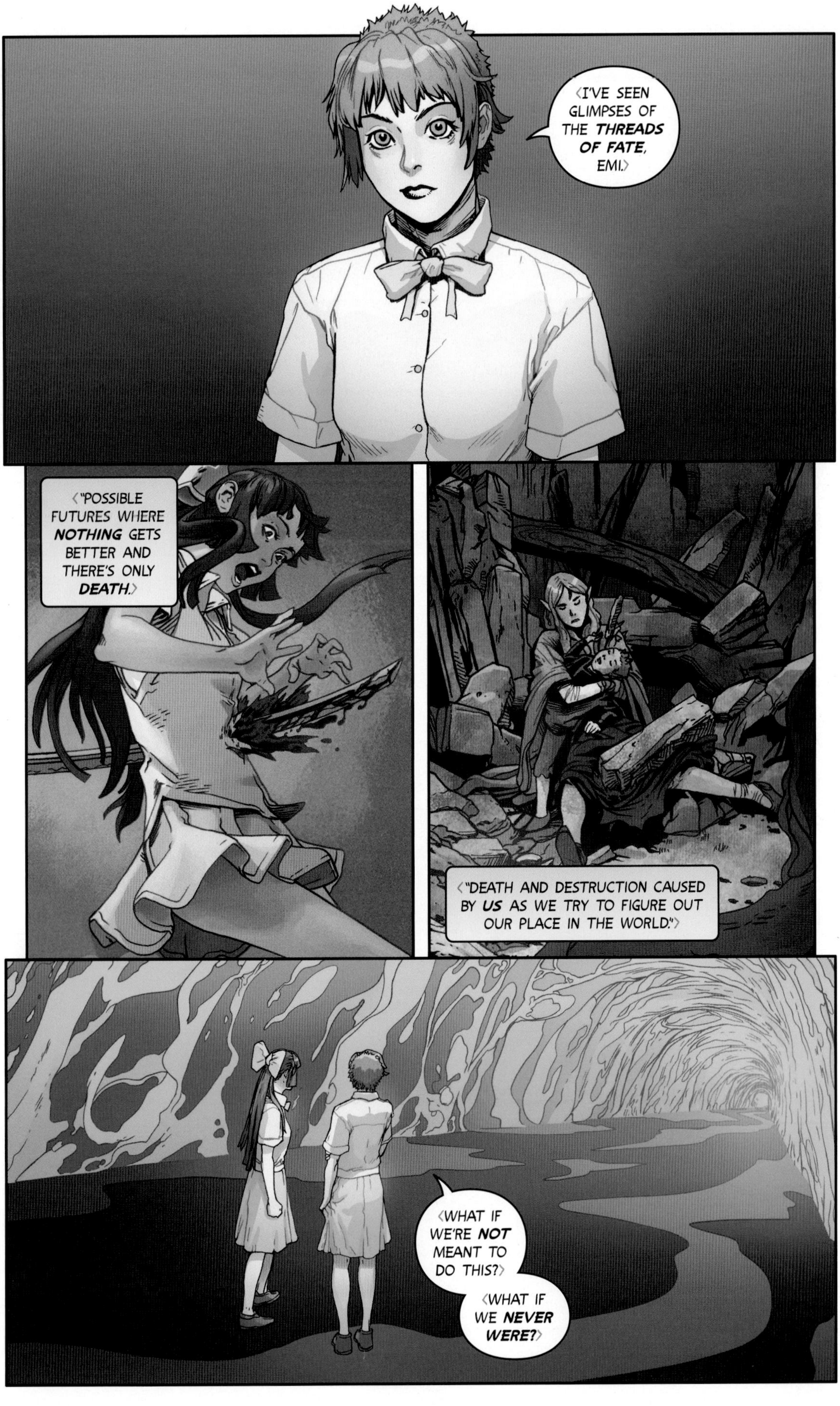

⟨I'VE SEEN GLIMPSES OF THE **THREADS OF FATE**, EMI.⟩
⟨"POSSIBLE FUTURES WHERE **NOTHING** GETS BETTER AND THERE'S ONLY **DEATH**.⟩
⟨"DEATH AND DESTRUCTION CAUSED BY **US** AS WE TRY TO FIGURE OUT OUR PLACE IN THE WORLD."⟩
⟨WHAT IF WE'RE **NOT** MEANT TO DO THIS?⟩
⟨WHAT IF WE **NEVER WERE?**⟩

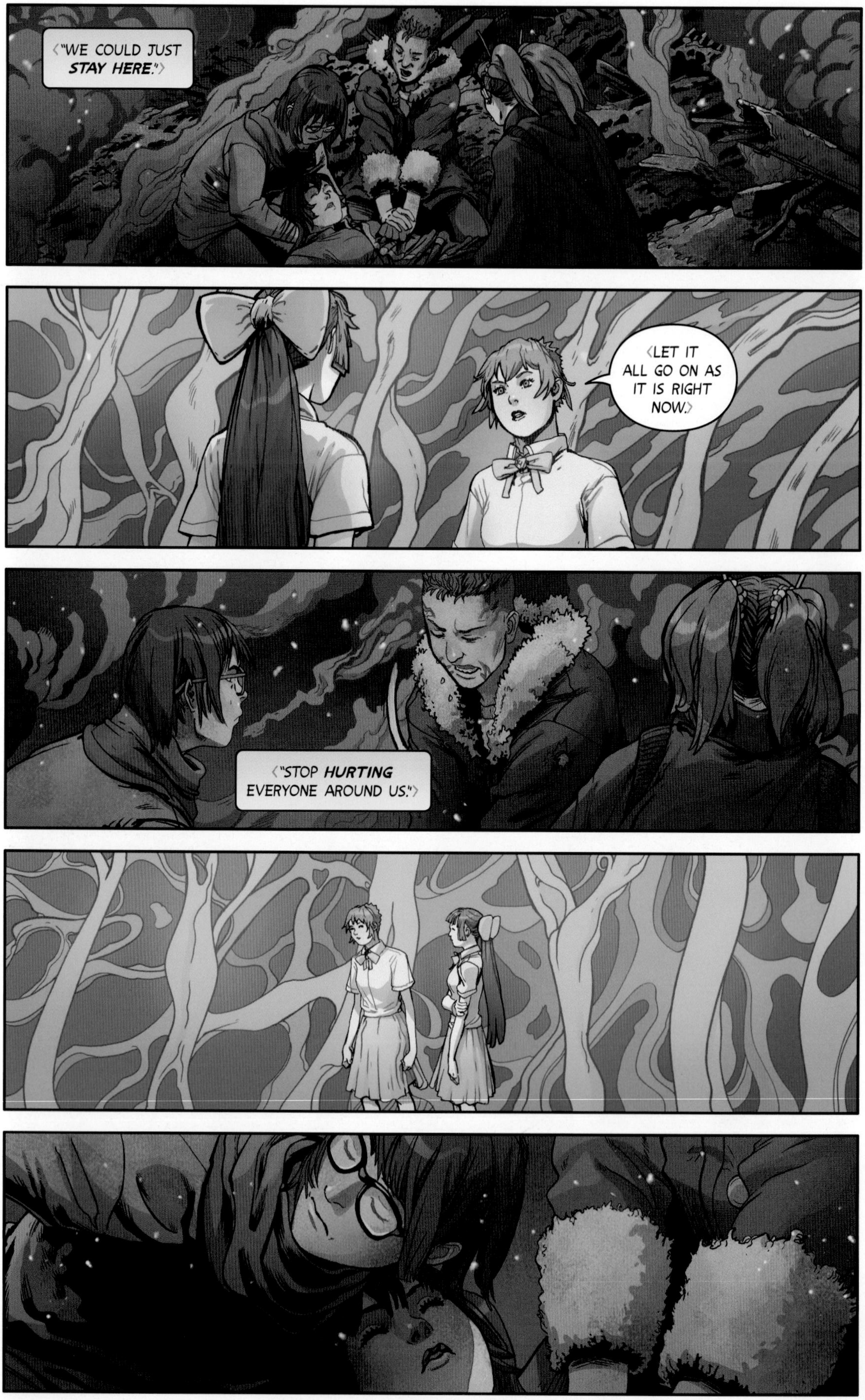
⟨"WE COULD JUST STAY HERE."⟩
⟨LET IT ALL GO ON AS IT IS RIGHT NOW.⟩
⟨"STOP HURTING EVERYONE AROUND US."⟩

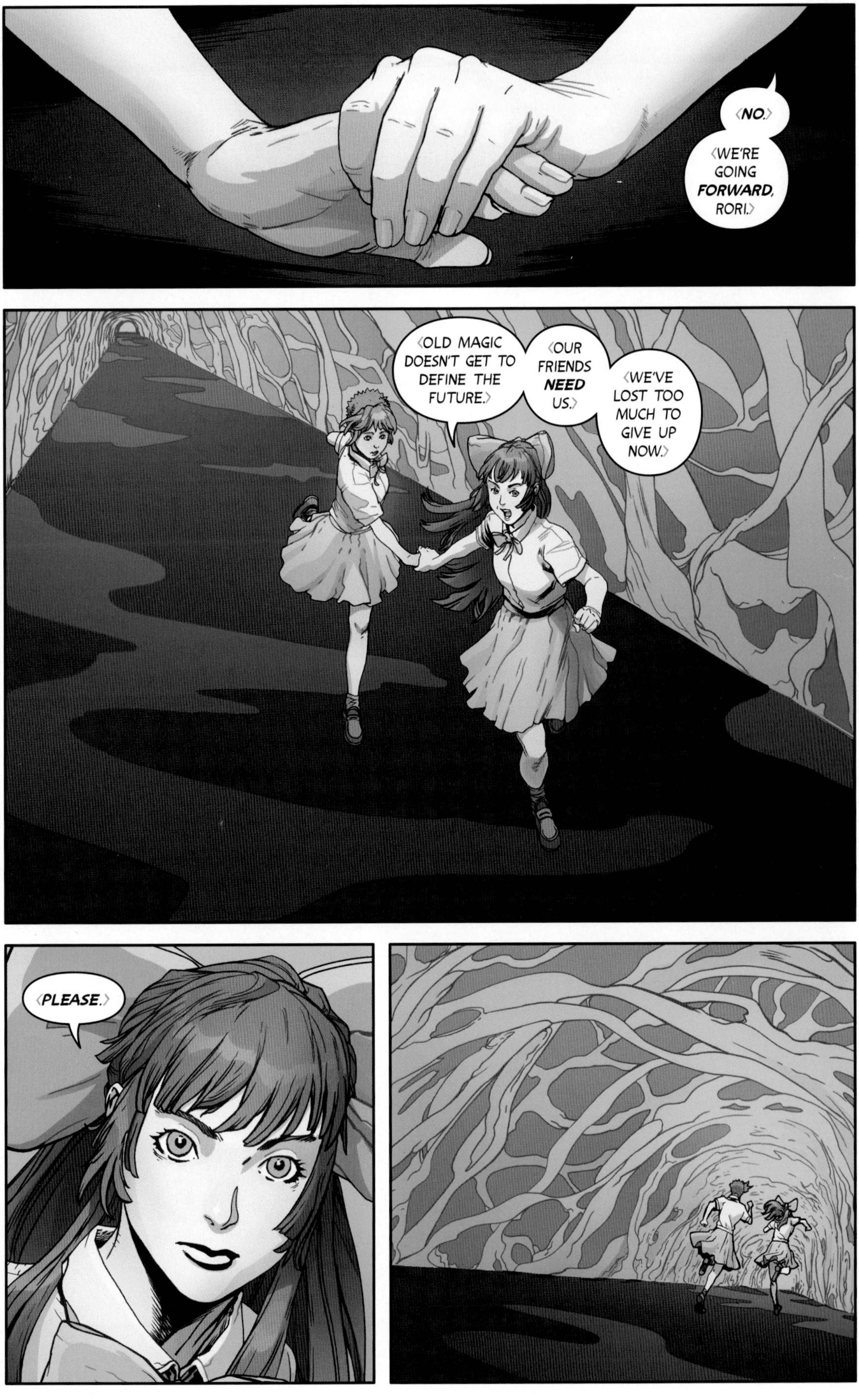
⟨NO.⟩
⟨WE'RE GOING FORWARD, RORI.⟩
⟨OLD MAGIC DOESN'T GET TO DEFINE THE FUTURE.⟩
⟨OUR FRIENDS NEED US.⟩
⟨WE'VE LOST TOO MUCH TO GIVE UP NOW.⟩
⟨PLEASE.⟩

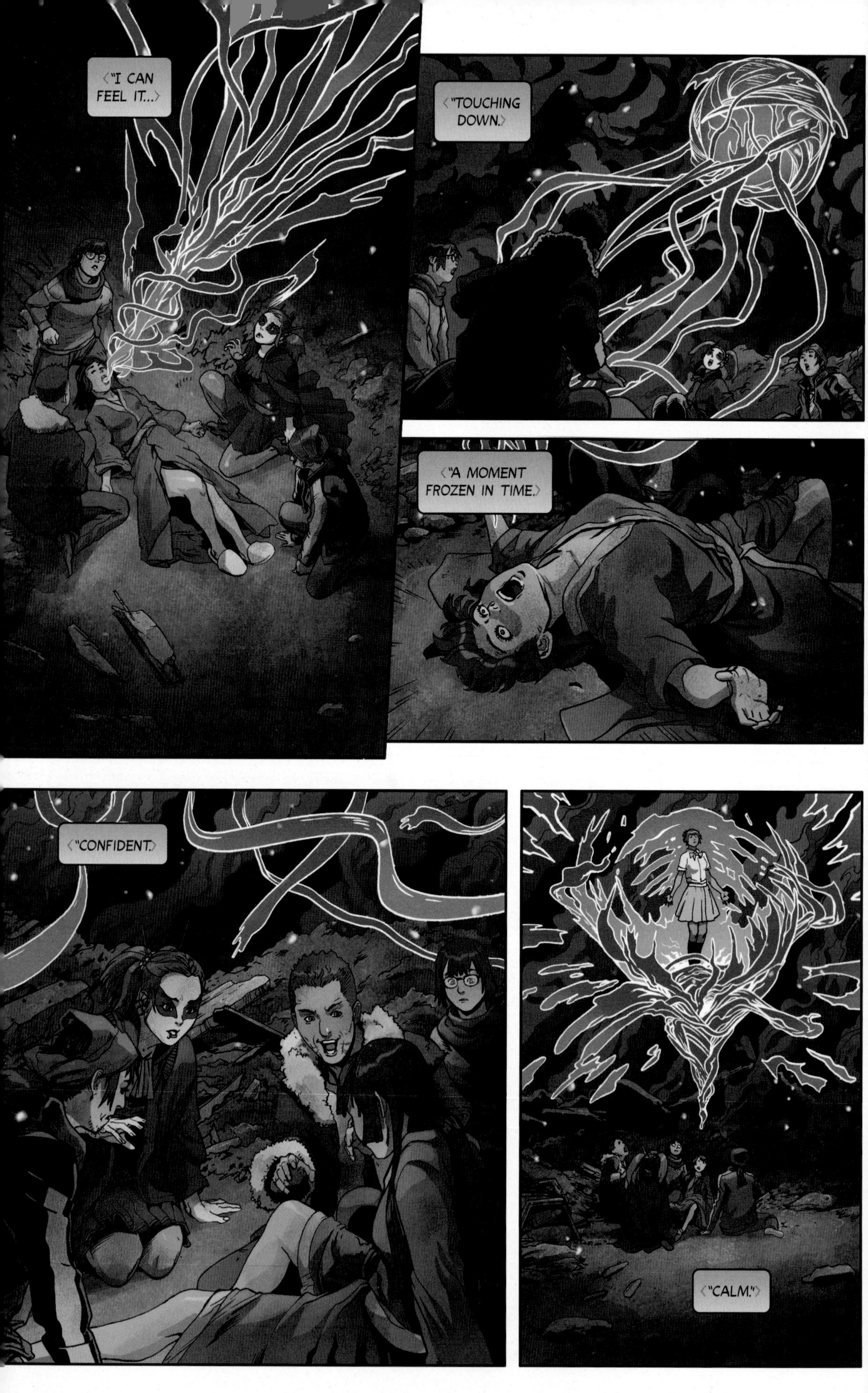

<"I CAN FEEL IT...>
<"TOUCHING DOWN.>
<"A MOMENT FROZEN IN TIME.>
<"CONFIDENT.>
<"CALM.">

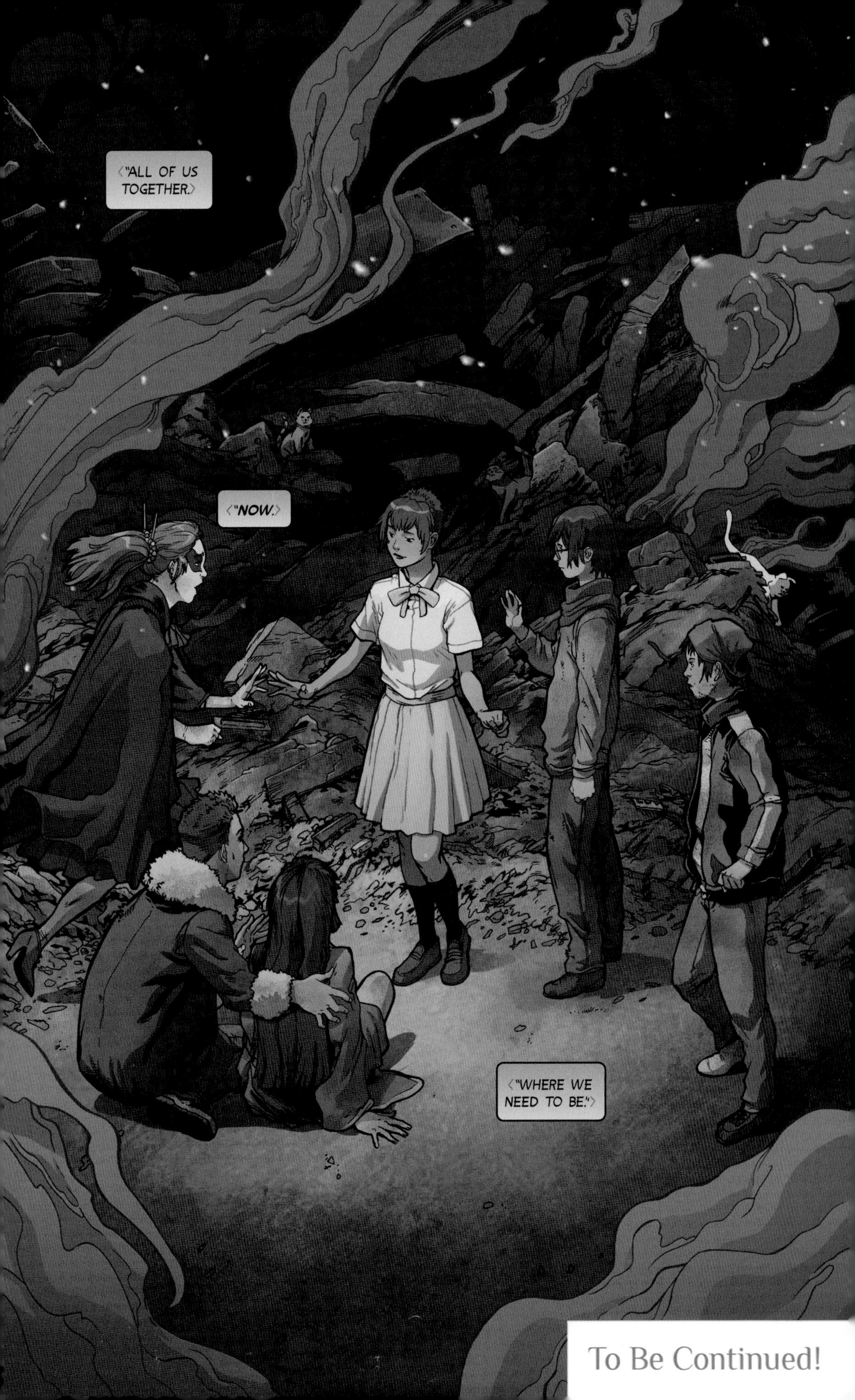
‹"ALL OF US TOGETHER.›
‹"NOW.›
‹"WHERE WE NEED TO BE."›
To Be Continued!

Paging Doctor Japan

One of the biggest shocks my wife Miyuki had when we moved to the US was that she had to pay for medical care. The idea that you might not go to the hospital because you couldn't afford it seemed wrong to her—imagine standing in a burning building and not calling the fire department because you were worried about the bill, or not calling the police after a robbery because the cost to investigate would probably be more than what was stolen. To an outsider from what we would call a "first world country," the concept of the US's bizarre pay-for-play medical system seemed completely insane.

After living in both Britain and Japan, I completely agree.

Japan has a National Health Care system. This means medical care is treated the same as police, fire stations, infrastructure maintenance, parks and recreations, and other vital services provided by the government. It is part of the citizenship package; you live in the country, pay your taxes—in return these basic needs are cared for.

We'll get into that later. First, a little history:

Like all civilizations, for much of Japan's history magic and medicine walked hand-in-hand. In an age when lightning strikes were attributed to the will of the angry dead, medical care consisted of incantations and exorcism. There were few illnesses that couldn't be explained away as the influence of yokai and bad spirits. Contact with China catapulted Japan into a more enlightened world. China's intricate medical practices were vastly superior to Japan's bone-rattling. From 608 CE, the aristocracy of Japan sent promising young men to be trained as physicians in Chinese herbal practices. This knowledge was then shared. In 982, Tamba Yasuyori wrote the 30-volume *Ishinhō*, a vast medical text based mostly on older Chinese manuals. The groundbreaking book dissected the human body into organs and parts, and attributed disease to an imbalance of yin/yang forces.

Across the ways and means of time, medicine slowly evolved to a system of humors and directions, and herbs and mysterious powders. By the time of the samurai, medicine had become a status symbol. The wealthy and aristocratic class carried around small medicine boxes called *inrō*. These inrō boxes were mini works of art, and hung by straps from the obi of those rich enough to afford them. The ability to dash out a smattering of rare headache powder was as impressive then as it is now to pull a bottle of 18-year-old Lagavulin whisky off the shelf. Medicine demonstrated your knowledge and wealth.

Of course, dealers in these medicines were not rich themselves; itinerates called kusuri-uri wandered the lonely highways of old Japan, a wooden back-pack on their backs filled with wonderful tinctures and ointments. They supplied frog eyeball extract and serpent skin for the rich and needy. Supposing they were on the up-and-up, that is. With their unlimited travel passes to get by the Shogun's strict laws and gates, kusuri-uri made ideal disguises for ninjas and other spies going about on their lord's secret business. Anytime you see a movie ninja dressed in black, realize that a more accurate portrayal would be a lonely, dirty medicine dealer with a heavy wooden pack on his back.

By the 16th century, contact with traders from Holland had brought even more scientific advances. Jesuit missionaries introduced some secrets, and Dutch physicians brought more, lending training where they were able. By the 18th century, Japanese medical practitioners were split between traditional Chinese herbalists and Holland-trained "Dutch Doctors" with books on anatomy and theories of internal medicine. By 1857, Dutch-trained physicians founded the medical school at the University of Tokyo. The government invested heavily in research, and by 1894 Japanese doctors had discovered the cause of the bubonic plague and dysentery. In 1901 they isolated and reproduced adrenaline.

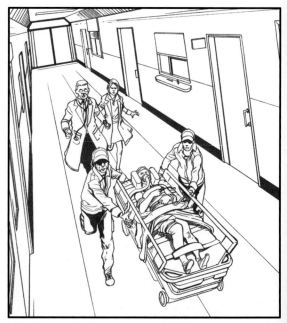

In the modern world, these twin paths of medicine have evolved together. Chinese herblore became the Japanese practice of *kanpo*, using natural ingredients from plants, animals, and minerals. With kanpo, your health is determined by reading your tongue, and a properly foul-tasting potion is prescribed for what ails you. Along with trips to your usual doctor, of course. There is no dichotomy here; most Western medicine is supplemented by regular trips to your kanpo physician. The result is the longest lifespan known on earth, with average ages stretching well into the 90s. Meeting a centenarian climbing a mountain is not an unusual occurrence. I have never met so many 100+ year olds as when I lived in Japan.

How did this wonderful system get established, you might ask? Well, like much of post-war Japan it was created by the United States. As the unchallenged victors, the small contingent of emissaries sent to rule Japan as the Supreme Commander of the Allied Forces of Japan (SCAP) were able to re-write Japan's constitution as an idealized society. Free from the anti-communist paranoia raging across the US, a small group of SCAP architects basically wrote the Japanese constitution as a leftist utopia, including provisions for women's rights and basic citizens' protections still unheard of in the United States. SCAP established the Council on Medical Education in 1946, and continued tweaking things until it created the modern Japanese health care system.

If you lived in Japan today, roughly 70% of all medical costs would be covered by the government. You can take out private insurance on the remaining 30% but if you absolutely can't pay there are ways around it that won't cripple you financially. Health care is focused on prevention rather than reaction, and there are mobile "doc in a box" checks that travel around giving you yearly checkups. Multiple studies have compared Japan's health care to the United States, and found that Japan's survival rates are higher.

I admit to waxing nostalgic here a bit; there are issues with the Japanese health care system, of course. I could tell stories about my broken leg and the doctor so nervous about his English ability that he broke out into the giggles every time he tried to treat me. And docs have a tendency to see medicine as the answer to everything. But the perfect system has not yet been created. Indeed, perfect cannot be the enemy of good. By almost any measurement Japan has excellent health care that is available to its population regardless of their income or citizenship status. In short, Japan is a nice place to get sick.

As a last example, indulge me in a brief story. If you have ever seen me at a comic convention, you might have seen my banner decorated with truly amazing balloon sculptures of the yokai Kitaro and his friends. Unfortunately, the recent Emerald City Comic Con was the last of these. My dear friend Hiromi has a brain tumor, and the cost of treatment would bankrupt her family. So they have decided to return to Japan where she can be treated for free—medical exiles from the U.S. where they have lived for many years.

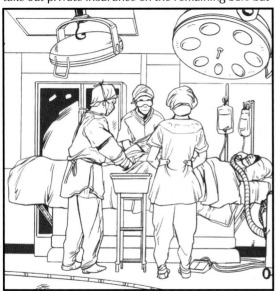

Sirens of the Irish Shores

Since the time of the Ancient Greeks, there have been folklore tales of oceanic femme fatales luring men to an early grave. These maidens of the sea have proven as lethal as they are beautiful, and the Irish mermaid known as the Merrow is no exception.

The name derives from the old Irish *Moruadh* meaning 'sea maid'. Although the literal translation is feminine, the term Merrow applies to both the male and female of the species. They are said to dwell in *Tir fo Thoinn*, or 'the Land beneath the waves'.

Merrow menfolk really don't have a lot going for them. They are hideously ugly to the point that the mermaids refuse to take them as mates, despite their genetic compatibility. There is actually very little documented about these loathsome creatures, however they have been described in folk tales as being covered in green scales, with green coarse hair and pointed, rotten teeth. They have blood-red beady eyes and their torsos and arms are stubby and grotesque. Merrow men are so bitter over their appearance and loneliness that they capture the spirits of drowned sailors and keep them incarcerated under the sea.

Merrow women, on the contrary, are absolutely striking. They have long, radiant hair, and from the waist down, have glistening verdigris scales covering quite remarkable fish tails. The beauty of the Merrow takes the breath of men away figuratively and literally. Their exquisite singing can mean both harmonious joy or death to those who succumb to the melodic enchantment.

Many men have been seduced into mating with the female Merrow and there are those with Irish surnames such as O'Flaherty and O'Sullivan in County Kerry and MacNamara in County Clare, that are believed to descend from such unions. Of course such relations were short-lived as the mermaid would become homesick for her subterranean way of life and would drag her suitor beneath the water.

Poor, unsuspecting males would be enticed into the sea by the bewitching music of the Merrow women and be pulled beneath the waves to live in entranced captivity. In the event one absconded, they would incur the wrath of the scorned Siren and be hunted and then drowned. If an escaped prisoner really antagonised their captor they would be angrily devoured, bones and all.

Written accounts of the Merrow women luring unsuspecting human Irish males date back to the ancient Annals of the Kingdom of Ireland, also known as the Annals of the Four Masters. Indeed, even the all-powerful demi-gods of chaos known as the Fomorians were not immune to their charms.

Roth was a Fomorian son carrying out his duties patrolling the coastal borders of the Fomorian lands. The Merrows took umbrage at his presence within their seas and took steps to ensure he would no longer pose a threat. The seemingly innocent beauties of the waters began their attack by lulling Roth gently to sleep with their enchanting melodies. Once he was sedated and clearly unable to fight back, they became bloodthirsty and homicidal. Violently they tore the poor misfortune limb from limb and joint from joint. Although much of him was consumed, the creatures sent his thigh floating over the current to what has now become known as the county of Waterford.

Of course sometimes on a bad day, there didn't need to be a catalyst to stir up the wrath and destruction of these ill-tempered wily sea maids. They would simply take pleasure in brewing up storms, shipwrecking and drowning innocent sailors for no other reason than crossing their watery path.

County Kerry lies on the Atlantic coast of Ireland and his strong links to the Merrow folk. Stories date back centuries and the most famous one of all involved a gentle fisherman who would rue the day he ever set eyes upon a Merrow woman.

Whilst walking on the beach, a young man by the name of Luty saw an incredible sight. There lying on the shingle was the most beautiful female he had ever seen. A woman in every way bar her fish tail that was floundering on the sand.

His kind nature took over from the disbelief and he realised quickly that the creature before him was in terrible distress. He lifted the woman into his two strong arms and carried her out to the waves. The Merrow was named Marina and she was so ecstatic at being rescued, her malicious nature was subdued and she granted Luty three wishes.

He asked for the ability to break any curses brought about by dark magic, to be able to command malevolent spirits to carry out charitable deeds and the power to make good things happen for those in need. The young man's selflessness impressed the sea maiden so much she added a final gift of prosperity to Luty and all his future descendants.

Luty was delighted and reached out to shake her hand. Sensing the pureness of his soul, her true wickedness came to the forefront and she began to seduce the unsuspecting hero with her alluring voice. A shocked Luty realised almost immediately what she was doing and reached into his pocket for his iron knife.

As with all fairy folk, Marina could be harmed with iron and he lashed out. The Merrow dived beneath the waves but not before uttering a terrifying promise to come back and reclaim Luty in nine years. Time passed and Luty married a local girl and had two sons. He took his youngest son fishing and as Luty reached the shore, Marina rose from the ocean depths and grabbed the poor man, dragging him down into the angry waves, and he was never heard from again.

The Merrow wear a special enchanted cap called a *cohuleen druith*. The garment and indeed the Merrow penchant for capturing the souls of hapless sailors was spoken of in the nineteenth century Thomas Keightley book of folk tales, *The Soul Cages*. The cohuleen druith holds the power of the Merrow that enables them to live under the ocean.

If you are fast enough to snatch the cap from the head of the siren before she enchants you, she is no longer able to descend under the waves and she is very much at your mercy. Of course if you are too late and your senses are ensnared – well I'm afraid you are doomed to an eternity in a soul cage, trapped at the bottom of the sea.

Tsukumogami – The Terrible Tools

The tale of the tsukumogami teaches one of humanity's oldest moral lessons—"My god is better than your god." It even adds a hefty side order of "How I worship my god is more correct than the way you worship that same god." That is quite a heavy message to pack into a mythology that is essentially a bunch of talking plates.

Japanese folklore says that when certain objects reach a 100 years of age, they can gain a soul. These objects—called *tsukumogami*—are traditionally household objects called *utsuwamono* or *kibutsu*, meaning cauldrons, containers, or receptacles of some sort. But they can also pretty much be anything used by people for 100 years. The world tsukumogami can be written in two ways, with the same pronunciation but with slightly different meanings. 付喪神 means essentially "tool spirits" and was most common in old Japan. In modern times it is more common to see 九十九神, meaning "ninety nine-year spirits," a reference to how old tsukumogami must be to come to life.

The origin of tsukumogami can be traced to a Muromachi period (1336 - 1573) picture scroll called *Tsukumogami-ki.* The scroll is an ancestor to modern comics, using words and pictures to tell the story of a bunch of discarded objects that set out for bloody revenge. It goes something like this:

When reaching 100 years of age, household objects gain life and consciousness. However, the big bowls and items of this story are having a less than happy birthday. During the New Year's ceremony of *susuharai* when old things are tossed out and soot is swept from the houses, these household objects find themselves tossed into the trash. Angry at years of neglect and finally being discarded, they band together into a tsukumogami gang and decide to get revenge. Only a single object raises its voice in objection, a set of rosary beads that served Buddhist novices for a century. The others beat the rosary beads until it shuts up, and then they go about their evil plan.

They head up into the mountains around Kyoto to establish a base. They even raise up their own deity, *Henge Daimyōjin*—the Great God of Shape-shifters. The tsukumogami build a portable shrine for their new god, and bearing it on their backs they attack the city at night (invisibly, because all yokai at the time were invisible). Marching through Kyoto, they proceed to kill and eat any hapless humans they meet. They even go so far as to attack the Prince Regent himself, who is saved by a Buddhist charm he carries. Encouraged by the effectiveness of his charm, the Prince summons the Abbot who made it for him and pleads for his help against these monsters.

The Abbot performs a set of rituals and summons a group of Buddhist deities who he sends to repel the tsukumogami. Driving them back to their mountain base, the animated objects are awed by the majesty of Buddha and instantly convert. Their new souls are saved. The Abbot then proceeds to give a little sermon about how following the *true* path of Shingon Buddhism—instead of those other discount brands—will lead to enlightenment in this life, and is available for all.

As you can see, *Tsukumogami-ki* is essentially a propaganda piece meant to show the power of Buddhism over the false gods of Shinto. If you have ever been under the illusion that Buddhism

and Shinto peacefully coexisted throughout Japanese history, then you have spent too much time wandering the "Asian" section of your local World Market. Long and bloody wars were fought over which was the true god of Japan, and multiple Buddhist sects enthusiastically killed each other over whose interpretation of the Dharma was correct. The old gods rarely peacefully step aside for the new.

Nothing in *Tsukumogami-ki* is accidental: The mountain base of the tsukumogami is the traditional home of Shinto spirits: The tsukumogami god, *Henge Daimyōjin* is ridiculous on purpose and meant to show how empty Shinto deities are that they can be made up on the spot and serve any purpose: The fact that most of the tsukumogami are *kibutsu*, pots and cauldrons and types of containers is important; cauldrons are a symbol of Shingon Buddhism. They represent a disciple whose mind is filled by a teacher, an empty receptacle waiting to be filled with wisdom.

Even the concept of inanimate objects with souls is an important part of Shingon Buddhism. They advocate the concept of *Sokushin Jobutsu*—meaning bodily enlightenment. To simplify it as much as possible, they take the concept of the omnipresence of Buddha to its logical extreme. Buddha permeates the universe, so every atom has a Buddha nature inside it. Thus, enlightenment is not limited to humans. Absolutely everything, from a blade of grass to your toothbrush, has an equal opportunity to reach the state of enlightened bliss called *satori*.

Needless to say, most of the subtle wisdom of the story of *Tsukumogami-ki* was lost on its readers. They came away with "Talking plates? Awesome!!!" and ran with it. There is some debate on whether the "100-year-old objects gaining souls" was an existing belief played upon by the author of the *Tskumogami-ki*, or if it was created just for that story. Some of the *Night Parade of 100 Demons* scrolls from the same time, like the *Hyakki Yagyō Zu*, also show objects running with the yokai wild pack. However, many of the transformed objects in the Night Parade are clearly not 100 years old. They are often demonic versions of musical instruments and contemporary objects, and there is no way to link them to the specific mythology presented in *Tsukumogami-ki*.

Like much in Japanese folklore, the final addition to tsukumogami legends was delivered by artist Toriyama Sekien. His fourth yokai encyclopedia,

Hyakki Tsurezure Bukuro (百器徒然袋, *The Illustrated Bag of One Hundred Haunted Housewares*) focused on tsukumogami. Inspired by Yoshida Kenko's classic book *Tsurezuregusa* (徒然草, *Essays in Idleness*), Toriyama created a number of tsukumogami yokai. Riffing off passages and terms used within the book. True to fashion, Toriyama gave little stories and personality to his creations. These are the tsukumogami we know today.

Welcome to the Land of Eternal Youth

Every self-respecting Irish man or woman knows the story of *Tir na nÓg*. Often simplified and romanticized as the 'Land of Eternal Youth', this island is believed to be the home of the demi-god race known as the *Tuatha Dé Danann*.

The origins and location of this enigmatic island remain as mysterious as ever. So how did Tir na nÓg become the sanctuary of a lost race of warriors and where is it now?

THE TUATHA DÉ DANANN

As the more cultured of the races of ancient Ireland, their diplomacy and education meant they frequently had the upper hand over rivals such as the Fir Bolg and arch nemeses, the Formorians. All this was set to change however, with the arrival of the Milesians.

The Milesians waged into a fearsome battle against the Tuatha Dé Danann and they were never going to settle until they had complete and utter domination over their rivals. Being the civilized nation they were, the Tuatha did everything they could to negotiate and seek peace and harmonious accord.

With no truce in sight the Tuatha did everything in their power to keep their stronghold including in-voking a mystical tempest to destroy the enemy. The crafty Milesians called upon a daughter of the Tuatha, the goddess Eriu and gained the land of Eire as their own.

What happened next to the Tuatha Dé Danann is a matter of speculation, however the outcome was always the same. A land of their own outside of space and time.

Regardless of how they got there, it goes without question that the Tuatha went underground. And this is where it gets interesting.

TIR NA NÓG

Sure, there's *Lord of the Rings* and the *Undying Lands*, but remember which one came first. Tír na nÓg is a land of beauty, natural abundance and first and foremost, immortality. Where it is, well that's another question altogether.

Generally, it is thought to lie on the Wild Atlantic Way off the west coast of Ireland, somewhere beyond the Aran Islands. It has to be remembered however, that it is a place made of mystical energy and its location is intangible.

Historical records show a Dutch navigator who settled in Dublin in the 17th century recorded seeing an island much described as Tír na nÓg. He sighted it off of the coast of Greenland which is some 1500 miles from the Aran Islands.

The island that appeared was protected by potent witchcraft and anyone trying to approach was pushed off course by powerful tempests and drowned at sea. Terrified to meet the same fate, the intrepid explorer made a full turn and headed south only to find the same island emerging on the horizon once again.

The terrain itself is a veritable landscape of waterfalls, mountains, forests and lakes. If you took the most beautiful and awe-inspiring Irish vistas they would not hold a candle to what awaits in the land of the Sidhe.

MANANNÁN MAC LIR

Manannán mac Lir is the Irish sea god and protector of Tír na nÓg. Much like Poseidon and Hades, his guardianship means the Land of Eternal Youth is well protected from unwanted visitors and the Merrow folk will raise the warning if anyone dares to cross the oceanic boundaries. If Manannán mac Lir permits, every 7 years a fortunate few will be blessed to see the land of Tír na nÓg emerge from above the waves.

REACHING THE LAND OF THE TUATHA DÉ DANANN

Legend says the goddess Danu assisted in the escape of the cultured race by hiding them beneath the mounds of the earth, otherwise known as sidhs, and disguising their location with magic. These sidhs were portals and the Tuatha Dé Danann became known as 'Aes Sidh' or 'people under the mound.'

Today that translates as 'Sidhe' or' faeries'.

As well as via coastal trickery, Tír na nÓg can be reached through one of the many magical faery portals dotted around the Emerald Isle. In fact, there is one not ten miles from my door called *Knockfierna* which translates as the 'mountain of truth.'

At certain times of the year such as Samhain, the veil separating ourselves from the Otherworld is at its thinnest and that is when access becomes possible. Remember though, all that glitters is most definitely not gold.

OISÍN AND TÍR NA NÓG

Oisín was a formidable warrior, one of the Fianna and the son of the legendary Fionn mac Cumhaill. What I should have mentioned is that the Sidhe were a devious lot and in particular the 'A Leannan Sidh' or faery sweetheart. She is known for luring unsuspecting male humans to Tír na nÓg, with them never to return home.

In this instance Niamh, daughter of Manannán mac Lir, failed in her mission. Whilst Oisín had fallen in love with his femme fatale, she in turn had fallen in love with the greatest poet Ireland had even known. Niamh carried him back to her land and they lived blissfully together. Time was an unknown quantity to those residing in Tír na nÓg and Oisín was shocked to find three hundred years had passed.

Desperate to see what was left of his people, Oisín travelled back on a white steed with Niamh's blessing. Her only warning was that he should not touch the land of humans, for that would be his demise, as mortality would take hold.

On arrival Oisín was devastated to discover all that he had held dear was gone. Miserable and lonely, he turned his magic horse towards Tír na nÓg. Just before he entered the waves he saw an old man needing help to move a boulder. Guiding his horse Embarr, he assisted in what would be his last act of kindness.

Oisín fell from his steed and instantly began to age. It is said Saint Patrick found him and before the Fianna warrior died of old age he recounted his tale of Tír na nÓg.

The Land of Eternal Youth has fluid boundaries and magical wards protecting the Tuatha Dé Danann from harm and invasion. They keep to themselves if you leave them be. If. Of course when the veils between worlds are at their thinnest, you may catch a glimpse of Tír na nÓg. If you are taken by a Leannan Sidhe and find your way home, just be sure you never set foot on this mortal coil again, because it will be the last thing you ever do.

The Red String of Fate

This story comes from long ago, from Tang dynasty China (618-907 CE):

"A young man named Iko was traveling about the country, when he came upon a waypoint town in southern Souki. In front of the gates to the town there was a mysterious old man. He sat in the middle of an enormous pile of books, all of which were illuminated by a moonbeam. The old man's books concerned themselves with the spiritual worlds. He was diligently reading them.

When Iko approached to ask what he was reading, the man told him that all human marriages were decided when the spirits were still in their raw state. Human beings were created as a pair, and an unbreakable red rope bound two souls together by the ankle. No matter the time or distance that separated them, any two people bound by this red rope would eventually be drawn together. This was their destiny.

Iko said that he had recently proposed marriage, but the old man told him it wouldn't work. He could see the red rope bound him to another. Iko was joined to a 3-year-old orphan girl, being raised by a vegetable dealer in that very town. Iko was enraged. He said this was a lie, and told his servant to locate and murder the child. The servant found her, and stabbed her with a knife between her eyes—then ran away in fear.

14 years later, Iko rose in position but was still unmarried. One of his superiors introduced him to a 17-year-old woman of astounding beauty, and they were soon wed. Iko was entranced by his new bride, and on their wedding night he noticed a small scar between her eyes. Asking about it, she replied that as a child she was suddenly attacked for no reason, but the knife only cut the skin before her attacker fled. Iko realized it was that same 3-year-old girl that he was bound to, and he came to realize that what the old man had said was true."

This is the oldest known story of what is called the unmei no akai ito (運命の赤い糸), the red string of fate. The legend comes from China, and concerns the lunar deity and god of marriage Yue Xia Lao (月下老). According to the stories, Yue Xia Lao binds two souls together with an unbreakable red cord wrapped around their ankles. As they wander through life, this cord may stretch or become tangled with others, but its draw is irresistible. The destined lovers will come together, and recognize each other as soulmates.

It's a romantic legend, and one that has spread across all of East Asia. In Japan the unmei no akai ito is found extensively in romance novels and comics aimed at young girls, who dream of their own red cord binding them to some handsome lover as yet unmet. Popular anime and manga like

Ai Yori Aoshi, *Free!*, and even *Naruto* are filled with the red cord, showing it tying together the often-convoluted collection of characters that populate the stories. Although in Japan it is usually tied around the pinky finger instead of the ankle as it is in China.

But the magic of the red string goes beyond frivolous romance—if a driving force in human nature can be called frivolous. There is power in red cords. Many cultures have recognized this; like the Jewish *segula* of a red wool bracelet knotted seven times and worn around the left wrist to protect from the evil eye and other calamities; or the knot magic of Celtic and Chinese traditions.

Across many cultures, across many times, weaving has also been seen as magical. The way that individual threads are deftly woven together to create a pattern is a metaphor for human society. We are all threads in the weave. We all combine to create the Great Tapestry of Life. And because we are so tightly woven, none of us have the distance required to see the pattern of the cloth. Or to know whose hand is doing the weaving.

In ancient Greece it was the Moirai who wove the threads. Three crones carefully measured out the thread of each person's life, determining its length and the role it would take in the pattern. Clotho spun the thread from her distaff. Lachesis measured its length with her rod. Finally Atropos chose the manner of each person's death before severing the thread with her sheers. Even the gods of Olympus were subject to their rule. In Norse mythology these women were called the Norns, and their names were Urðr (Wyrd), Verðandi, and Skuld. Other cultures have similar variants.

Japan does not have a mythology of weavers of fate, but acknowledges that act of stitching adds additional power. During the first and second world wars, Japanese soldiers were often equipped with *senninbari* (千人針; thousand-person stitches). These were prepared by mothers, sisters, and wives who would wander through town with a white belt, begging other women to stitch a single red thread on the belt, until a thousand women had given their blessing. Senninbari were worn as protection against bullets and other harm—a

powerful talisman combining the strength of the red thread with the power of binding one thread to another.

Belief in the thread runs deep. There are matchmakers who claim the power to see the thread, and whose services are in high demand. While researching this article, I asked my own wife if she believed we were connected by an *unmei no akai ito*. She looked at me like I was stupid—we met in a bar on New Year's Eve, while going up to order drinks at the bar at the same time. Two weeks later she moved in, and now we have been together ten years. What else could it be, she said, but the power of the red string drawing us together?

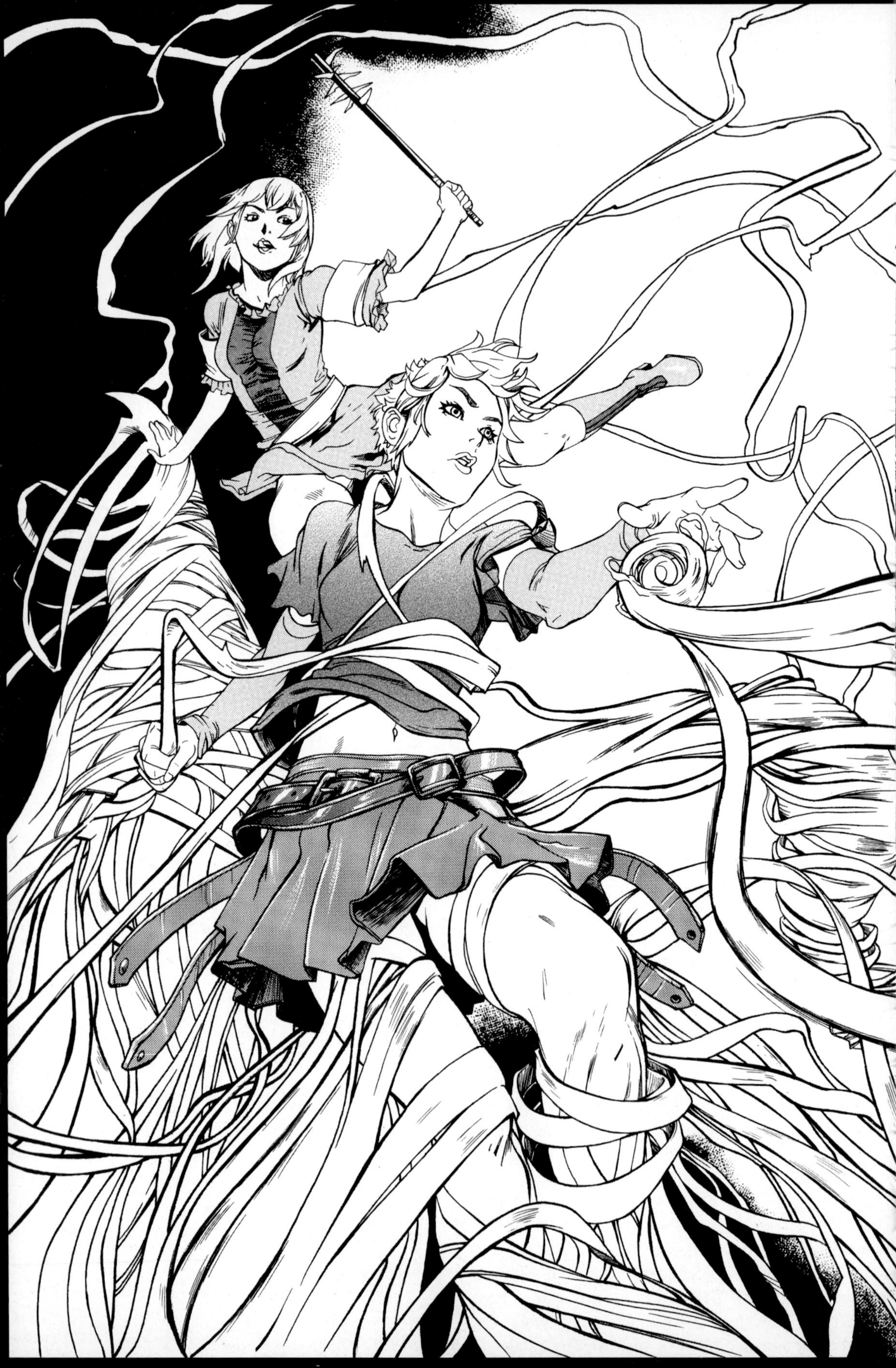

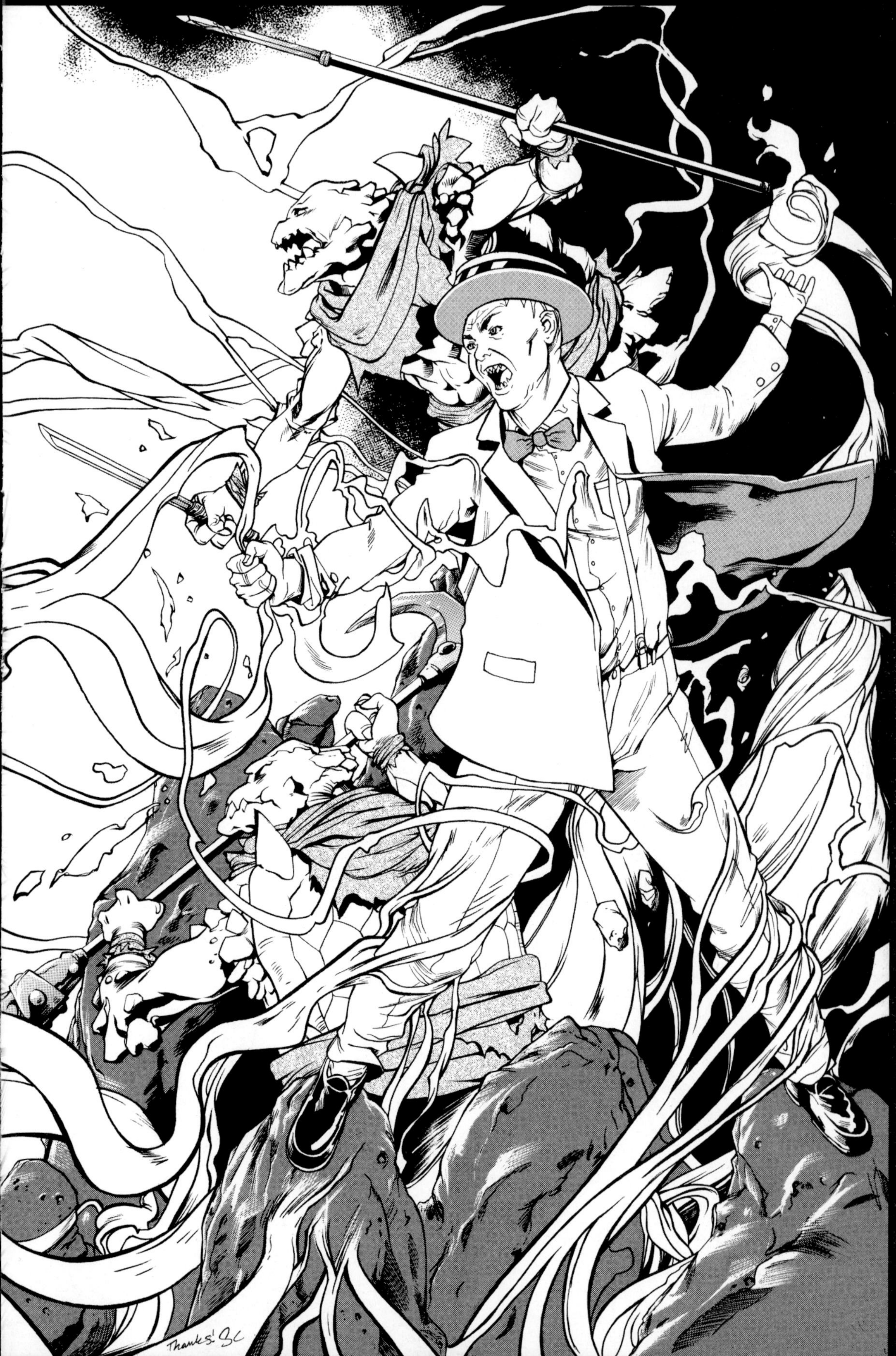
Thanks! BC

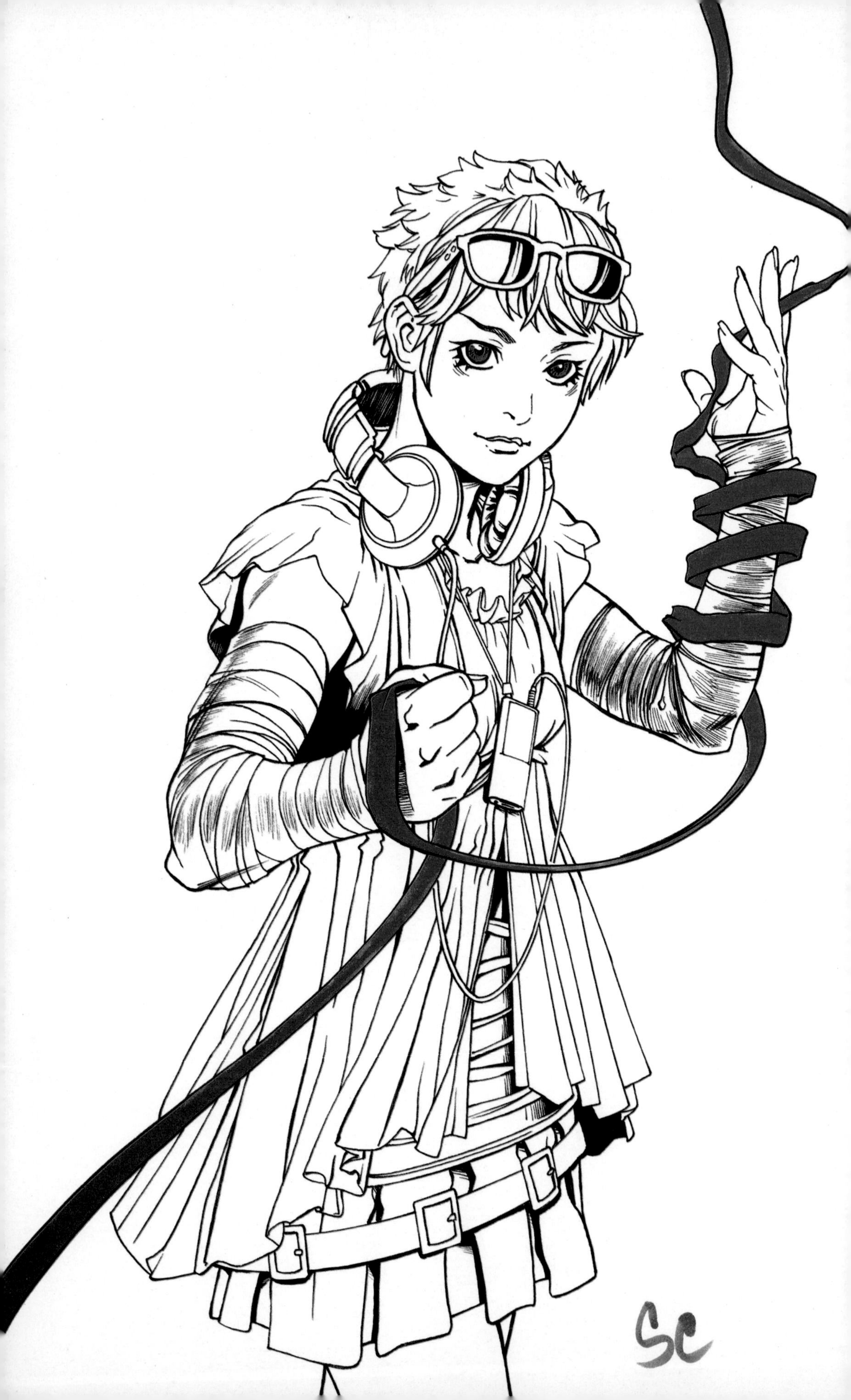
SC